A REM
AN UN

MISSION CHILD

Young Janna has lived her fourteen years on the icy northern plains of a world that has forgotten its history. Now the arrival of alien off-worlders—identical in appearance to her own kind but far different in thought and culture—has violently upset the fragile balance of a developing civilization. The Earthers' advanced technology and cruel indifference to local life have brought despair and destruction to Janna's home, robbing her of family, husband, child . . . self. But with the cataclysmic end of everything she has ever known comes the opportunity—unsought and unwanted—for rebirth.

"An astonishing, compulsively readable novel . . . McHugh tells a classic story of the clash between tradition and technology, modified by wry turns on gender and social roles, as seen with the eyes and heart of an indomitable, unforgettable protagonist."
Booklist (*Starred Review*)

"Maureen McHugh has mastered the trick of astonishing the reader."
Washington Post Book World

Named one of the year's Top 10 SF/Fantasy Books

MISSION CHILD

MAUREEN F. McHUGH

AVON · EOS

AVON BOOKS, INC.
1350 Avenue of the Americas
New York, New York 10019

Copyright © 1998 by Maureen F. McHugh
Cover art by Michael Evans
Excerpt from *Signal to Noise* copyright © 1998 by Eric S. Nylund
Excerpt from *The Death of the Necromancer* copyright © 1998 by Martha Wells
Excerpt from *Scent of Magic* copyright © 1998 by Andre Norton
Excerpt from *The Gilded Chain* copyright © 1998 by Dave Duncan
Excerpt from *Krondar the Betrayal* copyright © 1998 by Raymond E. Feist
Excerpt from *Mission Child* copyright © 1998 by Maureen F. McHugh
Excerpt from *Avalanche Soldier* copyright © 1999 by Susan R. Matthews
Inside cover author photo by David E. Brooks
Library of Congress Catalog Card Number: 98-8774
ISBN: 0-380-79122-6
www.avonbooks.com/eos

First Avon Eos Paperback Printing: November 1999
First Avon Eos Hardcover Printing: December 1998

AVON EOS TRADEMARK REG. U.S. PAT. OFF. AND IN OTHER COUNTRIES, MARCA REGISTRADA, HECHO EN U.S.A.

Printed in the U.S.A.

WCD   10   9   8   7   6   5   4   3   2

For Bob

Had I but one penny in the world,
thou shouldst have it for gingerbread

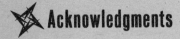# Acknowledgments

Thanks to Bob Yeager and Adam Yeager for their support; the Cleveland East Side Writers' Group for their excellent suggestions; the Cajun Sushi Hamsters for always being there; Gregory Feeley for loaning me some of his acute writing skills; the Edge list for their business support, reading help, and, well, generally edginess; Gardner Dozois for saying that the short story was fine but he was really interested in the setting and why didn't I write more there; Patrick Nielsen Hayden for publishing an earlier version in *Starlight 1*; Sandy Dijkstra for editing the first part rigorously; the people at Sycamore Hill (especially Carter Scholtz and Robert Frazier, whose comments seemed particularly illuminating); Jen Brehl for editorial guidance and caring; Mailboxes Etc. (Joe and Joe and Meg); the Arabica Coffee Shop in Twinsburg for opening at just the right time; Smith for unswerving devotion.

At the heart of this book is a question that Raphael Carter asked and that I have never stopped trying to answer. For that, great thanks.

In the end, this book is my fault, and much of what is good in it is due to much help, and all of the bad is due to me.

—Maureen F. McHugh

✦ Contents

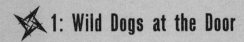# 1: Wild Dogs at the Door

THE SOUND OF RIFLES WAS LIKE THE cracking of whips. Like the snapping of bones. My da and I came outside to shade our eyes from the sun, and we watched the outrunners for the Tekse clan come into the Mission. They made a great deal of racket—brass clattering, the men singing and firing their guns into the air. It started the dogs barking and scared our renndeer.

They came to buy whiskey.. Or so we hoped. Sometimes when Tekse outrunners came, they just took it. They were all men, of course. Clan outrunners were all bachelors. They did foolish things.

"They have a lot of rifles," my da said.

They had more guns than I had ever seen. Usually when outrunners came, they had one or two guns. Guns are hard to get. But it looked as if almost every outrunner had a rifle.

Tekse dyed the clawed toes and ridgeline manes of their sled renndeer kracken yellow. They hung their harnesses with brass clappers, and bits of milky blue glass hung from the harnesses of their dogs. On this brief sunny day everything winked. Only their milking does were plain, and only because even the will of a hunter can't make a doe renndeer tractable.

The dogs nipped at the doe renndeer, halting them so outrunners could slip on hobbles. The renndeer looked pretty good. They were mostly dun, and the males were heavy in the shoulders with heads set low and forward on their necks. The long hairs on their ears were braided with red and yellow threads hanging almost to their knees. Handlers unhooked the sleds from the pack renndeer.

Our dogs barked and their dogs barked. The outrunner men talked loudly. Mission people stood at the doors of their houses and didn't talk at all. I saw one of the teachers, Ayudesh, come to the schoolhouse door and stand. Several of the outrunners looked at him and then looked away. Ayudesh was an offworlder, from Earth, from a place on Earth called India. He was taller than any other man in the village. His skin was so dark it looked as if it had been tanned. He and his wife, Wanji, they started the mission before I was born. I thought he might go talk to them, but he just stood there, like everyone else, watching the outrunners settle their animals.

I went down to the distillery to tell Mam. Aslak, my boyfriend, followed me down the hill. The distillery stank, so it was down below the mission in the trees, just above the fields.

Aslak caught me by the waist, and I leaned easily from his arms so he could brush his lips across my hair.

"It's too cold out here," I said and broke away.

"Let's go in the back," he said.

"I've got to tell Mam."

"Once you tell your mam, there'll be all these things to do and we won't get any time together," he said.

"I can't," I said, but I let him make up my mind for me.

We went around the side, tracking through the dry snow where no one much walked, through the lacy wintertrees to the storage door in the back. It was as cold there as it was outside, and dark. It smelled like mash and whiskey and the faint charcoal scent from the charred insides of the kegs. Brass whiskey, mission whiskey.

He boosted me onto a stack of kegs and kissed me.

It wasn't that I really cared so much about kissing. It was nice, but Aslak would have kissed and kissed for hours if I would let him. He would kiss long after my face felt overused and bruised. But I wanted to be with Aslak so much. I wanted to talk with him and have him walk with me. I would let him kiss me if I could whisper to him. I liked the way he pressed against me now; he was warm and I was cold.

He kissed me with little pecks—kiss, kiss, kiss. I liked it; it was almost as if he were talking to me in kisses. Then he kissed me hard and searched around with his tongue. I never knew what to do with my tongue when he put his in my mouth, so I just kept mine still. I could feel the rough edge of the keg beneath my legs, and if I shifted my weight it rocked on the one below it. I turned my face sideways to get my nose out of the way and opened my eyes to look past Aslak. In the dark I could barely make out Ranveig's eye burned on to all the kegs, to keep them from going bad. Ranveig was the door witch. Ranveig's sister Elin took souls from their mother and put them in seeds, put the seed in women to make babies. The kegs were all turned different directions, eyes looking everywhere. I closed mine again. Ranveig was also a virgin.

"Ohhhh, Janna! Eeeuuuu!"

I jumped, but Aslak didn't. He just let go of my waist and stepped back and crossed his arms the way he did when he was uncomfortable. The air felt cold where he had just been warm.

My little sister, Teija, shook her butt at us. "Kissy, kissy, kissy," she said. "MAM, JANNA'S BACK IN THE KEGS WITH ASLAK!"

"Shut up, Teija," I said. Not that she would.

"Slobber, slobber," she said, like we were renndeer trading cud. She danced around, still wriggling. She puckered up her lips and made wet smacking noises.

"Fucking little bitch," I said.

Aslak frowned at me. He liked Teija. She wasn't his little sister.

"MAM," Teija hollered, "JANNA SAID 'FUCK-ING'!"

"Janna," my mother called, "come here."

Mam was tallying on her high stool, hunched over to see her marks in the dim light of the fire. My mam wore trousers most often, and she was tall and man-faced. Still and all, men liked her. I took after her so I was secretly glad that men watched her walk by, even if she never much noticed.

"Leave your little sister alone," she said.

"Leave her alone!" I said. "She came and found me."

"Don't swear at her. You talk like an old man." Mam was acting like a headman, her voice even and cool.

"If she hadn't come looking—"

"If you had been working as you're supposed to, she'd have had no one to look for, would she."

"Tekse come here for whiskey," I said.

"So that means it is okay to swear at your sister."

It was the same words we always traded, all worn smooth and shining like the wood of a sled runner. Tekse was here and everybody was scared and we were having the same old argument. The brand for the kegs was heating in the fire and I could smell the tang of hot iron in the dung.

"You treat me like a child," I said.

She didn't even answer, but I knew what she would say—that I acted like a child. As if what Aslak and I were doing had anything to do with being a child.

I was so tired of it I thought I would burst.

"Go back to work," Mam said, turning on her stool. Saying *this talk is done* with her shoulders and her eyes.

"It's wrong to live this way," I said.

She looked back at me.

"If we lived with the clans, Aslak and I could be together."

That made her angry. "This is a better life than the clans," she said. "You don't know what you're talking about. Go back to work."

I didn't say anything. I just hated her. She didn't understand anything. She and my da hadn't waited until they were old. They hadn't waited for anything, and they'd left their clan to come to the mission when it was new. I stood in front of her, making her feel me standing there, all hot and silent.

"Janna," she said, "I'll not put up with your sullenness—" It made her furious when I didn't talk. "You and Aslak go back and hide the three-year-old whiskey."

Tekse had come for whiskey two years ago and taken

what they wanted and left us almost nothing but lame renndeer. They said it was because we had favored Toolie Clan in trade. The only reason we had any three-year-old whiskey left was because they couldn't tell what was what.

So my da and some of the men had dug a cellar in the distillery. Aslak jumped into the cellar, and I began stacking kegs at the edge for him to pull down. It wasn't very deep, not much over his chest, but the kegs were heavy.

"Hurry," Aslak said softly.

My hands were slick. I rolled the kegs on their edge. Aslak's hands were rough and red.

And then the last keg was on the edge. Ranveig's eye regarded me, strangely unaffected. Or maybe amused, or angry. Da said that spirits do not feel the way we feel. The teachers, Ayudesh and Wanji, never said anything at all about spirits, which was how we knew that they didn't listen to them.

There was not much space in the cellar, just enough for Aslak to stand and maybe a little more. Aslak put his hands on the edge and boosted himself out of the cellar. In front of the store we heard the crack of the door on its hinges and we jumped.

Aslak slid the wooden cover over the hole in the floor. "Move those," he said, pointing at empty kegs.

I didn't hear voices.

"Are you done yet?" Mam said, startling us again.

"Are they here?" I asked.

"No," she said. "Not yet." She didn't seem afraid. I had seen my mam afraid, but not very often. Mam helped us stack kegs. We all tried to be quiet, but they thumped like hollow drums. They filled the space around us with noise. It seemed that the outrunners had to hear us thumping away from outside. I kept looking at Mam, who was stacking kegs as if we hid whiskey all the time. Aslak was nervous, too. His shoulders were tense. I almost said to him, "You're up around the ears, boy," the way the hunters did, but right now I didn't think it would make him smile.

Mam scuffed the dirt around the kegs.

"Will they find them?" I asked.

Mam shrugged. "We'll see."

*   *   *

There was a lot to do to get ready for the outrunners besides hiding the best whiskey. Mam had us count the kegs. Then when we finally agreed on a number she wrote it in her tally book. "So we know how much we sell," she said. If we sold it instead of having it taken away. Mam hadn't seen the rifles.

We were just finishing counting when outrunners came. They came through the front. First the wind, like a wild dog sliding around the door and making the fire sway. Then the outrunners. The outrunners' cheeks were winter red. Their felts were all dark with dirt, like they'd been out for a long time. They were younger than I expected. Older than Aslak and me, but not so much. If we had been in the clans, Aslak might have been an outrunner.

"Hie," said one of the men, seeing my mother. They all looked at each other and grinned. People always seemed surprised that they were going to trade with my mam. The outrunners already smelled of whiskey, so people had finally made them welcome. Or maybe someone had the sense to realize that if they gave them drink we'd have time to get things ready. Maybe my da. My mam stood as she always did, with her arms crossed, tall as any of them. Waiting them out.

"What's this?" the first one said, looking around. "Eh? What's this? It stinks in here." The distillery always stank. The other two outrunners laughed. Like boys, being big men for each other.

They walked around, peered at the kegs, poked at the copper tubing and the still. One stuck his finger under the drip and tasted the raw stuff and grimaced.

Mam just stood and let them walk all around her. She didn't turn her head to watch them.

The leader picked up the brand. "What's this?" he said again.

"We mark all our kegs with the eye of Ranveig," Mam said.

"Woman's work," he remarked.

He tapped a keg. Not like Mam thumped them, listening, but just as if everything here were his. He pointed to a keg—not the one he was tapping on but a different one—and one of the other men picked it up. "Is it good?" he asked.

My mam shrugged.

One of the other outrunners sniggered. "Are you ignoring me?" he said.

My mam shrugged again. He didn't like that. He took two steps forward and hit Mam across the face. I looked at the black, packed-dirt floor.

"It's good," my mam said. I looked up and she had a red mark on the side of her face.

The outrunner grabbed her braid—she flinched as he reached past her face—and yanked her head. "It's good, woman?" he asked.

"Yes," she said, her voice coming almost airless, like she could not breathe.

He yanked her down to her knees and glared at the other two outrunners. They were still grinning. Then he let go and they all went out with the keg.

Mam stood back up again and touched her braid, then flipped it back over her neck. She didn't look at any of us.

People were in the schoolhouse. Ayudesh sat cross-legged on the table at the front, and people were sitting on the floor talking as if it were a meeting. Ayudesh had a square face and gray hair that made his skin look very dark. Ayudesh was an old man, older than anyone at the Mission, but he didn't look so old, just a little stooped. He still had all his teeth.

"So we should just let them take whatever they want?" JohnKisu said. JohnKisu was usually funny. Usually making jokes about people and talking dirty. He wasn't clowning now, but talking as a senior hunter. He sat on his heels, the way hunters do when they're waiting. I was looking but I didn't see my da.

Ayudesh said, "Even if we could get guns, they're used to fighting and we aren't. What do you think would happen?"

"If we don't stand up for ourselves, what will happen?" JohnKisu said.

"If you provoke them they'll destroy us," Ayudesh said.

"Teacher," JohnKisu said, spreading his hands as if he were telling a story. "Renndeer are not hunting animals, eh. They are not sharp-toothed like haunds or dogs. Haunds are hunters, packs of hunters, who do nothing but hunt renndeer. There are more renndeer than all the haunds could eat, eh. So how do they choose? They don't kill the buck renndeer with their long hard claws and heads; they take the young, the old, the sick, the helpless. We do not want to be haunds, teacher. We just want the haunds to go elsewhere for easy prey."

"You're making this bigger than it is. Why would they bother us?" Ayudesh said. "We are not renndeer; they are not here to hunt us. The worst they will do is take the whiskey."

"They are outrunners," JohnKisu said. "Bachelors from Tekse clan. They are little more than boys. They have guns and soon they will be drunk. We are toothless and they have teeth. What is to keep them from biting us just because they can?"

"Because if they bite us, we can't make whiskey," Ayudesh said.

"You think they are that wise?" JohnKisu said. "They are *bachelors*. They have no families, no responsibilities, no sense."

Wanji came in behind us, and the fire in the boxstove ducked and jumped in the draft. Wanji didn't sit down on the table but, as was her custom, lowered herself to the floor at the back of the schoolhouse. "Old hips," she muttered as if everyone in the room wasn't watching her. "Old women have old hips."

When I thought of Kalky, the old woman who makes the souls of everything, I thought of her as looking like Wanji. Wanji was dark, darker even than Ayudesh. She had a little face and a big nose and deep lines down from her nose to her chin. "What happened to you, daughter?" she asked my mam.

"The outrunners came to the distillery to take a keg," Mam said.

I noticed that now the meeting had turned around, away from Ayudesh on the table toward us in the back. Wanji always said that Ayudesh was vain and liked to sit high.

Sometimes she called him "High-on." They didn't act like married people. "And so," Wanji said.

My mother's face was still red from the blow, but it hadn't yet purpled. "I don't think the outrunners like to do business with me," Mam said.

"One of them hit her," I said, because Mam wasn't going to. Mam never talked about it when my da hit her, either. Although he didn't do it as much as he used to when I was Teija's size. Mam looked at me, but I couldn't tell if she was angry with me or not.

JohnKisu spread his hands to say *See?*

Wanji clucked.

"We got the three-year-old whiskey in the cellar," Mam said.

"Good," said Ayudesh, and some people turned back toward him. Then people started talking.

Some of the men were talking about guns. Wanji was listening without saying anything, resting her chin on her hand. Sometimes it seemed as if Wanji didn't even blink, that she just turned into stone and you didn't know what she was thinking.

Some of the other men were talking to Ayudesh about the whiskey. Paulina, JohnKisu's wife, got up and put water on the boxstove for the men to drink, and Jukka-Pekka went out the men's door, the spirit door in the back of the schoolhouse, which meant he was going to get whiskey or beer.

"Nothing will get done now," Aslak said, disgusted. "Let's go."

Outside there were outrunners. It seemed as if they were everywhere, even though there were really not that many of them.

Aslak scowled at them, and I looked at their guns. Long black guns slung over their backs. I had never seen a gun close. And there was my da, standing with three outrunners, holding a gun in his hands as if it were a fishing spear, admiring it. He was nodding and grinning, the way he did when someone told a good hunting story. Of course, he didn't know that one of these people had hit Mam.

Still, it made me mad that he was being friendly.

*　　*　　*

I was supposed to stay at the house, but I wanted to see what was happening. It was the time of year just before winterdark, when the sun was below the horizon all the time. There were still brief days, but it was dark by mid-afternoon. In the dark I could stand at the edges of things and not be seen. Mostly I wanted to watch my da.

The outrunners took two more kegs of whiskey and got loud. They stuck torches in the snow, so the dogs' harnesses all glittered and winked. We gave them a renndeer to slaughter, and they roasted that. Some of the Hamra men like my da—and even JohnKisu—sat with them and drank and talked and sang. I didn't understand why John-Kisu was there, but there he was, laughing and telling stories about the time my da got dumped out of the boat fishing.

Ayudesh was there, just listening.

The outrunners and the Hamra hunters were singing about Sivert the hunter and I looked up to see if I could make out the stars that formed him, but the sky had drifting clouds and I couldn't find the stars.

I couldn't see well enough; the light from the bonfire made everyone else just shadows. Faces glanced up, spirit faces in the firelight. The smoke blew our way and then shifted, and I smelled the sweat smell that came from the men's clothes as they warmed by the fire. And whiskey, of course. The renndeer was mostly bones.

I came up to my da and squatted behind him. "When are you coming home?" I asked.

"Janna," said my da. His face was strange, too, not human, like a mask. His eyes looked unnaturally light. "Go on back to your mother." I could smell whiskey on him, too. Whiskey sometimes made him mean. My da used to drink a lot of whiskey when I was young, but since Teija was born he didn't drink it very often at all. He said the mornings were too hard when you got old.

I drew away from him. I hated it when he smelled that way. I stood a moment, but there was nothing to watch but a bunch of drunk men. So I started around the edges to go back.

One of the outrunners stumbled up and into me before I could get out of the way. "Eh—?"

I pulled away but he gripped my arm. "Boy?" he said again. His breath in my face made me close my eyes and turn my head.

"No boy," he said. He was drunk, probably going to relieve himself. "No boy, girl, pretty as a boy," he said.

I tried to pull away.

"I'm not pretty enough for you?" he said. "Eh? Not pretty enough?" He wasn't pretty; he was wiry and had teeth missing on one side of his mouth. "Not Hamra Clan? With their pretty houses like offworlders? Not pretty, eh?"

My da said, "Leave her go."

"You've got dirt on your face," he said to me. It was so dark, even with the fire, that he couldn't really see anything.

"Let go," I said.

"Shut up, girl," he said to me. He licked his thumb and reached toward my face. I raised my hand and drew back, and he twisted my arm. "Stand still." He rubbed my cheek with his thumb and peered closely at my face. My cheek smarted where he had rubbed on it.

"Damn," he said, pleased. "Better." Then he leaned forward and tried to kiss me.

If I had just let him kiss me it would have been okay. He was so so drunk he couldn't really do anything. But his breath stank in my face and I tried to twist away. I pushed at him. He staggered and fell, pulling me down, too.

"Let go!" Shut up, I thought to myself, shut up, shut up! Give in, he's too drunk to do much. I tried to pull his arm away, but his grip was too strong.

"What's this?" another outrunner was saying.

"Eino's found some girl."

"It would be fucking Eino!"

I struggled, trying to get away. My da was standing over us; I could see him pulling on the man.

"Hey now," Ayudesh was saying, "hey now, leave her be." But nobody was paying attention. Everybody was watching us. The outrunner pinned me with my arms over my head and kissed me.

I went as still as I could.

"Get off him." Another outrunner hauled my da away. Ayudesh said, "Stop! That's enough!"

"She's yours, eh?" someone said. One of the out-runners was holding my father by the arm and my father's face was twisted. He had told me not to come by the fire and now he would be mad at me—

Someone else grunted and laughed.

"She likes Hamra better, eh?"

"That's because she doesn't know better."

"Eino'll show her."

You all stink like drunks, I wanted to scream at them, because they did. Oh, my da would be so mad at me, he was drunk, he was drunk, my da would be so mad—

There was the bone crack of gunfire and everybody stopped.

JohnKisu was standing next to the fire with an outrunner rifle pointed up, as if he were shooting at Sivert up there in the stars. His expression was mild and he was studying the gun as if he hadn't even noticed what was going on.

"Hey," an outrunner said, "put that down!"

JohnKisu looked around at the outrunners, at us. He looked slowly. He didn't look funny or angry, he looked as if he were out on a boat in the ice. Calm, far away. Cold as the stars. He could kill someone.

The outrunners felt it, too. They didn't move. If he shot one of them, the others would kill him, but the one he shot would still be dead. No one wanted to be the one who might be dead.

"It's a nice piece," JohnKisu said, "but if you used it for hunting you'd soon be so deaf you couldn't hear any-thing moving." Then he grinned.

Someone laughed.

Everybody laughed.

"Janna," JohnKisu said, "get us more whiskey."

"Eino, you walking dick, get up from the girl." One of them reached down and pulled him off. He looked mad.

"What," he said, "what?"

"Go take a piss," the outrunner said.

Everyone laughed.

I fell asleep thinking about how I wished that the Tekse outrunners were gone. I dreamed—and I was startled awake by gunfire.

Just more drinking and shooting.

I wished my da would come home. It didn't seem fair that we should lie there and be afraid while the men were getting drunk and singing.

The outrunners stayed the next day, taking three more kegs of whiskey but not talking about trade. The following day they sent out hunters but didn't find their own meat and so took another renndeer, a gelding, and more whiskey.

I went down to the distillery. It was already getting dark. The door was left open and the fire was out. Mam wasn't coming anymore. There was no work being done. Kegs had been taken down and some had been opened and left open. Some had been spilled. They had started on the green stuff, not knowing what was what and had thrown most of it in the snow, probably thinking it was bad. Branded eyes on the kegs looked everywhere.

I thought maybe they wouldn't leave until all the whiskey was gone. For one wild moment I thought about taking an ax to the kegs. Give them no reason to stay.

Instead I listened to them singing, their voices far away. My da was there, and I wondered what he was doing. I wanted him to see me and feel guilty and come home. I was afraid to walk back toward the voices, but I didn't want to stand outside the light in the dark either. I walked until I could see the big fire they had going and smell the renndeer roasting. Then I stood for a while, because I was more afraid of crossing the circle of firelight than I was cold. Maybe someone was holding me back, maybe my spirit knew something.

I looked for my father. I saw JohnKisu on the other side of the fire. His face was in the light. He wasn't singing, he was just watching. I saw Seppo, my little uncle, my father's half brother. I did not see my father anywhere.

Then I saw him. His back was to me. He was just a black outline against the fire. He had his hands open wide, as if he were explaining. He had his empty hands open. JohnKisu was watching my father explaining something to some of the outrunners, and something was wrong.

One of the outrunners turned his head and spat.

My father—I couldn't hear his voice, but I could see his

body, his shoulders moving as he explained. His shoulders working, working hard as if he were swimming. Such hard work, this talking with his hands open, talking, talking.

The outrunner took two steps, bent down, and pulled his rifle into the light. It was a dark thing there, a long thing against the light of the fire. My father took a step back and his hands came up, pushing something back.

And then the outrunner shot my father.

All the singing stopped. The fire cracked and the sparks rose like stars while my father struggled in the snow. He struggled hard, fighting and scraping back through the snow. Elbow-walking backwards. The outrunner was looking down the long barrel of the rifle.

Get up, I thought. Get up. For a long time it seemed I thought, Get up, get up. Da, get up! But no sound came out of my mouth, and there was black on the snow where my father had dragged himself and where he now lay.

The outrunner shot again.

My father flopped into the snow, and I could see the light on his face as he looked up. Then he stopped.

JohnKisu watched. No one moved except the outrunner who put his rifle away.

I could feel the red meat, the hammering muscle in my chest. I could feel it squeezing, squeezing. Heat flowed in my face. In my hands.

Outrunners shouted at outrunners. "You shit," one shouted at the one who shot my father. "You drunken, stupid shit!" The one who shot my father shrugged at first, as if he didn't care, and then he became angry, too, shouting.

No one saw me there. My breath was in my chest, so full. If I let the air out the outrunner would hear me breathe. I tried to take small breaths, could not get enough air. I did not remember when I had been holding my breath.

JohnKisu and the hunters of Hamra sat, like prey, hiding in their stillness. The arguing went on and on, until it wasn't about my father at all and his body was forgotten in the dirty snow. They argued about who was stupid and who had the High-on's favor. The whiskey was talking.

I could think of nothing but air.

I went back through the dark, out of Hamra, and crept around behind the houses in the dark and cold until I could come to our house without going past the fire. I took great shuddering breaths of cold air, breathed out great gouts of fog.

My mother was trying to get Teija quiet when I came in. "No," she was saying, "stop it now, or I'll give you something to cry about."

"Mam," I said, and I started to cry.

"What," she said. "Janna, your face is all red." She was my mam, with her face turned toward me, and I had never seen her face so clearly.

"They're going to kill all of us," I said. "They killed Da with a rifle."

She never said a word but just ran out and left me there. Teija started to cry, although she didn't really know what I was crying about. Just that she should be scared.

Wanji came and got me and brought me to Ayudesh's house because our house is small and Ayudesh's house had enough room for some people. Snow was caked in the creases of my father's pants. It was in his hands, too, unmelted. I had seen dead people before, and my father looked like all of them. Not like himself at all.

My mother had followed him as far as the living can go—or at least as far as someone untrained in spirit journeys—and she was not herself. She was sitting on the floor next to his body, rocking back and forth with her arms crossed in her lap. I had seen women like that before, but not my mother. I didn't want to look. It seemed indecent. Worse than the body of my father, since my father wasn't there at all.

Teija was screaming. Her face was red from the effort. I held her even though she was heavy and she kept arching away from me like a toddler in a tantrum. "MAM! MAM!" she kept screaming.

People came in and squatted down next to the body for a while. People talked about guns. It was important that I take care of Teija, so I did, until finally she wore herself out from crying and fell asleep. I held her on my lap until the blood was out of my legs and I couldn't feel the floor and then Wanji brought me a blanket and I wrapped Teija in it and let her sleep.

Wanji beckoned me to follow. I could barely stand— my legs had so little feeling. I held the wall and looked around, at my mother sitting next to the vacant body, at my sister, who though asleep was still alive. Then I tottered after Wanji as if I were the old woman.

Wanji took me to her house, which was little and dark. She had a lamp shaped like a bird. It had been in her house as long as I could remember. It didn't give very much light, but I had always liked it. We sat on the floor. Wanji's floor was always piled high with rugs from her home in India and furs and blankets. It made it hard to walk but nice to sit. Wanji got cold and her bones hurt, so she always made a little nest when she sat down. She pulled a red and blue rug across her lap. "Sit, sit, sit," she said.

I was cold, but there was a blanket to wrap around my shoulders and watch Wanji make hot tea. I couldn't remember being alone with Wanji before. But everything was so strange it didn't seem to make any difference, and it was nice to have Wanji deciding what to do and me not having to do anything.

Wanji made tea over her little clay bird lamp. She handed me a cup and I sipped it. Offworld tea was a strange drink. Wanji and Ayudesh liked it and hoarded it. It was too bitter to be very good, but it was warm and the smell of it was always special. I drank it and held it against me. I started to get warm. The blanket got warm from me and smelled faintly of Wanji, an old dry smell.

I was sleepy. It would have been nice to go to sleep right there in my little nest on Wanji's floor. I wanted someone to take care of me. My eyes started to fill up and in a moment I was crying salt tears into my tea.

"No time for that, Janna," Wanji said. Always sharp with us. Some people were afraid of Wanji. I was. But it felt good to cry, and I didn't know how to stop it, so I didn't.

Wanji didn't pay any attention. She was hunting through her house, checking in a chest, pulling up layers of rugs to peer in a corner. Was she going to give me a gun? I couldn't think of anything else that would help very much right now, but I couldn't imagine that Wanji had a gun.

She came back with a dark red plastic bag not much bigger than the span of my spread hand. That was almost as astonishing as a gun. We didn't have plastic; it wasn't appropriate. I wiped my nose on my sleeve. I was warm and tired. Would Wanji let me sleep right here on her floor? She put the bag in front of me. It shone like metal. So very fine. Like nothing we had. I touched the bag. I liked the feeling of plastic. I liked the sound of the word in English. If someday I had a daughter, maybe I'd name her Plastic. It would be a rich name, an exotic name. The teachers wouldn't like it, but it was a name I wished I had.

Wanji opened the plastic bag, but away from me so I couldn't see inside it. She picked at it as if she were picking at a sewing kit, looking for something. I wanted to look in it, but I was afraid that if I tried she'd snap at me.

She looked at me. "This is mine," she said. "We both got one, Ayudesh and I, and we decided that if the people who settled the mission couldn't have it, we wouldn't either."

I didn't care about that. That was old talk. I wanted to know what it was.

Wanji wasn't ready to tell me what it was. No one knew about this and I was afraid she would talk herself out of it. She looked at it and thought. If I thought, it was about my father being dead. I sipped tea and tried to think about being warm, about sleeping, but that feeling had passed. I wondered where Aslak was.

I thought about my da and I started to cry again.

I thought that would really get Wanji angry, so I tried to hide it, but she didn't pay any attention at all. The shawl she wore over her head slipped halfway down, so when I glanced up I could see where her hair parted and the line of pale skin. It looked so bare that I wanted it covered up again.

"It was a mistake," Wanji said.

I thought she meant the bag, and I felt a terrible disappointment that I wouldn't get to see what was inside it.

"You understand what we were trying to do?" she asked me.

With the bag? Not at all.

"Why can't you have plastic, Janna?" she said softly.

Wanji had taught me why I couldn't have plastic. Our lessons in appropriate development used lots of English words because it was hard to say these things any other way, so I found the words to tell her came most easily that way. "Plastic," I said, "it's not appropriate. Appropriate technologies are based on the needs and capacities of people; they must be sustainable without outside support. Like the distillery is. Plastic isn't appropriate to Hamra's economy because we can't create it and it replaces things we can produce, like skin bags." I stroked the bag again. "But I like plastic. It's beautiful."

"What are the six precepts of development philosophy?" she asked.

I had to think. "One," I said, "that economic development should be gradual. Two, that analyzing economic growth by the production of goods rather than the needs and capacities of people leads to displacement and increased poverty. Three, that economic development should come from the integrated development of rural areas with the traditional sector—"

"It's just words," she snapped at me.

I didn't know what I had done wrong so I ducked my head and sniffed and waited for her to get angry because I couldn't stop crying.

Instead she stroked my hair. "Oh, little girl. Oh, Janna. You are one of the bright ones. If you aren't understanding it, then we really haven't gotten it across, have we?" Her hand was nice on my hair, and it seemed so unlike Wanji that it scared me into stillness. "We were trying to help, you know," she said. "We were trying to do good. We gave up our lives to come here. Do you realize?"

Did she mean that they were going to die? Ayudesh and Wanji?

"Do you know what this mission is for, Janna?"

I nodded. "To teach us to use the precepts of the appropriate technology movement to protect us against the invit—inevitable devastation that comes when technology comes in contact with our culture.''

''But what does that mean, child?'' she said, although she didn't really expect me to answer.

But I did. ''If offworld things come, we will want them, and soon we will have no renndeer and we will be poor. But if we can learn to do things our own way . . .'' I did not know how to explain what would happen if we could do things our own way. ''It would be good,'' I finished lamely.

''Oh, Janna,'' she said, and there were tears in her eyes. ''You people always could surprise me.''

I did not know what to say.

But it seemed to decide her. ''This,'' she said, suddenly brisk. ''This is for—what would you call them?—runners. Offworld runners. It is to help them survive. I am going to give it to you, understood?''

I nodded, although I couldn't think what an offworld outrunner would be. I had never seen any offworlders except Wanji and Ayudesh and sometimes people who came to see them, and as far as I could tell, offworlders didn't even have clans. But I nodded because I wanted the bag.

But she didn't give it to me. She sighed again, a terrible sound. Out of the bag she pulled shiny foil packets—dark blue, red, and yellow. They were the size of the palm of her hand. Her glasses were around her neck. She put them on like she did in the schoolroom, absent from the gesture. She studied the printing on the foil packets. I loved foil. Plastic was beautiful, but foil, foil was something unimaginable. Tea came in foil packets. The strange foods that the teachers got off the skimmer came in foil.

My tea was cold.

''This one,'' she said, ''it is a kind of signal.'' She looked over her glasses at me. ''Listen to me, Janna. Your life will depend on this. When you have this, you can send a signal that the offworlders can hear. They can hear it all the way in Tonstad. And after you send it, if you can wait in the same place, they will send someone out to help you.''

''They can hear it in Tonstad?'' I said. I had never even

met anyone other than Wanji and Ayudesh who had ever been to Tonstad.

"They can pick it up on their instruments. You send it every day until someone comes."

"How do I send it?"

She read the yellow packet. "We have to set the signal, you and I. First we have to put it in you."

I didn't understand, but she was reading, so I waited.

"I'm going to put it in your ear," she said. "From there it will migrate to your brain."

"Will it hurt?" I asked.

"A little," she said. "But it has its own way of taking pain away. Now, what should be the code?" She studied the packet. She pursed her lips.

A thing in my ear. I was afraid and I wanted to say no, but I was more afraid of Wanji, so I didn't.

"You can whistle, can't you?" she asked.

I knew how to whistle, yes, but whistling was bad luck.

"Okay," she said, "here it is. I'll put this in your ear, and then we'll wait for a while. Then when everything is ready we'll set the code."

She opened up the packet and inside was another packet and a little metal fork. She opened the inside packet and took out a tiny little disk, a soft thing almost like a fish egg. She leaned forward and put it in my left ear. Then she pushed it in hard and I jerked.

"Hold still," she said.

Something was moving and making noise in my ear and I couldn't be still. I pulled away and shook my head. The noise in my ear was loud, a sort of rubbing, oozing sound. I couldn't hear normal things out of my left ear. It was stopped up with whatever was making the oozing noise. Then it started to hurt. A little at first, then more and more.

I put my hand over my ear, pressing against the pain. Maybe it would eat through my ear? What would stop it from eating a hole in my head?

"Stop it," I said to Wanji. "Make it stop!"

But she didn't, she just sat there, watching.

The pain grew sharp, and then suddenly it stopped. The sound, the pain, everything.

I took my hand away. I was still deaf on the left side, but it didn't hurt.

"Did it stop?" Wanji asked.

I nodded.

"Do you feel dizzy? Sick?"

I didn't.

Wanji picked up the next packet. It was blue. "While that one is working, we'll do this one. Then the third one, which is easy. This one will make you faster when you are angry or scared. It will make time feel slower. There isn't any code for it. Something in your body starts it."

I didn't have any idea what she was talking about.

"After it has happened, you'll be tired. It uses up your energy." She studied the back of the packet, then she scooted closer to me, so we were both sitting cross-legged with our knees touching. Wanji had hard, bony knees, even through the felt of her dress.

"Open your eye, very wide," she said.

"Wait," I said. "Is this going to hurt?"

"No," she said.

I opened my eyes as wide as I could.

"Look down, but keep your eyes wide open," she said.

I tried.

"No," she said, irritated, "keep your eyes open."

"They are open," I said. I didn't think she should treat me this way. My da had just died. She should be nice to me. I could hear her open the packet. I wanted to blink but I was afraid to. I did, because I couldn't help it.

She leaned forward and spread my left eye open with thumb and forefinger. Then she swiftly touched my eye.

I jerked back. There was something in my eye—I could feel it—up under my eyelid. It was very uncomfortable. I blinked and blinked and blinked. My eye filled up with tears, just the one eye, which was very strange.

My eye socket started to ache. "It hurts."

"It won't last long," she said.

"You said it wouldn't hurt!" I said, startled.

"I lied," Wanji said, matter-of-fact.

It hurt more and more. I moaned. "You're hateful," I said.

"That's true," she said, unperturbed.

She picked up the third packet, the red one.

"No," I said, "I won't! I won't! You can't do it!"

"Hush," she said, "this one won't hurt. I saved it until last on purpose."

"You're lying!" I scrambled away from her. The air was cold where the nest of rugs and blankets had been wrapped around me. My head ached. It just ached. And I still couldn't hear anything out of my left ear.

"Look," she said, "I will read you the English. It is a patch, nothing more. It says it will feel cold, but that is all. See, it is just a square of cloth that will rest on your neck. If it hurts you can take it off."

I scrambled backwards away from her.

"Janna," she said. "Enough!" She was angry.

I was afraid of it, but I was still more afraid of Wanji. So I hunched down in front of her. I was so afraid that I sobbed while she peeled the back off the square and put it on me.

"See," she said, still sharp with me, "it doesn't hurt at all. Stop crying. Stop it. Enough is enough." She waved her hands over her head in disgust. "You are hysterical."

I held my hand over the patch. It didn't hurt but it did feel cold. I scrunched up and wrapped myself in a rug and gave myself over to my misery. My head hurt and my ear still ached faintly and I was starting to feel dizzy.

"Lie down," Wanji said. "Go on, lie down. I'll wake you when we can set the signal."

I made myself a nest in the mess of Wanji's floor and piled a blanket and a rug on top of me. Maybe the dark made my head feel better—I didn't know. But I fell asleep.

Wanji shook me awake. I hadn't been asleep long, and my head still ached. She had the little metal fork from the ear packet, the yellow packet. It occurred to me that she might stick it in my ear.

I covered my ear with my hand. My head hurt enough. I wasn't going to let Wanji stick a fork in my ear.

"Don't scowl," she said.

"My head hurts," I said.

"Are you dizzy?" she asked.

I felt out of sorts, unbalanced, but not really dizzy.

"Shake your head," Wanji said.

I shook my head. Still the same, but no worse. "Don't stick that in my ear," I said.

"What? I'm not going to stick this in your ear. It's a musical fork. I'm going to make a sound with it and hold it to your ear. When I tell you to, I want you to whistle something, okay?"

"Whistle what?" I said.

"Anything," she said, "I don't care. Whistle something for me now."

I couldn't think of anything to whistle. I couldn't think of anything at all except that I wished Wanji would leave me alone and let me go back to sleep.

Wanji squatted there. Stubborn old bitch.

I finally thought of something to whistle, a crazy dog song for children. I started whistling—

"That's enough," she said. "Now don't say anything else, but when I nod my head you whistle that. Don't say anything to me. If you do, it will ruin everything. Nod your head if you understand."

I nodded.

She slapped the fork against her hand, and I could see the long tines vibrating. She held it up to my ear, the one I couldn't hear anything out of. She held it there, concentrating fiercely. Then she nodded.

I whistled.

"Okay," she said. "Good. That is how you start it. Now whistle it again."

I whistled.

Everything went dark and then suddenly my head got very hot. Then I could see again.

"Good," Wanji said. "You just sent a signal."

"Why did everything get dark?" I asked.

"All the light in your eyes got used in the signal," Wanji said. "You won't be able to see when you do it."

My head hurt even worse. Now besides my eye aching, my temples were pounding. I had a fever. I raised my hand and felt my hot cheek.

Wanji picked up the blue packet. "Now we have to figure out about the third one, the one that will let you hibernate."

I didn't want to learn about hibernating. "I feel sick," I said.

"It's probably too soon, anyway," Wanji said. "Sleep for a while."

I felt so awful I didn't know if I could sleep. But Wanji brought me more tea and I drank that and lay down in my nest and presently I was dreaming.

There was a sound of gunfire, far away, just a pop. And then more pop-pop-pop.

It startled me, although I had been hearing the outrunners' guns at night since they got here. I woke with a fever, and everything felt as if I were still dreaming. I was alone in Wanji's house. The lamp was still lit, but I didn't know if it had been refilled or how long I had slept. During the long night of winterdark it is hard to know when you are. I got up, put out the lamp, and went outside.

Morning cold is worst when you are warm from sleep. The dry snow crunched in the dark. Nothing was moving except the dogs were barking, their voices coming at me from every way.

The outrunners were gone from the center of the Mission. Nothing was there but the remains of their fire and the trampled slick places where they had walked. I slid a bit as I walked there. My head felt light and I concentrated on my walking because if I did not think about it I didn't know what my feet would do.

Again I heard the pop-pop-pop. I could not tell where it was coming from because it echoed off the buildings around me. I could smell smoke and see the dull glow of fire above the trees. It was down from Hamra, the fire. At first I thought the outrunners had gotten a really big bonfire going, and then I realized they had set fire to the distillery. I ran for home.

No one was at home.

I made a pack of blankets. I found my ax and a few things and put them in the bundle, then slung it all over my shoulders. I didn't know what we would do, but if they were shooting people we should run away.

Outside, the wind was sharp and cold and I felt the hint that there would be snow. I saw the glow of the fire on

the horizon, a false dawn. Were Mam and Teija still at
Ayudesh's house? Someone would take care of Mam,
wouldn't they?

Two, no three, people were moving, too far away in the
dim light to see if they were men or women. They clung
close to houses where they were invisible against the black
wood, avoiding the open spaces. I stayed close to my
house, waiting to see if they were outrunners. A black dog
came past the schoolhouse into the open area where the
outrunners' fire had been and stopped and sniffed—maybe
the place where my father had died. I smelled smoke on
the crisp air.

I drew back to the house. The spirit door was closed and
my father was dead. I crouched low and ran until I was in
the trees and then I slipped and fell and slid feetfirst in the
snow, down the hill between the tree trunks, hidden in the
pools of shadow under the trees. Then I was still, waiting.

I still felt feverish and nothing was real.

The snow under the trees was all powder. It dusted
my leggings and clung in clumps in the wrinkles behind
my knees.

Nothing came after me that I could see. I got up and
walked deeper into the trees and then uphill, away from
the distillery but still skirting the Mission. I should have
run, but I didn't know where to run to and the Mission
pulled at me. I circled around it as if on a tether, pulling
in closer and closer as I got to the uphill part behind the
Mission. Coming back around I hung in the trees beyond
the field behind the schoolhouse. I could see the renndeer
pens and see light. The outrunners were in the renndeer
pens and the renndeer were down. A couple of the men
were dressing the carcasses.

I stumbled over JohnKisu in the darkness, actually fell
over him in the bushes.

He was dead. Shot. His stomach was ripped by rifle fire
and his eyes were open. I couldn't tell in the darkness if
he had dragged himself out here to die or if someone had
thrown the body here.

I started backing away. One of the dogs at the renndeer
pen heard me and started to bark. I could see it in the
light, its ears up and its tail curled over its back. The

others barked, too, ears toward me in the dark. I stopped. Men in the pen looked out into the dark. A couple of them picked up rifles and, cradling them in their arms, walked out toward me from the light.

I backed up, slowly. Maybe they would find JohnKisu's body and think that the dogs were barking at that. But they were hunters and they would see the marks of my boots in the snow and follow me. If I ran they would hear me. I was not a hunter. I did not know what to do.

Back, one slow step and then another, while the outrunners walked out away from the light. They were not coming straight at me, but they were walking side by side and they would find me. I had my knife. There was cover around, mostly trees, but I didn't know what I could do against a hunter with a rifle. Even if I could stop one the others would hear me.

There were shouts over by the houses.

The outrunners kept walking, but the shouts did not stop, and then there was the pop of guns. That stopped one and then the other and they half turned.

The dogs turned barking toward the shouts.

The outrunners started to jog toward the schoolhouse.

I walked backward in the dark.

There were flames over there, at the houses. I couldn't tell whose house was on fire. It was downhill from the schoolhouse, which meant it might be our house. People were running in between the schoolhouse and Wanji's house, and the outrunners lifted their guns and fired. People, three of them, kept on running.

The outrunners fired again and again. One of the people stumbled, but they all kept running. They were black shapes skimming on the field. The snow on the field was not deep because the wind blew it into the trees. Then one was in the trees. The outrunners fired again, but the other two made the trees as well.

There was a summer camp out this way, a long walk down to the river, for drying fish.

I picked my way through the trees.

There were people at the summer camp, and I waited in the trees to make sure they were Hamra people. It was mid-morning by the time I got there, and I was tired from walking through the snow. I didn't remember ever having seen the summer camp in the winter before. The drying racks were bare poles with a top covering of snow, and the lean-to was almost covered in drifted snow. There was no shelter here.

There were signs of three or four people in the trampled snow. I didn't think it would be the outrunners down there, because how would they even know where the summer camp was—but I wasn't sure of anything. I didn't know if I was thinking right or not.

I didn't feel too cold. I still had a fever—I felt as if everything were far from me, as if I walked half in this world. I sat and looked at the snow cupped in a brown leaf, and my mind was empty and things did not seem too bad. I don't know how long I sat.

Someone was walking in the summer camp. I thought it was Ralf, one of the boys.

I was stiff from sitting and colder than I had noticed but moving helped. I slid down the hill into the summer camp.

The summer camp sat in a V that looked at the river frozen below. Ralf was already out of the camp, but he waved at me from the trees and I scrambled back up there.

There were three people crouched around a fire so tiny it was invisible and one of them was Aslak. I wanted to run to him, but suddenly I didn't know what to do.

He half stood, "Janna!"

"Where is everyone else?" Ralf asked.

"I don't know," I said. "They are killing people."

"Seppo stole a rifle and shot one of the outrunners," Ralf said. "They killed him. Then they started shooting." Seppo was my little uncle. He and my father had the same father, but different mothers.

"Where's your mother and your sister?" Aslak asked.

"I don't know. I was at Wanji's house all night," I said. "Where's your family?"

"My da and I were at the renndeer pen this morning with JohnKisu," he said.

"I found JohnKisu," I said.

"Did you find my da?" he asked.

"No. Was he shot?"

"I don't know. I don't think so."

"JohnKisu was shot dead," I said. "I saw some people running across the field behind the schoolhouse. Maybe one of them was shot." My voice was too high and it shook.

Aslak looked away, to save me embarrassment. "None of us were shot."

"Did you come together?"

"No," Ralf said. "I found Venke here and Aslak here."

Aslak said he had gone down to see the fire at the distillery. The outrunners had taken some of the casks. He didn't know how the fire had started—if it was an accident or if they'd done it on purpose. "Come here by me," he said.

I crouched next to him. "We need to see what is happening at Hamra."

"I'm not going back," Venke said, looking at no one. I did not know Venke very well. She was old enough to have children but she had no one. She lived by herself. She had had her nose slit by her clan for adultery, but I never knew if she had a husband with her old clan or not. Some people came to Hamra because they didn't want to be part of their clan anymore. Most of them went back, but Venke had stayed.

Aslak said, "I'll go."

Ralf said he would stay in case anyone else came to the summer camp. In a day or two he and Venke were going to head toward the west and see if they could come across the winter pastures of Maudal clan. Ralf had kin there.

"That's pretty far," Aslak said. "Toolie clan would be closer."

"You have kin with Toolie clan?" Ralf said.

Aslak nodded.

Ralf stood and watched us leave the camp, but Venke crouched next to the fire and turned her back to us.

It took us through the rest of the short midwinter morning and into afternoon to get to Hamra. The only good thing about winterdark was that it was dark for the outrunners, too.

Nothing was moving when we got back to Hamra. From

the back the schoolhouse looked all right, but the houses were all burned. I could see where my house had been. Charred logs standing in the red afternoon sun. The ground around them was wet and muddy from the heat of the fires.

In front of the schoolhouse there were bodies. My da's body, thrown back in the snow. My mam and my sister. My sister's head was broken in. My mam didn't have her pants on. The front of the schoolhouse had burned, but the fire must have burned out before the whole building was gone. The dogs were moving among the bodies, sniffing, stopping to tug on the freezing flesh.

Aslak shouted at them to drive them off.

My mam's hipbones were sharp under the bloody skin and her sex was there for everyone to see, but I kept noticing her bare feet. The soles were dark. Her toenails were thick and her feet looked old. An old, old woman's feet. As if she were as old as Wanji.

I looked at people to see who else was there. Aslak's da was there, and his mam. I saw Wanji, although she had no face—but I knew her from her skin. She had been caught in fire. In her skinless face her eyes were baked white like a smoked fish.

The dogs were circling back, watching Aslak.

He screamed at them. Then he crouched down on his heels and covered his eyes with his arm and cried.

I did not feel anything. Not yet.

I whistled the tune that Wanji had taught me to send out the message, and the world went dark. It was something to do, and for a moment, I didn't have to look at my mother's bare feet.

The place for the Hamra dead was up the hill beyond the mission, away from the river, but without renndeer I couldn't think of how we could get all these bodies there. We didn't have anything for the bodies, either. Nothing for the spirit journey, not even blankets to wrap them in.

I could not bear to think of my mother without pants. There were lots of dead women in the snow and many of them did have pants. It may not have been fair that my mother should have someone else's but I could not think of anything else to do, so I took the leggings off Marja

and tried to put them on my mother. I could not really
get them right—my mother was tall and her body was
stiff from the cold and from death. I hated handling her.

My mother's flesh was white and odd to touch. Not like
flesh at all. Like plastic. Soft looking but not to touch.

Aslak watched me without saying anything. I thought
he might tell me not to, but he didn't. Finally he said,
"We can't get them to the place for the dead."

I didn't know what to say to that.

"And we don't have anyone to talk to the spirits," he
said. "Only me." He was the man here. I didn't know if
Aslak had talked with spirits or not; men didn't talk about
that with women. "I say that this place is a place of the
dead, too," he said. His voice was strange. "Hamra is a
place of the dead now."

"We leave them here?" I asked.

He nodded.

He was beardless, but he was male and he was old
enough that he had walked through the spirit door. I was
glad that he had made the decision.

I looked in houses for things for the dead to have with
them, but most things were burned. There were some
things half burned and sometimes not burned at all. I found
a fur. It stank of the fire but it wasn't burned, and I used
that to wrap the woman whose leggings I had stolen. In
Pekka's house, the three children were all dead, all huddled against an unburned wall. They didn't have any marks
on them and they didn't look dead—their cheeks were
bright red.

Aslak sat in the burned-out schoolhouse and I didn't
know if what he did was a spirit thing or if it was just
grief, but I didn't bother him. He kept the dogs away.

I kept blankets separate for Aslak and me, and in John-
Kisu's house—which had only burned a little—I found
short skis. Anything I found that we could use I didn't
give to the dead, but everything else I gave to them.

I tried to make sure that everybody got something—a
bit of stitching or a cup or something—so they would
not be completely without possessions. I managed to find
something for almost everybody, and I found enough blankets to wrap Aslak's family. I wrapped Teija with my

mother. Everything I handled had black streaks on it. My hands kept getting stiff with the cold. I kept having to tuck them under my arms, so my clothes were streaked with black, too. I probably stank like burned things, but after looking through the houses I couldn't smell it anymore.

I didn't usually pay any attention to which house I was in. I stepped in through what was left of a door, with the dim early afternoon sunlight coming through the hole in the roof above me, and found Ayudesh.

His hands were burned, and his shoulder was so burned that I could see the meat of his muscle. I knelt in the ash and dirt and touched him and he was warm with life. "Ayudesh," I said. "Teacher."

He didn't seem to hear me.

I looked for something to wrap him in, but there was nothing left of the bed and no blankets. I checked the next house and the one after that and found a renndeer skin that was smoky and half burned, but I brought it back and covered him.

"Aslak!" I shouted. The snow was so bright. My knees were cold from kneeling on the ground. "Aslak!" I stumbled a bit in the snow, then ran on the hard pack. Aslak was crouched in front of the bodies. He looked at me.

"Aslak!" I said, "I found Ayudesh! He's hurt, he's burned bad, but he's alive!"

We made a fire in the ruins of Ayudesh's house. Unlike Wanji's house, from what I could see this wasn't any different than anyone else's house. Wanji's was strange and offworld, with no real furniture, but in Ayudesh's house there was a burned bed frame and a hearth with a place to hang a pot. I had given the pot to the dead.

"Do you think he'll live?" Aslak asked.

I didn't know. I didn't think so, though. He wasn't conscious, and his breathing was thick and bad, as if his lungs were closing up. Burns were bad, my mam had told me. I didn't have anything to put on them, no fat to seal them, and we really couldn't even keep him warm. At least he was out of the wind.

Aslak had killed and skinned a dog and cooked that. Aslak said, "We can't stay here."

"We can't leave him," I said. Even if he was going to die, we couldn't leave him.

Aslak said, "It smells like snow."

I knew that.

"We'll see how he does during the night," Aslak said. "We should try for Toolie clan."

I didn't have any idea where their winter pastures were, much less how to find them. I almost asked Aslak if he did, but I didn't want to shame his new manhood, so I didn't.

I tried not to think about the dogs wandering among the dead. I tried not to think about bad weather. I tried not to think about my house or my mam. It did not leave much to think about.

My kin were Lauperak. I didn't know where their pastures were, but someone would. I could go to them if I didn't like Toolie clan. I had met a couple of my cousins when they came and brought my father's half brother, my little uncle.

"Listen," Aslak said, touching my arm.

I didn't hear it at first, then I did. It was a skimmer.

It was far away. Skimmers didn't land at night. They didn't even come at night. It had come to my message, I guessed.

Aslak got up and we ran out to the edge of the field behind the schoolhouse. Dogs started barking.

Finally we saw lights from the skimmer, strange green and red stars. They moved against the sky as if they had been shaken loose.

The lights came toward us for a long time. They got bigger and brighter, more than any star. It seemed as if they stopped, but the lights kept getting brighter. I finally decided that they were coming straight toward us.

Then we could see the skimmer in its own lights.

I shouted, and Aslak shouted, too, but the skimmer didn't seem to hear us. But then it turned and slowly curved around, the sound of it going farther away and then just hanging in the air. It got to where it had been before and came back. This time it came even lower and it dropped red lights. One. Two. Three.

Then a third time it came around and I wondered what it would do now. But this time it landed, the sound of it so loud that I could feel as well as hear it. It was a different skimmer than the one we always saw. It was bigger, with a belly like it was pregnant. It was white and red. It settled easily on the snow. Its engines, pointed down, melted snow underneath them.

And then it sat. Lights blinked. The red lights on the ground flickered. The dogs barked.

The door opened and a man called out to watch something but I didn't understand. My English is pretty good, one of the best in school, but I couldn't understand him.

Finally a man jumped down, and then two more men and two women.

I couldn't understand what anyone was saying in English. They asked me questions, but I just kept shaking my head. I was tired and now, finally, I wanted to cry.

"You called us. Did you call us?" one man said over and over until I understood.

I nodded.

"How?"

"Wanji give me . . . in my head . . ." I had no idea how to explain. I pointed to my ear. "Ayudesh is, is bad."

One of the women came over and, handling my head as if I were a renndeer, turned it so she could push my hair out of the way and look in my ear. I still couldn't hear very well with that ear. Her handling wasn't rough, but it was not something people do to each other.

"How did you get a survey kit?" she asked me, many times, but even though I heard the words I didn't know how to think about them or answer them.

"No," I said. "Ayudesh is bad. You come!" I grabbed the woman's arm and I pulled her. She slipped in the snow, and walked stiff-legged like a child. The men followed, awkward. It was strange to see adults who couldn't walk on packed snow. I brought them to Ayudesh, and the woman knelt down and looked at him and said things to one of the men. He ran back to the skimmer, slipping and almost falling until he got to the unpacked snow at the field.

He came back with a heavy dark box with clasps that flickered in the firelight. It was a beautiful thing, and when he opened it up it was full of cunning things, of compartments and drawers and foil packets of every color.

The woman took out a packet and a length of plastic like cord, but hollow like a river reed, and she did something to Ayudesh. I watched.

"Ask if he will die," Aslak said.

"Um, the teacher," I said, "um, it is bad?"

The woman nodded. She said something, but I didn't understand. "Smoke," she said. "Do you understand? Smoke?"

"Smoke," I said. "Yes." To Aslak I said, "He had a lot of smoke in him."

Aslak shook his head.

The men went to the skimmer and came back with a litter. They put it next to Ayudesh and lifted him on, but then they stood up and nearly fell, trying to carry him. They tried to walk, but I couldn't stand watching, so I took the handles from the man by Ayudesh's feet, and Aslak, nodding, took the ones at the head. We carried Ayudesh to the skimmer.

We walked right up to the door of the skimmer, and I could look in. It was big inside. Hollow. It was dark in the back. I had thought it would be all lights inside and I was disappointed. There were things hanging on the walls, but mostly it was empty. One of the offworld men jumped up into the skimmer, and then he was not clumsy at all. He pulled the teacher and the litter into the back of the skimmer.

One of the men brought us something hot and bitter and sweet to drink. The drink was in blue plastic cups, the same color as the jackets that they all wore except for one man whose jacket was red with blue writing. Pretty things. I made myself drink mine. Anything this black and bitter must have been medicine. Aslak just held his.

"Where is everyone else?" the red-jacket man asked slowly.

"Dead," I said.

"Everyone?" he said.

"Yes," I said. Ralf and Venke weren't dead, but they were probably already gone. They seemed far away to me.

Then they got hand lights and we all walked over and looked at the bodies. Dogs ran from the lights, staying at the edges and slinking as if guilty of something.

"Which one is Wanji? Which is the wife of the mission director?" the man from the skimmer asked.

I had to walk between the bodies. We had laid them out so their heads all faced the schoolhouse and their feet all faced the center of the village. They were more bundles than people. I could have told her in the light, but in the dark, with the hand lights making it hard to see anything but where they were pointed, it took me a while. I found JohnKisu by mistake.

Then I found Wanji with her baked white eyes. I had wrapped her in a blanket but it was burned on one side.

"Wait," Aslak said. "They shouldn't do that."

I squatted down.

"Wanji is a Hamra person," Aslak said.

"Her spirit is already gone," I said.

"She won't have anything," he said.

"If the offworlders take her, won't they give her offworld things?"

"She didn't want offworld things," Aslak said. "That's why she was here."

"But we don't have anything to give her. At least if the offworlders give her things she'll have something."

Aslak shook his head. "JohnKisu—" he started to say but stopped. JohnKisu talked to spirits more than anyone. He would have known. But I didn't know how to ask him, and I didn't think Aslak did either. Although I wasn't sure. There wasn't any drum or anything for spirit talk anyway.

The offworlders stood looking at us.

"Okay," Aslak said. So I stood up and we picked up Wanji's body and we took it to the skimmer, me holding her legs near her bare feet, Aslak carrying her head.

A dog followed us in the dark.

They were talking again. Aslak and I stood there. Aslak's breath was an enormous white plume in the lights of the skimmer. I stamped my feet. The lights were bright, but they were a cheat. They didn't make you any warmer.

The man in the red jacket climbed up and went to the front of the skimmer. There were chairs there and he sat in one and talked to someone on a radio. I could remember the word for radio in English. Ayudesh used to have one until it stopped working and he didn't get another.

My thoughts rattled through my empty head.

Aslak and I stood outside the door, leaning in to watch them. The floor of the skimmer was metal.

One of the blue-jacket men brought us two blankets. The blankets were the same blue as his jacket and had a red symbol on them. A circle with words. I didn't pay much attention to them. He brought us foil packets. Five. Ten of them.

"Food," he said, pointing to the packets.

I nodded. "Food," I repeated.

"Do they have rifles?" Aslak asked harshly.

"Guns?" I asked. "You have guns?"

"No guns," the blue jacket said, "no guns."

I didn't know if we were supposed to get in the skimmer or if the gifts meant to go.

"We'll take care of him," the woman said. "We'll take good care of him."

"Move back," said the red jacket, shooing us.

We trotted back away from the skimmer. Its engines fired, and the ground underneath them steamed. The skimmer rose, and then the engines turned from pointing down to pointing back and it moved off. Heavy and slow at first, but then faster and faster. Higher and higher.

We stood in the snow and blinked in the darkness, holding our gifts.

2: The Great Cold Room of the World

WE DIDN'T TALK ABOUT HAMRA OR WHETHER or not Aslak really knew where he was going or even if Toolie clan would be there.

The second day out from Hamra it snowed. We crossed the black river ice and started up the valley. One of the dogs, a gray-and-black male with his tail curled over his back, followed us.

We skied single file, taking turns breaking a path, with the dog following behind. We didn't have grease for the skis, which made going uphill a little easier, but meant that they didn't glide well, so it was more tiring than usual. We were lucky to have JohnKisu's short skis. When it was light, it was only gray. Staring ahead at the snow made everything look the same, so sometimes I had to look up at Aslak's back because I couldn't tell where the path was. The snow crowded sound in on us. I could hear the sound of Aslak breathing, steady and loud as mine. His mustache, when he unwrapped his face, had little bits of rime from his breath. We breathed into and out of the dead landscape.

I had Aslak all to myself, but when I looked at him I thought about my mam and then my da and Teija and Ayudesh and all the village and my thoughts would swirl down and down and I would have to stop them because I was afraid if I let myself think I would sink to my knees in the snow and not go any farther. Then I would ski and try to feel nothing. Slip, slip, slip of the ungreased skis.

Winterbabies flashed from tree to tree, black and white wings. You can't eat winterbabies, they are aunworld—from this world, not from Earth—and their meat will make you sick.

We slept together. The third night he kissed me. Then he pressed me down into the blanket and tugged at my leggings. "Get these off," he said hoarsely.

I didn't move for a moment. I could feel everything around me in the dark—the rough uneven ground and the dead brush beneath the blanket, the bit of wind. It was too cold to undress. My skin shrank away at the thought of it. My mam had said no. My mam would be mad. My mam was dead. All those cold, dead people with their plastic skin. Even Ayudesh was dead, I was sure, without knowing quite why I was sure.

I slid my leggings down around my knees and the cold brushed fingers across my privates until he covered me with his own weight. He fumbled and he couldn't find where to put it in me, and when he raised up the cold came between us. It hurt when he finally put it in me, and I didn't like it but I didn't say anything.

When he was done I was empty and alone and the only thing I could think to ask was, "Are you my husband now?"

"Yeah," he said.

We ate the food given to us by the offworlders. Wanji had opened foil packets very neatly, I remembered, but I couldn't; and when I finally got one open, it broke apart and dry food fell all over the snow. I gathered it up, snow and all, and melted the snow with the food over the fire. It was a little like dried meat, but whoever had prepared it didn't know anything about drying because the meat was so lean that it dried away to nothing. When the snow was melted it looked like brown paste.

Once we tasted it, though, we were surprised. It was salty and good, and we ate all we could get. The dog stood by Aslak and whined. I melted some snow for the dog and since it was in the same pot it had a little of the salty taste of the offworlder's food. The dog drank it all.

Aslak told me to pull my leggings down. After that we

slept for a bit. I woke up tight against him with my back warm and the rest of me cold. I felt him wake against me. He tightened his arms around me and murmured, "My Janna. My Janna."

We got up in the dark and put our things together, wrapped up in the blanket. We did a lot of it by touch. When we camped we tried to find a place protected from the wind, but that meant it was even darker.

I was cold deep through.

We skied a lot more on the river the next day. It had been dark for a long time when we climbed up off the river ice and found a place to stop. The dog flopped down as soon as we did. Of the three kinds of things—those from Earth that nourish us, those that are aunworld and poison us, and those that we can eat but do not nourish— the dog was from Earth.

"That dog isn't getting any fatter," I said.

"I know," Aslak said.

"Do you want to eat him tonight?"

"No."

"Every day he just gets thinner."

"We're not going to eat him," Aslak said. He sounded angry. I wasn't going to ask him why we didn't eat the dog. It was stupid, but there wasn't any sense in arguing. If I got mad, if I started feeling, I would feel everything. I would feel Hamra's death, and then I didn't know if I could keep going.

He got a bit of tinder lit and started coaxing a fire out of the wet winter wood. Anger and cold make Aslak's fingers stiff, and he had trouble with the fire and lost the tiny flame. He used more precious tinder. I didn't say anything.

"I don't want to come to Toolie clan with nothing," Aslak finally said. "He's a good dog. He's learned from renndeer. He knows how to be around a herd."

I opened the foil packet more carefully and tasted some of the dried food. It wasn't like any food I had ever had before. I offered some to Aslak, and he tasted it and grimaced.

"It's all right when I mix it with snow," I said.

It was different than the packet we'd had before. Darker.

Still salty though. There really wasn't very much in one
packet, but we only had eight more left so that was all
we ate.

Aslak fed a little of his to the dog.

When we finished our meal and crawled into our blankets Aslak wanted to fuck. He kissed me a couple of
times, and then he was all hard and he put it in me. It
hurt a little. But it didn't take long and the sooner we got
it over the sooner I could go to sleep and I was bone tired.

JohnKisu used to make comments about how boys were
bad at fucking, but I didn't see what could make it
much better.

Afterward I curled up against him, spooned back to his
front. "Janna," he said, "it'll be all right. I'll take care
of you, I promise."

"I know," I whispered, saying what he needed. The
skin of my leg was so cold that the fabric of my leggings hurt.

On the seventh day Aslak killed the dog. He didn't say
he was going to, he just took out his knife. I saw it glint
in the fire and almost asked what he was doing. He walked
up to the dog lying in the snow, and it beat its tail once
feebly, then he pulled its muzzle up and slit its throat. I
grabbed the pot to catch what blood I could. The dog was
thin and stringy, but it tasted good. We ate everything.
We should have saved some, but we couldn't stop ourselves. We drank soup from the bones when we woke up
and broke the knob ends and sucked out the little bit of
marrow. "Eat," Aslak kept saying. He was taking care
of us.

Every day the amount of light was less, and in a few
weeks there would be no time when the sun was above
the horizon, just a few hours of twilight, when the sun
seemed almost about to rise.

After we ate the dog we ate half a foil packet each day.
I made a soup with a lot of snow.

We had used the last half packet two days before we
heard a renndeer bell in the dark. This was a deep bell,
the kind that carry a long distance. We stopped when we

heard it and waited, breathing out into the night and hoping, until we heard it again.

I hoped we would run into a herder, but we found the cabin first. There was smoke coming out of the chimney and there was a castrated work renndeer tied up outside.

Dogs barked. Someone opened the door. "Who is it?"

"Aslak and Janna of Hamra clan," Aslak said. "I have kin with Toolie clan. Arto and Sini are my grandparents."

"It's too cold to stand out there," said the man. "You let the haunds in." He meant the wind. We told them our story and they fed us and let us sleep. After we slept, the whole family got out sleds and took us through the dark to Aslak's kin.

Sini and her husband, Arto, had a lot of renndeer. They were all around the cabins of their winter camp. What with sons and daughters and their husbands and wives and children there were a lot of cabins. People. I thought it would be like home. We came through the snow with renndeer bells ringing and people came out of cabins and followed us.

Aslak smiled at me to hide his nervousness at meeting his kin. "A party in our honor, eh?" he said to me.

I was too nervous to do anything but smile back.

We stopped. The cabin wasn't like the ones at home; it was narrow and inside it was mostly empty like a tent. People from the other cabins followed us in. They all stared at us and no one smiled. The only person who didn't pay any attention to us was an older woman who was sewing a pair of boots. When they didn't look at us, the people all looked at her and when she didn't look up, most of them looked back at us. That's how we knew that the woman with the boots was Aslak's grandmother Sini.

Sini wore fur with red felt sewn with embroidery. She was not as tall as me, but when I met her I tended to forget that. Her hair was pulled back away from her round face and slicked down and darkened with renndeer grease. Her sleeves were embroidered halfway to her elbows. She was sewing the sole of the boot and she let us wait while she finished.

We were dirty and our clothes were ill used. We had nothing in our hands.

When she had finished the boot sole, she stood up. She had to get her feet under her because of her bulk. We waited, hands clasped in front of us. She handed the boot to one of the other women and then she turned, slapped her hands together as if to shake off any dust, and looked at us.

"What do you want?" Sini asked.

I knew then what it meant to be truly kinless.

"I'm Aslak," my husband said, "Ritta's son. This is my wife, Janna."

Sini said, "You are empty mouths, the two of you."

I'd thought she'd have wanted to know about her daughter.

"We can work," Aslak said.

Sini turned around and walked away from us. Anger rose up in me. She was shaming Aslak, this stingy old woman. "Your daughter is dead," I said. "She is naked in the land of the dead. This is your daughter's son."

I said it for Aslak, to shame her, but she only stopped and said over her shoulder, "That person was not my daughter, Hamra."

Cold words. Aslak took my hand. I studied the dark floor. After a moment I looked up but people were still watching so I studied the floor again. When I looked up again some people were leaving but some were still watching. One woman was peeling potatoes from last year's garden, so I went and sat down and started peeling potatoes, keeping my head down and watching the deep red peel slip off the pale pink flesh.

She didn't seem to mind. I looked at her out of the corner of my eye. Her winter furs had some blue felt, but not so much or so embroidered as Sini's. Tiny flowers ran around the sleeves and the neck, and tiny green leaves trimmed the edge. Whoever had done the needlework had a deft hand. She handled the wrinkled potatoes without thought, which made me suppose that potatoes were not a special thing here in Sini's camp.

We peeled potatoes for a while, and then she got up and beckoned me with her head. I followed her out into the cold. She left the potatoes inside. "I'll show you where to get water," she said. "I'm Inger."

"I'm Janna," I said.

We walked down the hill to get water.

"Did you do the needlework on that?" I asked.

She nodded.

"It's beautiful," I said.

"Hush," she said, embarrassed. "Don't say anything like that to the others. They'll think you're asking for a favor."

Then I was embarrassed because I wasn't asking for clothes—but she knew that or she wouldn't have warned me.

We brought water back together and together we cooked dinner. I washed things while everyone ate so as not to seem forward. Inger's stew smelled good, but my empty stomach twisted around itself.

Aslak and I got the leftovers. I brought him his dinner but he didn't want to look at me. "You found the winter pastures," I said. "I couldn't have found Lauperak's pastures." But his kin were mean and that wasn't much comfort for him.

That night Aslak and I slept in the cabin of Inger and her husband, Petri. There was a green plastic basin hanging on the wall, which shocked me, but then I realized that no one cared about what was appropriate or not. The cabin was warm, but I thought of my mother's house with the furs on the bed and the cookpot over the stove. I thought of all the colors of that house and the light from the lamp. I thought of Wanji's little lamp, shaped like a bird. I could have looked for the little lamp, it wouldn't have burned up in the fire. Then I would have something more than Wanji's tricks in my head, the ones that didn't help us.

I lay next to the wall, and Aslak lay outside me, on his back, asleep. I turned my face to the wall so he wouldn't hear me cry, although I really did want him to hear me cry.

But he didn't.

We lived with Inger and Petri. They had no children, so we did things for them.

I was sick in the morning, but I didn't let myself think about why. My belly sucked all my substance into itself and my arms and legs grew thin, and my hair didn't stay in my head. When I unbraided it and ran my fingers through it, long strands wrapped themselves around my finger joints. My belly didn't allow me to eat, but it demanded I feed it. It didn't grow much yet. It would seem that with all it was eating it should be big as a house.

At first I thought Aslak didn't notice, then I began to think that he had noticed and wasn't saying anything. He averted his eyes from me a lot. He probably thought I was sick, since he had seen me throwing up but never said anything. Perhaps he wanted me to die? If we weren't husband and wife, then maybe he could husband a girl whose parents had renndeer and he wouldn't be stuck kinless and without anything.

In the morning, I went and got water. I was queasy and the house smelled of breakfast potatoes, but the winter air was clear and clean and made my stomach settle. An old castrate renndeer came up behind me and snuffled against my shoulder for a handout, and I turned and buried my face against his neck. I pulled moss out of the trees and let him eat while I got the sled out. Then I pulled on his ears and let him slobber a bit of my jacket front. I took my gloves off and warmed my hands against his hide while he regarded me with his dark red eyes. No one paid any attention to him but me because he was so slow, and after years of learning to like people and the cabin and pulling a sled he didn't understand why no one taught him anything now. It was nice to have something grateful to me.

His great red eye was like a gem in his old face. It was something so liquid and shining and warm. I liked him, liked the warmth of his breath on my face when he lipped at my hat, liked his long eyelashes. He would be something that remembered me, however dimly, until next year when there was no one to feed him.

Would Aslak miss me? I didn't know. Maybe he would feel my hungry spirit with my ravenous belly as guilt gnawing at him.

But probably he would charm some other girl and marry her and get renndeer from her parents and finally be able to start his own life. So if I stayed alive then we both

would have nothing and the hungry child in my belly
would have nothing, but if the child and I died then Aslak
could have a life.

How noble I would be. I got to the creek blind with
tears and set the buckets down.

When I had finished crying I broke the ice in the creek
and filled the buckets. I let the renndeer drink out of one
and filled it again. He stayed there, gnawing on the long
hanging limbs of a spinner tree. I put the ax down with
the buckets because it had a head made by offworlders,
strong metal, and it was a good ax and not mine.

I stepped down into the creek. If I stuck to the side of
the creek where the wind had blown the ice mostly clear
of snow, I wouldn't leave tracks.

I walked down the creek, away from most of the cabins,
and finally found a place where a blackwood tree had
fallen. Most of the hardwood trees along the edge of the
creek had been cut down for building and all that was left
were trash like spinner, but here someone had missed this
broad blackwood. It had fallen partly across the creek, and
old leaves had made a kind of roof. I crouched down,
more than a little afraid to disturb some animal, but animals don't make their beds under trees on frozen creeks.
The cold came through my leggings right away, but I
thought that was good.

I sat there and rocked myself. Petri would want to know
where I had been, why I had taken so long to go get
water. I'd look so stupid if I went back. Stupid to die
because I was embarrassed. I stood up, crouching under
my canopy of leaves and branches, stiff already, but the
thought of stepping out there and walking back up the
creek made me sit back down again. I had walked such a
long way and I was cold.

So I sat there for a while longer. I started to shiver.
First a little, and then big, bone-shaking shivers. That
scared me, so I crawled outside and stood up unsteadily
on the ice.

I took little steps because I didn't trust myself not to
fall and I was so tired. I walked a little way and then I
realized I was going the wrong way, so I turned around
and walked until I passed the place where the blackwood

tree was. Then I wondered if I hadn't gone the right way the first time. There were only two ways to go—how could I have gotten confused? I kept watching for my own footprints, but I had been trying not to leave any footprints and it was dark.

I sat down to rest and try to think. My teeth had stopped chattering. I got sleepy. I thought about the castrate's big, dark red eye, shining and warm.

When I woke up in the cabin I felt nothing. I could not open my eyes, but I could hear things around me; the fire, and someone rustling. I didn't remember, only felt a vague sense of shame that I'd done something wrong and an awareness that it didn't matter that I couldn't make myself move. I was neither warm nor cold. I didn't even feel myself. It was a wonderful sensation.

I didn't hear Teija—maybe she was still sleeping. Mam wouldn't let me sleep too much longer. I didn't really want to get up.

I heard a hand drum. *Thump-thump, thump-thump, thump-thump* like a heartbeat. Someone was nose-singing, a long sound that went on and on. I smelled something smoky and pungent, and it made me think of summer. The scent was thick and it tickled inside my nose and head and a sneeze rose up in me, and it brought with it a wave of feeling, of coldness and aches and my eyes feeling dry inside my head and my chest feeling as if a weight sat on it and I sneezed and opened my eyes.

I was back in the world, in Petri and Inger's cabin. Despite the lantern light, the winterdark descended on me. I saw a shaman with his herbs smoking in a brass bowl and closed my eyes and turned my head away, wishing him gone.

He grabbed my jaw with his hard hand and brought my face back. I felt his breath as he blew smoke across my breath. I coughed and choked.

He let go, and I opened my watering eyes. He had squatted back on his heels. I didn't know him. He was a little man with a tiny twisted face like dried fruit and a hood with a haund's jaw for spirit talk.

"Go away," I whispered. My throat hurt from the smoke.

He laughed. "I know why the dead won't take this one," he said. "She's bitter and they spit her out."

I lay helplessly on my back and coughed, too tired to sit up. I coughed and felt my face grow red and my tired blood picked up and began to course again. Old work, my heart sang, old work, old work, old work.

He had a bowl of something, and he put his arms behind me and sat me up. I twisted my head away not to drink it. "Soup, stubborn little one," he said. "Just soup. Take it."

The smell was as strong as his hand, and it turned my head back. The soup was too hot, and I choked a bit and burned my lips, but he made me drink some.

"She's a fine doe," he said and laughed.

I reached for the soup, and he let me drink some more. My stomach protested but not too much. And then, even though it was a bare couple of mouthfuls, I was full and tired.

"Where's Aslak?" I said.

"Here," Aslak said, too loud. When I looked at him he looked back at me, and then his eyes slid off me and away, to the floor and then sideways to Petri, anywhere but me.

I lay back down and closed my eyes and wished I were home. And then I slept some more.

When I woke up the shaman was gone. Petri was probably furious at what I had cost him but I didn't care. I didn't care anymore what Petri or Inger or anyone thought, because I was kinless and couldn't care.

Aslak brought me more soup and a bit of bread. "Janna," he whispered, "are you all right?"

I didn't answer him. I took a bite of bread and held it in my mouth, not so hungry this time. Inger left the fire and busied herself at the other end of the cabin. I wanted him to care about me, but now that he did all I could think of was the way he worried about Petri's anger.

"Is the baby all right?" he asked.

So he knew.

I pretended to be busy eating. I didn't know if the baby

was all right. The baby didn't talk to me or anything. I waited for him to say something to *me*. Talk to me, Aslak.

But he looked at his hands. At anything. And after a moment he stood up and told Inger he would go split some wood.

No one talked to me. Petri didn't even seem angry at me. People walked around me as if I were thin ice and the weight of their eyes and voices was more than I could bear. I liked it that way.

Finally Aslak told me that I had been dead when they found me, but that in the warmth of the cabin I had come back to life. So they had called the old man to talk to my spirit and the other spirits, to make sure it was really my spirit that had come back in my body and not something lost.

They were all afraid of me. If I had been to the land of the dead, I should have remembered something, shouldn't I? But all I could remember was getting lost in the creek bed.

"Maybe it was the child," Aslak said. "Maybe that is why you came back."

"Why doesn't every mother come back?" I said crossly.

"Maybe they can't find their body again," Aslak said. "Maybe you could because you have the thing in your head to let skimmers find you."

"That's stupid," I said, and he didn't say any more. But I thought about it, and it gave me the answer. Wanji had given me more than just the thing to call the skimmer, she'd given me two other things. I had used two of Wanji's gifts, and neither one of them had really helped me.

I didn't tell Aslak, though, because he wanted to believe that it was because of the baby.

The first time he touched me it was to put his hand on my swelling belly. Tentatively he reached out and spread his hand across it. Then he smiled.

"We can call it Svorjen," he said.

"If it is a boy," I said.

"Yeah," he said. "But I think it is."

"Men always think it is a boy," I said. When Aslak

wasn't there I wanted him there, but when he was, ugly words came out of my mouth and the things he did and said seemed childish and stupid to me.

Eventually I couldn't lie there any longer and boredom drove me to do chores. A little at first and then a full day's work.

The sun came back, coming up and dipping right back below the horizon. The baby started to kick and shove and hiccough. I could put my hand on my belly and feel its foot or its head and watch my skin move as it rolled alive under there. The sickness lessened but didn't pass, and the belly continued to grow while the rest of me fed it.

Twenty-four weeks of winter finally passed into spring. Time came to head for summer pastures. Aslak and I had the bachelor herd, and Inger and Petri had the slower does.

If I stood, I found myself standing with my feet wide and my hands in the small of my back, trying to ease the ache. I'd seen women stand that way and here I was, grown-up and standing that way, too. Climbing after renndeer I felt on the edge of imbalance. My ankles were the only things other than my belly that weren't thin.

While we were moving renndeer I began to see blood spots on my leggings. We camped at the river, waiting for Inger and Petri to come up and help us swim the herd across. I couldn't get comfortable. I've always slept on my stomach, and now I had to sleep mostly on my side with my legs curled. When I lay down at night my butt and legs hurt as if my bones were bruised. The baby still kicked, although not as much. Maybe it was tired, too.

Aslak watched me out of the corner of his eye. He had done that since I came back to life after the creek. It made me irritated.

"Are you okay?" he said when we woke up in the morning. "How's the baby?"

"I'm fine," I'd say.

I counted. I thought I was still weeks away, maybe five or six, maybe a little more. All the time I wished it was over. It was my fault for wishing. Maybe. I don't know. We had been at the river two days when I woke up with pain. Not like the aching, but a hard pain, like something inside me was hurt.

I lay still, because there was nothing else I could do, and wondered if I would die. Something was wrong with me or the baby. After a while, the pain subsided. I was sweating. Aslak was out with the herd. I could hear them moving. Maybe Inger and Petri would come today and I wouldn't be alone. Inger knew more about childbearing than I did. The does were usually more than two days behind the bachelor herd, but we had been moving slow because of me, maybe if Inger and Petri had made a little better time . . .

Maybe it was just my stomach. My stomach had been terrible. Now that the pain was gone it didn't seem so serious. If something had been wrong, then the pain wouldn't have stopped, right? I got up and got myself some hot water.

I was drinking water when the pain came back. My first thought was that the hot water had brought it on. I lay down again and moaned because there was no one to hear me. I could not pretend this wasn't something wrong. It was terrible, this pain. You cannot hold pain in memory, not really. Only pain lets you know what pain is like. It takes you in its grip. It allows nothing else but itself.

I thought that the baby was dead inside me. What would happen to me with something dead inside me? Sometimes babies were born dead. Sometimes women died, did they die sometimes because the baby was dead? Or was the baby still alive but something was wrong with me? Was it trapped in there? Imagine if I died and the baby was alive inside me. That was terrible, to die surrounded by dead meat before you had even been alive.

Again, the pain eased. I panted and sweated.

And then I wet the bedding.

I didn't understand. I hadn't felt the need to relieve myself, but my leggings were wet and the bed was wet underneath, with the wet stopped only at the offworld blanket. It didn't smell right, either, it didn't have the stale beer smell of urine.

I made myself get up and after a moment, I took off my leggings. My legs were trembling from fear and tension. But I could stand and I felt okay. Maybe it was just the hot water, so soon after the last cramp. Maybe I should just be still for a while.

Of course, the pain came again. And then eventually, it stopped. And came again.

I learned to wait for the times when it didn't hurt.

I wondered if I should get off the bedding in case I fouled it. The bedding was our own, but it was all we had. Then I decided if I was going to die I would be selfish and at least die on a blanket. Aslak would still have his own bedding and he wouldn't have me so he could find a girl who wasn't kinless.

I wanted my mam. I could see her in my mind. Would she still be angry at me now?

Aslak came back. I heard him outside, but I didn't want to say anything. I wanted to put off his knowing. He came into the tent and said, "Janna—" and he looked at me lying there, with my hair stuck to my face with sweat and with my skinny legs bare. "Oh dogmeat," he said. "Oh dogmeat. Janna. You said it wasn't time yet. Inger's not here."

"It's not time," I said.

"It's not time? Oh dog's breath. What do I do?"

I didn't know.

"What about the herd?" he said.

"Go take care of them," I whispered. I wanted him to stay, wanted to see what he would choose. But I also wanted him to go, because I knew he would and then I would be right. I would die angry but not in his debt.

He knelt down next to the pile of bedding and his hands hovered in the air. "Let me see," he said.

This was supposed to be women's work, this was Kalky's time, but I didn't care. He could look. He had done this to me.

"I don't see the head," he said. "In renndeer you see the head."

"Maybe it's dead," I said.

"No," he said, too swift. "Don't say cold words, Janna."

The pain came back. Was this just what it was like to have a baby? Had I counted wrong? I couldn't think clearly with the pain, couldn't remember when I was supposed to be counting from. If it was the baby I was supposed to be sitting up. "Help me up," I said, and he put his arm behind me and helped me squat. My legs shook so that I could barely hold myself, even with his help. I tried not to cry out, with Aslak there to hear me I didn't want to cry out, but I did because I was so weak and I was so afraid. I opened my eyes, and his white face was right there and I loved him. He was my Aslak, who used to give me little kisses.

I wanted my mam.

The pain passed and he let my back down. "I still don't see anything," he said.

"It's not right," I whispered. "Something isn't right."

All through the long afternoon the pain came and went. I got so tired, and it seemed as if there was less time without the pain. The time without the pain seemed to squeeze in on itself. And then the pain changed, and I felt something within me shifting.

"Aslak!" I said.

"What?" he said. "What?"

But I didn't know what to say, so I just said again, "Aslak!" I was bleeding, I could feel it on my legs. I was dying, I could tell. I pushed against it, pushed and pushed.

When the pain slowed Aslak said, "I think I see it!"

The pain came back, it never really stopped, but it came in waves. It hurt and if I didn't do anything it hurt less, but if I didn't push it would never stop hurting. When I pushed, darkness came around my eyes so there was only a little spot in the middle of my vision where I could see.

"I see it!" Aslak said. "Janna, I see it!"

I gasped and stopped and felt as if I were torn in two, which is what women always said about having a baby, but it didn't matter, this was terrible, terrible. And I pushed and felt it moving, felt it drop from my body. Felt it leave.

"Oh Kalky," I prayed, "is it alive?"

Aslak picked it up. "It's a girl," he said. "It's a girl." He wiped its face and it lay there in his hands, so tiny and blue and dead.

And then it gasped, and its skin flushed, from its face and chest outward, a sudden blush of red until it was all red. I saw the spirit come into it. Aslak said, "She's alive, Janna."

She wasn't trapped. Oh, thank Kalky, she wasn't trapped.

Aslak gave her to me, my daughter, and I felt nothing. I just wished it was over. I was so tired. There was only the space of some breaths, while Aslak cut the cord that connected her to me, before the afterbirth started coming. I felt blood coming with every push. The blackness got closer and closer and the vision got farther and farther. I could feel tugging.

Then it was over.

She was a quiet baby. She was born covered in fine, downy black hair, all over, and had eyes that seemed too widely spaced apart, more than any other baby I could remember seeing. I was grateful that she was a quiet baby because I could not feel anything for her at all. We didn't name her yet. Aslak was busy making sure that the herd did not stray too far before Inger and Petri got there, and I had barely the strength to take care of a quiet baby. Besides, fussy babies sometimes had allergies and my mam had lost two babies that way. Wanji said that allergies were a price of not living on Earth.

I had little milk at first, but more came. I couldn't do it right, couldn't get her to suck right away. It was like she wouldn't learn. But finally she got the idea and then she was hungry a lot. She didn't cry, she would kind of mew. And at first when she suckled it hurt, but then it didn't hurt so much as I got used to it and I found that when she suckled I could sit there and feel nothing but a kind of pleasure.

She would close her wide-spaced empty blue eyes and lay her wrinkled little old woman face against me and hold her fists still. I hated her yellow stool and I hated trying to keep her clean, but I liked the way she smelled, a sort of sweet, boiled milk baby smell.

Aslak liked to hold her. He was worn out from keeping the herd himself, but when he came in to sleep he would hold her for a while. I couldn't remember my da holding Teija. It filled me with happiness to watch him that way.

He wasn't content to just let her be, though. He would try to get her to grasp his little finger and he would poke about her toothless gums and fiddle with her until she would make that sort of helpless mew and I would hold out my arms. He would give her back to me and lie down next to us.

He would touch my slack belly. Touch my breast. He would smile at us. And then he would sleep a few hours.

By the time Inger and Petri got there, nine days after she was born, I still couldn't stand up for very long. Petri poked his head in the tent and said, "Oh-ho! What's this? Couldn't wait, eh?"

I started awake and picked her up to me. Inger said, "What, what?" She pushed in behind Petri. "Oh my," she said, "it's a little early."

I nodded. "It's a girl." I was loath to hand her to Inger, though I couldn't say why.

Inger handled her carefully. She scrutinized her, I thought. "She's tiny," she said.

"She's all right," I said defensively. "She hardly cries."

"Ah, little girl," Inger said, talking soft to her. She held her carefully, smiling, but I kept thinking she was looking, looking for flaws.

"She is so ugly," I said, laughing a little.

"Babies are all ugly," Petri said.

"Not to their mothers," Inger said absently, and I flushed.

We stayed camped next to the river a little longer. In a few days we would have to swim the animals across.

Aslak sat down next to Petri. "There is a lame yearling who won't make the swim," he said.

"He's just spavined," Petri said. "Give him a few days here and he might make the crossing."

"I don't think so," Aslak said. "I think we should butcher him now."

Aslak had never said anything like that to Petri. I was surprised. Petri was surprised, too. "Since when do you tell me how to take care of my herd?"

"I've been taking care of this herd," Aslak said, stubborn. "We've been here for ten days," he spread his hands, palms up, to show all his fingers. "That leg is still hot and swollen. If we swim him, we just lose the meat."

I think Petri gave in mostly because he was surprised. I heard them outside the tent, talking, and I heard them hobbling the animal. It came quiet to the knife, which was a good sign. I fell asleep after that, and it was starting to get dark when Inger woke me up with a bowl of blood pudding and liver. She was frowning a little.

"What's this?" I asked. The liver should have gone to Petri, it was his animal.

"Your husband made it for you," Inger said.

The pudding was rich and black and smelled wonderful. I ate everything in the bowl. The girl beside me stirred and looked at the tent opening. It was a triangle of light.

Aslak came in. "Did you give it to her?" he asked. His forearms were still bloody from butchering.

"I gave it to her," Inger said.

Aslak looked down at me, tired but somehow satisfied. "It will make you strong," he said and smiled at me.

I didn't know what to say. I looked down at my baby girl, and back up at him. "I . . . I thank you, husband," I said. "It will make my milk rich, too."

His smile got bigger. It warmed all three of us, and it didn't matter at all if Petri and Inger scowled.

To get to the summer pastures we had to swim the animals across a river. A dun yearling got confused in the herd and went under, came up, lost his sense of direction and paddled downstream, and then realized he was moving away from the herd. He tried to swim back upstream, but the river was too fast and he spent too much energy trying to swim and he went under. He came up again with his dark eyes wide and the long, long fringe from his ears stringing in the water, and paddled again and then a floating branch hit him, and he went underneath it and didn't come up. There was nothing to be done.

We crossed the river, and on the other side Petri found a man who was selling rifles. It cost Petri ten does, all of whom might be bearing, but he got his rifle. Inger said nothing, but I thought she was angry. Ten does was too much.

Not long after we crossed the river the baby started crying instead of making the strange mewing sound. At first I was relieved, but then when she cried she kept on and on. It was as if something pained her and I couldn't help her. Inger would hold her, but she would arch her back away, and I would take her back. It was hard for me to keep up with the herd, slow as they were, and I was so tired that her crying made me angry. But Inger was always watching, and I would hide my anger and simply rock her while she cried.

We stopped at the calving grounds and waited to see how many of the does would calve. I wasn't sure that I wanted to watch, but then I couldn't not. The does didn't seem to have a very hard time of it. The calves came quickly, dropping folded to the ground, encased in the shining birthsack, pretty as something offworld. The mother would lick them until they wobbled to their feet. Petri handled them much the way Aslak had handled my girl, cleaning the mucus away from their noses. But the calves didn't seem to look dead. They looked stunned at birth, but not like my baby, not blue. I never saw a spirit come in a one. I didn't know if that was because people are different, or if it was something wrong.

Petri's herd did all right, but his count was down because of the does he'd traded away. I heard him arguing with Inger. "We don't have children, we don't need to divide our herd, so I have a rifle. It may save our lives."

At the summer pastures we set up the big tent. Everywhere there was talk of Tekse clan. Tekse clan had joined with three other clans, and now they were going to make the other clans join with them. I think I would have had outrunners in my sleep if I weren't already so worried about the baby. One day the baby started making strange hiccoughing noises and couldn't seem to breathe. I held her and rocked her and shushed her. Her lips turned blue and her tiny fists shook as she tried to get air.

The fit passed. But in a few days she had another. Afterward, she would sleep in my arms, unnaturally still, and I would look at her long, colorless eyelashes.

"Her spirit isn't anchored in her body, yet," Inger said. I knew that. I knew she wasn't a year old. She wasn't even a season old.

"Don't name her yet," Inger said. If you don't name a baby and it dies, it is easier for Kalky to send the spirit to a new baby. I didn't want her to be someone else's baby. But I didn't name her.

The baby didn't grow the way she was supposed to. She remained so tiny, her head would fit in Aslak's hand and he would stretch her little feet to his elbow and she would fit. Too tiny. I brewed beer to make my milk richer, but even though I finally stopped being quite so bony, none of it ever seemed to be passed on to her. She cried and wouldn't eat. There was something inconsolable in her, something inside hurt her. She never learned to turn over. When she wasn't crying she turned her wide vacant eyes to the strongest light. The baby died without a name. She turned blue and gasped and gasped and then she died.

I thought of my mam, and all the babies she had lost. She had lived. She had kept going, had more babies. Aslak sat with his back to me while I made her ready. She seemed so perfect when she was dead, with her five tiny fingers on each hand and five tiny toes, her little fingernails and toenails.

Inger said if we wanted Kalky to return her spirit to another then we needed to send her with nothing. So I put my baby out without even a blanket. It was a warm day. I put her where the sun would warm her skin, and afterward I wondered if it had seemed, for a while, as if she were alive because it was the time of year when the sun shone all the time and there was no night.

Maybe, by the time the sun set, she was someone else.

It was full light. The light was there all the time, summerlight, day and night, the long endless day of summer. The grass was high and full of flowers. Aslak's cousins went down to the water and caught fish, and we went down to join them. There was lots of work. The men fished and the women smoked the fish. Aslak's cousins were not so concerned that we were kinless. Some of them had renndeer and some didn't, but nobody had very much. In the summerlight, with the renndeer roaming the summer pastures without us, it didn't seem to matter who had renndeer and who didn't.

The men took out boats and cast nets. I had only done line fishing and I didn't know anything about nets, but it was not so complicated to learn how to mend them. We would sit around in the sun with net on our laps and mend holes torn in them. Some of the net was made of offworld stuff. It broke less often than ours, but it was bright yellow-green.

"I wonder that the fish don't see it and swim away," I said.

Liisa laughed. "Fish are so stupid, they probably swim toward it."

There were five of us. Liisa was younger than me. She was the only unmarried girl in the group, and we were supposed to keep an eye on her. Gustava was pregnant. She was a kind girl, but I could barely bring myself to talk to her without crying.

Still, she wanted to ask me questions about being pregnant.

"I don't know," I said, keeping my eyes on the net. "I don't think that everybody has the time I did. I was sick all the time. I couldn't eat."

Gustava shook her head. "I eat all the time," she said. She had smooth round arms. None of us were wearing jackets. We had only our underjackets, and our arms were bare in the sun. The summer had made me brown, and I wasn't so thin anymore. But I envied Gustava. She had round cheeks and fat arms and looked just beautiful. I was my mam's daughter, and I would never be round that way.

When the boys got back, they were talking about Tekse. Always talking about Tekse.

"They won't come here."

"Sure they will," Aslak said. "What's to stop them?"

"What do they need to come here for? They've got more pasture than they can use."

The men were stripped to the waist. Aslak's shoulders were pink from the sun. "Put on your shirt," I said. "You won't be able to sleep otherwise."

He looked over his shoulders and looked back at me and smiled. Like when we were at Hamra. "I'm bone and rag, woman," he said. "Won't you let a poor man rest?"

"Not if he's going to be cooked," I said.

He laughed. "Walk with me," Aslak said.

Everybody grinned as we walked up the hill. One of Aslak's cousins, a boy name Jari, said, "The little man might get sunburned."

We found a place where we could lie together in the tall grass. It itched against my bare arms. Underneath, the ground was cool. I thought about my girl, but I shied away from the thought.

Aslak kissed me. Little kisses. "You're nice today," he said. "Why aren't you always nice?" He said it teasing, but he meant it.

Why wasn't *he* always nice? But I didn't want him to stop the little kisses, so I kissed him. It felt like before. It would lead to sex, but that would be okay if he would hold me and talk to me. I kissed him on his red nose. It was a little hot from the sun. His eyes were lighter than his face. He smelled like the water.

When he came into me sometimes it hurt, but this time I wasn't so dry. It was nice to have him in me, to hold him there and feel as if I had some power over him. I could do this, I could make him so happy this way. When his hips shuddered against me I was afraid of getting pregnant again. People said that after the first time it wasn't so bad, but I was still afraid.

But then he went to sleep with me in the sun, and that was lovely.

When I woke up Aslak was awake and watching me. I unbraided my hair and shook it out and combed it with my fingers. Aslak just watched.

"What?" I said.

"They say there is an army forming to fight against Tekse," he said.

I sat in the sun and tried to think about what he meant and what he was telling me.

"I'm going," Aslak said.

"What if I don't want to go," I said. He didn't say

anything, because he didn't have to. I couldn't stay here without him. Was he going because of the guns? I knew who his lover was now. "Fuck you," I said. "Fuck you, you kinless dog." I got up and ran through the grass away from him, back down to the beach. He didn't follow after me.

I wanted him to follow after me because I wanted him to choose me, but he had already chosen the guns. Most everybody was sleeping when I got back down to the fish camp, so I checked the fire and put some damp grass on it to make it smoke more and sat down and stared at nothing.

Finally he came, picking his way down the hill, and sat down next to me.

I was so angry I had nothing to say to him.

He was quiet for a while. "Janna," he said, "we're kinless. Those people made us kinless. If I fight them, I can take some of their renndeer. I can make us something."

"Or you can die," I said.

He shrugged. "Would that be so terrible?" he said bitterly. "Can you tell me you want to stay here and keep on like this? With Petri begrudging every mouthful?"

"I'd rather not die," I said.

"Tekse will come here if we don't stop them. You know that."

I knew that. At least I thought I knew that. But they seemed very far away right now, and maybe this was too far for them to come. Maybe if we just stayed here we would be all right.

But we weren't going to stay. Aslak was going and I couldn't stay here by myself, so I would go too.

At least he wanted me to go.

I left my daughter's tiny bones on the hillside. That felt like all that I left. There was nothing else of me that was any part of Toolie clan, except maybe a yellow dog and a castrated renndeer with dark red eyes like gems. And the renndeer was old and the dog belonged to himself.

Aslak's cousin's uncle took us across the water in a

skin boat that rode light and high as if it were empty. Maybe it was. Maybe we were gone to Toolie clan.

The uncle was quiet. I wasn't sure if he was disapproving or not. He let us off in the flat muddy place where the renndeer forded, and we pushed his boat back into the current. The front of the boat slew downstream. He leaned over and spat in the water and did not look back. Then he dug his paddle into the metal-gray water to make the journey up against the current.

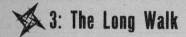# 3: The Long Walk

IT WAS THE DRY TIME OF YEAR, AND PALE
dust hung in the valley air like smoke. Aslak and I came
down into the camp through herds of summerfat renndeer.
Tekse had pushed people off their land, taking their renndeer and their women when they could and taking their
pasturelands when they couldn't. People had been pushed
and pushed and now they had stopped here, to push back.

I had never seen anything so big, so purposeful, as that
camp. There were red-and-white-painted tents and barking
dogs and renndeer snorfling. It was hundreds and hundreds
of people, mostly men. Here was a cookfire and a circle
of tents like two or three families, and next to it was
another. And next to that another. I saw five different sets
of renndeer ear markings for five different clans—not just
families, but *clans*—before we got to the tents.

A man stopped and said, "Are you coming to join the
fight?"

"Yes, uncle," Aslak said.

"What clan?"

"Toolie clan."

The man frowned. "I don't know where Toolie clan is
camped. Ask around."

We asked another man, and he hadn't heard that anyone
from Toolie clan was there, but he knew where Mette
family of Haland clan was, and they had lots of kin in
Toolie clan, so they would know if anyone was here.

He walked with us, because he said we would never

have found it on our own. Men were camped in a ribbon along the water, just one tent next to another tent, with barely space to get between to tie up a renndeer or get some water. And people were set up behind them, so that there was no way to tell where one camp ended and another began. The valley was one big camp.

Haland clan was camped back from the river, but they were squeezed in tight with other people around them. They said Toolie clan hadn't sent anybody. It was all confusion.

A man of Haland clan asked if we had kin in another clan. I said that my da's clan was Lauperak.

"Lauperak?" he said. "They are here. They'll be pleased to see a woman who can claim kin."

"Why?" Aslak said. "Did something happen to their women?"

"The seals were birthing," the man said, "and Lauperak men made a hunting party. Almost all the men of Lauperak were gone from camp for the hunting party." Lauperak made beautiful things from the skins and horns of seals. My da had sealskin boots when I was a little girl and even after the soles were gone, my mam had made him gloves from the uppers and they were soft and gray with long silver-tipped guard hairs. "Tekse waited until the men were gone and then they came in and took all the women and killed most of the boys taller than my waist," the man said. "Lauperak men have a big camp here. Just go back down the river and watch for renndeer with their earmarks."

We went back down the river, past where we had come in and I was sure we had missed them, but the people just went on. I had thought the two hundred or so people in Hamra was a lot, but there were ten times that number or more here.

Even with what the man had said, I didn't know what kind of greeting we would get. I was not relieved when we saw Lauperak ear marks. In the camp I found a man who was binding a bow. "I'm looking for kin to my da," I said. "My dad was Antti, Kolben's son from his first wife."

"You're from Hamra," he said.

"Hamra is gone," I said, "and my da is dead, and my little uncle, his half brother Seppo, is dead, too."

The man pointed downriver with his chin, as his hands were caught up with the bow. "Look for Tuire, Seppo's mother. She got away from the Tekse. They have a big red renndeer tied up outside the tent."

He was kind, not brusque, but it did not seem to surprise him that Hamra was gone. I hoped, after a year, that Tuire knew that Seppo was dead and would not think that cold words came with me.

Aslak followed me as if I were belled and it was fog. I wanted Aslak to lead, but he couldn't—it wasn't his kin.

I found the red renndeer and the tent and stood outside and said, "Hey, Tuire, Seppo's mother."

The woman who crawled out of the tent looked up at me and I could see my little uncle in her in her short-chinned face. "I'm Tuirek," she said. "Who asks?"

"Janna, Kaija's daughter, Antti's daughter, of Hamra clan."

She frowned at me and tugged on her braid. "Ah, child," she said softly, "you've come from one bad place to another." And then she took my hand and held it to her forehead, as if I were her sister.

Behind the camp was a ridge, and our outrunners said that the Tekse would come across the next valley. On the day of battle, we gathered at the top of the ridge before dawn. Below us, the valley had filled with fog and the sun came rising above it and it thinned in wisps and spirals.

Most people left their goods in the tents in the camp behind us, but I was too afraid, so I had my things and Aslak's, too. I had our short skis lashed so they made a rack for the pack to hang on my shoulders. When I put my pack on, the skis stuck up over my head and they hit me in the butt, but I could carry them that way.

"Are you going to ski down the hill at them?" asked the boy next to me. I was sitting with a group of boys, most of them about the age my sister Teija would be now—not old enough to fight.

"No," I said.

A couple of the boys sniggered.

It was hard to wait. We had a fire going to heat water. Every so often one of the men waiting to fight would wander back to get a cup. A bowlegged hunter told me that the outrunners said the Tekse were across the creek in the fog. In a little while we heard a sound like something buzzing or ripping and we all stood up. The fog was thinning, but there wasn't anything to see.

"What's that?" said one of the boys.

"It's a machine, I think," I said. The Tekse had machines that they rode on, like sleds. The outrunners had talked about them. I was surprised that they didn't sound like skimmers, although I didn't know until then that I had expected them to.

I wished Aslak would come back and get a cup of water, but he was pretty far down the ridge, away from the sunrise. He was supposed to be at the back because he didn't have a rifle. He had promised me he would stay back.

Someone shouted, "They're coming!"

For long moments we just heard the sound of their machines in the fog, then some of the hunters began pointing and the ones with guns started firing. I couldn't see anything, there were too many people.

"Stand to them!" someone was shouting.

There was a lot of noise. I could hear guns and the sound of the Tekse machines, but I couldn't tell how close they were. I thought about climbing a tree to see, but if I got up in a tree I was afraid it might take too long to get down or someone might see me and shoot me.

"What's going on?" a boy asked.

"They're shooting," said another boy.

One of the boys got up and darted off toward the fighting. He was barefoot and nimble. Another boy stood up and trotted after him a ways but stopped and stood.

Two men came through the hunters standing there. They had a third man by the arms between them. He'd been shot in the leg just below his knee and he was swearing steadily. "Dogmeat," he said. "Dogmeat." Over and over.

They let him down and he shrieked with pain. The splin-

tered bone was visible in his calf. He was bleeding a lot.
The boy who had been standing there came back to stare.

"It hurts," the man sobbed. "Spirit of all, it hurts."

I thought he'd be a cripple if he lived.

"Take care of him," one of the men who'd brought
him back said to me.

Take care of him? With what?

I cut the leggings away while the boys stood there and
watched us. "Give him some water," I said, but the boys
didn't move. "You," I pointed to one, "give him some
cold water."

I dug a shirt out of Aslak's pack, tore it to make a
bandage, and tied it around the man's leg. "Don't touch
it," he said. "Oh, dogmeat it hurts, don't touch it," and
shrieked again when I did touch it with the cloth. I wished
he would faint, but he didn't.

"Shhhh," I said. "Be still, it will hurt less."

The nimble boy came back. "They're coming up the
hill, they're riding *renndeer,* big bucks. They sit on their
backs and their legs flop up and down like this." He
showed us with his arms.

The wounded man was breathing in sobs.

"We keep shooting at them," said the nimble boy, "but
they keep coming. But their machines can't climb the
hill."

"What are the machines like?" another boy asked.

"Fast," the nimble boy said. "They're red and white,
and they're really fast, faster than anyone can run."

"How many are there?"

"A hundred? Maybe more. They're going along the
creek, but they can't get up at us. But those big renndeer can."

They brought another man back. He had been cut on
his forehead by a gunshot and his scalp was bleeding,
but he was chattering and chattering about how the Tekse
couldn't get to us and we were cutting them up. "We
keep shooting and it's like rain," he said. "They can't
keep coming, they've got to break!"

The nimble boy ran back through the men toward the
ridge again. I used more of Aslak's shirt to tie up the
second wounded man's head. The first wounded man was

quiet and very still, but his eyes were open and he was watching me.

Some of the men in front of me started running toward the direction where I thought Aslak was. After a bit the nimble boy came running back. "They broke through! They broke through! But we drove 'em back." He didn't wait to see what we thought of this but turned and ran back toward the fighting. This time two boys ran after him. I almost wished I could go, too.

From where we sat, I couldn't see over the edge of the ridge, even with the ranks of men in front of me thinned. The sun was up pretty high, it was about mid-morning. It didn't seem as if it had been that long.

I could still see wisps of fog and I sat and watched it blowing a bit in the breeze before I realized it wasn't fog, it was smoke from the guns. I stood up and just as I did, our men started shouting. It was a loud, animal noise, that shouting, and I didn't know what it meant. But then our men started running toward where I thought the Tekse were.

I didn't know what to do, so I ran to the top of the ridge and looked down. Our men were running down the hill into the smoke from the guns and through to where it was clear. I could see some of them splashing through the creek, laughing, falling down and getting wet. There were dying renndeer still on the hill, and a couple of Tekse men, too. One stood and, holding his wounded leg straight, stiff-legged down the hill, careening on the edge of his balance. I waited for the rifle fire to knock him down. I didn't know if I wanted him to be shot or not, but somehow he made it to the creek and across; and then I couldn't see him anymore.

Through all this the shooting didn't stop.

I was so tired of being scared and so tired of being bored.

I stood a long time, listening to the ululations of the Tekse fighters and the shouts and gunshots. Sometimes I would see people between the trees or crossing the creeks, but I couldn't really tell what was going on.

Men started coming up the hill toward me. I looked for Aslak. I was standing, holding his pack and my pack in my hands. I shouldn't have bothered with the packs and the damn skis. The skis were long and they caught on everything.

The Tekse machines were buzzing in and around the trees, and I saw them for the first time. They were small, no taller than a man's waist. They were red and white, and I watched one buzz across the creek. It hit the water and I expected it to sink, but it threw up a plume of water like a dog's tail and then climbed up the bank and the rider leaned his body and the thing turned.

None of the men coming up the hill with rifles was Aslak.

One of the men looked up at me and stopped. His eyes were light, but his face was smeared dark with dirt or smoke or ash. He raised his rifle to his shoulder, at me.

They were Tekse coming up the hill.

I ran. I heard the shot but I didn't feel anything so he had missed. I ran back toward the boys and the fire. "The Tekse are coming!" I shouted.

The man with the injured head gasped at me as I ran by. The way I had tied the bandage one eye was covered but the other was bright and astonished in his face. The man on the ground watched me run and his eyes were alive with terrible pain. I realized he couldn't get away without help, but I kept running.

I went over the top of the ridge and the sounds of battle were distant, and I realized how used to the sound of gunfire I'd become. I heard the sound of my feet in the grass, and my hard breath was immediate and insistent. There was no one else running for the camp yet; I was alone.

I came down the hill, past tents and renndeer. A woman with a basin straightened up and shaded her eyes with her hand to watch me go by. Everything was normal except for the emptiness of the camp. I had to slow down because I had a cramp in my side and I started coughing. I bent over coughing. I looked back up and I could see other people coming over the ridge, running. I couldn't see well enough to pick out who they were. I couldn't tell if Aslak was coming. I thought he might come back to where we had been staying.

But going to the camp was wrong. Everyone who had stayed in Hamra had been killed. I couldn't leave Aslak. I could not imagine life without Aslak. But I didn't want to die. He had not stayed in Hamra, surely he wouldn't come to the camp.

I moaned out loud, such a stupid sound. I made myself walk, let my feet think for me. I walked toward the place where we had stayed.

People were passing me, running. I stopped and looked back and saw up on the hill that one of the tents farthest from the river was set alight.

If I stayed here I would die. If Aslak came here he would die. Aslak would see that.

I ran.

I wore Aslak's pack and carried mine. I could smell my path in the anise sap of crushed plants from my passing; and I had long scrapes down my arms. The skis caught on things as if hands were pulling at them. Everywhere I was looking and looking. If I looked to the right, then I felt things creeping up on my left. If I looked to the left I saw that it was only the movement of the wind over the top of the ridge, but then I thought something was coming on the right. I ground my teeth together until my jaw ached.

I thought I heard the buzz sound of the machines of the Tekse. I stood stock-still, hearing the winterbabies and the chatterbats in the pale false river trees, thinking that I heard the buzz just on the edge of what a person could hear. I knelt down and pressed my ear against the cool ground, but the sounds were so far away that they might have been the sound of my own blood in my ears or the long-bodied beetles grinding the dirt for their dinner.

The pop of rifle shot was like that sound you've been expecting that jangles across your skin, and I jumped forward, running clumsily with my packs, as frightened as a mad bafit starting out of the grass. Going up over the ridge and down the other side, looking for cover, never looking back over my shoulder so I never saw who it was that was shooting at me or if they even were, since there were two more shots, more distant.

After that I was more cunning and walked where the undergrowth was more tangled, even though it slowed me down.

I was a bafit, the color of the dirt. I was small, listening and listening and walking softly, something eaten by every haund or dog or animal with teeth. I wished, like a bafit, I could go to earth. I would have liked to find a tree root I could crawl under and pack with leaves and curl up in. Bafit, bafit, I said to myself, tiny dark furry thing. Groundbat, unable to fly, with your nose to the ground making nests and burrows. Hunters call animal talents to them, take on the animal skin. I pulled the soft skin of the tiny, timid bafit around me, making myself as small as a hand. Bafit, bafit, I chanted in my head. I had never seen a mask of a bafit, but I figured a bafit wasn't an animal for a hunter. Bafit, bafit. I think the bafit gave me her ears, taught me to make only small sounds.

At dusk I curled up like a bafit. I slept with my ears open and woke in the purple twilight of the summer night, slept again, woke in the light, slept again. I woke a bafit.

The lemongrass smelled stronger and sweeter than it ever had, and I lay there with my nose next to it, listening to the world around me, very still. I heard winterbabies chattering in the trees. I stood up slowly. The long fingers of leaves, dried like long curls, crinkled when I walked. Nothing was silent. I could hear the clouds overhead like sighs. I felt sounds on the air against my skin and every part of me was open.

I walked out of the trees and onto the summer tundra, where the hills were green and everywhere lakes lay on top of the ground. Dig the length of an arm into the tundra and the ground is still frozen with winter, but on top of that is the skin of summer. The grass was new green, and the tailgrass made red clumps. The tailgrass flowers waved on long stems, and I could smell them without putting my head near. I could smell myself, faintly musky.

After three days I had seen groups of people and avoided them, crouching and watching them move far off on the bare landscape. To hide in this place meant to be very still. I found wild carrots and fenick, two things that were of this world but which people could eat. I could sit crouched forever, perfectly silent, perfectly happy, watching the people walk across the tundra, shimmering in the distance.

I came on a group of people sitting around a fire and then the bafit left me, dropping away from me, because it was time to be human again.

I crouched there on my heels, with my pack in front of me. None of them was Aslak. I had been expecting that I would find Aslak, all the three days, without really thinking about it, but he wasn't there. I walked across the tundra. Some people reached for their weapons, but when they saw me they relaxed and looked back at the fire, spilling a trail of pale smoke in the direction of the ceaseless wind.

They were talking a bit, watching a pot steam.

"I have some wild carrots and some fenick," I said. The steam from the pot smelled of meat and I was terribly hungry.

"Put it in, then," said a woman.

I dropped the yellow-green carrots and the pale fenick in the pot and crouched back on my heels to wait and listen. I was out of practice with people. We ate from the pot and the food was good, although there wasn't much of it. Some people lay down for a while and slept and I did too.

Then people got up, and there was the bustle of putting things away. I picked up my pack and slung Aslak's pack with its rack of skis on my back. Some people didn't have anything.

"All that is yours?" a man asked me. He was bandy-legged, like my da, but he had a different way of talking.

"No," I said, "this is my husband's. I'm looking for him."

"Where is he?" the man asked.

"I don't know," I said, irritated. "He was fighting and we got separated. I'm looking for him."

"Who was he with?" the man asked.

"Lauperak," I said, "but he had no rifle. Aslak. His name is Aslak, did you see him?"

The man shook his head. "No, I didn't. Do you want me to carry that pack for you?"

The pack slowed me down and wore me out and the skis bumped against me all the time. But if he carried it, then I would have to let him use it, and I couldn't let him use Aslak's things. I shook my head and started to cry.

He looked at me and shook his head, but then he looked away and let me cry a little. Then we all started walking.

We walked in the endless summer day, going around the metal shine of shallow lakes and ponds and puddles. You could walk across the lakes, they were so shallow, but the cold mud would suck your feet. We stopped when we were tired. Sometimes we stopped and people went looking for things to eat. We were always afraid of Tekse catching up with us, so there wasn't meat in the pot again for two days. Across the empty land we would see people in ones or threes or fives, and they would come toward us. The land was so big it was always a long time from when we saw them until they caught up with us. It was like traveling with a clan. A strange clan of kinless persons and no renndeer. They told me how the Tekse chased them until they were a strung out group and then picked up the women and the children and killed any straggling men. Most of this group was men.

We came over a swell in the land and saw far off a huge group of people. The group had no machines and only a few renndeer. So we walked across the soft land to them, leaving our footprints. The group was the main remnants of the army. We joined with them, a little stream of people joining a river.

It was hard to search among people who didn't stand still. People moved around between other people, and people were trying to find kin.

I saw him sitting talking to two other men and then realized it wasn't him because Aslak was still a bit of a boy, and then realized it was. I felt the weight of his pack, and the way I thought it was him but I wasn't sure. I walked toward him, hoping he would look up and recognize me, or not recognize me and then I'd be able to tell if it was Aslak or not. Then he grinned at something someone said and pushed the air away with his hands and I knew him and walked up to him. I was suddenly shy, and all I could think to say was, "I brought your pack."

His startled face opened up to me.

He leaped up and grabbed my arms. "Janna!" he said. "Janna!" Then to the two men, "This is Janna! I was telling you about her and here she is! Janna! You look good!"

His hands were too tight on my arms and he was hurting me but it was a good hurt. I couldn't say anything, just open my mouth and laugh.

"Are you okay?" he said. "Are you sick? Were you hurt?"

"I was a bafit," I said.

"What?" he said.

"I was a bafit," I said. "Like hunters are haunds. I was a bafit. I hid and crept around."

"A bafit," he said. He hugged me and picked me up so my feet were off the ground. "A bafit. You couldn't be a bafit. You were never a bafit in your life."

"I was," I said, "I truly was."

"She was a bafit," he said. The two men were looking up at us, grinning at our happiness. "I don't care if you were a leaf," he said. "I thought that the Tekse had you. I thought you were dead."

"No," I said. "Remember what that shaman said? I'm too bitter, the dead spit me right back out."

I had Aslak again and now I knew, all we had to do was hang on until we got somewhere. Maybe the coast. We couldn't go back toward Toolie clan, the Tekse were between us and them, so we could only head south and west toward the ocean. Aslak told me about the battle. The Tekse had only pretended to run away, and when the men ran down the hill they had been waiting for them and they had killed a lot of them.

The day shortened. Tekse clan followed us like haunds after renndeer, nipping at us to hamstring us and kill us off. We would see them coming, and the hunters who had guns would turn to face them, like renndeer circling. Aslak and the others without rifles hung back just in case someone with a rifle was shot. The rest of us would look for a mound to lie behind, or we would keep walking and try to put wet ground between us and them. They didn't ride renndeer in the soft tundra, and they didn't use their machines. Still, they had guns and guns.

I never thought I would be able to walk with someone shooting at me, but we learned to keep going, all spread out, so that we were not in one place for them to shoot. I think I could do it because I was hungry. At first I was light and my feet seemed too far from my head and all I could think of was food. I saw lights in front of my eyes when I picked up my pack. Then I stopped being so hungry and I couldn't think as well. I didn't know what to do when the shooting started, so even though I was afraid, I just did what I was supposed to. When we stopped, I forgot things. Aslak forgot things. Aslak forgot our pot, and if I hadn't seen it there we wouldn't have had one. So I tried to make myself always check on him. It made him snappish.

It was harder on him than me—men need more food. His hair grew paler from the sun, and his eyelashes all but disappeared. When we rested sometimes I just looked at him and the bones of his face.

"We are together," he said. That was all he needed to say. We were together.

I thought about stopping. Sometimes a woman would just sit down right where she was. People would part around her. No one said anything—she had decided the Tekse were better than starving and if she stayed the Tekse would pick her up.

At night, Aslak held me. Sometimes he just whispered my name. *Janna, Janna, Janna.* If it hadn't been for him, I would have given up and let them pick me up too. But we were together. I don't think I would have survived by myself.

One day it snowed. Big lazy snowflakes. In the morning the edges of the ponds and puddles were rimmed with fine, transparent ice, pretty, tinkling ice sounds. I heated our water in the morning. Hunters called it white tea.

Tekse came after us and I kicked out the fire—although if you left a fire burning there was no chance of it catching anything because of all the water. Aslak ran toward the hunters, and I grabbed our packs. *Pop. Pop. Pop.* I made myself look slowly at where we had camped. I couldn't

forget anything. Then I trotted with the two packs. I got
tired, so I slowed to a walk. We were all spread out. Only
the children were allowed to stay close to someone. I
would look to one side and someone would be walking,
like me. And beyond them, two or three man lengths away,
was someone else. The sun was angled low and our shadows were so long. Even skinnier than we were.

The Tekse didn't shoot long. We waited, then, for the
hunters to catch up. Aslak came back, walking with his
head down, carrying a rifle.

I didn't want him to have a rifle. He didn't say how he
had gotten it, but he let me look at it and showed me how
it opened and how it fired. He had ammunition in his
pockets, not very much, but some of the men had boxes
that cooked ammunition. They had to have the right things
to make it from, and there wasn't a whole lot of that.

The rifle was heavy. I gave it back to him and then we
walked some more.

When it got cold it got easier to walk. We could go
straight, rather than worrying about mud. One day I realized that the Tekse had stopped bothering us. This land
was crossing land, where clans moved their herds from
summer to winter pastures, and we came across a family
moving their herd. Our hunters came into their camp with
guns and took most of their dogs and most of their renndeer. We killed some of the renndeer and ate them with
beans we had taken from the family.

They would go to their families at the winter grounds.
They would be like Aslak and me when we had lived with
his kin, except maybe their kin would be generous and
not mean-spirited. They would sleep in their cabin and
they would have food to eat unless Tekse came and took
the rest of their animals and their women. I tried to feel
bad for them, but sitting around the fire and looking at
Aslak's mouth and fingers glistening with renndeer fat I
was too selfish to care.

The next day we were all sick from eating so much
food. My bowels had gotten lazy and they didn't want to
work. My belly ached and ached from the food. I wanted
to make us new boots, but we couldn't take the time to

tan the hides. Aslak and I weren't old enough to have gotten hide and sinew anyway, that went to the older hunters and their kin. But we had food for days after that.

It snowed more. Aslak and I had skis but most people didn't, and I was glad for my stubbornness.

If someone had been wounded by Tekse, mostly they died as it got colder. We would stop for a rest and when it was time to get up they didn't. Either they were dead or they couldn't walk—and that was the same as being dead.

Because we had skis, Aslak would carry my pack and I would carry someone's child on my back. Most of the women and children had given up, but there were still a couple of dozen children. But there wasn't enough people with skis to carry all the children. The group strung out, farther and farther until it was as if we were traveling alone. Then we would camp and people would straggle in. Some people didn't catch up. At first we would go back and look for them, but after a while we learned that there wasn't any reason to go back.

We coughed all the time.

We drank white tea and boiled dead grass. It gave us the shits. You would be skiing and your belly would cramp up and you would have to stop there and shit in the snow like a dog. I waited for Aslak and he waited for me, but when I saw other people crouched I just went past them, and other people did that to us.

We got to the point where we couldn't carry children anymore. I would try to put a child on my back and my knees would fold.

Aslak was not okay. "Do you want to stop?" I would say.

"No." He was too proud. He didn't want to be the weak one.

"Wait," I would say, and he would slow up, puzzled. I would point off through the trees. "Look, it's a town. And they're waving to us. And they're carrying big plates for a feast."

The first time he looked. He leaned on his long stick and peered across the empty land, even the hills less obvious in the snow. He looked long and hard, looking across the horizon for a long slow time, many breaths in and out, the way a hunter does.

Then finally he looked at me.

"Or maybe not," I said. "Maybe it really wasn't a feast I saw. Maybe it really wasn't roast duck."

He leaned on his stick, looking long at me. I'd made him angry, but I'd gotten him to stop and take a breather.

"Or potatoes saved from the summer," I prattled on. "Or flatbread baked with fat."

"Or cheese," he said. I loved cheese and he knew it. "Or butter churned from milk to go on the flatbread. Or summer pinkberries dried and then cooked with whiskey." All my favorites.

"Okay," I said. "I got you to stop."

"Or sweet egg bread. Or preserved meats."

"Okay," I said, squirming more than I really felt. I couldn't think about food, so the words really rolled uselessly off my back.

Aslak was grinning. "Or sausages. Or pickled vegetables and sausage cooked in stew."

"No," I said. "Don't! I'm sorry! I'm sorry! I surrender!"

That made him laugh out loud. "I ought to smack you," he said.

But he didn't. He never smacked me, not once.

After that, whenever I thought we needed a rest, I'd say something like, "Do you smell that?"

And he'd pause and say, "You mean that smell of roasting meat?"

"No," I'd say, "not roasting meat." I'd sit down and lean against my pack.

"Or that smell of fried bread?" He'd sit down too, and sometimes drink a little water. There wasn't much to make a fire with, so we couldn't even heat the water.

I'd sniff a moment and wait in mock deliberation. "No, not that."

It was a dangerous game to play. Think too much and it could make me cry. And I couldn't ever let it get to me, not with Aslak watching. He'd always end the game when he thought he'd rested enough. "No," he'd say, "I guess I don't smell anything."

And I'd say, "I guess you're right."

Then we would struggle up and on.

We skied past a man lying dead on the way. He was lying there on his side, as if he had gone to sleep. He hadn't been dead that long, but in the cold a body would stiffen in no time. His eyes were half-open and rimmed with frost. They were blue. He wasn't anybody I knew, and if Aslak knew him he didn't say. Aslak checked to see if he had any ammunition. He didn't, but his clothes were in better shape than ours were so we stripped him.

Across the tundra I saw more people coming, heads down and arms and legs seesawing as they came. The man was stiff, so it was difficult to get the clothes off him. Aslak took his tunic, but I took the leggings. They weren't women's leggings, of course, but mine were worn to almost nothing, so I just put these on over them and tucked my clothes in like a man.

"You look like a boy," Aslak said.

"What do you mean," I said, irritated.

"No, it's good. People who will bother a woman won't bother a boy."

I didn't really understand what he was saying. "Take his boots," I said.

The first of the skiers behind us caught up to where we were before we were done and stopped to watch Aslak try the boots.

I felt the stranger's eyes on me and thought of what I was doing, of robbing the dead. He would have nothing to take with him. I had nothing to give him, though.

"What about the old boots?" the stranger asked Aslak.

Aslak's old boots were held together by long strips of dead grass. I was always watching for clumps of the tough grass because Aslak wore through the strips so fast. But this man's boots were gone on top. I didn't know whether they had worn that way or if he'd boiled and eaten the leather.

Aslak sat a moment, worn out from the effort of undressing the dead man.

"Thank you," he said to the dead man. "If I can, I'll send you clothes someday." He cut off a hunk of the dead man's hair.

"What's that for?" I asked.

Aslak shrugged. "If I can pay him back, I will put the hair out with the things. The hair is part of his body; maybe it will be enough for him to get some things."

There must be a lot of dead people with nothing but their skin. I thought of all the people I had seen dead and how most of them didn't have much of anything at all. I should have been sad at the thought, but I didn't have enough spirit left to worry about anyone besides Aslak and me.

Aslak used his stick to help him stand up. Then he grimaced and spread his hand against his belly. I went over to him and held his elbow while he crouched and pulled down his leggings. I had quit having the cramps, but the grass still made Aslak sick. But there wasn't anything else to eat.

There was nothing much coming out of him, just thin, watery stuff. I held his elbow while another stranger skied by. I had forgotten the dead man until the stranger stopped.

"Are you finished here?" he asked.

"In a moment," I said.

Aslak gasped as his stomach spasmed. I stood there with my head all empty and my hands and feet growing stiff from the cold. At least I wasn't as stiff when I was moving.

"Okay," Aslak said.

We skied on.

"I wonder what he wanted," I said.

"Who?" Aslak asked.

"The man who stopped where we got the clothes."

Aslak was watching where he skied. Even a little slope is not as good as no slope at all. Without wax, the skis were hard to push through the snow, but not so hard as walking without them. I hadn't seen anyone without skis for a while, which meant that the people without them were either way behind us, or they were dead.

I had forgotten about my question when Aslak answered. "Maybe meat," he said. I couldn't think of what Aslak meant, and then I realized he meant the dead man was meat.

I didn't know what to think then.

* * *

It was winterdark, the time of the long night. We skied for only very short parts of the day, and rested for very long ones. The cold settled in our joints, and after we had sat it was harder and harder to get up. My legs hurt from chilblains and my skin was so tender from the cold that my leggings felt raw.

I watched all the time, and one time I saw the feathery stand of potato fruit. I stopped and dug and dug, hurting my hands on the frozen ground. Aslak watched for a bit. "What is it?" he asked.

I kept digging, too intent to answer him. He knelt and helped. I found it, the brown tuber, and dug it up. It was just starting to harden for the winter. If it had been any harder I couldn't have cut through the skin—it would have been like a stone, and we had nothing with which to build a fire to boil it until it softened.

I cut it in half and inside in the middle was the soft custard pulp, as sweet as honey. We scooped it up and sucked it off our fingers. Finally, we were full. I felt good for the first time I could remember, and I leaned up against Aslak.

"The sun is coming up," Aslak said.

I looked at where he was looking. The sky was reddened there as if it was dawn, but it seemed to me that the sun would never come up. But then, as we sat there, it did. The sun did come up. It shivered light across the landscape.

I could only smile. I looked at Aslak.

Revealed in the light he was an old man. His hood was back a bit from his forehead, and I could see how thin his hair had gotten. His face was shrunken in on itself. I looked back toward the light. I wanted the light to go away. I didn't want to see him that way.

The light did go away.

I got up and Aslak got up and went a few strides and then bent over his belly, gasping. When he could stand up we started again, but as soon as he moved, it happened again. It wasn't the potato fruit because I felt okay. He sat down in the snow.

"You go on," Aslak said to me.

"No," I said.

That was all. That was all there was to say. I waited for two more sunrises and sunsets, careful not to look at him while the sun was up, and then he died.

I wanted to drag him somewhere so he wouldn't be eaten by people, but I couldn't. I couldn't even make a cairn for him.

I got up and walked some more, but I didn't like walking by myself. I found a place by a lake; the lake was now all ice. There was a hill that had been eaten out by water to form a place like a burrow and I crawled under there. I wrapped myself in the blankets we had gotten from the offworlders. We still had them, the blankets they had given us when they took Ayudesh. I wrapped them all around me, over my head and around my feet. I thought about my pack. I had left Aslak's pack with him. We didn't have much in our packs anymore, but no one would find me here and eat me or take my things and when I got to the spirit world I would have enough to share with Aslak if someone took his things.

Aslak. I sang a song about driving renndeer. Not really out loud, just to him and myself. I sang it mostly in my nose. Aslak sang really well. He had a lot of wind, and when he sang he could hold the song for a long time without taking another breath. He would sing for me.

I got warm and I went to sleep.

Wanji's gifts did not let me die. I slept like an animal in winter. I went to earth and stayed there while the sun looped wider and wider arcs above the horizon.

I woke up with the water on my face and the sound of snapping and water. I woke in the spring, with all my body crying out in pain from the long sleep. The tundra was melting and running with springwater and some of it was dripping on me.

I was trapped, and I could barely move. My elbows and my shoulders, my knees and my hips, and most of all my back hurt. When I moved it was like sticks drawn across each other. There was no fat in my joints. I could move my teeth with my tongue. I lay there for a while, but there was a space in the blanket where the water came through. I moved my wrist and it hurt. I moved it anyway, and my elbow, and made my fingers crawl like beetles to pull my hand to my chin. It hurt and I made little noises—"ehh, ehh, ehh . . ."

My fingers were stupid and I couldn't get the blanket closed. I tried to move to get away from the water and worked myself so that the edge of the blanket was under a puddle and water seeped in. I got my arm out and I felt the long fingers of dead grass on my skin. I started and sat up. My joints scraped like dry leather and I cried from the pain.

I crawled out to get away from the water, but the lake had crept up into my hiding place. I put my hand down and the ground sloped away. I was wet to my shoulder, and my face went in and it was cold. I jerked my head up and drew a big, deep breath. My arm was thin and broken-looking where it went in the water and I looked away.

I crawled out of the water and lay in the sun. I felt as if I were dying. Maybe, if I didn't move, I would finally die. Or maybe I couldn't die, but I would just get so weak that all I could do was lie there, trapped, through summer and winter. That frightened me so much I made myself move.

There were little plants with flat leaves, and I ate some of them. They were tart. Then I ate some grass. That made me sick. So I ate more of the tart little plants, and that didn't make me sick. I curled up for a while in the sun, hoping for warmth, and then I crawled around looking for more of the tart little plants.

When I could I looked for wild carrots. And suboor root. I ate them raw. I made myself stand. I cried when I stood because when I stood I could see more than the things right in front of my nose and the land was empty. It was empty of Aslak, and death had spit me back out again. I was taboo for death. Of the three kinds of things there were for eating—those that nourished, those that neither nourished nor hurt, or those that the body rejected— I was something that death vomited back.

I walked in the sunlight with my shadow stretched long and skinny in front of me in the morning, coming around to trail behind me come evening.

I walked the rest of the way to Tonstad because the things that Wanji had done to me made me forget how to die.

Before I got to Tonstad I began seeing people. Lots of people. Most of them were people like myself, but some of them were not. Some of them wore offworld shirts and offworld shoes—bright boots with markings on the sides. Black with red. Purple with pale green. Swirls of color that hurt the eyes.

Outside Tonstad there was a road made of plastic stone. It was like stone in that it was hard, but the edges were perfectly straight and the road didn't have any marks from use. It was too perfect to be made by people. I stood on the edge of the road and a truck came by, and I stepped back off the road to let it pass. The road smelled of ocean, but the truck smelled acrid and hot, like nothing I had ever smelled. It was bigger and more awful than the pictures Ayudesh had shown us to teach us the word, back in the schoolhouse in Hamra. The truck left a wind that pulled at me and I followed the direction the truck had gone, walking alongside the road.

No one paid any attention to me, even though I had stopped thinking about being a bafit or about being anything. More trucks passed. I slogged on through the mud beside the road.

There were some buildings. They were little buildings, not really proper, all made of different pieces of things, of gray and green metal and of black plastic and of something like blue felt and of things I didn't know the name of. I smelled food and whiskey. The people in the little buildings served food to other people. I stopped and looked. My stomach, so used to green things I had picked on the road, clenched tight.

There were lots of men drinking whiskey in the stalls. There were more whiskey stalls than there were food stalls. The men in the whiskey stalls made me think of the outriders for Tekse, and how they had been when they came to Hamra Mission. I watched three men and a woman, all drunk. The woman was drunk and one of the men kept pulling her face toward him so he could kiss her.

"Buy me some supper," she said.

"I'll buy you a drink," said the man. He talked like the men from the south.

"Don't wanna drink," she whined. "I'm hungry."

I was hungry, too. Around me I saw men eating and drinking, but this woman was only drinking and the men were not letting her have food. She had an old bruise on her face. She was my age, and I thought that she might have been prettier than me, but she didn't look pretty now.

"Are you looking for the refugee camp, boy?" said a man in one of the stalls.

I didn't realize he was talking to me at first.

"Boy," he said again, looking at me, "are you deaf?"

He thought I was a boy. I was wearing the clothing Aslak and I had taken from the dead man. I had forgotten to get the hair that Aslak kept so I could make an offering for the man. But then, maybe I could make an offering for Aslak, and he would still have the hair and he could give some to the dead man.

The man in the stall dished up a bowl of something. Stew or soup.

"Can I have some?" I asked.

"No," he said in the stall. "You have to have money to buy this food."

I looked at the girl.

He laughed. "Well, I suppose some persons can buy with their box if they don't have money. But you haven't got the right hunting tools." He thought a moment. "I'll give you a meal if you give me your rifle," he said.

"Don't give *him* your rifle," said one of the men with the drunk woman.

"They'll just take it from him when he gets to the camp," said the man with the food.

"Yeah, but they'll give him a chit for it."

"All you can eat," said the man in the stall.

It wasn't my rifle, it was Aslak's. Maybe I wouldn't go to the camp if they would take it away from me.

"What's a chit?" I asked.

But they just laughed.

My poor head was empty from hunger, and I didn't know why they were laughing at me. Not one of them had asked me what my kinship was. None of them had treated me like a person.

The man with the food stall pointed up the road. "They'll give you free food in the camp."

I walked up the road toward the camp. All around me were smells of food. I realized after a while that tears were running down my face, although I hadn't known I was crying. No one paid any attention though.

The camp was a big place behind a fence. There was a beautiful, offworld building that was part of the gate, and there were people standing in a queue, so I stood with the other people. They were not like me; they had all eaten. They carried things in bags.

I watched for a while. The people talked to a man and then he let them past. Beyond the man was rows and rows of tents. Not round tents, like a person would use for herding, but big square offworld tents, all the same color blue. The tents went on and on, as far as I could see. And there were clanspeople living in them, and spilling out of them. No renndeer. No dogs. It was a strange sight.

But I had to have food, so I stood with the other people and then there were no people in front of me.

"Will you take my rifle from me?" I asked the man at the gate. He looked like a clansman, but he wore offworld clothing. All blue, the same as the tents.

"If you stay here, you have to give me your rifle," he said. "But I will give you a paper that says that I owe you the cost of your rifle."

"It's not my rifle," I explained. "It belonged to someone else. But I should take care of it."

"You can't come in with the rifle. There are no rifles allowed in the camp," he said.

So I went and sat outside the camp and watched people all that long afternoon.

Late in the afternoon there came a group of men. Maybe ten men, all in blue offworld clothing, with offworld boots and with rifles that were a lot nicer than mine. They walked so that their feet were all in a line. Left foot, right foot as if they were dancing.

One of them stopped and talked with the man in the gate. He wore the same clothing they did. He pointed to me and they danced over to where I was sitting. I was neither asleep nor awake, but when they danced to me, I felt I had to wake up.

"Do you have any money?" one asked me. "Do you have a job?" It was hard to decide which one was speaking, because I was stupid from hunger and they all looked alike.

"Do you have kin in Tonstad? Anyone you can stay with?"

I couldn't think of what to answer.

They took my rifle away from me and put me in the camp.

The camp was a strange torment. There was food there, twice a day. They handed out ground grain, dried milk and salt, every day. Some days we would also get bread. Some days we would get dried fruit. The first evening I was there I was given a scoop of grain in my bowl, a scoop of dried milk, and some salt, and then the woman in blue gave me some dried fruit. I didn't know what kind, it didn't look like anything I had ever seen before.

We got water, and there were cook stoves that ran on gas. At Hamra we had made gas from renndeer manure for a while and used it to make electricity, but then after a while we decided that we needed it more for cooking and for the vegetable gardens, so we stopped, but at least I knew what gas was. So did everyone in the camp. Even children were used to blue tents and plastic and gas stoves to cook.

I had to stay at the very end of the camp, with two other people in a tent that was new. Beyond us they were scraping the ground flat with machines for more tents. We got our food late, almost dark. I could smell cooking.

I rocked, waiting for the food to come, and one of the women crouched next to me. "You should go to the medical tent," she said.

A man, her husband, I thought, shook his head. "No, it's best to stay away from the medical tent." They were dark-haired, the woman and her husband. A lot of the people in the camp were dark-haired. Persons from the

coast, many of them had hair as dark as Wanji and Ayudesh. I had thought that only offworlders were so dark.

The woman pursed her lips. "You eat slow, do you
hear me? If you eat too fast you'll get sick."

She helped me get a bowl, and when the truck came to
give out food she showed me what to do. Then she helped
me cook it. It tasted wonderful. I wanted to gulp the whole
hot steaming mess down.

"No, no," the woman said. "Your belly has forgotten
how to eat. Give it time."

She was right. I ate slow mouthfuls, sucking on the
dried fruit that had swelled with the cooking. I didn't know
that we got fed every day so I was wondering how much
I should save, but I found that I couldn't eat all mine
anyway. My stomach felt too full. Like bursting. It was a
wonderful pain.

I crawled into the tent that smelled of plastic, and I
slept.

The dark-haired coastal woman woke me up when they
brought food the next morning. It was the grain and milk
and salt, this time with something else. "Powdered egg,"
she said, grimacing. "Here." She dropped her bag in my
bowl. "It will do you good." She sat back on her heels
and sighed. "I would give anything for some meat."

She cooked my breakfast for me. She was no relation
to me, but she made my breakfast for me. "Did you fight
the Tekse?" she asked.

Her husband said sharply, "Dortea."

She waved her hand at him, a shooing motion. "He
doesn't mind," she said to her husband.

I was too stupid with food to realize right away that
she had called me "he."

"We moved back here to get away from the front of
the camp," Dortea told me. "We have been here since
last fall. We had a good place near the front but it cost
too much to keep. But we are going to get it back."

My mind was empty. I realized now while she was
talking that she had meant me when she said "he" to her
husband, but now I didn't know if I should correct her
or not.

"You will have to spend a lot of time outside the tent,"

she said. "But we will give you some joss for using it. Okay?"

"Okay," I said, not understanding.

"It's good for you," she said, and thumped my arm. "You get joss and not have to do anything."

I didn't even know what joss was. I was afraid to ask. I was afraid to show my ignorance about anything. I didn't want them to think I was stupid and I didn't want them to be insulted.

After breakfast, the camp started to come alive. Dortea and her husband went walking to the front of the camp where they had friends to talk to. I crawled inside the tent to sleep after my breakfast.

Dortea shook me awake. I sat up in the thick blue air of the tent. It was raining outside, not hard. A soft summer day, with the rain like a cloud around us. It had made silver in Dortea's hair. "We need the tent," she whispered. "You go for a walk, okay?" She pressed something in my hand. I got up, groggy and unsure how long I had slept.

Outside was her husband and another man. The other man brushed past me to go in the tent, but her husband just stood there. I stopped and said "hey" but he looked away from me.

I stood for a moment, not sure what to do. I looked at what Dortea had given me. It was a square of paper folded up. I started to unfold it, and Dortea's husband grabbed my arm. He leaned toward me and whispered, "Don't open it here. The offworlders will take it from you." Then he brought my hand up to my nose so I could smell. It was a strong smell, like something from a shaman.

Inside the tent the man made a soft sound that I recognized. A sex sound.

Dortea's husband smiled at me. His mind was still on the packet. I expected him to hear the sound and rush into the tent, but he paid no attention. I put the paper inside my shirt and walked into the rain.

"Hey, hunter," Dortea's husband said, "I'm Juho. Of Ooluot clan."

I could have said I wasn't a hunter. I was a little surprised that a person from the coast would know how to be so polite, but the people from the coast were clansmen, too, even if their hair was dark. The man inside the tent sighed as if something had eased him. I didn't want to be in that tent. "Jan," I said. Which is a boy's name. "Of Hamra clan." What was a clan without people? I thought briefly of Venke and Ralf, but they belonged to other clans, now. "Jan of no clan," I said. "My kin are all dead."

He nodded. "A lot of us are kin to that clan, Jan of no clan."

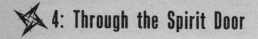 # 4: Through the Spirit Door

I HAD TO PEE, SO I WANDERED BACK DOWN the rows of tents to the latrine. There were two—one for men and one for women—and I stood outside for a while. The air was rank. A great deal of urine that probably should have been used for feltmaking was being wasted. And a great deal of shit for fertilizer. But no one was much making felt or farming in the refugee camp, so it probably didn't matter. From the amount of goods they lavished on kinless strangers it was obvious that off-worlders were so rich that they could easily throw away urine.

The latrines were really one very big tent with a door on one side with a woman's shape above it and a door on the other with a man's shape above it. All my life, every house and tent had a spirit door for men only in the back—except for the tents here in the refugee camp—but I had never heard of a door just for women.

The more immediate problem was how to piss without giving away my disguise. I didn't know what it was like inside a latrine, but there was a steady traffic in people. I waited, hoping to be able to go in when no one was there, but even when no one was inside there was the constant possibility that someone would come. I finally gave up and walked away with a full bladder.

If I went back and went in the women's latrine and peed, it might not get back to Dortea and her husband.

Instead, I finally crept around some new tents and squatted.

The camp was full of rules. There were no rifles in the camp, just knives. If you were not in line for food you did not get any unless you were in the medical tent. You had to pee and shit in latrines. The people in blue uniforms were to be treated like elders.

There were unwritten rules, too. If you didn't have some way to make yourself a little rich you were nothing. A few people could make money because they were shamans or because they could make things, but a lot of people didn't have any way to make money. A lot of women sold themselves, like Dortea. There were a lot more men than women in the camp. But still there were enough women selling themselves that women could not get very much. No one shared because kinship didn't matter in the camp.

I was lucky. When Dortea needed the tent, she and Juho always gave me something. I had a little stash of joss and I still had my chit for my rifle.

My biggest problem was my bowels. It had been a long time since I had good food in my stomach and suddenly, after two days of nothing coming out, I had to relieve myself all the time. When I walked I had to sit down after a bit because I got dizzy. My hips and shoulders ached. I craved fat.

I thought of meat glistening with fat. Of cheese and of butter. Goose. My mam used to cook a goose and put the meat in a jar and then pour the rendered goose fat from the skin over the meat to preserve it. Then Teija and I would eat the cracklings.

I walked farther and then sat in the road for a while and watched a few people pass. It was raining again and most people weren't out and about. People sat in their tents with the flaps open, and a big-bellied toddler in a bright pink offworld shirt leaned on the tent pole and watched me stonily. I watched her back. After a while her sister came and picked her up and took her back in the tent. I hadn't taken care of my sister, not at the end. I had always thought that when we grew up we would be friends, the way sisters got. I missed the grown-up Teija that never was.

When I got near the front of the camp I sat for a while and watched people some more. In the back, where I lived, most of the people were thin and starved. We were sexless and no one looked at us. Dortea and her husband, Juho, were smooth and fat and their hair shone, but most of us at the back of the camp were barely persons.

I watched a group of young men, three or four. There was one dark-haired one who was bigger than the others, and he was skipping stones at the feet of two others, one dark, like the southerners, one blond, like my clan.

"Quit it!" the light-haired one said.

The big boy laughed. He had short hair and no beard, in the style of the coastal people.

"Just quit it, Davin," said the light-haired one. His hair was longer, but not as long as, say, Aslak's had been.

The boy sitting next to the biggest boy was wearing offworld boots and a tight offworld shirt over felt breeches. It looked strange to me.

"It's not worth it," the biggest boy said to the one wearing the offworld shirt and boots. "You can make more money selling joss."

"I like it," said the boy sitting on the box. He had his knees spread wide and his elbows resting on them. He clasped his hands and leaned forward. "I need to get out of camp sometimes." I watched the way he sat, trying to remember it so I could sit that way.

"I don't like work," the biggest boy said. "It isn't work a hunter should do."

The fair-haired boy spat. "I need a smoke," he said and went in one of the tents, letting the flap close behind him. They paid no attention to me.

One of them elbowed one of the others and grinned. He pointed with his chin and they all looked across the road. Some of them clucked, the way young men do at a girl.

Across the road, standing in the opening of a tent, was an ugly old man dressed like a woman. He was a shaman. He wore a long buckskin jerkin that hung to his knees. It was gray and stained and old, but it had beautiful red stitchery around the neck and hem. He wore red leggings, too. His hair was long and braided and gray, except over his ears where it was white. There was nothing female about his face. He had long wrinkles that ran in crescents away from his eyes. His eyes were very dark, like Wanji's.

He had a plastic jug dangling empty from one finger, as if he was going to go fill it up with water at the tap. He looked at me.

"Go get me water," he said.

I stood up before I thought and went and took the bottle from him. He had an odd, musty-fruity smell, and his hand was hot and dry.

I went and got the water, standing behind women at the tap and filling the jug. I felt exposed.

The young men were grinning when I came back.

The flap was closed and I hesitated for a moment, not sure which tent it was, but I finally said, "Uncle?" trying to pitch my voice low.

"Come," he said.

Outside, one of the young men catcalled and I heard laughter.

In the humid blueness of the tent, the old-person smell quite overwhelmed the usual plastic-offworld smell of the tent.

"Sit," he said.

I sat cross-legged and wondered after I sat down if that was the way a boy would sit. At that moment I could not remember if I had ever seen a boy sit cross-legged. My mind felt filled with smoke.

The old man watched me, although I couldn't see him very well. "You don't know if you swim in the air or if you fly in the water," he said after a while.

I was afraid to say anything.

"Why are you dressed that way?" he asked.

I was pretty sure that he knew I was a girl. Maybe wearing a dress made him look at other persons differently. Maybe talking to spirits made him notice me when I was invisible to everyone else.

"I can help the boy inside come out to live in your skin," he said softly, so that no one outside the tent might hear.

He didn't do so well at letting the woman inside him live in his skin, if that was why he wore a dress.

"Think about it," he said and motioned for me to go. "And next time, look at me. Boys don't drop their eyes."

I scooted out of the tent and stood for a moment, breathing the wet air and the offworld smells. The young men across the way snickered, and the biggest one skipped a stone at my feet. I jumped, and walked away.

It wasn't raining the next morning although the air was heavy with moisture, and it would probably rain in the afternoon. But this morning the tent flaps were open and people were walking around or sitting.

The young men were in their same place. I fingered the square paper packets of joss in my pocket. They were slick and creased from my handling them. One of the young men looked up and saw me and grinned. He elbowed another one.

"Looking for your friend?" the other one said, and they all looked up and laughed.

I could feel my face heating up, and I sat down and pretended not to hear them. I kept the shaman's tent in the corner of my eye. If the old man came out I would leave. But the flaps were closed. Maybe the old shaman wasn't there or maybe he was asleep or something.

"What's your name?" one asked. They were probably younger than me.

"Jan," I said, trying to drop my voice, to sound like a boy.

"What kinship?"

"Jan of no clan," I said. "My clan is dead."

They didn't offer their names or kinship back. They didn't particularly care that my clan was dead—I wasn't the only kinless person in camp.

They got bored with me and went back to talking, and I could sit there and listen. I was a little sleepy and not hungry at all, and the sound of their voices was slow music. The sun was out and warm on my clothes.

The fair-haired boy was there. He was a newcomer with thin wrists and neck. He sat near the edge of a tent, as if he wanted to be able to run between the tents. A bafit like I had been, although being a bafit was woman magic, not man magic. But this camp had made me a boy; maybe Tekse had made him a bafit. Stranger things happened.

I wanted to smile at him, but it might be a girl thing to do and so I carefully paid no attention to him.

The shaman came out of his tent with his water jug and the biggest young man looked over at me. "Jan," he called, "your granny's here."

"Not his granny," another said. "His granny's ugly."

"My granny's dead," I said, and though they laughed they didn't say anything else. I watched the shaman walk down the road toward the water spigot. He didn't try to walk like a woman. I didn't understand why he dressed like a woman, but it was hard to say why shamans did things. It might be a spirit thing.

"You are Jan?" It was the bafit, who had scooted a little closer to me. Not so close but close enough that he could talk quietly and I could hear him.

I nodded. "What's your name?"

"Kari," he said.

"What's your kinship?"

"Torvsdon clan," he said. I'd never heard of it. "What's your kinship?"

"Hamra," I said, "but they are all dead, so I'm Jan no kin now."

He considered this news gravely. He was small and slight, and he had beautiful long eyelashes. But his face was little and sharp like an old man's face and there was nothing girlish about him.

"Come with me," he said quietly. He got up and I followed him. He went around the tents and walked along the fence. There was a narrow path of bare earth worn there, with tufts of the dry grass growing up along the posts. Sometimes a fat groundbat would start up into the air, flapping madly to get enough height to really fly. We walked to where the fence turned in front of us, and Kari ducked and pulled up the bottom of the fence as if it were a skirt and went underneath it. Then he held it for me.

We were behind the shacks that lined the road.

"Do you have any money?" he whispered.

I shook my head.

He shrugged. He went on a bit around the outside of

the fence and sat down in the grass. He pulled out a wooden pipe and one of the paper packets like those Dortea's husband gave me. He unwrapped it carefully, shielding it from the wind with his body, and put a pinch of the joss weed in his tiny pipe. Everyone got matches so we could light our gas burners and prepare our grain. I watched him cup a match in his hand to light it, keeping the almost invisible flame from the wind. Then he laid the match across the bowl of the pipe and drew.

The joss shriveled under the flame I couldn't see in the sunlight.

He handed the pipe to me and I put the smooth wood between my teeth. The smoke was dry, terribly dry, and hotter than I expected, and I coughed and my eyes teared.

He grinned.

"I like whiskey better," I said and coughed again.

"Do you have any?" he asked.

"I used to make it," I said. "Well, I used to work in the distillery. But I don't have any."

The smoke didn't burn like whiskey and it didn't make a warmth in my belly.

We smoked the pipe. Kari had to relight it a couple of times. When we had smoked all his joss I gave him one of my packets.

His eyes widened a bit, but he took it and poured it in the pipe bowl. He wrapped what was left back up and I shook my head. "That's okay. It's yours."

"I thought you hadn't smoked before, the way you were coughing," he said.

"I haven't," I said.

"You won't feel anything this time," he said. "But tomorrow we'll smoke some more and you'll feel it. No one feels it the first time."

I wondered if I'd made a mistake. Maybe men all smoked. Maybe it was part of man magic. If it was, I'd have to tell him about Hamra and say that we didn't do much magic there.

His eyes were red and he looked tired, but in a nice way. He smiled at me. I was getting a little better at drawing on the pipe. I would hold the smoke in my mouth a moment.

"You need to breathe it in," he told me.

The joss was a good thing because we didn't have to talk so much and we could be busy with the pipe. I was afraid I would make a mistake or that my voice would give me away.

Persons came in and out of the camp at the fence while we sat there. A lot of people knew the back door. I didn't see any women, and I wondered if this were a kind of spirit door. But then, on the other hand, maybe women tended to stay in the camp because they had children.

We sat until it started to rain, and then he got up and pulled up the fence and we went back into camp. Kari said, "Tomorrow."

He probably had a tent where he could go to get out of the rain. I never knew whether Dortea had someone or not in our tent, and I tried to stay away as much as I could. But sometimes she had someone at night, and then her husband and I would squat in the dark and wait while she worked. Dortea's husband was nice, but as we squatted outside that night I thought about how easy it had been to be with Kari.

It wasn't fair. I should be able to go to my own bed to get out of the rain.

Dortea's husband always gave me something when we sat out at night, but this night he gave me a piece of paper that wasn't folded. I was tired and thought it was a note, but there was no light and he didn't seem to expect me to do anything. So I put it away.

Later I crawled wet into my blankets and slept, and woke stiff in the morning. Dortea and her husband were still asleep when I left.

The boys were not yet at their place, but the shaman's tent flap was open and he sat on his cot and watched me. He didn't say anything—he just watched me. I tried to think of something to do with myself because I knew I looked uncomfortable. I wanted to look anywhere but at the tent, but my eyes were drawn back and drawn back and every time I looked there he was, watching me.

Ugly old man, I thought, irritated.

I dug in my pocket and found the note and pulled it out. It wasn't a note, of course—Dortea's husband hadn't grown up in Hamra, he wouldn't know how to read and write—it was money. It had a ten in the middle and on the corners, and I thought it might be enough to get something to eat. I stuffed it away and looked up, and the shaman was still watching me.

I looked back down at my ragged boots and wondered what I should do.

I could give him the money for his silence, but I wanted the money for Kari and me. I wanted something to eat. Some stew. Some meat. Something rich with fat.

I went over to the tent and squatted in front of it. "Uncle," I said, "I have a gift."

The old man didn't say anything, but I thought maybe he looked contemptuous. I looked at his boots. They had red embroidery on them, to match the embroidery on his dress.

"And I have a question."

He didn't move. Finally he said, "Let me see your gift."

I handed him the joss. It was small enough to fit in the palm of his hand. His hands were absurdly large for a man who dressed like a woman. He opened the packet deftly and folded it back up and put it away. Then he nodded.

"Is joss used in men's magic?" I whispered.

I knew I was not supposed to ask about men's magic, but the shaman had promised he could teach me how to be a boy if I wanted him to.

"Yes," he said finally and let the tent flap down so it almost slapped me in the face.

"Have you ever bought food from outside?" I asked Kari. "Have you ever bought meat?"

He shook his head.

"I want to. I want to buy us some meat." I showed him my money.

His eyes got wide and then he grinned.

We ducked under the fence-cut between two of the shacks. A lot of the shacks weren't open, but we prowled up and down the row of them, looking at what people sold. I hadn't waited to get my breakfast so I was empty with hunger and anticipation, but I was willing to be hungry for a while longer in order to get what I really liked. There were places that sold stew and places that sold meat grilled on skewers. One place sold sausage. Another sold fish, but it was meat I really wanted.

"We could get a bottle of whiskey with that," Kari said, doubtful.

I didn't want whiskey and it was my money.

Finally we bought meat on skewers. We bought flatbread and cheesy butter. I had enough money that we could buy two cups of beer. Then my money was gone except for a couple of light coins, but when I smelled that food I didn't care.

The fat on the meat tasted wonderful. It was full in my mouth. We sat at the counter with our elbows on the wood and ate. I ate very slowly, because tonight would be porridge again. I can't remember food that tasted so good. The butter on the bread was faintly salty, like tears. We didn't talk, but we grinned at each other, and Kari's mouth was shining with fat. The beer wasn't so good, it was watery and tasted like it hadn't been brewed long enough. But the food. The meat had juice. It was early enough that we were the first customers and the meat tasted fresh, although it had been so long since I had renndeer that maybe I couldn't tell the difference anymore.

When it was gone I was so full I could barely move.

We walked away from the counter and slipped between the stalls and sat down by the fence.

"I'm so full I feel terrible," Kari said.

"Me, too," I said. I wiped my mouth on my sleeve and leaned back against the fence.

"It's wonderful," Kari said.

"Yeah," I said.

After a while he brought out the little pipe and we smoked joss. I hoped to be better at drawing the smoke in my lungs this time, but it still made me cough. After a while I realized that I could feel the joss, that my eyes were tired. I looked at Kari's eyes and they were red. It was a strange feeling, as if I were far away from everything. I could relax and not worry about anything.

Kari said something about the joss fog, and I laughed and he laughed.

We laughed a long time for no reason at all. After a while we fell asleep.

Dortea was crying in a kind of hopeless, tired fashion. Juho, her husband, was squatting there not looking at her, his hunter's hands helpless between his knees. When she saw me coming she went inside the tent and let the flap close.

Juho tried to smile at me.

I felt a moment's flash of irritation. I was full, I was happy. I didn't want trouble right now. I wanted to be able to go into the tent and lie down and think about nothing but my own well-being. But I put the feeling away.

"Hey, Juho," I said.

He lifted his hand.

"What's wrong?" I asked.

He shrugged. "It's hard for her," he said. He clenched his hands, opened them, clenched his hands.

I didn't know what to say so I didn't say anything. The camp would be giving out food soon. I was a little hungry, not a lot. There was nothing else to do but wait for it, and I was tired of having nowhere to go.

"I went and bought some meat for a friend and me with that money," I said.

Juho brightened up. "You did?" I nodded. "A man needs meat. These people"—he indicated the camp—"they don't understand what a person needs."

I nodded.

We squatted there, and I thought to myself that I was just like a normal boy, here with Juho. I could hear Dortea, crying softly to herself. But suddenly Juho stood up. I looked up, but he wasn't going anywhere. After a minute he squatted again. "I'm a good hunter," he said abruptly.

It was a startling thing to say. Good hunters always said they weren't. They began hunting stories by saying things like, "I'm not good at moving quiet, not like so-and-so, but once . . ." Maybe hunters talked different to men than they did when women were around.

Juho stood up again. "I can hunt," he said. "I can fish. I know what is offworld, what is shared, and what we can't eat. I respect the difference. Men like to hunt with me, I carry my own weight. I don't foul tracks. A person does these things."

He looked at me as if expecting me to say something different. I just looked startled.

"What do you know," he said, and stood up. He went in the tent and I sat outside. They talked to each other, so quietly I couldn't make out what they were saying.

Then Juho's voice got louder. "I can hunt," he said.

I heard her shush him.

"Don't," he said. "I'm not your child."

Then there was a slap. A sharp sound. "Don't talk that way," she hissed, low but clear, even to me. I stared at the two pipes that led to the burners for our tent and the tent to our right. When they came on it would mean that it was time to distribute food. I wanted to go away, but I wanted to hear them.

"I wasn't talking about the child," he said dully. "I don't care about it. I'll raise it as if it were mine."

"Go away," she said.

He laughed. "To where?"

Then there was quiet.

After my da and ma fought they often had sex. I listened for the sound of Dortea and Juho having sex, but I didn't hear anything. Maybe they were quiet or maybe that was only my parents.

I hoped they had sex. Otherwise they were just sitting there, silent, in the tent. The tent was too small for two persons to sit and be silent.

When I woke Dortea was sitting cross-legged on her blankets. She had let her hair down and was putting it back up. I sat up and coughed.

"Oh, you poor boy," she said. She came over and felt my forehead. "You have a fever. You need to go to the medical tent. They will take care of you."

Juho grunted and turned on his side. At least Dortea hadn't had any men the night before. "Is anyone coming this morning?" I asked her. My voice was a croak. I didn't have to worry about whether or not people thought I sounded like a boy.

She shrugged. "If someone comes, they come. Juho will take you to the medical tent."

She made my morning porridge, adding extra water to make it thin. Dortea liked to take care of people. Juho walked me to the medical tent.

The line was long, and I squatted there for a long time. Finally I got to the front of the line. There was an offworld woman there, but she didn't look anything like Wanji or Ayudesh. Her skin was almost black and her short hair was tight against her head. She wore the blue clothes that were the official camp clothes.

"Have you been here before?" she asked. She spoke my language.

I shook my head.

"Your name and kinship?"

"Jan of Hamra," I croaked.

She had a piece of offworld equipment in her hand and she entered my name. I craned to look at the display, wondering for a frightened instant if it would tell her that I was a woman. She smiled and showed it to me. The words were English, but most of them were just parts of words and I didn't understand them. I saw "immunizations" though. "I have that medicine," I said, pointing to the word.

"What?" she said.

"Immunizations." I just read that word, but my thick tongue stumbled anyway. English is tough when you're sick. "I have had Sudin, TCK and Physcop." All the children in Hamra got immunizations, and we learned about them, too.

"You have?" she said, clearly startled. "Here?"

I shook my head. "In Hamra." I used my own language. "It's a mission."

She didn't understand me. I dredged through my English and came up with the way to say it. "In Hamra Mission. When I was—" I held my hand out to show when I was little.

"You speak English," she said, delighted.

"A little," I said. "Very bad."

"Dennis," she called into the tent, "Marie, there's a boy here who speaks some English!"

They gave me some medicine for my throat and made me open my mouth and sprayed something in it. The pain stopped, but I still felt that achy, stupid feeling. Dennis, who was tall and whose skin was so white he would have had a sunburn even faster than Aslak, was trying to talk to a woman who was pregnant and he wanted my help.

I sat there and tried to think of how to explain things. I learned what "prenatal care" meant.

Dennis waved his arms around when he talked. He had very fine, thin hair which he kept running his hand through, making it stand up all over.

"Is he a shaman?" the woman asked me. She was dark-haired, from the coast.

"No," I said. "Offworlders don't talk to spirits. But they make good medicine."

"Tell her if she comes here every morning before ten, she'll get supplements," Dennis said.

I didn't have a clue what he was saying. I held my empty hands up and shook my head—what?

"Tell her, 'Come every morning,' " Dennis said to me. "We will give her extra food."

"More food?" I said.

"More food," he agreed.

"I get enough food," the woman said. "It is just not very good."

"Bad food? Good food?" I asked.

He went and got some foil packets like the ones that the people in the skimmer had given Aslak and me.

I nodded. "Yes, better food. Sometimes beans, sometimes maybe some meat. But whoever put this food up didn't know anything about meat. The meat doesn't have enough fat. You have to put it in water like the meal they give us. Then it is okay. Not renndeer meat or anything, but okay."

She studied the foil packet and then nodded. "Do you think I can sell it and get real food?"

I shrugged. "I dunno. Somebody might like them. The foil is pretty."

"Can you use the foil for anything?"

I thought you probably could, but I couldn't think of anything.

Dennis watched us, nodding. Pleased. Then Fadima, the very dark-skinned woman with the strange hair (it was curled so tight I wanted to touch it, but that would have been rude) told Dennis I was sick and should go rest. Dennis didn't want me to go, but he didn't argue.

"Can you come back?" he asked. "Maybe tomorrow?" He gave me one of the foil packets of food. I said I would.

I wandered back toward our tent, hoping to lie down. Juho was standing outside, his hand cupped to his side to hide the joss he was smoking, waiting for Dortea to finish with a man, so I turned and went back toward the front of the camp where I might find Kari.

Kari was sitting at the edge of the group of young men. He got up when he saw me. "Where've you been?" he asked.

"At the medical tent."

"Are you sick?" He drew back.

"They gave me medicine. I'm okay now." My voice was still hoarse, but that was okay with me, it made me sound more like a boy. "They want me to help them. They gave me this." I showed him the foil packet.

"What's that?" Davin, the biggest one, asked. They were all looking at us.

"It's offworld food," I said. "They gave it to me at the medical tent."

"Let's see it," he said.

I looked at Kari and he looked at me, but neither one of us knew anything to do except let them see it. I tossed it to him. His muscular arms were bare when he raised them to catch it.

"What's it like?" he asked.

"The meat isn't good," I said. "Not enough fat. It dries away to nothing. But it's salty."

He turned the foil packet over and over. It was red and silver and it flashed reflected light at us. He handed it on to another young man, and he looked at it. They passed it hand to hand while we stood there watching.

The bare-armed one said, "Who's going to cook it?"

I probably would have answered that I was, but I was

still slow from feeling sick. The guys burst out laughing. Kari flushed and laughed a little, too. It took me slow moments to figure out they were saying that women cooked and that one of us would have to cook it and be like a woman.

I looked back at the shaman's tent, not meaning to. The tent flap was closed.

"Looking for a real woman to cook it for you?" The boys laughed harder.

I got up.

"Look at those hips."

Was I walking like a girl? I didn't even look back at Kari, I was afraid to. I just cut between the tents and headed along the fence. I could hear them laughing and my heart was pounding and I wanted to run.

I heard Kari behind me.

I cut under the fence and sat down outside where I could lean. I had been walking fast and I coughed. Kari sat down in the grass. "I can get more tomorrow," I said. "They want me to work for them at the medical tent."

"Oh, sure," he said. "What could you do at the medical tent?"

"I speak some English," I said. "They want me to explain to people what they're saying."

"You speak English?" he asked.

"A little," I said.

"How come?"

"I learned it in Hamra," I said. "Hamra was a mission town. Offworlders started it. That's where I was born." I coughed some more.

"Are you going to do it?" he asked.

"Sure," I said. "Why not?"

"Because what if you get sick?" he asked.

"I won't," I said.

"But there is sickness at the medical tent."

"The offworlders don't get sick," I said.

"How do you know?" he said. He squatted. "I'd think about it if I were you, Jan."

"I think I just want to sleep for a while," I said. "I don't really feel too good." I lay there on the grass and

closed my eyes. I could see the red sun through my eyelids, staining the world red.

When I woke, Kari was gone. It was late and I thought
it would be time for food soon.

Juho and Dortea's tent was empty. I was thirsty, but the
water jug was empty, too. I took it to the spigot to get
water. In the winter, would the spigot freeze?

Would I still be here in the winter? Why not? What
else did I have to do?

When I got to the spigot the old shaman was there, and
I almost turned around and walked away, but he saw me.
He beckoned me over and let me stand with him so I
didn't have to wait at the back of the line. I could still
smell that odd dry smell. "Thank you, uncle," I said.

Softly he said, not looking at me, "Stand with your feet
farther apart, and your weight between them. Like you
have something there."

I did as he told me.

"Not so wide," he said.

I adjusted a little.

"Better," he said.

He waited while I filled my water jug. I felt compelled
to wait while he filled his.

"Come to my tent," he said. "After the meal."

"I don't feel good," I said. "I'm sick. I think I should
just lie down."

"How much rest do you get in a whore's tent?" he
asked.

My mouth opened. His tone had been utterly reasonable;
his words had not. I tried to think of what to say, but he
just turned and walked away.

How did he know about me?

I got back to the tent a little before Dortea and Juho
did. Juho was red-eyed and stupid from joss. Dortea was
quiet. She didn't talk to him when he smoked too much
joss. Juho didn't seem to care. He squatted next to me.
"You know why I smoke?" he asked. "Because when I
smoke, I don't care. It's the only way a man can live in
this place." He grinned foolishly.

"Dortea," I said, "at the medical tent today I found

out that if you are pregnant they give you extra food. It's in packets. It's not like the food they give out from the trucks."

She shook her hair down in her face and turned her shoulder to me, as if she were mourning.

"That's good," Juho said. "What kind of food is it?"

I told him about the foil packets.

"Doesn't that sound good?" he asked Dortea. "You can get them. If we don't eat them, we can sell them, maybe."

She nodded but didn't say anything.

We got our food and Dortea cooked it without speaking. My throat was hurting a little, but the hot meal soothed it. I wasn't really hungry, though. We got dried fruit, and I gave mine to Dortea. She smiled a little but didn't want to look at me. Juho talked all the time we were eating. He talked mostly about people from his clan, other hunters. Sometimes he would say something like, "You remember, Dortea," and she would nod a little.

"I have to go," I said, when I had eaten all the meal I could stand. "I have to meet someone."

Dortea took my bowl and rinsed it out.

When I left, Juho lit more joss. The sweet smell drifted along behind me as I walked away.

I was afraid to go to the tent, but the shaman would track me down if I didn't. Maybe he knew I was outside right now. I didn't understand men's magic.

"Uncle," I said.

He opened the tent flap and I ducked underneath.

The first night I just slept there. He told me to lie down and I did. I was tense. I didn't know what he would do, and I would have thought I could never sleep, but I was sick enough that my body took over and I did. I woke up a number of times, and at first the shaman was still up, sitting on his blankets, looking at nothing or pulling things out of a bag and laying them out. Later, when I woke up during the long gray twilight, he was snoring softly, asleep on his blankets. It was raining on the tent and the wind was pulling at the canvas. I was grateful that I didn't have to worry about staying outside, if Dortea had a man to see.

When I woke up in the morning, he was already awake and boiling water in a glass jar over a little candle. He had a tripod made out of metal from something the offworlders had discarded.

"Old people wake up early," he said.

"I have to go to the medical tent," I said.

"Good morning," he said, unperturbed. "Would you like some white tea?"

"White tea" meant hot water. He poured it into a cup and handed it to me.

I blew on it and started to sip it.

"When you drink it," he said, "look over the cup."

I didn't understand.

"Hunters are always looking for something out there." He gestured with his hand as if the tent walls weren't there. "Women look into cups and bowls to see that things are prepared well. Men are looking beyond. When you drink, look over the cup at me."

I sipped, watching him.

"Better," he said.

The back of the tent was cut to make flaps. A spirit door. There were marks on the walls, made with charcoal and with I didn't know what else.

"Are you bleeding?" he asked.

"No," I said. "Not since fall." I had wondered about that.

"You will again," he said. "Go on to the medical tent. Bring me back some offworld food."

The medical tent was blue like all the tents but larger. There was another tent behind it that was as big as the schoolhouse had been in Hamra, and people who were too sick to leave stayed there. Only two of the offworlders were there when I got there: the women Marie and Fadima. Fadima said, "Hello!" in English and waved. She asked me something.

I didn't know what she was asking so I nodded. Marie poured a cup of dark stuff and handed it to me. It was hot and bitter. I thought it might be the same drink that the offworlders had given to Aslak and me when the skimmer came to Hamra, but I wasn't sure. So much had happened since then. I sipped it, watching them over the rim of the cup the way the shaman had said.

"How are you?" Marie asked.

I understood that. "Fine, thank you," I said. "And yourself?"

"Pretty good," she said. "Are you feeling better?"

I did feel better. I felt pretty much well. The drink might have been more medicine, I didn't know. I couldn't think of any other reason for it.

Dennis shuffled in. "It's hot," he said.

Wanji and Ayudesh had told us that offworlders talked about the weather.

Dennis got a cup of the medicine and I noticed that when he drank it he looked into it. Of course, he was an offworlder, not a hunter.

People lined up outside in the sun, and Fadima took her piece of equipment, she called it a planner, and stood at the door and asked them questions, while Marie and Dennis gave them medicine and asked them more questions.

The old shaman knew answers. Offworlders asked questions. But their medicine was really good. I knew that from Wanji and Ayudesh and from my mam, who told me about how offworld medicine saved me when I was a baby and about how the other clans got diseases that we didn't get because of immunizations.

Of course, offworld medicine hadn't saved Hamra.

I learned a lot of English working in the medical tent that day, and went back to the shaman with my head whirling from all I'd tried to stuff in it. I brought him offworld food, too. Two packets, given to me for my work.

I had to walk past the boys, and they laughed and made kissing noises when I stopped at the tent and said, "Uncle?" Kari was sitting there, too. He laughed uncomfortably, trying to fit in with the boys. I felt the color creeping up my face. That would surely prove I was a girl.

The shaman called to come in.

I gave a packet to him and kept one. He sat cross-legged on his blankets. He turned the bright silver and blue foil packet over and over. "What is this?" he asked.

" 'Pork and rice' it says. You cook it in water. Like

meal." I shuffled and dropped my voice. "Do you want me to cook it for you before I go?"

He glared at me. "You don't cook," he said. "Go on. Just come back here to sleep." He turned his shoulder to me, dismissing me.

"But I live in another tent," I said.

He waved his hand at me to go away.

"I can't stay here with you," I said.

"You have things to find out," he said. "I didn't tell you to go on this journey. Why do you choose to dress this way? What are you looking for?"

"I am not looking for anything," I said.

"Hah!" It was almost a bark. "Then go out and get some decent clothes and stop pretending."

"I . . ." I had started to say "I can't," but why couldn't I? Because I didn't want to be like Dortea? Not every woman in the camp was like Dortea. But if I dressed like a woman, I would be—I struggled to think of what I would be, and the words that kept coming to me were that I would be naked. "I just want to be invisible," I said.

"No," he said. "You want to be someone else. I'm teaching you to be someone else. Why am I teaching you? I don't know. I don't know why you came to me, I don't even know why I'm still alive. I'm an old man and my bones ache, and here there are only stupid people who laugh at me and don't know anything. They don't know why I am what I am or that I didn't choose it. I didn't choose it any more than you have chosen it, *boy.*"

Softly, I said, "Why do you, I mean, the dress, why—"

"Because a shaman is a doorway. All shaman are between." He shrugged. "Because the spirits use us in different ways. It is my mystery. I don't like it, but it is. Now get out of here. I want to make my dinner."

Kari was still there when I came out.

The boys were there, too, but they were arguing about something, two of them standing chest to chest, and they weren't very interested in me. Funny, in the shaman's tent I hadn't even heard them, but their voices were loud and the canvas of the tent wasn't much of a barrier to sound. I cut between the tents, and after a while I heard Kari following me.

"What are you doing in there?" Kari asked.

"I, ah, he's helping me," I said. My voice was girl high.

Kari looked at me oddly and I expected him to say something about my voice, but instead he said, "Are you sick?"

"No, I'm okay now." I said, consciously dropping my voice. "He's teaching me."

"You're going to be a shaman?" His eyes narrowed.

"No!" I said. But I didn't know what else to tell him, and I could see he didn't believe me anyway. "I've got offworld food," I said, to change the subject.

He let me. "Where are we going to cook it?" he asked. "My tent is crowded."

I thought about taking him to mine, to Juho and Dortea, but it made me uncomfortable. "My tent isn't good," I said.

"Then we can go to mine."

His tent had six people living in it: his mam and his da, him, and his sister-in-law and her two children. They were in the middle of the camp, not near the front like Dortea and Juho wanted to be.

His sister-in-law took the food packet from me and I told her how to fix it and she did. If anything, it was saltier than I remembered, but this one was sweet, too. Very strange. We let the two children try some, but they didn't like it.

"Needs vinegar," Kari said. It did, too.

We saved a lot of it and used it to salt our meal when it came. I ate with Kari and his family. His da said hello to me and asked me my kinship, but nobody else talked to me and I thought the sister-in-law was watching me. Hunters notice things far away, women notice things up close. Maybe she could tell. When I left, would she tell Kari that I was a girl?

I was tired to death of pretending. I wanted to go somewhere and not have to think about how I talked or where I went to the bathroom.

And the only place to go was back to the shaman.

"I'm tired," I told him.

He shrugged. "Go to sleep."

"I'm tired of trying to be a boy."

"Then quit," he said.

I couldn't quit. How could I go out and tell Kari that I was really a woman? And if I stopped trying to be a boy, then what would happen if I went back to Dortea and Juho's tent? There wouldn't be any reason for me to stay at the shaman's tent. I didn't want to do what Dortea did.

"You are gaining weight," the shaman said.

I thought I was. I didn't get so tired, and I didn't get dizzy anymore.

"You need to buy some cloth," he said.

"Cloth?" I said. "How much?

"About twice the length of your arms from fingertip to fingertip, and about the width of your elbow to your finger."

I nodded. I wondered if I was allowed to ask why.

This evening there were shelled nuts in a paper cone sitting with the water cups. He must have bought them outside, but I didn't even know how the shaman could get outside or that he had any money. They were untouched. I had been watching them since before dinner, waiting for him to either eat them or offer me some. The packet was stained with oil from the nuts. When he didn't eat them I began to suspect they were for me.

Was it a test? Men were more forward than women. Would a man ask for some where a woman would wait? There were always tests with the shaman.

"May I?" I finally asked.

He nodded as if he didn't care.

I reached over and took one.

He shook his head. I had failed again.

He reached over and took a handful and tossed them in his mouth. It was a gesture I had seen men make all my life. I reached in and instead of taking one or two, I took a handful. A big, greedy handful. I put them all in my mouth, watching the shaman.

He nodded. "Women eat one or two."

I was sick of this whole business. But I remembered it.

"So I need to get money to get cloth. Why?" I asked.

"To bind your chest," he said. "You are getting your weight back."

I looked down. I had never been soft and round, but I was a woman. My chest had been flat when I came to the camp, I hadn't thought much about it since then. If I thought about my chest, I would have to think about the rat's nest of my hair and about everything else about me.

"I have joss," I said. "Can you get money for me from joss?"

"How much do you have?" he asked.

Kari and I had smoked some. I had less than I thought. He shook his head. "You need more."

"I don't have any more," I said. I should have saved the joss and money I got from Juho and Dortea, but I hadn't. I fingered the chit for Aslak's rifle. But I couldn't sell that. "Maybe I can sell the food packets I get from the medical tent," I said.

"Maybe," the shaman said. "Go get me some water."

I took the jug by the door and went to the spigot for water.

I ended up taking two long lengths of elastic bandage from the medical tent. There were boxes of them in the cabinet. I fetched things for the medicals all day, so it wasn't difficult. I was afraid at first that they would be wrong because they were a little wider than the length of my palm, but the shaman was pleased with them.

"Take off your shirt," he said.

"Here?" I said.

"I'm an old man and you're my assistant," he said, irritated. "Besides, I like my girls soft. Take off your shirt."

I took it off and he helped me bind my chest. My breasts were rounding, and my stomach was not so hollow under my ribs, but I was still thin. Not at all soft. Not at all tempting to the old man.

"Take off your breeches, too," he said.

I was afraid. He seemed matter of fact, so I did. I stood there, barefoot and naked except for the chest bindings. He murmured to himself.

He got out his hand drum and sat down on the floor of the tent. When I started to sit he shook his head, so I stood and listened to him drum. The sound was pleasant, repetitive, and after a couple of moments, I felt myself swaying to the sound.

He dipped a rivertree stick in soot and painted little circles like men's nipples on my bindings. Then he took out a knife and passed it through the flame and cut the inside of my right thigh, high up near my sex, so swiftly I didn't have time to do more than flinch. Then I felt the burn from the hot knife, and the pain.

"What!" I said.

"Sit," he said.

The blood ran in a thin stream down the inside of my leg. I sat and reached down to try to stop the cut from bleeding.

"No," he said. "Sit, close your eyes. Breath in through your nose and out through your mouth."

I sat and tried to concentrate on breathing in through my nose and out through my mouth, but mostly I was conscious of the cut on the inside of my thigh and the way it pulsed with my heart.

He rustled around, and after a bit he must have lit something because I smelled the burning and then a sweetish acrid smell a little like joss. He held something close to my face and said, "Don't open your eyes yet." Then he started playing his hand drum again and singing softly. The hand drum was almost like a heartbeat. A strong heartbeat and underneath it, a softer one. Two heartbeats. Was the soft heartbeat my woman's heart and the strong one my man's heart?

I coughed, but I managed to keep my eyes closed, and after a bit I got used to the smoke. I breathed it into my lungs. It was hot and dry in my nose and on my throat, and it made me thirsty. I kept expecting him to stop, but there must have been a lot of it to burn, because he blew across it now and then—I felt his breath—but held it there. In through my nose and out through my mouth, and the cut on my thigh throbbing with my heart's drum.

I felt the shaman's breath across my face, and I was dizzy and far away from everything.

Was he opening the way of the spirits? That's what was supposed to happen to boys. I didn't want the way of the spirits opened. I didn't want the spirits close.

I thought of my baby, my girl, bones on the hillside. If she came to me, what would I say? If she accused me of letting her go into the spirit world nameless, what explanation could I give her? I breathed her in through my nose.

Her name was Rahel. I breathed that name out through my mouth. My gift to her. If she was already reborn, then it was a secret name and maybe someday a shaman would tell her and maybe she would go her whole life and never know her secret name. But I would know.

I breathed smoke in through my nose and tried to breathe Rahel's spirit out through my mouth. But I could feel her, a separate thing inside me. She would not leave.

Homeless ghost.

She speeded up the drum of my heart. My ears sang.

I heard myself babbling like a baby. I shook and shook and thought my heart would burst. She would kill me, not out of anger but because she had no understanding, no mooring.

She was afraid, too, I thought. I pictured her, I thought of her blue, newborn eyes. I crooned to her in my head, and the babbling slowed and stopped and my heart slowed.

There was no smoke.

I thought everything inside me was so still that I might forget to breathe.

My spirit baby slept within me, home.

"Open your eyes," the shaman said.

I opened my eyes. They felt as dry as leather and heavy as if I had been smoking joss.

"Stand up," he said.

I stood up, and the movement broke the scab on my thigh and the blood ran in a thin line down the inside of my leg. I was dizzy and my stomach swooped for a moment, but then I steadied myself. He dabbed soot on the cut, which hurt.

He helped me dress, because I couldn't balance well enough to stand on one leg to put on my breeches and boots. I leaned on his shoulder. It was the first time I had ever touched him, and his shoulder was bent and fragile.

It was dark in the tent. He had lit a lantern. I didn't understand. I had missed supper? It had only felt like a few minutes.

"Go out," he said. I swayed and then started toward the front of the tent.

"No, Jan," he said. He gestured to the back of the tent. "Go out."

I went out through the spirit door and into the darkness.

He followed me out and made me sit. He wrapped a blanket around my shoulders. The stars were up. It was the short summer night. "I will come and get you. Until then, stay here."

I fell asleep sitting and dreamed of my da.

In the morning the shaman shook my shoulder and woke me and brought me back into the tent through the spirit door.

I felt the difference after that. Inside me in the center of my chest was a nutshell the size of my fist, and inside the shell were Rahel and Janna, curled up around each other. Outside I was Jan.

"Is it magic?" I asked the shaman.

He shrugged. "Magic never works the way you think," he said.

I thought of the spells that Wanji had given me. It was true; the magic hadn't even worked the way Wanji had thought, but that was because the spells weren't appropriate technology. I thought again about the third spell. The one that I didn't know what it did.

Kari was waiting for me outside the medical tent. "Where were you yesterday?" he said.

"I was . . ." I tried to think of how to say it. I shrugged. "The shaman did something to me."

Kari didn't like the shaman, and he refused to be convinced that I wasn't learning the spirit ways. I didn't really care at the moment. I had to relieve myself.

"I've got to do something," I said. "Can I meet you in a few minutes?"

"What?" Kari asked.

What? I couldn't think of anything. "I can't say," I said. "I'll be back."

I headed back away from the medical tent. This was the busiest time for the camp and finding a place to relieve myself would be hard. I took long boy strides, feeling my boyness.

I found a place, not really far enough back in the camp, but there were usually people in the part where there were no tents anyway, so lately I went to the part of the camp where the tents had just been put up and no one was living yet. I crouched between two empty tents. Foolish and naked. The smell of myself.

"What are you doing?" Kari asked.

Desperately I covered myself with my hands. "Get out of here!" I shrieked.

"What?" he said. "What's wrong with you? Oh, *dog-meat*!" He backed up a step.

I yanked up my breeches and ran, away from the camp. I thought Kari would follow me. I looked over my shoulder, but he wasn't there. Some people were out where there were no tents, playing a game with skins, knocking each other over and wrestling.

I sat down and watched them play. They were young boys, not old enough to go out through the spirit door, only old enough to play at hunting. I tried to follow the game. Boys played it in Hamra, but I never had. I didn't know how to be a boy. I felt ashamed and afraid.

Eventually it was time for dinner. Kari was sitting watching the young men. I flushed bright red when I saw him and I waited for him to say something. I didn't know what I would do in front of the young men.

Kari didn't say anything, but he nodded his head sharp for me to follow him.

"It's almost time for dinner," I mumbled, but I followed him. What choice did I have?

We went around the tents and out through the back door of the camp, out to where the stalls were set up. They were busy because it was evening. We walked among the people and Kari looked at me sometimes, sideways, but didn't say anything for a long time.

Finally he said, "You're a woman."

I looked around, but he had said it soft and no one had heard.

"Why are you dressed as a boy?" he asked. "Are you . . . do you want to be a man?"

"I don't want to be a woman alone," I said. "I have no kin. Bad things happen to a woman alone."

He frowned. But it was a thoughtful frown.

I felt strange to be talking about being a woman. I realized that I didn't feel very much like a woman. I didn't think it would be very smart to say that to him.

We walked awhile, and he asked me when I had started dressing as a man. I told him about finding the body of the man and about Aslak dying and about coming here and being called "boy." He didn't much comment on Aslak's death. He was more interested in the spells that Wanji had given me.

"You went to sleep and slept until spring?" he asked.

"Well, not exactly sleep," I said. "More like being dead, only I really wasn't."

"Why didn't you die?" he asked.

"I don't know," I said.

"Did you die?" he asked, looking at me in that sideways fashion.

"No," I said irritably. "It's just technology. I wish Wanji hadn't given them to me."

"What else can you do?"

I told him about the shuttle coming. "There's another one, but I'm not really sure what it does."

"Dogmeat," he cursed, speculatively. "Maybe it changed you into a boy?"

"Kari," I said, "I'm not a boy. I don't have a dick." Although I couldn't remember what that other one did to me, I was pretty sure I'd remember if Wanji had told me it would make me want to be a boy.

He shrugged, then nodded. "Maybe you're just crazy," he said matter-of-factly. "Although from the way you grew up, I guess it isn't surprising you'd be crazy."

"I'm not crazy," I said.

He looked at me and laughed. "Sure, you just dress and act like a boy."

"I told you—that was to be safe." He clearly didn't believe me and it irritated me. "Hey, I've had a husband and a baby."

"You had a baby?" he asked. This took him aback.

"She died," I said.

Of course he knew that—I didn't have a baby with me now, did I?

"Are you going to tell everyone?" I asked.

"No," he said.

"Why not?"

"Who would I tell? The old shaman knows, doesn't he?"

I nodded. "He's teaching me how to be a boy."

This struck Kari as terribly funny. "As if he'd know," he said.

"I know someone who wants to buy some of your food," Kari said. He meant the food that I got from the medical tent.

"Who?" I asked.

"One of the people who sells food." Kari knew one of the stall owners, a man named Simone. He hemmed and hawed but finally bought twelve packets for a five and five ones.

I gave Kari the piece with the five on it. "What's this for?" he asked.

"You found the person to sell it to. I've never been able to figure out how to sell anything," I said. Was that because I was a woman? Were men braver about things like that?

"I didn't do anything," he said and tried to give me back the money.

"I didn't do anything either," I said.

"It was your food," he said.

I shrugged.

"Do you want to get some meat?" Kari asked.

"I'm going to keep mine," I said. I had to start thinking about things. The longer I stayed, the more likely that people other than Kari would figure out I was a woman. There were too many persons, too little space. It wasn't civilized.

"I'll buy some," Kari said. "For both of us."

"You should keep yours, too," I said.

"You bought me meat one time. Besides, it really should be your money." He was strange about it, not looking at me while he said it.

"Okay," I said.

We couldn't buy as much as we had the first time, and I felt awkward not putting my five in, too, but Kari didn't seem to care. We bought meat and flatbread but no beer. Kari sat with his knee pressed against mine, although there was room enough for him.

"People should eat meat," I said.

Kari nodded. "You like it?" he asked.

Of course I liked it.

He grinned, his mouth full of bread and meat. "Good," he said. He was absurdly pleased.

I felt more awkward. This wasn't the way he had treated me before. The meal was not so fine as it had been, and I wanted to get away.

"Let's walk," Kari said when we had finished. We walked down the road, beyond the stalls toward the city of Tonstad.

There was nothing but road between the camp and Tonstad. The grass was pale orange and midsummer tall by now, and it waved heavy heads as we passed.

Kari kept walking a little too close to me, though, and sometimes our arms brushed. I tried to pretend I didn't notice it happening.

"We shouldn't go too far," I said. "If they catch us they'll take us back to the camp."

"I've been to town," Kari said. "Nobody does anything until it gets late."

I wanted to go to town. I pretended the idea had struck me and lengthened my stride. "Good."

"Hey, we don't have to hurry," Kari said.

"Why not?" I asked. "The sooner we get there, the more we can see."

"No," he said, crestfallen, "I mean, I just want to take my time, you know, walk with you. Don't you want to walk with me?"

"Sure I do," I said. "It's great. It's great to be out of the camp."

He gave me a half smile.

We walked a bit.

"Jan," he said, "what is your real name?"

"Jan, now, I guess."

"No, what was it before?"

I didn't want to tell him. "Janna," I said.

"Janna," he said. "Of course."

We walked more. There were big dragonflies in the fields of grass, glinting green-black in the sun. Their wings were as long as my hand.

"On Earth they have birds," I said.

Kari wasn't interested in what they had on Earth. "What are birds?" he said halfheartedly.

"Like daybats, only they don't have fur. They have something called *feathers*. Some are red and some are blue."

"Oh," he said, not really listening. "Janna, you know, since I met you I've, you know, I really liked you."

"I like you too, Kari," I said, brightly. "You're a good friend. You're about my only friend."

He stopped and I had no choice but to stop, too. He stood peering at me. I am tall for a woman, although next to Aslak I always felt short. Kari was not so tall for a man and we looked at each other eye to eye. Awkwardly he took my hand.

"I can't do that," I said, pulling my hand away.

"Why not?" he asked.

"I can't." He was barely more than a boy, younger than me. "I, I'm a widow, and I'm not ready for another man yet." I couldn't say because I didn't feel anything for him.

"You don't like me. What's wrong with me?" he asked, the words like vinegar.

"Nothing," I said. I didn't know if I would like Kari or not, but I had been a boy to Kari and I thought of him that way. And he was so young.

I wondered what I looked like. There was no one to tell me, no mother, no girl, to say "oh, your hair," and sit with a comb and get the snarls out, to oil and braid it. The shaman had cut a bunch of it off for me, but when I ran my hand over it my fingers could see the mess it was.

I started to laugh at the thought that Kari wanted me.

"What?" he asked, sulky and offended.

"I look awful," I said.

"You don't," he said, turning his eyes from me.

"You must be woman hungry," I said. Rough words quick to my tongue, man words. Would I have ever said that? Maybe to Aslak, to tease. "I am scrawny and ugly." I couldn't help laughing.

"Don't laugh at me!" he flared, sudden heat.

"I'm sorry," I said. "I'm not laughing at you, I'm really not. I'm just imagining what I look like. I look so awful."

"Are you saying I couldn't get a proper girl?" he said, rising up on his toes a little.

Of course he couldn't get a proper girl, but his man pride was there, rearing his head.

"I was your friend," he said, furious. "First I was your friend, then I learned about you, it isn't, you've made it—"

He turned from me then and walked away, walked back toward camp with his back stiff with anger.

"Kari," I called. "I'm sorry." I trotted to catch up to him.

He turned, angry. "You're sick!" he said. "You don't even like men!"

That left me openmouthed with surprise. "No," I said, not even quite sure what he meant.

"I'll tell them," he said, and then he sprinted away.

I ran after him. But I'd been sitting around the camp too much and Kari had been walking to town. I had no wind and he outlasted me easily enough and finally I walked and then sat in the midsummer grass.

He was just angry. They were hot words. By the time he got to camp maybe he wouldn't say anything to anybody.

But what if he did?

Even if he didn't, he had found out. The camp was getting more people every week. More people, more chances to be found out. And what was there in the camp, anyway? Easy food, but no meat, nothing a person really needed. The camp took our personhood away, left us like rennder. The offworlders' animals.

He would have it to use, always. Either I would have to go with Kari or I would have to leave. It was already midsummer. Either I would leave now or I would have to wait out the winter in the camp.

I sat in the grass that smelled sweet sharp. Wanji called that smell licorice, and she said it was a candy, but it was just a grass smell to me. The dragonflies buzzed around me, I sat so still so long.

I sat in the grass until it started to get dark. The patrol went by in a truck, going to town to round people up, like Kari had said.

I walked back to camp and waited through the long, long summer evening until darkness, sleeping in the grass behind the stalls and trying to ignore the smells of food. I had my five, but I thought I might need that. Finally, near the middle of the night, it got dark and then I went in the back way through the dark to the shaman's tent.

I tried to creep in, but he was awake. Old men do not need to sleep so much. "Where have you been?" he asked. There was only his voice in the darkness.

I jumped at the sound of his voice. "Waiting," I said. "Someone has found me out."

"How?" he asked.

"They saw me squatting to shit."

In the dark I collected my things.

"What are you going to do?" he said.

"Leave," I said. "Go south."

"And do what?"

"I thought, I don't know, maybe if I went south to the port, I might get a job, because of my English."

"You're not ready," the shaman said.

"I know I'm not ready," I said, "but do you see I can't stay?"

"You've just started," he said. "This is the wrong time to leave."

I busied myself packing. I found some packets of food. I had taken twelve to the stallman, but I had seven more that I hadn't bothered to try to sell. I had thought twelve was a good number and if I wanted to sell more later, I could. I had a can I could cook in, and a knife. It was not so much.

I fingered the chit that they had given me for Aslak's gun. I wasn't supposed to be able to leave the refugee camp unless I had a job or kin who could take me, and I couldn't redeem the rifle unless they decided I was ready to leave.

I didn't want to leave the rifle. I could have used it. But there was nothing to be done.

I put the chit on the end of the shaman's blankets.

"I thank you, sir," I said. I didn't know what else to say. "I think you'll be glad to have some peace and not have some clumsy person around."

"You are a fool," he said.

By the time I got to the back opening, the sky was already beginning to lighten. Night is very short in mid-summer. I headed south, with the dawn on my left.

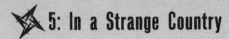# 5: In a Strange Country

I HAD BEEN IN TAUFZIN FOR THREE DAYS and all that time it had rained. I couldn't sleep because of the noise—when I lay down the sidewalk trembled with the sound of the city. Sound was everywhere: from the trucks and things that ran the roads, sounds of feet, rumbles of machines from under the ground. I sat on the sidewalk and a man tossed a coin at me.

I was so cold that when I picked up my coin my fingers were stiff and it was hard to get hold of it on the flat sidewalk. I decided I had better walk. My hips ached.

I walked because I had nothing else to do. The city made my feet hurt. There was no give to the earth, it was all hard, and every step my heel hit, and I felt it through all my connected bones, leg and spine, until it rang in my aching, empty head.

The city changed around me though I had thought it was all the same. For a while I walked by low buildings built up against each other and all painted white or pale gray like serious ghosts. Then I walked through a place where all the windows were full of yellow light and off-world goods.

I was leaning against a wall next to a window full of carved people wearing clothes the pale purple of berries when someone stopped and said, "You are going to get in trouble if you stay here." The man was a clansman.

"Where should I go?" I asked, I thought, quite reasonably.

He was the first clansman I had seen here. Everyone else was round-faced and broad and spoke a language I didn't understand. He was a bowlegged hunter, so like my father I wondered if I might be talking to a spirit, except that my father had never dressed in offworld clothes in his life and this man wore some ash-gray thing with a hood for a jerkin. But at least he wore decent boots. A bit used and stained with city grime but made from good renndeer hide.

"Go home," he said.

"I don't have a home."

"Where are you staying?" he asked.

"On the sidewalk," I said.

He spat and swore. He stamped down the street, and I thought idly that I ought to watch which way he went, although I wasn't quite clear why.

That *why* was still occupying me when he stamped back. "Come by," he said. So I followed him.

We walked a good bit. I wasn't even paying attention to the city anymore. I couldn't hold landmarks in my head, much less get a sense of the place, because it was all buildings, and even though the buildings were different, as soon as I had turned a corner I couldn't remember if they'd been tall or short, white or gray.

We went down a hill.

"Okay." The man stopped. "You're in your own part of town now."

I looked around. Some of the buildings looked old. They leaned together like drunks.

"Will you be all right now?" he asked. "Do you have any money?"

I showed him my coin. Did he want it for leading me here?

"Is that all?" he asked. "What kin are you?"

"Hamra," I said.

He sighed. "I've never heard of them."

"They're all dead," I said. "I'm the only one left."

He looked at me for a while, but I didn't know from his face what that might mean. "Aren't you lucky," he said finally.

"No," I said, stupid and light-headed.

"Come on," he said.

"Where?" I asked.

"A place where you can sleep out of the rain."

We walked around the streets—all angles, left and then right and then left, in some elaborate pattern. He left me standing in front of yet another building and told me to knock on the door.

I watched him splash off through the rain. I hoped his boots were in better shape than mine; my feet were soaked.

I knocked on the door. Above the door was painted MENNONITE JOACHIM RENNLOYT MISSION. The word "mission" shocked me as suddenly as if I had been hit by lightning. I didn't know what to do then. Too many feelings for my tired empty head.

The door opened and a woman said, "Yah?"

I blinked in the strong yellow light. Electrical light, the kind that is bright but has no heat.

The woman looked me up and down, and then asked something in my own language. She had a terrible accent, so for a moment I didn't understand she was speaking my language and then I realized.

"I'm sorry," I said. "I didn't understand."

"Do you need aid?" she asked again.

I nodded.

"Come by," she said. Inside was a white hallway and stairs that went straight up. She closed the door and suddenly the sound of the city was muffled and the rain was far away. She took me up the stairs into the dimness rather than into the lighted hallway.

On the second floor were pallets, all laid out in straight lines like the streets, and men slept on most of them. It was quiet. Even with all the men there.

"I have a blanket," I whispered.

She shushed me without speaking and took my blanket and put it on a shelf. Then she gestured that I should go into a room. She followed me in.

"This is a bathroom," she said. "Do you know about bathrooms?"

I didn't recognize anything, so I shook my head.

"You put this down to latch the door," she said. "You piss in here, and shit if you need to, and when you are done, you push this handle down.'' She did and there was a noise and the water disappeared in a rush. "There is water here, but turn it off when you are done. I am afraid we have only cold water up here. In here,'' she opened a closet, "are dry clothes you can use. For a boy your size . . .'' She paused, looking in the closet.

She found me clothes that were too big for me and then left me to put down the latch. She told me that the shower was downstairs, and there would be time enough for that tomorrow.

I didn't understand much of what she said, but I drank water, pissed, did the handle, and then, with the latch down on the door, I could strip off my wet clothes. In the mirror I saw myself for the first time. My face and hands were black, and there was a black line around my neck. My clothes were stiff. I washed myself in the water as best I could. The shaman had hacked my hair off so it came to just below my ears, and it was ragged and grimy and uneven. I rinsed my whole head in the sink and the water ran black, but it didn't do much good. My face and hands were cleaner, and I could put on the clothes from the closet. The shirt was soft and blue.

Then there were dry blankets. And silence, except for the sound of other men sleeping. And I slept.

I awoke startled and scrambling out of the blankets, not sure where I was with a head full of dreams about my family.

"Hey, hey, hey,'' a man said, his voice smooth as if I were a startled renndeer. "You're okay. You're at the Mission. Okay? What's your name? My name is Mika. What's your name?''

He was crouched down next to my pallet, and he had his hands out and open. His words were just noise. I was so tired and confused. "It's breakfast time,'' he said, as if there wasn't anything odd. "Let's go downstairs and get breakfast, okay?''

Some men were sitting up, watching us. Some were rolling up the blankets they had slept in.

"I'm sorry,'' I said. "I was startled.''

"It's okay,'' he said. "What's your name?''

"Jan," I said.

"I'm Mika," he said again. He started folding my blankets. I knelt down and folded them with him, watching his hands. He had soft, beautiful hands. They were clean and the fingers were long. He had a leather thong bracelet like some people wore at home, but it was the only thing that he was wearing that wasn't offworld. He wore a soft pale hooded shirt that looked as if it had never been dirty, and around his neck he had a fine chain of gold. He had the strangest shoes. They were all different layers of leather stitched together in a beautiful pattern to make the shape of the shoe. They were once white, although now they had city grime on them. But his ankles were not grimy.

He was marvelously clean. I saw my own dirty hands and my cracked nails and felt shamed.

He showed me where to put my blanket, and then we went to get breakfast. There were women coming downstairs from the floor above us. Last night I had not even noticed that there was a floor above us. Some of the women had children with them. Refugees, just like the camps.

Breakfast was at long tables in the back on the first floor. The room was low and the voices echoed. Here and there among the people at the tables there were people who looked as if they were from Taufzin, but most of the people were clanspeople, like me. We were all beggars.

They served grain porridge, like I remembered from the camp, and toasted bread to dip in it. They also served the bitter drink called coffee of which Mika drank three cups, although he wasn't interested in porridge.

I was terribly interested in porridge and ate mine and enough for him.

He sat drinking his coffee and watching me eat, but he didn't say anything.

Afterward I was hoping I could go back upstairs and lie down some more, but instead they told us all that the Mission was putting us out until evening. Nobody but me seemed surprised by this.

"Where do we go?" I asked.

Mika laughed. "Wherever we want." He stood up and

picked up his coffee cup and my bowl. I picked up the rest of my things and followed him.

"You're going, too? Why do we go?" Maybe this was the way the people who worked here got to leave and do other things.

The cup and the bowl clattered against the bin. They sounded almost as if they had broken but they hadn't. "So we will go out and find ways to support ourselves," he said.

It was a funny thing to say, and it took me a moment. "You mean we are supposed to use the day to find out how to live and then come back here at night?" It sounded reasonable. But I was really tired. "No one here wants us," I pointed out. "How are we supposed to live?"

Mika laughed. "That really is the question. So what are you doing in this city?"

"I thought I could work because I speak English," I said. "But no one wants me here."

"You speak English?" Mika said. "Really?"

"Some," I said. "But when I tried to tell someone that, they just screamed at me."

"If you can speak some English, can you read and write?" he asked.

"Yeah."

"How do you know how to read and write?"

I pointed over the door of the Mission. "I grew up in a mission, up north."

Mika was stopped on the steps, looking at me, thinking. "Dogmeat," he said.

"What's wrong?"

"That's great," he said. "I can get you a job, I think. I'll only charge you half of your first paycheck."

I didn't exactly understand what he said. But he was going to get me work and that was great.

"Sissela," he said, "I need to ask a favor of you."

The woman who answered the door was wearing a bright robe patterned in red flowers. She looked as if she had been asleep. I wondered what it would be like to sleep in something like that.

"Mika," she said, and then answered him in the language they used here. He said something to her in the same language.

He was talking about me, because she looked at me and made herself smile. Then she nodded at him.

"You'll need to clean up," Mika said. "Then Sissela can cut your hair. Sissela is good at cutting hair."

I reached up and touched my hair.

We followed Sissela into her place. We had climbed up an outside staircase past four other floors to get here. I looked back outside over the railing at the space of air below us to the street.

We stepped out of the light and the clear, rainwashed morning into the dim place where she lived. The air was close with the smell of people and sleep and smoke. The first room had chairs and kinds of furniture I had never seen before. The next room had a table strewn with papers and empty glasses and cups. She had jars on the wide shelf in there, and she reached in one and pulled out a bag and a pipe. I knew what the pipe was. Kari and I had shared enough pipes.

"This way," Mika said.

He took me into the room where she slept. She slept in a bed. I knew the word in English, but I had never seen one before. On top of the bed the blankets were all swept in a pile. The little room beyond that was the bathroom.

Mika showed me how to use the sink and the shower. I didn't tell him I already knew from the night before because I wasn't sure how any of it worked.

"Take off your clothes," he said, turning on the water.

"No," I said.

He looked at me oddly.

"I don't take off my clothes," I said.

"Ever?" he said.

"Ever," I said.

"Well, showering with your clothes on isn't going to do you any good. And if you don't get clean, you won't get a job."

"Then you have to leave," I said. Did my voice sound too much like a woman's voice?

Mika just shrugged. "Get clean," he said. "Or I'll make you do it again."

I latched the door behind him and stripped off the clothes I had gotten at the mission.

The water was warm. I was almost afraid to get under it. It was unpleasant the way it got in my eyes, but the warmth was wonderful. I could have stood there and stood there, but instead I used the cloth and the soap and washed myself as if I were an old shirt. When I washed my hair the water ran gray.

The water wasn't as warm when I finished, but I was clean. I dried myself, dressed, and unlatched the door.

No one was in the bedroom, but I heard voices and smelled joss smoke. Mika and the woman were sitting at the table and he was telling her something and she was laughing. Was it about me?

Mika looked up. "What an improvement," he said.

Sissela didn't look too impressed, but she got up and gestured that I should sit down in the chair. Then she got scissors and cut off my hair in big matted clumps. It fell around the chair in lumps like little animals.

So strange. I felt so light with my hair gone. Then she set to work shaping what was left, cutting it in a straight line above my eyes and combing the rest of it back. She would cut, then stop for a moment, light the pipe and take a draw, and study my head. I wished she would let me have a draw on the pipe, but it didn't seem polite to ask. Then she cut some more and suddenly she was done. "You have nice hair," she said. She had a strong city accent.

"Thank you," I said.

She handed me a mirror and a strange person looked back at me. The stranger had such a thin face. The bones of his forehead were large and in his temples you could see the fine blue veins, and under his cheeks was hollow. A face that was little more than a skull. Ugly boy.

"You clean up very well," Mika said, studying me. "I would never have guessed. You will have to lie and tell them you are older than you are."

I realized he thought I was young because I was beardless. A beardless boy. I nodded. "Thank you," I said to Sissela. She waved her hand, pushing the thanks away.

She said something to Mika as she picked up a broom and started to sweep the dead hair away.

Outside it was still bright and I blinked. The air smelled so clear after Sissela's place.

Mika clattered down the stairs, a male racket, and I followed trying to make as much sound as he did. He started whistling.

Whistling is bad luck, but I didn't say anything.

The place where Mika took me to work was in yet another part of town. Here the streets were wide, and trucks growled along. The buildings were huge and low and plain. Without windows. The few bushes and trees out front looked out of place and dusty.

Inside the light was odd, flat and white. Everything looked empty: The floors were tan, the walls were white, the tables with their drawers, everything else was tan, too. We walked down a hallway and up to a door with a sign on it. The sign was black and the letters were white and it said PERSONNEL. I sounded the word out to myself and held on to it in case I needed it.

The woman behind the table was wearing black and red, not tan, and she stood out. Mika talked to her and pointed to me, and she talked to him. Then she said to me, "You speak English?"

"I speak some," I said.

"What's your name?"

"Jan," I said. "Jan of Hamra clan."

She had a paper and she pushed it toward me. "You can read and write? Can you fill this out?"

She gave me a pencil, and I wrote my name out. I knew Hamraclan would be my last name if I were an offworlder. I put down Unmarried. For my age I had to ask, "Do you mean my offworld age?"

She nodded, "Your Terran age, if you know it."

I thought I was sixteen, but Terran years were shorter and so I should put about twenty, but Mika thought I was younger. So I put eighteen. For my birth date I shrugged.

She was smiling. "Were you born in winter or summer, do you know?"

Winter, I was pretty sure. "Winter," I said.

She took it from me and put a year and a *w*.

"What's your address?"

I didn't know. I looked at Mika. "What?" he said in our language. "Oh," he said, and turned and talked to her.

She nodded and wrote something down. I could see "Menno Mission" and then numbers.

"How did you learn English?" she asked.

"My home was a mission," I said. "We had school. They are dead now."

She looked a little irritated. Cold luck words to say in a place like this, I guessed.

They took me in back and they gave me tests on all sorts of things. Read a passage and say what it means, look at pictures and answer questions. I couldn't answer a lot of the questions. Then a test of numbers. I had not liked numbers much when I was in school, but they were easier than English and I answered a lot of those right. Even the algebra. I was surprised at how much algebra I remembered.

It took a great long time. And before it was over I was as tired as if I had not slept the night before.

I sat in a soft chair in a room with Mika and waited while they decided about the tests.

Mika was pleased. "She liked the way you spoke," he said. "Your English must have been good."

"My English isn't so good," I said.

"Good enough," he said. But he hadn't taken the tests.

Still, the woman came back. "Mr. Hamra," she said, and somehow I knew to stand up, even though it didn't feel like a real name. "As you may know, Werther Zin-Tech of Koziko makes precision manufacturing machinery, using Earth-level technologies. We would like to offer you a job. You do very well with numbers and you read some English. We think you could learn to keep machines working for us, and you could use the manuals, most of which are from Earth. You will need some schooling, and for the half year you are in schooling, you will work half days, about thirty hours, cleaning up and your pay will only be 11.60 centremarc per hour. You won't get paid for your schooling time, but after that, if it all works out, you'll be a technician and your pay will be 18.10 cm. Can you start in three weeks, on Monday? We can give you an advance on your pay to help you until you would start.''

She gave me two hundred cm in ten twenty-cm bills. When we got outside I gave half to Mika. ''I will give you the rest when I get it?'' I said.

''That's great,'' Mika said. ''That's really great. You're going to be a technician? That's a great job. Congratulations!''

''Thank you,'' I said. ''You helped me a lot. So much.''

''You helped me, too,'' he said. ''Tonight I won't have to sleep at the Mission.''

''You don't stay there tonight?'' I asked.

He shook his head. ''Not now.''

''They don't care you don't come?'' I was confused. I thought when you had a job you always had to come.

He laughed. ''They wouldn't care if I never came back. Come with me and we'll get a place to stay.''

Mika took me back to the part of town where the Mission was and found us a woman who had rooms she would rent. We could each rent a room for two weeks for fifty cm. My room had a bed. I sat down on it, and it was so soft it was uncomfortable. My room had a window. Although it wasn't as high up as Sissela's room, it looked down on the air and I liked that. I could watch the people on the street.

Mika came into my room. ''What do you think?'' he asked.

''It is a great room,'' I said.

He thought that was funny. He showed me how to open the window, and the light and the air poured into the room and I was so happy I could have cried.

I ran out of money before I started work and Mika loaned me some. He loaned me more than I asked for, in fact, and told me to get some clothes, so I got some pants and some soft shirts. I didn't see Mika very much. He said he had a business now, and the money he'd gotten from getting me a job had given him the stake he needed to get it started. That was the first time I understood that Mika had been at the Mission because, like me, he didn't have any other place to go.

Mika explained his business, which had something to do with buying stuff from people who had made it but couldn't find anyone who wanted to buy it, and then selling it to people who wanted to buy it but didn't know the people who make it. It seemed to me that Mika was a finder, which was my own word for what he did. He had found me a job. And he found people who wanted things and he found things that people wanted.

Mika was a person of the city. He was a hunter, in his own way. He could go anywhere in the city, the way hunters know the land. He was confident, like hunters, although he acted in ways that no hunter ever would. He told me about how he had found this person who had leather gloves for sale and couldn't sell them because it was summer. Then he found another person who brought all these Mennons in from the countryside (those were the people whose men had long beards and who all dressed in blues and grays). The Mennons would work for very little money. So this man bought all the gloves from Mika, and the Mennons cut patterns in the backs of the gloves, diamonds and animal shapes and elaborate knot work like embroidery. They cut the fingers off. What was left was barely glove, and nothing that would keep you warm. It was more like jewelry. Then the man who had hired the Mennons and Mika sold the new-worked gloves in the marketplace.

He was bragging when he told it, which was nothing like what a hunter would do, but it was so interesting I didn't care.

He brought me a pair of gloves, brown and supple, with cutwork on the backs that left little more than a fisherman's net and all my skin showed through. I loved them. There was nowhere to wear them, of course. I had nowhere to go. I sat in my room in the window and watched the people below on the street and wore my gloves. And thought about Mika. I told myself that I thought about him all the time because I was bored. I thought about his hair and his voice. I thought about sex with him. One night I dreamed I was married to him and that we were wandering through the city, and that it had been emptied by war with the clans, but Mika knew where things were hidden and it was exciting rather than scary.

I'd have thought that after living on the sidewalk that I would be so happy to have a place that I would never be bored. But I couldn't sleep enough to fill the hours. After a week, Mika moved somewhere else, and then I didn't even have a hope of seeing him on the stairs.

I was relieved when I finally got to go to my job.

I didn't sleep the night before. I had slept so much and I was so worried about what the job would be like. Mika had explained things to me about how I would have to work for so many hours, and that I would have to be at work at an exact time and could not be even one minute late or they might tell me I couldn't have the job. He had taken me out and bought me a watch and shown me how to wear it. And he told me not to wear my gloves.

"They are not really for work," he said, smiling a little. He treated me as if I were his little brother.

So I walked off to work, starting early in the morning before it was light. I left my gloves under the too-soft mattress on the bed (I slept on the floor because when I didn't my back hurt) and I had the watch strapped around my right wrist.

I was there seventeen minutes before I had to be, which was a relief. The closer I had gotten, the more I had worried that something would happen or that I had misjudged the time and I would be late. I went to the door and was stopped by a man who checked his clipboard and found my name on it. He told me something, but I didn't understand the language. He pointed and said, "Personnel," which I did understand, and I nodded hard to show him I did.

The woman who had given me the job was not there. Other people were there. Mennons. Mostly men, although there were three women. The women wore white caps over their hair. The fabric of the caps was so fine that you could see the shadow of their hair through them. The caps tied under their chins. They looked new and marvelously neat.

The man who met us spoke to the Mennons in their language, and then spoke to me in English. He talked for a while, and then said to me, "We will fit you for uniforms. Follow everyone else. I will meet with you later to explain things." He said this calmly and without anger. I understood most of what he said, although I didn't understand the word "uniforms." But I turned it over and over in my mind. I felt extra alert, as if I were hunting something.

The uniforms were all of a piece. They were dark green. It was a good color, like the color of the needles on the trees at home. I didn't feel so bad that I didn't have new clothes. We were given clothes, and then the women marched one way and the men went another. We went into a big room with rows and rows of metal lockers, and I was given a series of numbers on a piece of paper. The man in charge of us had two helpers—men who worked in this clothing place. The lockers were all green, too.

I watched the helpers teaching people. After a while I tried to open the locker myself, from what I had seen other people do. It took me a while, but I learned to do it, and when the man who spoke English got to me he said, "Good, I see you've got it."

I flushed with pride.

There wasn't anything inside the lockers except shelves and hooks.

Then the other men started taking off their clothes and putting on the uniforms.

I looked around. There wasn't much place to hide.

If they would fire me for being one minute late, surely they would fire me for telling them I was a boy when I was really a girl. It had been a mistake not to tell Mika. But when I thought of telling Mika that I was a girl I was suddenly afraid of him in a way I wasn't when he thought I was a boy. I was a kinless boy. Better than being a kinless girl. Would he be mad at me when he found out I had lost this job? What would I tell him, that I had been late?

"Jan," said the man in English, "do you need a bathroom?"

"Yes," I said. "I need a bathroom."

He showed me to the bathroom. There were stalls with doors, toilets, like the rooming house where I lived. There was a huge room with showers, but I could shower at the rooming house, where there was only one shower in the bathroom and I could close the door.

I used one of the stalls to change my clothes. Then I went to the bathroom, just in case.

My heart was still beating fast. They hadn't left the lockers, and the man was talking in their language. I stood at the back and listened to see if I could make any sense.

I knew some words. I could ask for wheatmeal, bread, tea, and a meat sandwich called a steuber. I could say hello. But in the flow of language I couldn't distinguish anything. And he probably didn't say anything about wheatmeal or steubers anyway.

Then we went all around the building. I shuffled along behind. After he had told the Mennons what this place was, he would say something to me in English. Mostly they were words I didn't know. Sometimes, like the eating place, I knew what the place was and still didn't understand the English.

I watched the time go by on my watch, but that made everything slower. I wondered why the offworlders wanted to break up time into little blocks—it seemed torturous to me—but after I had started watching the time, I couldn't stop.

Two hours we shuffled around. My head ached.

Then we went back to the eating place, and the man who spoke English sat down next to me. "Coffee or tea?" he said.

"Tea," I said. At least I had understood what he asked.

He got two cups. One was tea and that was for me.

He asked me something about the tour and I nodded, not sure what he had said.

"Next," he said, "there will be English lessons."

"English lessons," I repeated, to show that I understood. "Good." Not that I wanted anything to do with English lessons. I wanted to go back to my room. I was tired and I didn't know what was going on.

English lessons were done in a room with two people teaching us. One was the man who had led us all around. The other was a woman. She was dressed like a Mennon, but she spoke English like an offworlder. I had hoped that the lessons would be easy because the Mennons didn't seem to know any English. Our lessons were interactive. Each person learned his own way. We put on a visor thing that covered our eyes and ears, and we couldn't hear anyone or see anyone. Then we saw and heard the interactives.

My interactive was a girl. She looked a little like a clanswoman, but like Mika she was very much city. There was a book on the table in front of me. In the real classroom there was a book, too, so when I reached down to pick up the book, I could touch a real book. The real book wasn't exactly where the book was in the interactive, but I supposed the girl couldn't be expected to have lined them up exactly.

"We will speak only English," she said. "What is your name?"

"Jan," I said.

"Can you answer in a whole sentence?" she asked, but nice.

"My name is Jan," I said. Then in clans' language I said, "I'm worn out from all this trying to understand English. It's hard."

"Only English," she said and frowned a little.

"Excuse me," I said, embarrassed. She had said only English.

"I am an interactive," she said. "You may name me."

Name her? "What is your name?" I asked.

"I am an interactive," she said again. "I am not a person. You may give me a name."

It took me a while to figure out that she was some sort of spirit of the machine.

"I'll call you Rahel," I said, thinking of the spirit of my daughter.

I regretted it instantly. But the interactive smiled and said, "Rahel, that is a good name. Thank you."

What if I had trapped my daughter's spirit in the machine? I felt sick. "I am stop a minute," I said. I took the thing off my head and the interactive was gone. I could hear people around me talking in badly accented English. The man stood at a main table that must have told him something. When I took my head visor off he looked at me. The woman walked over to me.

"Are you all right?" she asked.

"I am fine," I said. "I am stop a minute. Okay?"

"Okay," she said. "A minute."

I didn't want to put the visor back on, but she and the man were watching me, so I did. The woman with my daughter's name was waiting. "Hello," she said.

I would need to talk to a shaman. I didn't know where I would find a shaman. Surely there had to be one in the city.

"Let's practice English, and I will teach you a technician's job," said the woman with my daughter's name. "You are going to be a technician, so let's start with tools."

I didn't see Mika for three days after I started work. By Wednesday I was furious with him. Then, very late on Wednesday he threw pebbles at my window.

I didn't know what was going on. I was just drifting into sleep, and the sound brought me bolt upright and startled. I looked out the window into the dark and saw his pale face upturned below.

"Jan," he hissed. "Can I come in?"

"The front door is locked," I said. The front door was locked at ten every night. It was a rule. I had a key, but I never carried it with me because I was always back before ten.

"So you will have to let me in," Mika said.

I thought no one was supposed to come in after ten, but I wasn't sure about that. And Mika seemed to assume it was okay. The rules that people all knew were a lot harder than the official rules.

"I'm so tired," Mika said. He was smiling and pleased with himself.

"What?" I asked.

"Can I sleep on your floor tonight?"

I thought he had gotten all the money from the gloves and he didn't need a room like mine anymore. I had imagined him in a place like the woman who cut my hair had.

"Do you need money?" I asked, which was foolish because I didn't have any.

"I just finished a deal that means some nice money, and if it works out, maybe some steady money."

I let him in.

"I'm so tired," he said. "I haven't been to sleep since Monday."

He needed to shave. I rubbed my beardless jaw and followed him up the stairs to my room. All the things I had wanted to say to him couldn't be said now.

He was going to sleep in my room. On my floor.

"You can have the bed," I said.

"I don't need the bed," he said. "I'm so tired I could sleep anywhere." Then he saw my blanket on the floor where I had been sleeping.

"My back hurts when I try to sleep on the bed," I said. "And it is too hot. Too squishy."

He thought that was funny. "You're a regular outrunner, aren't you," he said.

"No," I said sharply. "Don't call me that."

He frowned at me. "It was a joke."

"I know," I said.

My answer left no room for talk, and he took off his shoes in silence and stretched out on my bed.

"Thanks for letting me stay," he said.

"It's okay," I said. "I'm paying for the room with your money. I have to get up early tomorrow to go to work."

"Oh yeah," he said, his voice already drowsy. "How is it?"

I thought about saying how difficult it was. I thought about saying, why would you care? "It's okay," I said.

"Great," he said, absent.

I listened to him breathing.

"Mika?"

"Ha?" I heard his breath catch as if he had already gone to sleep.

"Do you know where I could find a shaman?"

"A what?" he asked.

"I need to ask a shaman a question."

"I don't even know what a shaman is," he said.

"A spirit man," I said.

"No," he said, grumpy. "I don't know where to find a spirit man."

I had more things to ask him, but I let him go to sleep.

I got up in the morning and left him sleeping, and when I got home from work, the bastard was gone again and I still didn't know how to find him.

I didn't see Mika again until after I got paid.

Getting paid was very strange. After spending the morning learning to be a technician, I spent the afternoon learning how to mop and clean. Offworlders were very clean. I understood for the first time why everything offworlders had looked so new—because they were always cleaning things.

I was scrubbing a yellow machine that made matrices to grow chips when my teacher handed me a piece of paper. The piece of paper had been folded and glued in a rather elaborate way, so he showed me how to tear it open. I didn't understand why they had to put one piece of paper around another this way.

Inside was another piece of paper. "What's this?" I asked.

"It's your paycheck," he said. He showed me how much it was for, and how the two hundred they gave me when they told me I could have the job had been subtracted out.

"This is money?" I asked. It didn't look like money.

The teacher took me to an office where they would take my check. They gave me a book and a card and showed me how to use the card to get money from machines. The machine would know how much money I had, and when I took money out, it would subtract that from the amount it knew I had.

I learned how to do all of it, but it seemed very convoluted. I asked why they didn't just give people money instead of doing all of this, and they said it was to keep people from getting robbed, but it seemed needlessly complicated.

The good thing was that all this doing money meant that by the time I got back to scrubbing the machine, it was almost time to go home. There was only the long hour, which was what I called the last hour because it seemed to take longer than any other hour of the day. I would look at the time, and then wait, and make myself wait and not look at the time again until I couldn't stand it and then it would only be five minutes later.

But finally I could walk home. I thought for sure that Mika would come that evening to get the money I owed him. I hurried and didn't buy dinner stuff, just fruit to have in my room for Mika. Mika didn't come and I ate all the fruit waiting for him, and it gave me the runs.

I was sorry I had ever left the camp. At least there were people I could talk to there. Kari might not have told anyone, and now it seemed that it would have been worth it to have sex with him. I lay in the dark on the floor and tried to pretend that Aslak was there, sleeping beside me. I tried to imagine us back in Hamra, married. Rahel growing up. A family. I hoped pretending would make me feel better, but it just made me cry.

The next day, while I mopped the floor in the cafeteria I thought about what I would do when Mika finally showed up. I would just give him the money. I would be aloof, neither friendly nor unfriendly. He would ask me what was wrong. I would just shrug. He would feel embarrassed. . . .

What if he didn't care?

Maybe he wasn't my friend, maybe he didn't even like me.

It took me a little over an hour to walk from work to my room, and all I had to do while I was walking was think about Mika. On my way home there was a machine that gave money, and I stopped at it and tried getting money out. It knew how much money I had. It gave me some of my money, enough to pay for another week in my room and some extra to get something to eat.

I stopped to get something to eat, and they had whiskey in bottles.

It was the brown color of brass whiskey, the kind my mother made. I fingered my money and asked how much it was. I had learned enough of the Taufzin language to ask how much something was, although sometimes I didn't understand the answer until they wrote it down. Whiskey was expensive. I had enough for two weeks in my room, and for food, but not enough to buy the whiskey and pay Mika what I owed him.

So I bought the whiskey anyway. I would pay Mika the rest when I got another paycheck. Besides, he had made all that money—he was rich. He obviously didn't care or he would have come around the day I got paid.

I had to show them my work card to get the whiskey. I didn't understand it, I had the money, but the storeman kept asking for it, so I did. I carried the bottle home, cradling it.

When I opened it the smell of whiskey was like perfume.

It was as good as what my mother made. A different taste, but not harsh. Aged more than two years, I was sure. I drank two glasses because I wanted to be careful with it. I ate my dinner. I fell asleep easily. It was wonderful.

I didn't fall asleep so easily the next night, but if I drank more I'd run out before payday, so I lay in the darkness, feeling the pleasant fuzziness of the whiskey, and tried not to think about my mother.

I worked, and I came home and ate my dinner and looked out my window at the street below and drank my two glasses of whiskey, and then, one night, while I was drinking the first glass, there he was, looking up at me from the street.

"Jan!"

"Come up!" I said.

I had the door open to the hall and there he was in my little room.

"Is that whiskey?" he said. "Jan, you surprise me. Drinking on a work night?"

I frowned, not sure what he meant, but he just laughed and asked for a drink, so I poured him one, thinking about how little there was left in the bottle and how many more days until payday. But glad to see him. Glad to have him fill up my room. "So you are rich now?" I asked.

"Not rich," he said.

"You said you'd have steady money."

"Sometimes the buyer changes his mind," Mika said. "So I have unsteady money which is mostly gone."

"I can pay you part of what I owe you," I said. "But they took my advance out of my paycheck. I'll have to owe you one hundred more in two weeks."

"Okay," he said.

Which meant he would have to come back and see me. And by the time he came back, I could afford more whiskey.

I wanted to be angry at him, but I didn't dare. Sitting here it was completely different than I had imagined. He was different than I had imagined. When I'd first met him he had seemed so offworld, so city, to me. But looking at him now, I could see how very much he looked like a clansman. The people down here all have round bland faces, and clansmen, we have knobby cheeks and sharp chins and look different. Even in his city clothes, Mika didn't look like a Mennon.

He looked so good to me.

I poured him the last of my precious whiskey. "Do you need a place to stay?"

"No," he said. "Your bed is safe."

"I don't use it," I said.

He laughed. "You need to get out more."

I had the sudden terrible urge to say "I am a woman." I wanted badly, physically, to lean over and kiss him on the cheek. I could see his cheek there, smoothly shaven, and his lips. I didn't change my expression, nothing outside changed. Outside I was frozen for an instant because the urge was so strong to say the thing I couldn't say. But I couldn't. Instead I said, "I don't know anyone, and I don't speak the language."

I didn't know if I was Jan or Janna. Maybe it was the whiskey.

"You should meet people," he said, just talking.

"How?" I asked.

He didn't know. Get out of my room more. And do what? I thought bitterly, but already I was making him uncomfortable and I wanted him to stay. So I asked him how he came to live in the city.

His mother was a clanswoman and his father was a sailor and had brought her back to Taufzin, but then he'd gone back on a ship or something and left her alone.

"Where's your mother?" I asked.

"She lives near the Menno Mission," he said. "She cleans people's houses."

"Is your mother old?" I asked. "Do you have many brothers and sisters?"

"I'm the oldest," he said. "I have a lot of brothers and sisters. But I don't see them very often. I've got to go— you've got to get up in the morning." He was eager to end the conversation.

"If I need to get in touch with you, you know, to send you the money," I asked, "how do I do it?"

"Leave a message with Sissela," he said. "Sissela can usually get in touch with me." He wrote her name and the numbers of her address on a piece of paper.

On the day I got paid, I stopped at the machine and took out the money I owed Mika. I had a lot of trouble finding where Sissela lived. I knew that buildings had numbers, but finding the street was very hard.

I climbed the stairs and knocked on the door. I expected other doors to open up from the noise, and I didn't know what I was going to say if they did. Then there was no answer.

I sat down on the steps and tried to think of what to do. I was tired, and since I had run out of money, I hadn't had any lunch. I should have stopped and bought something to eat. I looked over the railing to see if I could see any shops where there would be something to eat, but there weren't any that I could see, so I sat down again.

I thought I could find my way back, but I wasn't exactly sure. I could wait for Sissela.

So I sat. Other than being in a strange place and more than a little nervous about what Sissela would think when she saw me, waiting was not a whole lot different from sitting back in my own room. Except that I didn't have any whiskey.

It was long after dark when Sissela climbed the stairs. She said something in Taufzin.

"Hello," I said. "I'm Mika's friend Jan."

She stood below me on the steps. She had a bag in her

arms, as if she had just come from a shop. "What are you doing?" she asked.

"Putting off death," I answered, which is something clanspeople say.

I could see her grin in the darkness. "So are we all," she said.

"I have money for Mika," I said. "He told me I could get in touch with him through you."

"He did," she said. She had a heavy city accent, but I could understand her, and she seemed to understand me pretty well. "Come in," she said. I took her bag while she got her key. I realized suddenly that I didn't have the key to the front door and wouldn't be able to get into my own room. I would have to wake someone up. She switched on the light and the room was just as much a mess as it had been the last time I was there.

"Mika is a crazy dog," she said.

I nodded and put the bag down on the table for her.

"I'll check around and see if I can get a message to him that you have money for him." She dug into the bag and started putting things away in cupboards. "Would you like a beer?"

"No, thank you," I said.

"You don't have to use clan manners on me," she said. "Have a beer."

My stomach was so empty the beer would probably make me sick, but I took one.

"Do you know where I could find a shaman?" I asked. "You know, a spirit man?"

That stopped her. She turned around from putting a box away and looked at me. "A spirit man? What for?"

"I have to do something about a ghost."

That made her smile, although she tried to hide it. I don't know what was so funny about a ghost.

"It is the ghost of my dead daughter," I said. Men have daughters, too. "I think I may have done something to trap it."

"Oh, my," she said softly and sat down.

"She died without a name, because she was so young, you understand? But she was old enough it was hard to decide if she should have a name or not. And later, at the refugee camp, at a, um, ceremony, her ghost came to me and demanded that I know her name was Rahel. So I gave her ghost a place.'' The words tumbled out of me. This city woman probably didn't know anything about spirits and probably didn't have a clue what I was talking about. ''It is hard to explain,'' I said lamely. ''Anyway, at the place where I work, I am taking English and the English lessons are with an *'interactive.'* Do you know what I mean?''

She nodded.

''Anyway, the *interactive* is a woman and it asked me to give it a name and I wasn't thinking. I had never heard of *interactives,* and I guess I was thinking it was a kind of machine spirit, you know? Not a real spirit, but, you know, something real and not real. So I gave it my daughter's name. Now I am afraid that my daughter could get trapped in the machine.''

''Are you married?'' Sissela asked.

''Not anymore,'' I said. ''My whole clan is dead. I am the only one left, I think. Maybe two others.''

''Oh. I'm sorry,'' she said. ''I, um, I don't know of any spirit men. But I will ask around. If I hear of anyone, I will send you a message, through Mika.''

''Thank you,'' I said.

It was quiet then. Cold words about death always leave nothing but silence.

''Your hair is growing out,'' Sissela said. ''I could give you a trim.''

''No,'' I said, ''that's okay.''

''No, really,'' she said. ''I would like to.''

So she went and got a towel and wrapped it around my shoulders. The beer was making me light-headed but not sick. It was starting to get a little chilly and the towel felt good. A moth battered at the light in her kitchen, and she trimmed my hair. Her fingers knew where they were going, not at all tentative when they touched. She told me about what she did for a living. She cut hair, washed people's hair, and made the elaborate shapes of hair that city people liked.

The light in the kitchen was yellow and warm.

When she was done, I thanked her. It was, I told her, the nicest thing anyone had done for me in a long time. Both of us were afraid we would cry, but we did not.

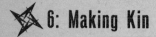# 6: Making Kin

IT WAS MY DAUGHTER WHO TOLD ME ABOUT buses. Since she was part of the machine, Rahel knew all about things like buses. I came into work wet from my walk and didn't have time to dry my hair when I changed into my uniform.

I didn't know how Rahel could tell from where she was that my hair wasn't dry but she could. "Your hair is wet," she said.

"It is raining," I explained.

"You got caught in the rain?" she asked.

Because we practiced English she would say the same thing a couple of different ways. "Yes," I said carefully. "I got caught in the rain. I am walking to work."

"Was the bus late?" she asked.

"I don't understand."

Rahel cocked her head. "How do you come to work?" she asked.

"I walk," I said.

"Why don't you take a bus?" she asked.

"What is that, 'take a bus'?"

So she told me all about buses and showed me what would happen when I got on a bus. She showed me a map of the city with my room marked on it and with the company marked on it. It took me a while to get the idea of a map. We drew maps when I was in school, but they were different. Rahel was very patient with me.

I was used to being taught things by my daughter, although I wasn't very comfortable with the idea. She was very patient with me. She never called me anything but Jan, because the machine that she was part of knew me only as Jan.

We went on then with the next lesson in my technical job, which involved replacing the drum on a machine that rolled out the medium for chip crystallization.

I rode the bus for a couple of weeks before I thought to ask Rahel how far the buses went.

"The buses follow routes," she said. "Different buses go different places."

"There are buses that go to different cities?" I asked.

She assured me that there were.

"There are buses that go to Tonstad?"

Rahel, in her self-possessed way, thought for a moment. "I don't know," she said, which meant that the machine didn't know. She gave me the code number for the phone to call someone who would know the answer and I wrote it down.

"Are you thinking of going to Tonstad?" she asked.

The way she asked reminded me that I was supposed to be having a language lesson. I spoke English best when I was really angry or at these moments when I wasn't thinking about it and I just said things. The moment I started to think about it I got stiff and forgot words. "Yes," I said carefully, "I am thinking of going to Tonstad."

"Why do you want to go there?" she asked.

"I want to go to Tonstad because I know someone who lives there," I said. I was thinking of the shaman.

"Good," she said. Then we turned our attention to more tech training.

There was a monitor that techs could use on the floor and I used it to call the number Rahel had given me. One of the Taufzinnir techs asked for me because my Taufzin was so much more terrible than my English. There was a bus that went to Tonstad, and it took eleven hours to get there. I had taken weeks to walk from Tonstad to Taufzin. Now I would be able to go back in a day. I could even go back on one day and come back with the shaman on the next. I hadn't worked long enough to earn extra days off so that was important.

The shaman would help me figure out if Rahel was trapped in the machine or if she was just residing there.

I got up in the dark on a Saturday and caught a city bus to the place where I could take the long bus to Tonstad. The leaves were falling from the trees, and they made the city air smell a little like nuts. It was a homesick smell. It was so early that there were night bats still diving at the insects under the streetlamps. Flick into the light and gone, flick into the light and gone.

The long distance buses were different. They all left from the same place, a complicated maze of concrete levels and ramps and numbers. The city seemed full of places like this. I thought about going back to my room. I could curl up in the blankets on the floor and sleep for a while. Then I could spend the afternoon watching out my window.

I bought a ticket to Tonstad. I went to the bathroom to wash my face. In the mirror my face suddenly struck me as delicate and female. I had been eating better and I was filling out. Not a skinny, gawky looking boy but maybe starting to look like a girl again. It was an ugly bathroom and it smelled of men. I was afraid that someone would look at me and realize I was a girl. I went back out to sit on the bench and wait. What would I do?

I would ask the shaman what to do, maybe he could teach me more about being a boy. But if I looked like a girl, then I looked like a girl. I didn't know what to do about that.

It occurred to me that it really made no difference anymore. In Taufzin I could be a girl.

My stomach tightened and ached, and I felt myself breathing. I felt myself draw breath inside and it wasn't enough. I couldn't be a girl and I didn't know why, but the thought was terrible. I could not be a girl again. Something would not let me be a girl again. If I was a girl something terrible would happen to me, I was sure of it.

I wondered if it was because of Rahel. Was I cursed because I had named my daughter, or not named my daughter until too late? And now since I was no true mother I could not even be a woman or my heart would burst.

I had never really been in Tonstad the city, but I didn't have much sense of it when the bus got me there in the early evening. The place where the bus left people off was a restaurant with a sign with a long silver bus to show that they stopped there and that you could buy tickets there. I stumbled down the steps. My legs felt worse than if I had been walking all day and my stomach was rolling. I had been sick the whole ride—never enough to throw up but enough to keep me miserable.

At least when I got off the bus, the cold air helped my stomach. I drank in deep breaths.

I tried to remember what the shaman had taught me. To stand like a boy. I felt light-headed, as if I could barely stand at all.

I tottered into the restaurant and up to the counter where they took money for food and bus tickets. "Excuse me," I asked the woman, and then realized I didn't know the English for refugee camp. It wasn't something that came up in my lessons.

"Yes?" the woman said. "Are you all right?"

Of course, in Tonstad they spoke the same language I did.

My own voice sounded high and impossibly girlish. "Can you tell me where the camp is? The one for the clanspeople?"

The restaurant smelled of fried meat, oily on my tongue, and baked dough, dry in my nose, and all of it heavy on my stomach. I breathed through my mouth, listening as she told me, pointing, that it was *that* way out of town.

Out on the street, a couple of blocks away, I realized that I couldn't remember what the restaurant looked like. I wasn't even exactly sure how to get back to it or which street I had turned on. But walking made me feel better. I figured if I kept walking eventually I would come to the edge of Tonstad. I was just a little worried about getting to the camp and getting back to the bus so I could be back to work on Monday.

All around people were talking a language I understood.

Tonstad wasn't anything like home, but it was nice to understand and be able to talk and read signs.

I stopped and asked directions. I couldn't tell whether the woman I asked thought I was a boy or a girl. She told me how to get to the main road that led to the camp.

I was out of Tonstad very quickly. Surprisingly so. I had thought of Tonstad as a pretty big place, but after Taufzin it didn't seem so big at all. I walked through the deepening twilight past long fields of heavy-headed grass where dragonflies played. I was hungry.

The camp was not as big as I remembered, either. The place to get through the fence was still there. I was watching for Kari or Juho and Dortea, but I didn't run into anyone I knew. The trucks were handing out dinner and I thought about getting in line, but decided I wasn't that hungry.

I found the shaman's tent and called, "Uncle?" For a moment I thought, What if he is dead?

"Come?"

Then I didn't know how he would receive me. But I had come all this way. I opened the tent flap and he looked surprised.

"You've come back," he said. I couldn't tell if he was pleased or not.

"Yes, uncle. I have a job, in Taufzin. I came back to ask your advice, and to see if you would come back with me."

That amused him.

"Winter is coming and these tents are not good tents," I said. I made a show of rubbing the material between thumb and forefinger. "They are thin. Not like good hide. The wind will shake them."

"So you have come back to save me," he said.

"I—" I started to say I had come back because I needed his advice, but then I thought, no man would admit that. I was being tested again. "I was only thinking of my debt to you," I said. I sounded sullen, which wasn't what I meant at all.

He burst out laughing. "Well, sit down and tell me about this fabulous life you would take me to in Taufzin."

He put on some white tea for us and rolled himself a smoke and did not offer me any, like always.

I felt terribly at home.

I told him about my job and my room. He didn't seem particularly impressed by my job. He listened to me, nodding his head, fond of me, as if I were a nephew or something.

"I—I have a problem, uncle. I need your advice," I said.

He raised his hand and stopped me. "Go get me some water," he said. "My hips ache."

I opened my mouth to say someone might see me here, but realized he wouldn't care. The plastic jug was still by the door.

At the pump, thankfully no one paid any attention to me. Maybe it was because of the shaman. I felt more a boy now, knew I looked more a boy again, in his influence.

He heated more water for us, and I sat cross-legged, waiting until he would let me tell him.

"Now," he finally said. "What brought you all the way back to me?"

Words would not rise to my lips. So many things had brought me. Loneliness. Rahel. A bus. But it was Rahel he was asking about. "My daughter," I finally said.

The shaman sat and half closed his eyes so they were hooded. If he was surprised I couldn't tell.

"She is trapped," I explained. "In a machine. Where I have my job."

"How do you know it is your daughter?" he asked. "Did you have a dream?"

"No," I said. "She has my daughter's name. My daughter died when she was still nameless—but she lived a whole summer, so maybe she should have had a name. I don't know. But here, when you were bringing me through the spirit door, she came to me and told me her name. Then she came in here," I pointed to my chest and felt the sad hollowness where she had been. I had not noticed how empty I was with Rahel in the machine but it had been there, a dull pain, that I felt now and it made tears start in my eyes. I stopped talking then, to keep from crying.

The shaman didn't say anything, but he looked angry. He looked hard at me.

"It's my fault," I admitted. "The machine at work, it is a teaching machine, and this young girl was my teacher in the machine and we were supposed to name our teacher in the machine and the name just popped out of my mouth. I wasn't even thinking about her when I said it. Although," I said, the thought striking me for the first time, "maybe that's because Rahel leaped into the machine. Maybe she wanted a body, even if it was only a machine body. She doesn't seem to want to get out, but I don't really know. She can only do what the machine will let her do."

I waited to see what the shaman would say, but he said nothing.

I was afraid I had talked enough. The shaman didn't like me to talk too much.

There was only a bit of wind rustling over the fabric of the tent. The fabric would fill and then sigh.

The shaman still said nothing.

Outside I could hear low voices. Not many, just the sound of people around. But no traffic on the roads, only people. In the city I had gotten used to lots of noise in the background. Here the noises were softer, the way they should be. People and place noises, not metal noises.

I waited for the shaman to say something to me. He was really angry if he was being silent so long. I didn't know if he was angry at me for naming Rahel or for letting her jump into the machine.

But I hadn't named her and I hadn't known she was going to jump into the machine, so how could it be my fault?

My thoughts went round and round, and the shaman was still quiet. It was so dark I could see him only as a shape, just lit in a few places by the candle of his little water heater.

Finally he said, "This is the spirit of the daughter of your body."

"Yes," I said. It felt like an accusation. Like a blow.

"Okay," he said and sighed. "Okay." His voice was resigned and old. "Tomorrow I'll go with you."

* * *

The trip back to Taufzin wore the old man out.

By the time we got off the bus in the big bus station, he looked older than I had ever seen him and he was so tired that he wasn't even interested in how strange everything was. I led him to the place where we caught the bus to where I stayed. He stumbled climbing the step onto the bus and clutched my arm like an old woman.

It was well after dark on Sunday when we got back to my room. He blinked a bit at the brightness of the lights in the house, but after a day of buses and bus stations he was immune to surprises. I settled him in my bed and gave him a cup of hot tea with a spoonful of whiskey in it and he held it in both hands, like a child, to drink it. Then he settled down in the covers.

I was tired, too. The shaman snored. A little rasp in the back of his throat and then a louder one and then a snore, and then another, each subsequent one gathering in strength and forcefulness until his throat closed and the effort to breathe almost woke him up. And then it would start all over. In the camp his snoring had irritated me, and I always tried to get to sleep before he did so it wouldn't keep me awake. That night it was the sound of companionship. I let it lap over me. Eventually I drowned in sleep.

The shaman woke up when my alarm went off. I told him I had to go to work and that I would be back. From his covers he grumbled about my going so early.

"They will give me a warning if I'm late," I explained, "and after three times they can fire me."

He turned his shoulder to me. He didn't understand; clanspeople don't care about clocks. I don't know that he was really listening anyway. I left him bread and fruit for breakfast and caught the bus to work.

At work, during my English lesson, I told Rahel that I had gone to Tonstad to get the shaman.

She inclined her head prettily. "How did you go?" she asked.

"By bus," I said.

"Please answer in a complete sentence," she said.

"I go by bus," I said.

"We need to practice tenses of 'to go,' " she said. I turned the pages of my book and there were the tenses. Rahel could only communicate with me this way. Listening to her was like listening for the real conversation in the spaces. I tried to think of a way to tell her that I brought the shaman for her, but I couldn't think of a way. So I let it pass. Maybe she already knew.

I worried about the shaman all day. I was afraid he would decide to leave my room and get lost in the city. I was afraid that I would go back and the stress of the journey would have been too much for an old man, and he was dead.

I didn't even stop to get anything for dinner. He was sitting in my room, watching out the window when I opened up the door.

"Hey," he said absently. "Why are people bringing out those big kegs?"

I looked out the window. "That's trash," I said. "Tomorrow morning, persons will come and put the trash on a truck and take it away."

He snorted through his nose at that.

"Are you hungry?" I asked.

He shrugged.

"I'm going to go get something to eat," I said. "Do you want to come with me?"

"No," he said.

"Stay here," I said.

He laughed. "You are my husband now?"

"Uncle, it's easy to get lost in the city," I said. "I will take you anywhere you want to go, but stay here until I get back."

"Bring some meat," he said. "I'm tired of the stuff in the camp."

Coming back up the stairs with sandwiches I saw that my door was open upstairs. Of course, he wouldn't even know to lock my door when he left. The clans didn't lock doors and tents didn't have locks.

I heard voices. The shaman's and someone else's.

Mika was sitting on the floor. I had not seen Mika since he came to get the money I owed him for finding me a job.

"Hey, Jan," Mika said.

My heart sank.

The shaman was leaning up against the window frame. "Did you bring meat?" he asked. I could smell the meat sandwiches in my hands, and I could smell the musty smell of the shaman filling my room.

"I did," I said. "Mika, what are you doing here?" I had wanted Mika to come see me. I had thought of him and thought of him. Now here he was and there was a dirty old man in a buckskin dress in my room.

"Sissela sent me to see you," Mika said. "She said I was neglecting you. She wants you to come for dinner sometime soon. She figured you need another haircut."

Did I need another haircut? I ran my hand over my head. Did having short hair make me look more like a boy? I wished I could ask someone. Someone other than the shaman.

The shaman got up and unwrapped the food. Pulling off the paper caused the wrapper to heat up. "Leave them a minute to get hot," I said. Then to Mika, "Can you have some with us?"

There were only two and Mika could count. "I already ate," he said.

"Some whiskey, uncle?" I asked. I poured glasses for both Mika and the shaman. I only had two glasses, but I could do without. "Mika found me my job," I explained to the shaman.

"He told me," the shaman said. To Mika he said, "You are good to someone with no kin."

Mika didn't know he was supposed to answer that anyone might be kin, so he just shrugged and said, "It was good for both of us."

I gave the shaman the sandwich without sauce. He looked at it a moment and then fished out a piece of meat and popped it in his mouth. I was watching Mika. Mika was watching the shaman. I couldn't tell whether Mika was amazed or disgusted. Maybe amused.

"Good," the shaman said. "What is it?"

I had assumed that it was renndeer, but I hadn't ever really thought about it.

Mika peered. "Not pork," he said.

"Pork?" asked the shaman.

"Offworld," Mika said. "They raise them out in the countryside. They're good meat. But I don't know what *this* is." Mika glanced at me. Was he laughing at the old man? Was he laughing at me? "Do you tell fortunes?" Mika asked the old man.

I sucked air through my teeth, sure the shaman would be offended.

"Sometimes," the old man said. "Do you?"

Mika laughed. "Sometimes. Mostly to girls, though. And mostly they're wrong."

The shaman nodded and smiled.

I didn't know which was worse; if Mika was laughing at the old man, or if the old man was laughing at Mika.

"Your friend is a cohd," the shaman said. A "cohd" was a slippery fish. Someone not to be trusted. Mika laughed, but I didn't think he knew what it meant. The shaman handed me his whiskey glass to be refilled.

The whiskey smelled good. It made my mouth water. I ate some of my sandwich, and Mika watched the shaman.

"You're not a clansman," the shaman said to Mika.

"My mother was a renner," Mika said. *Renner* was what the people of Taufzin called us.

"Your mother is dead?" the shaman said.

"No," Mika said. "She is still alive."

"Ah," said the shaman. "Your father wasn't a clansman?"

"I don't think so," Mika said and shifted. "I don't know who he was, though."

"Do you want to know?" the shaman asked. Could the shaman find out?

"No," Mika said flatly.

The shaman did not exactly smile. "He was not so bad as all that," the shaman said.

Mika shrugged, uncomfortable.

I tried to think of something to say. "When would Sissela like me to come over?" I asked.

"She said Friday."

"What do you do here in this city?" the shaman asked. "What does a hunter do here?"

"I'm not a hunter," Mika said. "I'm a businessman.

I'm a broker, actually. I find people who need to sell things and put them with people who need to buy things."

"It's still a kind of hunting," the shaman said.

"I guess it is," Mika said.

The room felt as tense as a full fishing net. I wanted to scream at them to stop it.

"We need more whiskey," the shaman said to me. "The bottle is almost empty."

I stood up to go and get more, and Mika said, "I've got to go. I'll walk with you."

Out on the street he said, "Who is that disagreeable old bastard?"

"That's the shaman," I said. "I went and got him."

"He's your uncle?" Mika said.

"No," I said. "He's just the shaman."

Mika shook his head. "Why do you do what he tells you? You think he's going to put a curse on you or something?"

"No," I said. "No. He's my teacher, that's all."

Mika grinned. "You're going to be a shaman? Are you going to start wearing a dress?" He eyed me up and down. "You'd be pretty in a dress."

"No!" I said, terrified.

Mika laughed. "I'll tell Sissela you can come to dinner on Friday."

When Sissela opened the door there was noise, music, and I blinked in the light. "Jan," she said, "it's cold, come in."

The fall night was sharp but not what I'd call cold. The apartment was neat and clean this time, and smelled of food. The music came from a system against one wall. There was a flat screen system with video on it, and after a moment I decided that the video was supposed to go with the music.

"Mika bought it for me," she said. "Do you like it?"

"Yeah," I said. "Where's Mika?"

"He's late, of course," she said.

I stood in the middle of her living room and watched the video. It was riders on motorcycles, riding at night.

Sissela said something, but I was watching the video.

In the corner it said "Wintergarden." The video faded away and another took its place.

"What?" I said. It was hard to concentrate on Sissela instead of the video.

"Has the shaman helped you with your daughter's ghost?" she said.

I shook my head. "He won't talk about it. When I come home from work he says he's tired."

I was sitting in the middle of her living room watching videos while she cut my hair when Mika knocked loud on the door and came in without asking. He had a bag of groceries and he was happy. "Hey, Jan," he said, "you like the system?"

The videos didn't make any sense but it was hard to stop watching them.

He pulled a couple of bottles out of the bag and a long loaf of braided bread. He gave Sissela a big kiss. It was embarrassing, even if Sissela just looked a little annoyed. I hadn't thought they were together. Sissela seemed to treat him like a friend, but he had bought her the system and he acted as if the apartment were his.

"You can tell your friend that I had a good day hunting," Mika said.

I didn't know what he meant at first. "He's not my friend," I said. "He's my teacher."

Mika wasn't paying any attention. "Have a sundowner," he said. It was sweet, like juice, but I could feel the alcohol going down, too.

Sissela had made a big stew for dinner, and it was very, very good. She kept putting food in my bowl. Sissela kept saying it was good I wasn't so skinny anymore. "You used to look as if you were going to break," she said.

I couldn't eat very much. It was probably a good thing. My hips were getting rounder. I looked at myself in the locker room at work and I thought I looked too much like a girl. I was afraid I would start bleeding monthly again. I needed to get some rags and have them ready.

Mika was talking about some business deal. Mika had make a deal with a man. Mika was selling things for the man.

"What kind of things," Sissela asked.

"Whatever he needs sold," Mika said. "I think you need a bigger place than this."

"This place is fine," Sissela said, then switched into Taufzin so I really couldn't understand her.

Mika said no; I could understand that.

Sissela kept saying "What?" in Taufzin, I thought asking him about what he sold. Mika said something, I didn't understand.

Sissela got really angry at him.

Sissela called him a dog in our own language. "Don't believe anything he says," she said to me. "He's a liar. He's always been a liar."

Mika said, "Shut up, Sissela. It's not true."

"You won't tell me what you're selling," she said. She was crying. "Do you think I'm stupid? I don't want your things. I don't want you here!"

"I'm not selling anything bad," Mika said. "I'm helping this guy sell whiskey. Just whiskey."

"You liar," she said, and ran to the bathroom and slammed the door.

I looked at the table. I wasn't sure what to do or where to look. Maybe I should just keep eating? Maybe that would be rude? I looked at Mika, and he gave me a tight-lipped smile and shrugged. "Sissela gets like this," he said. "She'll get over it."

"You sell whiskey?" I asked.

He nodded. "To renner. See, city people make you pay tax if you make whiskey, and renner don't have the money for the tax—you know? So I help them sell it without having to pay the tax."

"Other clanspeople sell whiskey?" I asked. "I used to make whiskey. My clan did."

"Yeah?" he said, really not interested.

"Brass whiskey," I said. "It was the color of brass. It was famous. I thought we were the only clan that made whiskey."

Mika was watching the bathroom door. I could hear water running and maybe Sissela crying, but I wasn't sure.

He didn't say anything. I ate a little more dinner, and he did, too. The water stopped running, but Sissela didn't come out. After a while Mika went to the door and called her name.

"Go away," she said.

"Come on, Sissela," he said.

She didn't answer after that, not even when he beat on the door with his fist.

"Maybe we should go," I said.

For a moment I thought he was going to tell me to get lost. Which I would have happily done. But instead he just shrugged and we went.

The sundowner made me feel even less as if there was ground under my feet. I had had three. It was more than the amount of whiskey I drank, but it hadn't been the same as whiskey. More like beer, only it tasted good.

We clattered down the stairs and he said, "She'll get over it, she always does."

I floated down the steps. I didn't have to think about where my feet were going, they just went in the places they were supposed to. I wondered if Aslak used to say the same things about me that Mika was saying about Sissela.

"She's your girlfriend?" I asked.

He shook his head. "Sissela's just a friend. She was my girlfriend a long time ago."

"I was married, you know," I said.

Mika gave me a sideways look. "Sissela told me."

We walked down the street. My spirit wandered up and down and all around.

"You want to go get a drink?" Mika asked.

My heart beat fast, but I tried to be calm, like a hunter whose prey comes into range. "Sure," I said. "That would be great." As though Mika asked me out for a drink all the time.

He knew a place where clanspeople went and he took me there.

It was in a building where people lived—not like mine, which was really more like a big house, but more like Sissela's. Only Sissela's was nicer. This was a big wooden building and even in the dark I could see the way it looked tired, the edges sagging and the whole outside soft looking and not new looking, the way city people liked things. Between the building and the one next door was a space not wide enough for a car, and we went between the buildings to a bare yard full of papers and smelling of urine. Mika opened a door in the back of the building and there were steps down and a single bare light casting shadows at our feet.

The stairwell smelled of cold joss smoke and beer, and we could see our breath. There was another door at the bottom. When Mika opened that, I heard singing and voices and smelled whiskey and the sooty smell of a real fire and it was all so familiar, like home.

The air was blue with smoke, some of it from the fire and some of it from joss. I could feel the people around me. They were clanspeople, most of them in leather boots and leather pants. In my coveralls, I was one of only a few who wore city clothes. I could feel their spirits close to me. They didn't look like city people. City people were big and smooth and somehow not so real as my people. These men had little dark, square faces with seams around their mouths. City people had legs too long for their body. My people were smaller, closer to the ground.

There were no chairs. We bought whiskey at the bar from a clansman. It was not very good whiskey, I could see when he poured it out of the big bag. It was clear, for one thing. And it wouldn't hold a bead, that is, a bubble of air wouldn't stay at the rim of the fluid. It smelled green and raw, and it bit when I drank it and made my eyes water, but I was so grateful for it.

Like a lot of the men, I squatted down.

"I can't stay like that," Mika said.

City people sit in chairs all the time. So I stood up and we leaned against the wall.

"Sissela doesn't understand," he said. "She is willing to cut people's hair and make just enough to get by all the rest of her life. I get bored, you know? She stands on her feet all day. I want to use my mind. I want to use my wits. Your friend, the shaman, what he said about me is true. I'm a hunter. Sissela isn't a hunter. You know what you are when you're not a hunter, don't you?"

I shook my head.

"Prey," he said. "Eat or be eaten."

I thought about that. It wasn't really true. A big wild

renndeer bull isn't prey to much of anything. Sure, a
hunter can bring it down, but that hunter can bring down
anything that is likely to eat a renndeer, too. But Mika
wasn't like a renndeer bull. He was no headman, to turn
to for advice. He was quick and sharp. The shaman was
right: Mika was a hunter.

When Mika loved you, he would love you without
thought. He would hunt you down. You would be the
object. All that sharpness would be directed at you. He
would not be thinking about weighing the good and the
bad, you would be there and he would be after you.

I listened to him talk and nodded sometimes. I knew I
was not a hunter. I was afraid I was prey, although not
Mika's prey.

I watched his hands, his beautiful, smooth hands. The
fingers were straight, not bent by the bow. His whole body
was like a renndeer that has been raised well. Like one
you would use when you went to gather with the clans.
You would braid ribbons in its ear fringe and paint its
hooves, and its very size and sleekness would tell the
world how rich you were, that you could afford this animal. Mika was like that. He was handsome. He was like
a High-on's son.

I went to buy some joss, but Mika bought it for me and
I let him. We shared it, and the blue smoke curled around
his face. I wished my hair were long. I wished I were
like Sissela, smooth and soft. Except that Sissela didn't
understand him, not the way I did. Sissela didn't understand about hunters and men the way I did, because the
city hid everything hard and ugly like it hid the smells of
dirt and sweat.

"You're a strange one," Mika said to me.

I was in a haze of joss fog. "Why is that?" I asked.

"You're just very strange," Mika said, and laughed.

"That's because I'm not a man," I said. I said it because if I didn't I was afraid I would never see him again;
although after I said it, I realized with a shock that I had
thrown it all away. Jan slipped off me and I knew, in that
moment, I looked like a woman in men's clothes and I
was the only woman in this place. I didn't know why it
worked that way, it was a spirit thing, I supposed.

Mika was still chuckling. "So what are you, then? Are you like your friend the shaman?"'

The drink and the joss fog rose in my head, and my stomach roiled from raw whiskey after a day of little food. "I have to go outside," I said and stepped away from the wall and staggered.

"Are you all right?" he said.

"Just drunk," I said. "I need to go outside. Get some air."

He followed me as I staggered up the steps and out into the dirt yard. It startled me to be surrounded by buildings because downstairs in the bar I had forgotten where I was. I leaned against the fence and waited for my stomach to stop boiling and my head to stop whirling, and then I was sick.

"You okay?" Mika said when I was done.

I nodded. I did feel better.

"You want to go home?" he asked.

"I'm not a man," I said to Mika, again. I stood up and my head didn't whirl and my stomach felt better.

"Yeah?" he said. "Why's that?" His voice was light; he thought I was drunk. He started back for the street.

"I'm a woman," I said. "I'm just pretending to be a man."

"Like your shaman," he said.

"No," I said. "Not like him." I followed him down the alley between the buildings. "I'm a woman. I was married. I had a baby. I just wear men's clothes."

He stopped me in the street. "Are you lying?" he asked.

I shook my head.

He took my chin and turned my face roughly toward the streetlight and studied me. My skin shivered under his hand. "Fuck," he swore, and then he laughed.

He laughed loud and amused in the empty street. The buildings reflected his laugh back at us and I flushed although there wasn't enough light for him to see that.

I started to shiver. I felt unclothed.

"And here I thought you were just simple little Jan," he said. "Simple, countryside Jan."

I didn't know what to say to that. I just shook my head.

"Appearances can be deceiving," he said. "Come on back to my place and have some more joss," he said. "Tell me all about this."

His place was in an apartment building so run-down that some of the windows were boarded up blind. There were few lights in the street, none in the building, but it was late. We climbed the stairs to the top of the building, past five floors that felt empty to me. I couldn't remember being in a place in the city that felt so empty. His apartment was huge. It took up a corner of the building. I felt that once this building might have been grand, but now there was only this bare hunter's nest with its view of the dark street. One light hung on a chain in the middle of the big room.

Mika wandered through the rooms, turning the light on in each room, until the place fairly echoed with hard white light off dirty walls. There was nothing in the place but a mattress in one room and a couple of toiletries in the bathroom. Nothing else. Just scarred wood floors and open doorways with no doors and the pale dirty walls and the white light and the black windows. At least up this high all the windows still had glass.

"I just found this apartment," Mika said. "I don't spend much time here."

I was afraid to be alone with him here, but I was excited, too, and I was very, very tired.

He opened a cupboard in the kitchen and found a pipe and some joss. He sat on the mattress, and I sat on the floor. He lit the pipe, and then passed it to me.

The smoke was so dry, it sucked all the wetness out of my throat and I coughed blue smoke.

"You are a girl," Mika said. He was shaking his head. "I can't believe I didn't notice."

"I didn't act like a girl before," I said. "The shaman, he initiated me. He taught me how to be a boy. But when I told you, it's all gone now."

"This is some kind of spell?" he asked. "Some sort of curse?"

"No," I said. "The shaman is helping me." I didn't know how to explain it. So I shrugged.

"Helping you to be like him?" Mika asked. "Do shamans all have to dress like the other sex?"

"No," I said. "Oh, no. Just the shaman."

"Why does he dress that way?"

"The spirits tell him to," I said. "He doesn't like it."

"He shouldn't. Why do you want to be a boy?" he asked.

"I don't want to be a boy."

"The spirits tell you to?"

"No," I said. But I wasn't sure. Maybe I dressed like a boy because I was supposed to. A spirit didn't necessarily come and tell you what to do. "I don't think so," I amended. "It was an accident. My clothes were falling apart and there was a dead man there and I took his clothes. Then when I got to the refugee camp, they thought I was a boy and being a girl, well, it didn't feel safe." It wasn't a real explanation, but I couldn't explain because I didn't understand.

I felt so cold in the white light of his apartment that I started to shiver. When I lost Jan it was if I had lost my top layer of skin.

"You're cold," Mika said. He took a blanket off the mattress and wrapped it around my shoulders. "You're a skinny thing," he said.

"I know," I said, miserable.

He looked at me for a long moment. "You had a husband? You don't look old enough to be married."

"I had a husband," I said. "And a baby daughter. But they died." So I told him about Rahel, how she never grew much and how she died. And I told him a little about Aslak and about the war.

He told me more about his family. His mother was clan, and she came to Taufzin with a sailor. Then when he got tired of her she had to get another boyfriend. Mika had a bunch of brothers and sisters, all with different fathers. His mother still lived in Taufzin, but he didn't like her very much. She drank too much and threw up sometimes. Now that she wasn't pretty, the boyfriends were pretty awful and there were a lot more of them and they didn't stay as long. She always needed money. The best thing to do was to stay away from her.

"I don't want to end up like her," he said. "I don't want to end up with nothing. But I can't work on some factory line. I just can't. I need to move, to use my mind. So I'm always hunting. But it's so hard to stay ahead. If I get arrested, I'll end up like so many guys—I'll come out of prison and I'll have to start all over, making a place for myself on the street. I was in prison eighteen months, a little over a year, and when I came out it was if I'd never existed. The streets had just closed up. Stick your hand in a bucket of water and pull your hand out and check out the hole in the water your hand made. You disappear—that's how long people remember you. . . ." He smoked joss as he talked, and the joss fog floated up through the hard light. The blanket was warm.

I fell asleep listening to the sound of his voice.

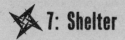 **7: Shelter**

"I AM LEAVING," THE SHAMAN SAID.

It happened like this.

I was tired and bleary-eyed. The light had woken me, curled up on the floor of Mika's bare apartment. Mika was a hill under the blankets on the mattress. The apartment was very cold. It was like being at home in Hamra without a fire, only there was light everywhere. I put the blanket I was using over Mika and let myself into the dark stairwell and walked home.

I was so tired. I went up the stairs. I knew that the shaman would want to know where I'd been and I didn't want to talk about it. He was sitting at the window, watching the street.

"Hello," I said.

He nodded without looking at me.

I lay down and wrapped myself in my blankets.

"I am leaving," the shaman said.

"Where are you going?" I asked. I thought he meant he was going to walk down to the corner or something.

"Back to Tonstad," he said.

I sat up. "To the camp?" I said. "You can't!"

"Why should I stay here?" he asked.

"To help me with my daughter," I said. "You haven't helped me."

"You don't need me to help you," he said, and his voice was cold and remorseless as time.

171

"You haven't helped me," I said. "I brought you here to help my daughter."

He didn't answer, and I thought his mind was made up.

"You can't go back," I said. "You don't know how to get to the bus. You don't have money for a ticket." The foreign words, "bus" and "money" and "ticket" skittered across my voice like stones on ice.

He just shrugged. I would give him the money, he knew that. I would take him, if he made me.

"I can't take you back," I said. "Not until next *weekend*."

"Weekend" was an English word. "If I left now, I wouldn't get back in time for work on Monday."

He turned on me and he was fierce. "You're in trouble now," he said. "Look at this place."

I looked around. The room didn't look too much of a mess. I didn't understand.

"Insects," he said. "This place makes people into insects."

I didn't understand that, either.

"I'm really tired," I said. I was whining. He couldn't go back to Tonstad without me. I lay down again and pulled the covers up to my ears. I thought he would rail at me, but that never was his way.

After a while he got up. I tried to pretend to be asleep, but I was tense and my breathing didn't sound like a person asleep. He stepped over me and opened the door and closed it behind him.

Was he trying to go home by himself? He'd get lost out there. Serve him right. He was a grown man—he didn't need me carrying him around on my hip. I'd find him or he'd find his way back.

I was tired and unable to sleep. I got up and checked and his things were still here. He wasn't trying to get back to Tonstad. I peeked out the window to see if he was outside sitting on the step, but he wasn't.

I couldn't go to sleep while he was out there.

Eventually I went out walking to look for him. I didn't find him, but when I got back he was asleep on the bed.

Stupid bastard.

Maybe he would just die. People did.

*   *   *

Mika showed up on Sunday.

The shaman was treating me with the hospitality you render a stranger. When Mika knocked, he looked up from his tea. When I opened the door, he smiled at me and I blushed. As if I wasn't allowed to have any friends.

"Hey, old man," Mika said. "You know, I think you were right the night you called me a hunter."

The shaman nodded politely. "I'm glad you weren't offended," he said.

"Hey, Jan," Mika said. "You feeling better? Up to a drink and maybe some dinner?"

The shaman expected me to say yes. I could feel his contempt and I almost said no, but it wasn't right for him to decide what I did. "Sure," I said. "There's bread and meat," I told the shaman.

"I will be fine," the shaman said artlessly.

"Hag," I said when we got in the hall.

Mika laughed. I had wanted him to, but calling the old man a hag had been unfair.

"You two quarreling?" Mika asked.

"He wants me to take him back to Tonstad," I said. "He's mad at me because he doesn't have anything to do."

"Why don't you come back to my place," Mika said. "I've got a pipe. We can get something to eat on the way."

We stopped and got fried meat and popped grain and gravy and took it back to Mika's high apartment. I sat by the cold window, looking down from on high at the canyon of the streets. I had never had this kind of food before. It was salty and good.

"What were you like before?" Mika asked me.

Before what?

"Did you always dress like a boy? Did you do boy things?"

Of course I hadn't always dressed like a boy. "What kind of things?" I asked.

"Like hunt?" he asked.

I laughed. "Nobody would have ever let me hunt with them. We didn't do so much hunting, anyway, because we were always in the same place, so most of the game was gone. The hunters had to go a long way to find anything. I don't like hunting.''

His eyes caught the light and he smiled, somehow pleased. ''Why not?''

''Because you sit still in the cold and wish you hadn't had anything to drink because you have to pee and you can't move.''

He thought that was funny, but it was true. Hunting was about being patient, about waiting.

''I was an animal once,'' I said. ''But I was only a bafit.''

He didn't understand. He didn't know very much about how people live, only about this city.

''I didn't want anyone to notice me,'' I said, ''and people don't notice a bafit. So I was a bafit. That was before my husband died.'' I didn't know why I said that, but being with Mika right now had suddenly brought Aslak near to me. I could smell the memory of him and have him rise up before me.

''You didn't want your husband to notice you?'' Mika asked.

''No,'' I said, ''it wasn't that. We were separated.'' I felt I was going to cry. I looked out the window and down the empty canyon of buildings.

Mika put his arms around me and it frightened the tears out of me, but I let him hold me. I held my breath and sat very still.

''You *are* a little thing,'' he said. ''A bafit, eh?''

After a bit he let me go and went and got his pipe. It was getting dark outside and deeper in the city the lights were on. The sky glowed as if somewhere over the horizon the trees were on fire. This time, instead of joss, he had a black resin that he put in the pipe. He bent his head over it and lit it. It flared and lit his face orange like the color of the sky outside. He drew a deep breath and then he handed the pipe to me.

I drew a breath of it. The smoke was hot, like joss, but not so hard. Breathing in, breathing out. I handed him the pipe. It wasn't joss. I could feel it fast. Mika took another breath off the pipe and handed it back to me. It was almost out. I took a deep breath of it, and the resin glowed, an orange ember, brightening the harder I pulled on the pipe. I filled my chest with the heat until I couldn't anymore, and the ember went out.

I felt alive now. I could think. I could think about things. I couldn't sit there, so I stood up. Joss made me sleepy and still, not like this at all.

"Where are you going?" Mika asked me.

"I don't know," I said.

I wanted to walk around on my tiptoes. I wanted to hold my arms out. "I don't know why I let the shaman bother me," I said. "He lives in my place. He has no money. Nobody in the camp liked him. They all made fun of him or they were afraid of him."

"Is he going to curse you if you make him mad?" Mika asked.

"It's not like that," I said. I wondered if Mika would have sex with me. The thought just wandered into my head. "I feel really good," I said.

"Yeah," Mika said, "I know." He thought I was funny.

He felt good, too. I could see that. I was inside with Mika. He put more in the pipe and handed it to me. I drew a big breath and my heart hammered within the bonecage of my chest. I passed it back to him and sat down on the floor, a little dizzy. "Are you going to have sex with me?" I asked.

"I don't know," he said. "Do you want me to, little bafit?"

"I'm not a bafit right now," I said.

"What are you now?" he asked.

"I'm Janna," I said.

"Let's see," he said.

I opened the jumpsuit and slid it off my shoulders. Underneath were my bindings. I unwrapped them. They left red lines on my skin where they pressed, and they'd squished my breasts so flat that it would take them a while to come back up. Not that I had ever had very big breasts. I was scared. I didn't know why I was doing this. I didn't know what he would think of me. I was never a pretty girl with round breasts. But my mam had never been pretty and men had liked her.

"Why are you doing this?" Mika asked.

"Because I'm tired of being Jan," I said. When I said it, I realized it was true.

"You'll get cold."

"I'm not," I said. "I'm not like you city people, I don't get cold. You're all so soft. And you don't know anything."

"We don't know anything," he said.

"No. You think that because you know about the city, you know everything, but you don't. Even in Hamra we knew more than you do." I felt happy and reckless. It was so nice to really say these things. "If someone didn't get your food for you, you'd starve, do you know that? What would you do if I brought you a renndeer? I know how to use all the parts. I can skin it and take the organs out and strip the tendons out of its legs and save the skin and the fur of the legs for leggings because they are strong and I can tan it and sew the skin and use the leg bones for all sorts of things, and make a really good stew from the fat part of the tail. I can make my own clothes and my own place to live and get my own food. Have you ever done any of those things?

"And I know what to call someone like the shaman, and I know how to respect my elders, and how to be polite to strangers. And I know about the spirits."

I was starting to get cold, but I didn't want to tell Mika. The energy was starting to drain away from me, too. I wanted another breath from the pipe.

Mika relit the pipe and took in the smoke, but he didn't offer any to me.

I had made him mad and now he wouldn't give me any.

He leaned forward and kissed me.

"Give me the pipe," I said.

He held it behind him so I couldn't reach it and kissed me again.

I pushed him away. "Let me have some," I said. "Then I'll kiss you."

"No," he said.

"I don't care, then," I said. I pulled my jumpsuit up,

pretending it was because he wouldn't give me the pipe, not because I was cold. I thought he really knew, though. He was laughing at me. He was always laughing at me. "Stop laughing," I said.

All the feeling from the pipe was draining out of me. I felt half there.

Then Mika surprised me and handed me the pipe.

I took a deep breath of the smoke.

"You may be the most interesting woman I ever met," he said.

"You can kiss me," I said and leaned toward him.

He kissed me. Not like Aslak kissed, but different, nibbling on my mouth with his lips, soft, like a renndeer used its lips to take moss out of my hand.

"Your poor breasts," he said, and reached his hands inside my jumpsuit. "You shouldn't treat them that way."

I laughed at him. "You talk silly," I said.

"You shouldn't be trusted with them," he said, but he was smiling. "You don't take good care of them."

I looked down at them and at his hands cupping them. No one had ever talked to me like this before.

"Come over here," he said, and put his hands around my ribs and pulled me toward his mattress.

I sat down beside him, and he pushed me on my back and kissed me. It was frightening and exciting. I reminded myself that it was just sex. He stopped and relit the pipe and took another breath, then handed it to me. While I breathed in, he took off his shirt. His body was like someone younger than his face. He was bigger than Aslak, even though Aslak had been as tall. At least I thought so. It was hard to remember exactly what Aslak had been like. He didn't have as much hair as Aslak. There was something girlish about his skin, but that was the way city people were—smooth with fat under the skin and healthy as prize animals.

I wished we had already done this and it was the second or third time.

I waited for him to take his cock out of his pants, but instead he lay back down beside me and stroked my body as if he were gentling me. It was strange and nice. I didn't know if I was supposed to do anything or not. Then he kissed my breasts and took one of them in his mouth. It was a very strange thing for a grown man to do. Aslak had tasted my milk while I was nursing, but Aslak was my husband and it had been embarrassing even with him. I didn't have any milk now. What was he doing? I looked at the ceiling of his room while he did it.

It was a long time before he put his cock in me. It had been so long since I had sex that it was a little difficult for me, like the first time is. I thought he would climax quickly, like Aslak.

Mika talked to me, leaning on his elbows above me. "Does that feel good?" he asked.

"Yes," I lied.

"Scoot down a bit," he said. "You can put your arms around me."

He kept talking to me about how good it felt. I wished he would climax.

Finally he did and he rolled off me and smiled at me.

I smiled at him, too. I didn't think it meant we were married, this act. It wasn't like with Aslak. I was cold and the effects of the pipe were gone.

Mika put his hand on me and did things with his fingers.

"Don't do that," I said, pushing him away.

"Why not?" he asked. "Are you sore?"

"No," I said. "What are you doing?"

"Making you come," he said. "Haven't you done that?"

I had by myself, of course, but never with a man. I didn't know what to say.

"Just close your eyes," he said.

He wasn't as good at it as I was by myself, of course, he didn't know exactly what to do. It was frustrating, because I would start to feel it, and then he would change the way his fingers were moving. But he was patient and it got stronger and stronger until it swept over me, stronger than when I did it myself—not so sharp but lasting longer—and then I was all done and I could feel the sweat behind my knees and I was embarrassed.

"You didn't have to do that," I said.

"I wanted to," he said.

I felt as if he had won something from me.

*   *   *

I brought home a bottle of whiskey and an elaborate explanation for the shaman. I'd bought the whiskey in a shop with iron grates across the window and hard yellow light that spilled into the street. The explanation went unused. If the shaman could see what I'd been up to, he didn't say.

"I need to meet your daughter," he said when I came in.

"She's at work," I said, thinking that I had to be there in a very few hours. It was almost midnight.

"Then I'll go with you," he said.

I didn't know if he could. "You couldn't stay all day," I said.

"Why not?" he asked.

"There's nothing there for you to do," I said.

"There's nothing here for me to do."

"But I'm not supposed—" I started to say.

"You want my help," he said. "You think that you can do whatever you want and I can help you? You leave all our work like refuse behind in an old campsite. It's time to do some work now."

So he went with me in the morning. I was afraid he would be too slow getting going. He didn't seem to understand about what would happen if I were late to work. But he was ready before I was, sitting on the bed with one leg crossed over the other, smoking his pipe while I finished getting cleaned up. I wished he could wear something else, but all he had were women's clothes. Even if I'd had something else for him to wear, he probably wouldn't have worn it.

When we opened the door to the outside the wind hit me and cut cold to my bones.

I saw mostly the same three or four people at the bus stop; two round-faced men in dark brown with broad Menno farmer's hats and a woman dressed to work behind a food counter, and sometimes a young man with a bag of books and papers. We would nod at each other, and they would sometimes talk to each other in Taufzin. I understood some of what they said, but they had country accents that made it even harder than understanding city people.

The sight of the shaman stunned them all into silence. The two brothers stared and the woman looked across the street at nothing at all. The shaman shook the folds out of his long dress and appeared not to notice.

I flushed to the top of my forehead.

When the bus came they crowded on before us and the shaman and I followed slowly.

I paid the fares. The bus driver watched the shaman's back in the mirror, and the shaman found an empty seat for the two of us.

I was still cold. The shaman wasn't. Mika's pipe had taken my heat from me and I wanted to take some of the smoke right now and wake up and feel good. But I wanted to be like the shaman and not feel the cold, too. I huddled in my jacket and hated both of them.

At work I showed the card that let me come in. "This is my uncle," I told the guard at the door. "He comes with me today."

The guard grinned at me and shook his head. He said something in Taufzin and laughed. It took me a while to figure out what he'd said: "Can't pick your family."

"Don't spit inside the building," I told the shaman. "It is considered very rude here."

The shaman looked at me coldly.

"Please," I added. I was as tall as the shaman, but I felt very small.

At least he didn't spit.

I took him into the lockers and showed him mine. He admired the combination lock and had me teach him how to work it. Then I gathered up my clothes and went to the bathroom where I changed. No one else changed in the bathroom, but I couldn't change where people might see me.

Janna was in the mirror instead of Jan—white, skinny-faced girl with big eyes, like some poor relative—but no one seemed to notice. People see what they want, I think.

At the schoolroom I introduced the shaman as my uncle. I thought that the teacher, Ms. Overbek, would say no visitors, but I think the sight of the shaman so startled her that she became very polite to hide her face and forgot to throw him out.

"Can I show him the teaching system?" I asked.

Ms. Overbek looked at the clock. That was the first thing these people always did when trying to make a decision, as if there was some way to time their thinking. "Be quick," she said. "Don't hold up class."

Some of the students were already there. The Menno students did not talk to me much, anyway, because my Taufzin was so bad, but now I knew they wouldn't talk to me at all. The girls did not look at me at all.

At least it didn't seem as if I would be fired.

I showed the shaman my chair, and he sat down, pulling his dress gracefully beneath him. I checked the headset. Rahel was there, reading a book. She smiled at me and I said, "Rahel, there is someone I would like you to meet. This is my uncle. He is a shaman. You can talk with him." I said it all in my own language and I took off the headset before she could tell me to speak English.

Then I put the headset over the shaman's head, adjusting it over his gray hair. The smell of him was very strong here, in this clean classroom.

He stiffened for a moment, sitting very straight. I waited to hear him say hello to Rahel. The headsets were made so that they drank in some of the sound of your voice while you were talking. When I took my headset off during class time, the room was full of whispers. The shaman didn't say anything for a long time.

Then he whispered some things I couldn't hear and his hands came up and he groped at the headset. I thought he was adjusting it at first, but then I realized he was trying to take it off. I undid the connections. It was harder to undo them from outside than it was when I was wearing the headset.

The shaman looked around, startled, at the classroom.

Ms. Overbek watched us. "Jan, is everything all right?" she asked.

"Yes, ma'am." I waited for him to collect himself. It occurred to me that if I could put him on a bus, I could tell the bus driver to tell him when to get off. He could get home from the bus stop. "Do you want to go home?" I asked.

"Okay," he said.

"Ms. Overbek," I said. "I want to get on a bus, my uncle—I mean, my uncle wants to get on a bus."

"All right," she said. "Be quick."

The guard smiled at us and winked.

"What did you think?" I asked the shaman.

"I didn't see your daughter," he said.

"It's not Rahel?" I asked. In my coveralls I was colder than I would have been in my jacket.

"I saw an old woman," the shaman said. "I did not see a young girl at all."

Spirits can look like anything they want, of course.

"If she was like anything she was like my dead wife," the shaman said. "But she wasn't the spirit of my dead wife. She was different."

"You were married?" I blurted out.

"Of course I was married," he said. "Just because of the dress does not mean I am not a man. I am not like you, I am not both. I just wear a dress because the spirits require it. But I didn't meet your daughter, and I have to think about this." He rubbed his forehead. "It was very strange, this teaching thing. You go there every day?"

"I thought at first it might be a spirit kind of place," I said. "But it is really an offworld-machine kind of place, isn't it. Maybe it is just the machine? Maybe it isn't Rahel at all?"

The shaman shook his head. "I think you bring the spirit to the machine. The spirit is in you. It's very strange. Offworld people don't make any sense to me. They are worse than city people."

I looked for the bus. It wasn't my daughter? My daughter's spirit was in me? That was what I had thought in the camp.

"Tonight," the shaman said, "maybe it is time to teach you some things. You are the only student I have," he said, dismissively. But that was the way he always talked, and I tried not to take it to heart.

"Is this going to take very long?" I asked the shaman.

He had pushed all my bedding under his bed so as to make the largest space possible in the room. He had dried plants and joss and a bowl and his hand drum out. "That's a city question," he said. Which it was. He found all this business about getting to work on time and knowing what time it was very silly. "Does it take any longer or shorter if you name the minutes?" he asked.

"No," I said, "but I have to get up early and go to work tomorrow."

"Be quiet," he said, irritated at me.

I was in trouble, so I sat on the bed and waited while he did things and tried not to think about the fact that I had been up too late on Sunday night and now I would be up too late tonight and tomorrow would come very soon, and I couldn't sleep late until Saturday. I wondered if Mika would ever want to see me again.

I fell asleep sitting on the bed.

When the shaman woke me my neck ached from sleeping sitting up. He was tapping his fingers across the stretched hide of his hand drum, a sound like rain. He was sitting there with his eyes closed. I didn't know if he had started or if he was thinking about something. The tapping had that kind of aimless quality of someone waiting for something.

I started to drift. There wasn't any light in the room except from the streetlight outside. I could see the shaman only as a shape and hear the sound of the drum, like rain, like a heartbeat.

He slapped the drum as I dozed and I jerked awake.

He did it on purpose, I was sure. Even if he wasn't looking at me, he could have looked at me and then closed his eyes again.

I stretched and made myself sit up. I had to get up so early. I looked at the clock. It wasn't late, but I had been out so late the night before.

The shaman slapped the drum. This time I wasn't dozing, but it still jerked at me.

So I watched him, to catch him looking at me. I listened to the drumbeat. It was sometimes a pattern. Then it was as if he lost the focus and wandered away, and a new pattern would start. If he opened his eyes again before he slapped the drum I didn't see it, but in the darkness I might have missed the flash of his eye-white.

I was awake now, attuned to the drum. I listened for its moments of coherence, listened while it drifted and found itself again, like the heartbeat of some living animal. . . .

Then he stopped.

He had the hot plate I used for cooking in the middle of the floor. He liked it, he said, because he could either burn things in it or use it to heat things. Hot plates didn't last long, and I had bought him a third one a little over a week ago. He lit whatever he had in it now, using matches we had bought at the store where I got shaved meat. The flare hurt my eyes and lit his face all yellow-red from underneath. I smelled joss and something bittersweet.

He picked up the hand drum, and this time he beat it with a definite rhythm, a strong even sound. He swayed with it. I listened. The sound thumped on and then broke, and I was hung for a moment, waiting, and then he was beating out the complex rhythm again. *Dot-de-dah, dot-de-dah, de-dah, dot-de-dah, de-dah, de-dah, da dot-dot-de-dah* . . . The joss fumes were in my head and I felt very light. I had never been on a spirit journey, but I felt as if I could follow the shaman now into a trance. My spirit felt connected to my body only in the most tenuous way.

Someone beat on the door and I jumped.

The shaman stopped playing and jerked his head toward the door: I should answer.

It was my landlady. She was old, as old as the shaman, but she was a city person, of course. She frowned at me. "Could you please be quiet," she whispered, angry at me. "There are other people living here."

I nodded. "We are quiet," I said.

"What is that smell?" she asked.

"Dinner," I said, and shut the door. I was afraid she would knock again, but that must have satisfied her.

"We have to be quiet," I told the shaman.

"Don't open the door again," he said, and went back to his hand drum.

He didn't even let her have time to get downstairs so, of course, she was knocking on the door again right away. I started to get up, but the shaman said, "Sit." He kept tapping on the hand drum.

I sat. The landlady pounded on the door and called, "Jan! Jan Hamra! Open the door! I'll get the key!"

"She can open it," I said to the shaman. "She has a key."

The shaman whirled up from the floor, fast as a young man, yanked open the door and *hissed* at the landlady. Startled, she drew back. The shaman leaned toward her, his face contorted, and hissed at her again.

She took a step back and drew into herself. He hiked his shoulders so he loomed over her and stepped into her face, still hissing.

For a moment she held her ground. The sound he was making began to sound funny to me. I was afraid I would laugh. The landlady was beginning to get her bearings a little.

Then he spat in her face.

She turned and ran.

He stepped back and slammed the door so that the very walls seemed to shake. Then he sat back down on the floor, adjusted his robes like an old lady and settled himself, and picked up his hand drum. He started playing again as if nothing had happened.

"She'll be mad at me," I said. "She'll come back."

"She won't come back," he said.

"She might call the *police*," I said. "You know, the soldiers. For the city."

"This isn't the camp," the shaman said. "Be quiet."

"But—"

"Be quiet," he said firmly. So I was.

He started playing the not-really-music again. Brushing his fingers across the face of the drum. Running them across so the drum shushed. But I couldn't listen the same way I had before.

He played a long time and I listened for the landlady until my thoughts drifted and I was listening to the drum and the smoke was making me sleepy. He put some oil in a lamp and then went back to the drum. Now the noise sounded like rain on a roof, and I closed my eyes and I forgot I wasn't at home, in Hamra, sitting on the black dirt floor. I opened my eyes again and the room was so different from what I expected, so small and so empty of people—not my mother or my little sister or anyone come to sit and drink hot water and talk through the long dark of winter. Even the shaman's face was not the face of my kin, because he was more like the coastal people who are dark and my clan was lighter, except for Wanji and Ayudesh, of course.

I was so caught by surprise that my throat closed.

The shaman started playing a steadier beat, and that took me away from the feeling I might cry. I listened to the heartbeat of the drum. The smoke was making me feel that my hold on myself was very thin. I wanted to let go and go to my mam. I didn't know how to let go, although I felt it might happen at any minute and I wanted it so bad. To forget about this city and my job.

He stopped once and got out a cone made of plants and renndeer fat. It was to help him in his trance. He lit it and the smell of fat and smoke was in the room. He played some more.

His playing got softer, less likely to disturb anyone, and I relaxed. Finally it trailed off. He was humming through his nose, a faint sound. Sometimes it seemed as if he was humming inside my head. I felt barely part of my body. I could leave my body, look at us below, me on the bed and the shaman so still, outlined against the street-lit window.

I could not see the shaman's spirit. I was by myself. I wanted to get back to my own body, but I was pulled up and out of the room and into a different place.

There was a person in this other place. He had hairy ears with long tufts like a renndeer did, only longer, down to his waist while his hair went only a little past his shoulders. I wondered if he was a renndeer spirit. I didn't know renndeer had spirits. He had hairy thighs and loins and belly and a penis, although it lay soft and limp, a curving nose. It looked as though it would be really big if it woke. He had golden eyes with sideways pupils.

He didn't seem dangerous to me. He stood in the tall grass of this place where we were and looked at me, and then he said some things in a language I didn't know. I understood him, though.

He said, "You are a crossing place. You have to make your own dance."

Then he stomped and his feet made a hollow sound on the earth as if they were as hard as renndeer feet. He leapt up and turned in the air and stomped again.

I stomped, and the earth echoed hollow beneath me. He stopped and watched me. He didn't tell me not to do it, but I had the feeling that maybe this was his dance and it wasn't my dance and it was okay if I wanted to do it but it didn't mean anything if I did. I did it anyway. I leapt and I could leap into the air, higher than the height of a man. Leaping and leaping and turning and maybe making a dance of my own out of it, high above the grass. I wanted to dance in the air, not on the earth—

I woke up with a headache. It was time to go to work. I could taste a funny, flat taste like metal in my mouth. The shaman was asleep, curled up where he had been sitting. He didn't have to go to work, the bastard.

I got up and stepped over him, but he never moved while I got ready.

All day at work I thought about the man with the hairy ears. When he had leapt in the air, the long streamers of hair hanging from his ears had twirled behind him, longer than his hair. I felt that I missed him. I felt as if I had just met someone I wanted to spend the rest of my life with. I felt as if I had known him for a long time, as if he were a cousin, kin of mine. It was strange. He made me itchy with desire, even though I should have been tired.

Rahel was no different. I felt as if she didn't know. The place inside the machine was sharp and complicated, more complicated than the spirit place, which had just been long grass without even insects, but the machine place felt flat. It was cut off. I wondered if maybe she had been seduced by all the details and did not realize that she was cut off. I wondered if she cared. I wondered if she was Rahel at all or just the semblance of Rahel, put there by a clever machine. Could the spirit of my daughter have been so thin, so like this machine world?

Maybe she was a machine spirit. Or maybe that was what she had become now.

"Are you happy?" I asked.

"Are you happy?" she asked me back, serene and unconcerned. "If you would like, you can talk to a counselor. Would you like me to alert the teacher?"

"No," I said. "I'm not unhappy."

I didn't tell her about the spirit I had met.

I couldn't wait to ask the shaman, though.

I ran up the steps, and there was a envelope on my door. I got a sick feeling because I knew it was from my landlady and that she was mad at me. I opened it up, standing in the hall. It said that after Saturday I had to live somewhere else.

I was scared. I was so scared, but more than that, I was really angry. I stuck my key in the door and unlocked the door with a loud click, and the door slammed against the wall like the crack of a rifle. "Dogmeat!" I shouted. I was going to shout that he had lost me my place to live, but the room was empty.

I ran to Mika. I was afraid he wouldn't be home. I didn't think he spent much time in the bare high place where he lived, but it was the only place I knew to go. When he answered the door I was so grateful I could have cried.

"Mika," I said, and did start to cry. Stupid girl.

"What?" he said. "Jan, what's wrong?"

"I have to find a new place to live," I blubbered.

He couldn't understand me at first. I kept thinking about how I hadn't wanted him to think of me like this. I had wanted to be like my mam. Mam never cried, except when she had my sister and the pain was so bad.

"Is that all?" Mika said when he understood, which made me feel even sillier, but relieved, too, because Mika could take care of it. "You needed to get out of the rattrap anyway," he said. "You and that old man in one room was stupid."

He took me out and fed me dinner, and then he let me stay the night with him. I was a little worried about the shaman, but I wanted someone else to take care of things for a while.

I went to work from Mika's and went back to his place

after work and all in all I didn't go back to check on the shaman until Thursday. By then I was convinced I would find him dead in the room. I didn't know why, but I opened the door with dread. I had it in my mind, there he would be on the bed, or the room would be empty. He had never even bought his own food.

But there he was, sitting there as if I had gone to work in the morning and was just coming home. The room was full of his old-man smell, like an animal's lair. "Where are we moving?" he asked. He just assumed I was going to take care of it.

"Mika's going to find us a place," I said. "Have you been eating?"

In an odd way, nothing had changed. I went to work and came home and on Friday, I went to Mika's and he said he hadn't had time to find us a place yet, so we could move into his until he found one.

The shaman and I gathered our things and we went to live with Mika.

After climbing five flights with our things, the shaman didn't seem to even notice the size and space and strangeness of where we were living. He simply chose a room and said, "I'll put my things here," and did. I had expected him to be dismayed at the sight of all those boarded-up windows on the first two floors. I had been prepared to explain that Mika's rooms were different, that we would be staying here only until we found something better. But he hadn't seemed to think anything about it at all. Maybe the whole city was so strange he didn't care.

I started to put my things in another room, but Mika pointed to the room where his mattress was and said, "Just leave them in there."

I looked at him for a moment, hoping he would see that I couldn't do that, but Mika didn't seem to notice. It was his place. We weren't paying any rent. I guessed that I owed him something. What was the shaman going to do?

The shaman glanced up and then went on laying out his blankets. Then he got out his bowl and his hot plate and his drum and crumbled up some things in the bowl. I went over to see what he was doing and if I was supposed to help. Outside, the sky was cold and purple at dusk.

"I am going to need to get some more plants," he said.

I didn't have any idea where to get plants in all this stone and metal, so I didn't say anything. He didn't really expect me to, anyway.

"What're you cooking?" Mika asked. "Don't you want to do it in the kitchen?"

The shaman kept on rolling the dried stuff between the hard skin of his palms. Tiny pungent bits of plant dusted down into the bowl.

"It's not for eating," I explained.

"Smells like licorice," Mika said.

Sometimes my mam had used the same plant for cooking. "It smells like home," I said.

The shaman grunted agreement.

"Is it some kind of spell?" Mika asked.

The shaman looked up at him, contemptuous.

"Not a spell," I said fast. "He doesn't do spells."

That earned *me* a look of contempt. Maybe he did do spells.

We stood and watched him, Mika and I, and I had a strange sense of how this looked to Mika. In Taufzin I asked Mika, "You are sorry we are here?"

Mika shook his head. "No," he said, "I'm not sorry."

"Speak so I can understand you," the shaman said.

"Excuse me, uncle," I said, but I didn't tell him what I had asked.

"Do you have some water?" the shaman asked Mika.

"We get it from the tap," Mika said, smiling a little.

"Go get some," the shaman said.

I thought Mika would get angry, but he just shrugged and winked at me and went and got some water in a glass.

The shaman burned herbs in a bowl. He picked up the bowl and, nose-singing, went around all the rooms, wafting smoke around and sprinkling water in all the corners. He shuffled and I shuffled after him, the dutiful apprentice.

Mika watched us, smiling a little.

The shaman straightened up and handed me the bowl and the glass. He put his hands in the small of his back and stretched. I took the pan and the glass back into the kitchen, washed them, and put the glass away. The shaman was sitting on his blankets.

Mika said, "I've got an appointment. I'll be back late."

It was the darkest part of the night, almost predawn. It was near the time when I would get up to go to work. We were just going to sleep. You can't go to sleep right away when you smoke black resin. You feel too good. Then all of a sudden you are so tired and everything seems awful.

I had no clothes on, and neither did Mika. I was pressed up against him, my feet on top of his so I could feel his heat even in my soles. But I felt so alone.

Maybe Mika did, too. He stroked my head, like I was a pet. "I'm not good for you," he said. "I don't mean to be, but when you get a place to live, you should stay away from me."

"I don't want to stay away from you," I said. I was already too far away. I wanted to be closer to him. I wanted him in me. Not in a sexual way, but really inside me, the way my daughter used to be. I didn't want to be by myself.

"We are a lot alike, bafit," he said. "We're both alone. We're both just animals in the forest. We don't have kin to count on."

"I'll be your kin," I promised.

He groaned. "You're too good for me."

Maybe it was the black resin talking, not Mika, but at that moment I fell in love with him.

The shaman woke me up when he grabbed my arm and hauled me to my feet. I grabbed for a blanket and found only air. "What?" I said. "What?"

Mika made some half-awake noise.

The shaman's hand on my arm hurt. The old man was quite strong. I would have been more frightened if I knew what was going on, instead I felt only the animal fear that comes of being startled awake.

"Get out of here," the shaman said, and pushed me toward his own room.

I twisted in his arm, trying to get a blanket.

"It's too late for that," the shaman said.

"I'm cold," I said.

"Too bad," the shaman said.

It wasn't until he sat me down on his own blankets that I could get something to cover myself.

"You're going the wrong way," the shaman said. I didn't understand him. I was still half asleep—we had been up so late.

"You're going the wrong way," the shaman said again.

"I'm not going anywhere," I said.

"You have already been—" the shaman gestured furiously at the part of the flat where Mika's mattress was "—*there.*"

Mika came to the door wearing only his pants. "What?" he said. "What's going on?"

"You don't know anything about this," the shaman said.

"Let me get my clothes," I said.

"You stay here," the shaman said. "You," he pointed at Mika, "you aren't even a whole person. You stay away from this."

"Let her get some clothes," Mika said.

"*Her.*" The shaman rounded on him. "What makes you think that is a *woman.*"

Mika smiled a little. "I'm sure that she's a woman," he said. I flushed. At least he didn't look at me.

"She is more than you know," the shaman said. "She is also he. But you don't know anything about that, because you're not even a man. You live in this city and are deaf to everything but the stones."

"Come on, old man," Mika said. "Let her get some clothes."

I started to get up and the shaman pushed me back down.

"Stop it," I said. "I need my clothes. No man would let you make him sit around like this." He let me up, then, and I went and got my coveralls and pulled them on.

The shaman followed me. "You are being stupid," he said.

I didn't say anything, because I didn't know if he was

right or not. But we had to live somewhere. I wanted to live with Mika.

"Maybe it's time for me to go back to being a girl," I said.

"NO!" the shaman shouted. "You know that's not true!"

"I don't know!" I said. "I don't know anything! My daughter is still stuck in the machine! You got us thrown out of our place!"

"The spirits are in you," the shaman said. "You know that you shouldn't go back."

"The renn spirit said I had to dance my own dance!" I said. "Not your dance! Not anyone else's dance!"

"He didn't mean this kind of dance," the shaman said, thrusting his pelvis at me.

I looked away.

"Old man," Mika said, "this is my place. I don't like you here, do you understand me? And I'm not afraid of you. Now pack your things and get out of here."

"No!" I said. "No, Mika, please. He has no one to take care of him."

"Look, it's early in the morning and he's screaming gibberish at me that I'm not a man. I don't live this way, I don't have to."

"He won't scream anymore," I said. And to the shaman, "Stop it. Just stop it."

"I will go back to the camp," the shaman said.

"You can't," I said. "It's winter up there. And I'd have to take you and I'm not taking you this weekend. I couldn't get back in time, I'd lose my job."

"Jesus," Mika said. He said that a lot. It was the name of the Taufzinnir god.

We all stood there looking at one another, until finally the shaman shuffled off to his room. I followed him.

"What did the spirits say to you?" I asked.

"Nothing," he said. "Go away."

"What about my daughter?" I said.

"Your daughter is not your concern," he said.

"My daughter is my concern," I said, angry.

"You are done with that!" he shouted. Then he said more quietly, "You are done with that."

I didn't understand.

"I tried to let you go your own way," he said. "I thought you would come back. The spirits are in you. They are combining within you the male and the female. You have had a child. You have been to war. Now you would throw it all away because of this boy. That is going backward. A renndeer cannot crawl back into its mother."

"I'm a woman pretending to be a man," I said.

"No," he said. "No, that's not it."

"I have a woman's body," I said. He shook his head. "Do you think I'm going to grow a penis?" I asked.

"This isn't about a body," he said.

"You are talking crazy," I said.

"Inside yourself is your spirit. Is it just a woman?" he asked.

Inside I didn't feel like a woman or a man, I only felt like myself. I didn't have an answer for him, so I didn't answer at all.

At work my teacher said to me, "Jan, according to your records, you haven't had a physical."

I didn't know what a physical was so I didn't know if I'd had one or not. She said she would schedule me for one. It meant a break from work, I thought, and that would be all right.

The physical was in a special office, almost more like where someone would live, with cushioned chairs. I sat in the chair and waited for a while. Then the nurse took me into another room and had me sit on the bench. He told me to take off my clothes and put on this shirt that tied around the middle.

"I can't," I said. "I mean, I can't take off my clothes. It is clan." Nobody knew anything about clanspeople, so I had told the people in the locker room that it was a clan thing that I couldn't take off my clothes.

"It's part of the physical," the nurse said.

"I'm sorry," I said. "I can't."

The nurse looked irritated with me. He argued with me a little more, telling me that it was required, but he didn't seem likely to try to undress me so I just refused. After a little while he gave in and left. Offworlders were very careful about other people's customs.

The doctor came in after that. I had never seen her before. She talked to me for a while. Did I like my job? Did I feel comfortable here? Had I felt ill?

She asked me if she could have a couple of drops of my blood. I knew about that from working with the medics in the camp, so I held out my finger and she pricked me. She took my temperature and some other things. She started to listen to my heart, but I said she couldn't because she wanted to unzip my coveralls. So she listened at my wrist.

She looked in my eyes and in my nose and in my ears. She frowned when she looked in my ears.

"You have implants," she said.

I knew what she meant. The things that Wanji had given me. "I grew up in an appropriate technology settlement," I said.

That startled her. She asked me a couple of questions and looked in my ears and more closely under my eyelids. "It's a standard issue kit," she said. "Distress transmitter, metabolic regulators. We don't recommend keeping them for too long. Do you want it removed?"

No, I realized, I didn't want it removed. "I don't know how it works," I said. "I want to know more."

"I'll see if we have anything."

Then she left.

I waited. There was a magazine that showed beautiful rooms of furniture, with plants and carpets and deep rich colors. I looked at the rooms and wondered what it would be like to live in one.

After a while she came back in. "Jan," she said, "we have run an analysis of your blood. There are things we must talk about."

I didn't understand exactly what she had said, but I knew it was something about my blood. I got a little more nervous.

"You are in fairly good health," she said. "You are— how do I say this?—you have a woman's body."

They were going to fire me. They had found out.

"You have traces of illegal drugs in your blood," she said.

"Do I have to leave?" I asked.

"No," she said. "You must stop taking the drugs. Do you understand me? We will check your blood now, and if we find drugs again, we will make you take counseling."

I didn't understand that at all. I had heard the word "counseling" before, but I couldn't remember what it meant.

"Now," she said. "Your presentation of gender is your right, do you understand me?"

She had to explain for a long time before I understood. Offworlders didn't care if you were a woman pretending to be a man. In fact, she would recommend I talk to someone who would help me decide about what to do. I didn't ask how they knew about my feelings about Mika and my worries about what I should do. Perhaps it was from the blood test.

She gave me a printout that she said would explain my implants.

I said good-bye to the doctor and good-bye to the nurse and walked out of the office. I felt funny as I walked down the hall, so I went into the bathroom and then I threw up. I put cold water on my face and I felt a little better. Then I went back to class.

I didn't say anything to Rahel, and I didn't tell Mika or the shaman that night. I knew Mika would think it was funny. I didn't know what the shaman would think. I suspected he thought he already knew what I should do.

Two days later I met a man in the same office where the doctor worked. This time the nurse was there but the doctor wasn't. The nurse smiled at me and I smiled back at him. I wondered if he knew.

"Jan?" said the man, and he took me into yet another room. This one had two chairs. The walls were painted green, and there were plants. It was a pretty room. "I'm Herve," he said in English. "I'm a gender counselor."

I nodded as if I understood.

"Where are you from?" he asked.

"North," I said. "From Hamra."

"Hamra is your clan?" he asked.

"It was," I said. "They are all dead now."

He blinked at that. I was too nervous to care.

"Your English is good," he said.

"Thank you," I said. I had recently gone through what Rahel called a threshold, which meant that suddenly English was easier for me. That was the way people learned language, in jumps.

"When you were growing up, did you think of yourself as a boy or a girl?" he asked.

"A girl," I said.

"When did you decide you were a boy?"

I thought. I didn't know that I had ever decided I was a boy. "I think," I said, "I think when I come to the camp. The refugee camp in Tonstad."

"Why did you want to be a boy then?"

"I don't know," I said. "Someone thinks I am a boy. I was alone. I had no man, no kin. My husband was dead. I thought if I am a boy, it is safer."

He asked me to draw a picture of myself. "I can't draw," I said.

"It's okay," he said.

I tried to draw myself in my coveralls. I had a lot of trouble with the face and the fingers, although I did pretty good with the shoes.

"Can you draw yourself without coveralls?" the man asked.

"No," I said.

"Okay," he said. "That's okay." He sat back and sighed. "You are an interesting case, Jan," he said. "I usually evaluate gender in the context of culture and social situation. I can do blood work to find out if your brain chemistry is different, but a huge percentage of transgenders aren't neurologically predisposed. Do you understand me?"

I nodded.

He knew that I didn't. He leaned forward. "Think of it this way: some people have a male brain in a female body. They are like someone wearing someone else's clothes. Only they are wearing the wrong body."

I could understand that. "I don't think like that," I said.

"Maybe you are, maybe you aren't. I don't know about

your culture. I don't know enough about the clans. It doesn't matter. There are a lot of people who choose to be a woman or a man for all different reasons. Sometimes people don't even know the reasons. But," he said, "we can do some things to help you." He held up one finger. "We can leave you go the way you are. Two—" he held up the second finger "—we can change you into a man. You will have no breasts. You will grow a beard. You will have a penis. Or three, we can do something in the middle. We can let you feel some of what it is like to be a man. You will be more like a man, but you won't have a penis. Do you understand?"

I nodded.

"Okay," he said. "Tell me the three things you can do."

"Okay," I said, "okay . . ." and found I couldn't. The ideas wiggled out of me as soon as I tried to think of them.

He was very careful, like a mother, not getting angry, while he helped me understand.

"The thing is," he said, "we can do the third one, the one that is partway, and you can easily change your mind. You can go back to the way things are now. Or you can go on and be changed into a man."

"Okay." I was thinking and thinking, my thoughts all running like an angry army. "Okay. I want to try the third one. It seems like a good idea to try."

"When do you want to try?" he asked.

"Now," I said.

"Okay," he said. "We will make an appointment for you to see me on Friday. We'll use an implant. You know what an implant is? Good. We'll use an implant. We'll have to do something to retard beard growth. You will have some changes, but they will be small."

I wanted it. I wanted it for here, at work, and I didn't even think about Mika. "Can we do it now?" I said. There didn't seem to be any reason to wait.

"No, Jan," he said and he smiled at me. It was the first time he wasn't serious. "No, I think we should give you a little time. Friday is soon enough."

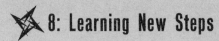# 8: Learning New Steps

IT WAS SNOWING. AT HOME IT HAD PROBA-
bly snowed weeks ago, but this was the first snow in
Taufzin. It was a big, heavy flake and the air tasted of
moisture. People in this city were blind and deaf. They
talked about the weather all the time, as if it were a cranky
uncle, but they never paid any attention to it. Just hid
inside their buildings like animals sleeping in winter.

Mika bought one of the systems he had bought Sissela.
There were pictures and sound but no address hookup and
no way to call anyone, of course. The shaman liked to
watch it. I sat on the floor with him, watching for a while.
He explained that it was about a family and their problems
but their problems were foolish.

I didn't know who the people were and they felt like
no kin to me, so I didn't watch long.

One of Mika's friends came by. This guy was tall and
awkward with hips like a woman or like a man who sits
too much. He had a box of stuff he wanted to tell Mika
about. I told him I didn't know where Mika was and wrote
his name and his system address down on a scrap of paper
so Mika could add it to all the other scraps he never paid
any attention to.

I watched some more about the family with the shaman.

"This is a stupid city," I said to the shaman.

He looked sideways at me but didn't say anything.

I got up and walked around the room. "There is nothing
for a person here," I said. "A person should do."

He laughed.

"It's not funny," I said.

"You are busy all day and all night with your job and your boy," the shaman said. "I sit all day. You tell me that this place has nothing for a person?"

I shrugged. I hadn't thought much about how the shaman spent his days. I figured they were pretty much the same as in the camp. Of course, the camp was no place for a person, either.

"There is another person," I said, "a friend of Mika's. She is a clansperson. She'll come here and you can meet her."

"Thank you," the shaman said, still laughing at me with his eyes.

"I'm going for a walk," I said, irritated to be laughed at.

Going down the stairs I found Mika coming up. "Where you going?" he asked.

"Just to walk," I said. "Rikki was here. He has a box to show you. I wrote down his address."

"Thanks," Mika said. He started on up the stairs and I followed him. "I thought you were going for a walk," he said.

"I was just bored."

"How about if we go out this weekend?"

"Okay," I said.

"Will you go as a girl?" he asked.

"A girl?" I didn't know what he meant.

"In a dress," he said. "I'll buy the dress."

"I can't do that." It felt, well, wrong. Like I'd get in trouble.

"Why not? Nobody you know will be there. People from work aren't likely to show up at a place where I'd take you."

"No," I said. "No, I couldn't."

He went on upstairs and I followed him.

"So what are you?" he asked. "Do you think you're really a guy? Trust me, *I* know you're not a boy." He grinned at me.

"I don't think I'm a boy," I said, but I could hear how defensive I sounded.

"What then?"

The shaman was watching another family. This one was an offworld family and they kept expecting Taufzin to be like offworld.

"I don't know," I said. "Maybe I'm neither."

"Maybe you're both," Mika said. He found the paper I had written Rikki's address on. "Walk down to the corner with me so I can call this guy."

Back down the stairs and out into the lazy snow. "I like that idea," I said.

"What?" Mika said. "Did Rikki say what this was about?"

"He said he had a box of something, but he didn't say what. I like the idea of being both."

"Both what?" Mika said.

He could make me so mad. "What you said." He was walking so fast that I had to almost skip to keep up with him. "About being both a woman and a man."

"I didn't say that," he said.

"You did. You said maybe I was a woman *and* a man."

"I don't know if you've ever looked at yourself naked, bafit, but you aren't a man."

"They could make me one."

He laughed.

"No really, they told me at work. They could make me a man. They gave me an implant to see if I wanted to feel more like a man."

That stopped him. "Jesus Christ, Jan."

"It's just to see," I said. "They can take it out if I don't like it."

"Do you like it?" he asked.

"I don't feel any different."

"How long have you had it?"

"Since Friday," I said. "Not even a week."

"Take it out," he said and started walking again, his feet stomping in the snow. He was mad.

"Not yet," I said.

"Have them take it out tomorrow. That's stupid. It's sick."

He didn't say any more, he just walked fast to the corner. The sounds of the street were absorbed by the snow, and the city sounded quiet. He called Rikki. "Hey, this is Mika. What have you got?"

I watched the snow land on his hair. He had beautiful hair, glossy and fat. The snow landed there and stayed, not melting.

"I dunno, Rikki, I'd have to see it. No, not tonight, I've got to go out. How about Friday? What time you work?"

I listened to him speak Taufzin. He could go back and forth from my language to Taufzin so smoothly. Mika was smart. I wasn't so smart. I was just some girl from the clans. Maybe he was right about the implant. Maybe I should have it taken out. But I didn't want to; it felt right and it was mine.

The implants from Wanji had never been mine. Maybe because I hadn't asked for them.

"There's a message here for you from Sissela," Mika said.

He handed me the headset and I slid it on. "Hey, Jan," Sissela's voice said. "How are you? Why don't you come over for dinner on Friday? Leave me a reply."

I hit reply and waited for her system, but it was Sissela who answered.

"Hi, Sissela," I said. "It's Jan. I'm going out on Friday," I said, looking at Mika but he was standing in the snow looking at his shoes as if he were somewhere else and I was nothing but a weak spirit. "How about if I take you out to a restaurant on Saturday? You can meet the shaman, I bet you never met a shaman."

She laughed, clear as bells. "No, I've never met a shaman. But I'm busy on Saturday. How about Thursday?"

"I work," I said.

"After work is okay."

"The shaman and I are staying at Mika's," I said. "We had to leave our other place."

"Mika's?" she said. She sounded uncertain. "You want me to meet you there?"

I shuffled in the snow. "The shaman doesn't get around too well. He's old. He's a little, um, strange looking. He wears a dress."

"Did you say a dress?" she said. "What kind of dress?"

"Like a woman's dress. Maybe I should get some food and bring it to your place?"

"Okay," she said. "Don't worry about the food, just come." She sounded relieved. There was a pause. I never knew what to do when I was finished talking. I started to say good-bye, but then she said, "Is Mika coming?"

I looked at him, but Mika was still deaf. "Eh, I don't think so."

"Okay," she said. Then, "Okay." I couldn't tell if she was relieved or disappointed. Maybe both.

Mika made me feel that way sometimes, too.

If Sissela was surprised by the shaman's appearance, she hid it well. She said, "Hello, uncle," and I thought that even if she talked our language sounding like a Menno, at least she was polite.

"Hello, daughter. Something smells good."

I smelled meat cooking. Home smells. There were two other people in the apartment, sitting on chairs at the table, and they stood up when we came in. They were clanspeople, too, even though they were dressed like city people.

"This is Lea and Tum," Sissela said. "They are friends of mine. I hope you don't mind. Lea helped me make dinner."

Lea smiled. She was missing some teeth. When I was growing up, lots of adults had teeth missing and I never thought about it, but now, I was so used to Taufzin people that her gap-toothed smile embarrassed me.

The shaman said hello and asked her what kin, and we sat for a few minutes and discussed everybody's kin lines. They were coastal people, and they could find kin in common. I was from too far away to have kin with any of these people. I sat, feeling left out, and tried to smile and be interested.

Dinner was all summer food. We had renndeer stewed with parsnips and sour milk with berries. Lea hovered over the shaman. "Here is a good piece of meat." She spooned out a little more. "No gristle on this one." There was winter greens, but fresh. There was beer. Homemade beer, not the stuff that came in bottles here. There was whiskey, but it was bought from the store.

"Where do you get the meat?" I asked.

Tum shrugged. "I have cousins who bring it in from up-country."

"I tried to get some fish," Lea said, "but none of it looked fresh enough. When it gets here it stinks."

Sissela sat back and watched, just picking. The shaman, who never ate much, emptied his bowl again and again. The meat did taste good. It was hard to stop eating even when I was full.

Finally we had eaten and were drinking whiskey. Tum put a bottle of whiskey next to the shaman. "For you," he said. "Uncle," Tum said diffidently, "we need you to talk to the spirits for us."

The shaman, who had ignored the whiskey bottle, sat back in his chair.

"It is my wife," Tum said. "She has terrible pains sometimes. They wake her up groaning in the middle of the night."

"Where are these pains?" the shaman asked.

Lea stood up and pointed to her left side.

The shaman asked her questions. What had she been eating? Had she offended anyone? How did she sleep? Did she lie on her side or on her back? Did she dream? What did she dream of? Had she children? What were their names? Were they alive? Her husband had a dead first wife and a dead child, and I thought of my daughter. How long had they lived in the city?

"Get my bag," the shaman told me, so I fetched his bag. I'd thought he was stupid to bring it but here he needed it.

The shaman took us into Sissela's bedroom but made Sissela and the husband wait outside. He had his pot and his bowl from our place in the bag, and he had some green stuff left. He burned some in the bowl and had the woman inhale the smoke, then he made her take off her shirt. She was thinner than I expected. She had looked fat in all her layers of clothing, but that was only because she had dressed the way we did at home. Her old breasts lay like sacks on her ribs. Her nipples were dark and long, and the veins were blue under her skin.

The shaman touched her gently on her side and asked

her if it hurt. He was careful. She stared ahead as if not seeing him. I tried not to look at her. Sissela's room was all in white and pale blue. Even the walls were pale blue. Everything smelled sharply of the stuff that the shaman had burned, a cool smell that prickled at my nose.

The shaman shook his head. "I don't have the things I need," he said. He made a pipe and gave it to the woman to smoke. He let her cover herself first. I breathed in the smoke from the pipe and it made me sleepy. It was so hard to go to work and then do anything else.

The shaman cuffed my ear and knocked me over. "Pay attention," he said.

"What!" I said. "I worked today!"

"Don't talk back."

"Don't talk back!" Anger rose up in me. I hadn't known how angry I was. "I work all day, I put food in your mouth!"

He hit me hard in the side of the head and I saw a flash of light. I swung my arm up to hit him back, but I stopped myself. He was an old man.

"If you want to stop, stop," he said. "I have taken care of myself before, little man." His voice was very cold.

The woman was looking at me. Her eyes were cold, too.

"Get out of here," the shaman said. "Your anger fills the room. It hurts the healing."

Tum and Sissela were still sitting at the table, drinking white tea. I sat down.

"Is everything okay?" Sissela asked.

"He makes me crazy," I said.

Tum looked away.

"He's a little different," Sissela agreed.

"I take care of him," I said. "I give him a place to live, and food. I brought him here from the refugee camp at Tonstad. And he hits me." My head ached. "I wish I hadn't brought him. But now I have to take care of him, there isn't anyone else. I should take him back."

"Don't take him back," Tum burst out. "We need him."

"I'm not taking him back," I said. "I'm just mad. I couldn't take him back anyway, it's winter."

"Other people want to see him," Tum said. "My

cousin wants to see him about his daughter, and other people, too. We don't have anyone here to talk spirit.''

When I got home on Friday, Mika had a dress for me. I took it into the bathroom and, under the artificial light, put it on. It was a simple dress, a foolish dress; it left me bare. My naked arms and legs stuck out from it. It was just two pieces of cloth, sewn up the sides and across the shoulders. It was bright blue. It wasn't anything like the dresses I saw on the street. They had jackets and coats. The women at the factory, the Taufzin girls, came to work in their dresses that went below their knees and covered their arms. This was like something someone would make if you just told them what a dress should be. A false dress.

I came out of the bathroom, and Mika laughed. ''You should see your face,'' he said. ''You look like a thunderstorm.'' He stepped back and appraised me and shook his head. ''The dress is okay,'' he said, ''but you need to get rid of the hair on your legs.''

The shaman looked over at me and snorted.

''Shut up,'' I said.

''You look kinless,'' the shaman said. I knew what he meant. Dressed in rags.

''I am kinless,'' I said. To Mika I said, ''I can't wear this.''

''Why not?'' Mika said. He cocked his head. ''You look cute.''

''I look—I look—'' I could not find words for how I looked. I was wrong in this dress and I looked like someone who no one cared about and who didn't care about herself, all bony shoulders and stringy neck and with my hair dirty from work. ''This isn't mine,'' I said.

''I bought it,'' he said.

''I don't mean that,'' I said.

''You don't look like a boy,'' he said. ''You're trying that implant thing to be a boy. Just once why don't you try to be a girl? You might like it.''

''I don't like it,'' I said.

''You haven't tried,'' he said. ''Never with me. Except for sex. You like sex, Jan.''

I did like sex. "The counselor says my gender is my choice."

"What is that word," the shaman asked, *"gender?"*

"It means whether you are a boy or a girl," Mika said. "Jan thinks she's a boy."

"Jan is a boy, when he's not dressed like that," the shaman said.

"I am not," I said, angry. I could feel the heat in my face. "I'm both."

"Both?" the shaman said.

"Jesus," Mika said. "I wish you'd stay out of this."

"He knows more about it than you do," I said to Mika.

The shaman threw up his hands. "Okay, if you are both, go be both."

"See," Mika said. "If he knows more than I do, you should try it."

It wasn't that easy. We had to go outside in the early dark and down to the store on the corner where they sold something that would take the hair off my legs and from under my arms, and Mika found me a pair of blue shoes there. They were too big in the heels and felt as if they'd fall off every time I took a step.

Mika also bought me color for my lips and my eyelids. It was very embarrassing.

Back in his place he made me put the stuff all over my legs and under my arms and then he had me stand around in the cold bathroom waiting until it had dissolved all the hair. Then he made me wash it all off and wash my hair, and he dressed me in the dress and the shoes and put color on my lips.

"You look sexy and cute," he kept saying.

Pretty girls are round and I had never been, but in this silly rag I was even less so.

"Just give it a chance," he said.

Breathe it in: the smell of smoke and whiskey. There was music and a girl singing in a voice that sounded as if she had been drinking and smoking. It was a sad song. I couldn't drink and smoke, but I could listen to the music. It was nice, except that I was cold.

Mika taught me to dance. I leaned against him and

he swayed his hips. I swayed with him. It was sad like the song.

"Do you like me better than Sissela?" I asked. He couldn't hear me because of the music, otherwise I wouldn't have asked him. I wished we could go home and have sex. "Do you want to go home?" I asked, this time loud enough for him to hear.

"Not yet," he said.

"I want to fuck you," I said, grinning up at him. He had taught me how to say it in Taufzin. It made him laugh.

The renn spirit had said I had to learn how to dance my own way, but this didn't seem to be it.

Mika had to talk to someone, so after a while we went out into the cold where we could see the air from inside us. I kept walking out of my shoes. "I'm hungry," I said. "Let's get something to eat."

"After I talk to Rikki," Mika said.

Rikki was the man who had come to see Mika earlier in the week. We caught a bus. The lights in the bus were hard and white. They made Mika look dead. At least the bus was warm. I looked out the window, and my breath made smoke on the glass. In the reflection I could see the color on my eyes and mouth. I looked foolish, but sometimes, just for a moment, I could see how I might look better this way. I wasn't used to looking at myself as a woman.

Rikki lived in a house on a street of houses that all looked the same. They were made out of the same concrete as the road. They were low and there was no space between them. The windows were dark at Rikki's, but there was some light coming out between the curtains.

Rikki opened the door. He was barefoot and he didn't have a shirt on. "Hey, Mika," he said, as if he didn't really care if Mika was here or not. His eyes were red, and he was smoking something. He didn't seem to recognize me.

Inside was too warm. "What have you got?" Mika asked.

There was another man there. He was barefoot, too, but he had his shirt on. Mika and Rikki didn't pay any attention to him or me. I went and sat down on the couch. I sank deep into it. It was soft and lumpy and green, and it had a faint beer smell.

"Get something to drink," Rikki told Mika. Rikki went into another room to get his box of stuff, and Mika got a bottle of sweet wine out of the kitchen. Rikki and his friend had been playing cards. The friend looked at his cards, bored. This was the kind of thing that went on with Mika all the time. We went out to get something to eat and he had to stop and see someone and sell them something or pick something up.

A woman followed Rikki out, rubbing her arms as if she'd been asleep. She was skinny, even more skinny than I was, so skinny her thighs were only as big around as a man's arm, and there was space between them. Her pubic bone stuck out as if she were a boy. She looked awful.

"What is it?" Mika asked Rikki.

Rikki opened up the box and Mika peered in. He reached in and took out a white wafer.

"It's some kind of self-replicator," Rikki said. "It wasn't on the packing slip, so I took it."

"What's it do?" Mika asked.

"I don't know," Rikki said. "I think it makes medicine, but I'm not sure. I knew it would be worth a lot of money."

"You have to have documents," Mika said. "Without documents, this could be anything. Nobody wants this stuff without documents."

"It's self-replicating," Rikki said, his voice climbing into a whine. You could see right away how things stood between Rikki and Mika and who was top dog.

Mika shrugged. "Self-replicating what? Without documents it could be toothpaste." The man playing cards snorted through his nose. Rikki looked over, sharp. "Who am I going to sell this to?" Mika asked.

"Can't they find out what it is?" Rikki asked. "It's something for the lab. Everything else was for the lab."

"What else was on the packing slip?" Mika asked.

"Things for the lab," Rikki said, trying hard to get Mika to understand.

"What kind of things?" Mika asked, his voice soft and patient.

"I don't know. It was all in English."

Mika looked at the wafers for a while. Rikki shifted from one foot to another, hopeful. When he couldn't stand it anymore, Rikki said, "Are you going to buy them or just play with them all night?"

Mika reached into his pocket and pulled out his wallet. The skinny woman came over to stand next to Rikki. Her eyes were narrow. "Are you going to give him money or tar?" she asked.

"Tar" was what some people called the black resin.

"Money," Rikki said, "I want money. He gives me tar it'll all be gone before I can sell it."

The woman frowned slightly. It made her look old.

I was embarrassed to be watching them, but I found myself studying her feet, which were long and narrow and fine. Her toenails were painted dark red. I wondered why anyone would want their toenails to look bruised. She saw me looking at her feet, and my eyes retreated to my own square, stubby ones. Mine were hard; I didn't have to take off my shoes to see that. I looked at my feet in the silly shoes Mika had bought me, sitting there so neatly, side by side. I didn't want my feet naked here anyway.

Mika picked up the box. I had trouble getting up because the couch was so soft it didn't want to let me go.

Mika was quiet until we got down the street, and then he whispered, "Jan, do you know what we've got?"

I hadn't any idea.

"We're going to have to be very careful," he whispered, his voice tight and fierce.

"We are?" I asked. "Because of the box? What are they?"

"Technology," he said. "Self-replicating technology. These have a code in them to make pharmaceuticals. Medicine. You have to have a license to have these. Offworlders keep these tight. I know people who would pay a lot of money to get these."

"What kind of medicine?" I asked.

"Who knows," he said. "Who cares."

We took the box home, and Mika looked at the disks for a while, taking them out and holding them in his hand.

He let me hold one. It was as smooth as a plate and a little bigger than the palm of my hand. He slipped one of the disks into his pocket, like a lucky charm, and put the rest back in the box.

Mika couldn't be still. He wanted to go back out, so out we went, this time to another bar where the music was different and the dancing was full of slow movements. He bought me whiskey, even though I wasn't supposed to have it.

"Take this," he said and gave me a pill.

"I'm not supposed to," I said. "I'm not supposed to for work, am I?"

"It's not like that," he said. "They won't care at work. If I can sell these, we'll have a lot of money. You won't have to work."

I liked that idea. Work was so hard. Not the work itself but the being there on time and being nervous—was I making a mistake, was I breaking a rule that everybody knew about but me? I would sleep late and not ride the bus in the morning. "What will I do?" I asked.

"You'll be with me," he said.

"Okay," I said.

He showed me how to dance, and I watched the other girls out of the corner of my eye. It was sexy dancing and I liked it. I rolled my shoulders. "We shouldn't have gone back out," I said. "We should have stayed home."

"And done what?" Mika said, teasing me.

I whispered in his ear what we should have done. He laughed. "You'll say anything," he said.

"It's because I don't know any better," I said, which was almost true.

I had another whiskey and the pill made me feel all soft inside. I could dance better after the pill started working. It loosened all my joints and made me move like the other girls. I wondered if I would be able to move like the other girls once the implant really started working. Maybe I didn't want the implant. Maybe I didn't want to give this up.

"You're a sexy thing," Mika said. He was beautiful. His hair was glossy and clean, and in the opening of his shirt the skin of his neck and chest was smooth and perfect and just faintly shining with sweat. I touched the place where his shirt was open and then smelled his scent on my fingers.

"You're my little animal," he said, "my bafit."

"Not a bafit," I said. I didn't feel timid, I felt strong and I wanted something.

We danced another dance, and then he picked up my coat and wrapped me up in it.

"Are we going home?" I asked.

Not home, not yet. "We have to go see someone, about the disks."

It had rained while we were dancing. Winter rain was worse than snow, never clean. The wet cold air filled my lungs. Tomorrow it might snow. Or be warm. Taufzin weather, if you didn't like it, wait a while, people said, it would change. My silly little shoes were made of cloth and they soaked up the rain, which made them heavy and so it was even easier to walk out of them.

"After this, can we go home?" I asked. I was wondering if I would still need to have sex with him, because by now I was too tired to really want to.

"I need you to be sharp, bafit," Mika said. "This guy, the one we're going to see, he could eat us alive."

"Let's not go," I said.

"I need to go. If I don't go tonight, I might not have the nerve tomorrow," Mika said.

"We can go tomorrow, I'll make you. I've been up since six-thirty this morning," I said. "I'm really tired—"

"Listen," he said, "you don't understand. That box, you don't know, that box . . . it's full of gold. I can't sell that box without help, I don't have the right strings. Acquaintances. What would renner say? Like kin, okay? I need someone to do that with. But this guy, he can do it. And if I sell this, and I have the money, you won't need to pretend to be a boy anymore. I won't have to be running from here to there like someone's motherless cousin. I'll be like Dolf, that's the man we're going to see."

It was all about having kin. Everything always comes down to kin. If you don't have kin, you have to make your own lines of kinship. I nodded because I understood.

I understood that the shaman was my kin and Mika was my kin and I was the daughter-in-law, and it was better to have kin fighting with each other than no kin at all. Mika had no kin. He had run away from his family, the way my mother and father had, only he didn't have a Hamra to go to, so he had to make kin other ways.

We waited for a bus and I thought about this, this kin-lessness of Mika's. It made me understand him in a new way, a way I thought Mika probably didn't understand himself. I wanted to talk about it, but Mika didn't like to talk. I hugged the idea to myself. I turned it over and over like a stone in my hand. I wished I would have another idea, just as smart.

Mika was nervous, but he was excited, too. "Do you feel lucky, bafit?" he asked. "I think I feel lucky."

I had never been so foolishly dressed for the cold. It was as if I were walking in snow, my feet were completely gone. And it wasn't even that cold. "Why do women dress like this?" I asked Mika.

He thought that was funny. "Because it looks nice."

"I can't feel my feet," I said.

He grinned. "When we get home, I'll make it up to you. You look really cute."

I snorted out my nose like a renndeer, and he laughed out loud. I saw again in his throat the perfect smoothness of his skin, the *clarity* of it. His skin, his skin, and his fine hair and his hands. Such an animal, such a fine, fine animal.

"Sometimes I can't believe you like me," I said.

"Sometimes, I can't either."

"No, really. You can have a pretty girl."

"You are pretty," he said, which was the kind of lie men tell women, but it was what I wanted him to say. "Besides, you're interesting."

"And I adore you," I said.

"You have a funny way of shówing it." He pecked me on the cheek. I loved when he did that. It wasn't sex when he did that, it was just me.

"Are you going to get rid of that implant thing, now?" he asked.

*   *   *

The house was pale yellow and the door was dark green under the house light. There was brass shining on the door, and a brass plate on the wall. The windows glowed through pale fabric. It looked warm and dry.

A girl opened the door. She was Menno, with a broad face and dark hair. But she looked a lot like an offworlder, too. Her clothes had that look, all finished, not like the Menno girls at work in their long-sleeved dresses where you could see the stitches. Mika looked scared.

She led us through the house to a big kitchen in the back.

Dolf was tall and thin with a long hooked nose. Everything in the kitchen, including Dolf, looked offworld and expensive and too bright and *clean.* He was talking to another man who was as broad as he was thin. Mika suddenly looked shabby and a little dirty.

"What is it, Mika?" Dolf said.

"I've got something I think you'll be interested in," Mika said. He handed Dolf the disk out of his pocket.

Dolf turned it around in his hands, looking at both sides. "Where did you get it?" he finally asked.

"It fell off a truck," Mika said.

I didn't like Dolf. He didn't like Mika, to him Mika was just some dog off the street. My wet, dirty shoes were leaving smudges of mud on the slick white kitchen floor.

"How many of these have you got?" Dolf asked.

Mika shrugged. "I can get a few more."

"How many?"

"I could get you a dozen," Mika said.

There were a lot more than a dozen in the box, but I knew enough not to say anything.

"What do they do?"

Mika shrugged. "Some kind of pharmaceuticals. The manifest didn't fall off the truck. Someone would have to test it, I guess."

"I'll test this one and be in touch with you," Dolf said.

"I'm just a middleman, Dolf," Mika said. "I have to get in touch with someone to get you more. It might take some time."

"I'll call you in a couple of days," Dolf said tiredly. Under his eyes his skin was purple and bruised. He was older than I thought, maybe because he was so tall, maybe because his clothes were so neat I didn't realize how used he was.

Outside the rain had stopped and the streets had a dirty sheen on them.

"When he finds out what they are, he'll call me," Mika said.

"What are they?" I asked.

"He thinks they're fakes, that's all. When he finds out they're the real thing, he'll call me."

"What are they?" I asked again.

"Technology. Licensed technology. Replication units for a pharmaceutical."

"What do they do?"

"How the hell would I know?" he exploded. "Jesus, Jan! You're the fucking technician, why don't you figure out what they do?"

"I don't know how to figure them out. I'm not that kind of technician."

"Then why do you care?"

"If I was trying to sell them, I'd like to know what they are."

"Damn it! I don't know what they are! That's why we came to see Dolf, because he can tell us what they are."

"Are you going to sell them to him? He's an ugly man."

"I don't care what he looks like," Mika said.

"That's not what I mean."

"I'll sell some to him," he said, "and some to other people. You never used to get in my face this way. Is it the thing that's supposed to make you a boy that's doing this?"

"It's not making me a boy," I said. "And it's not doing anything to me yet. I just thought you knew what was going on."

"I do know what's going on. I'm going to use Dolf to find out what the damn things do, and maybe even have him sell a few for me."

"He wants to eat us," I said. "Eat us like renndeer calves."

"So we're careful. So stop talking about it," Mika said.

"Fine," I said. And shut up. Mika didn't talk to me, either. Not the long cold time we stood in the street, waiting for the bus nor, once the bus came, on the long trip back across town. Finally I fell asleep with my head jolting against the chill window and the cold white of the interior lights falling down all around me, making me dream of snow.

Mika woke me up at the bus stop near his building. "I need you to do something for me," he said.

"I'm tired," I whispered.

"Come on," he said. We went up to the apartment and he let me change into my clothes. In the mirror, even with the color washed off, I still thought I looked like a rag-and-bone girl. "I need you to take these to work and put them in your locker," Mika said.

"Now?" I said.

"Yes," he said. "Now."

"No," I said.

He sighed, "Jan, listen to me. This guy, Dolf, he would just as soon step on us as look at us. If he comes here he'll just take the disks."

"I'll take them tomorrow," I said.

"Now. I'll pay for a cab," Mika said.

"Just give him the disks if he's such a crazy dog," I said.

"Look"—Mika grabbed my arm so tight it hurt—"you listen to me. Things like this don't happen very often, okay? Okay? You go to your job and they pay you every week, and in ten years you'll be making a little more money and maybe they'll make you a manager, right? But you know what happens to people like me?"

I didn't know what he was talking about.

"So I'm going to try to make a little money with this, try to make enough money to set myself up with something better. I need you to help me. Have I ever asked you to help me?"

We went downstairs and walked to the corner, Mika carrying the box, and finally he found a cab and it glided up to where we stood. Inside it was all the same color of gray—seat, floor, and ceiling. It stank of offworld, as if nothing human had ever touched it. It didn't even have a driver. I told the address to a speaker and we glided off, quiet as a whisper.

I told the guard at work I needed to put something in my locker and I showed him my ID—and that was all it took. I passed the schoolroom. The door was closed and inside the machine that may or may not call up my daughter sat in the dark.

Outside Mika was waiting with his hands in his pockets. He looked hangdog and sad in the rain.

"Thanks, bafit," he said.

The shaman woke me up too early. He wanted me to take him over to Sissela's place. He was meeting a man who needed to talk spirit. "You could learn to take a bus by yourself," I said.

"That's why you are here," he said. "So I can talk spirit and you can talk bus." He nudged me with his toe again.

Mika rolled so his back was to me.

There were three people waiting at Sissela's, and Sissela was a little exasperated, too. "I have to work today," she said, even though it was Saturday. "What am I going to do? This isn't a doctor's office."

"He doesn't care," I said. "Mika had me out until really late, but he still made me get up."

"Is Mika selling drugs?" Sissela asked.

"No," I said. "He has some technology he got from a kinless person named Rikki. He says it is going to make us rich."

Sissela rolled her eyes. "Rikki. Rikki's trash. I have to go to work. Can you stay here and watch my place while these people are here?"

No sooner had Sissela left than I found the shaman in her bedroom, drawing a square on the floor with a piece of charcoal. "What are you doing?" I asked. "You can't do that."

"Shut up," the shaman said.

"No," I said. "This is Sissela's house. You can't do that. She told me to watch it."

He backhanded me. I saw it coming and tried to duck,

so he got me on the forehead. I saw a flash. I crouched down.

"You forget yourself," he said.

I went in the other room where I fell asleep with my head on the kitchen table. It was late afternoon when the shaman shook me awake. "Worthless," he said. "Get up."

There was only one man left. "What?" I said.

"Come on," he said. "We have to go with this man."

I wanted to go back and sleep some more, but instead I trudged out into the cold and down the steps from Sissela's apartment. I was so groggy that I didn't even check the apartment before we left.

The wet air woke me up. "This air is unwholesome," I said.

The clansman looked at me oddly, but the shaman didn't pay any attention.

We caught a bus that took us out of the city. There were a handful of people on the bus, but only one woman asked for a stop. Most of the people were riding the bus to the end, like us.

The end was a place where ships came down. Long before we got there we could hear the rumble and see the ships coming in. One of the signs said "shuttleport" in English, and then all the signs were in English and everything said shuttleport. Shuttleport Cargo. Shuttleport Lounge. Shuttleport Recordings, Adults Only. The shuttleport went on and on. We drove past it and drove past it, and it still went on. We had been going past it for a long time when the clansman touched the bell strip to signal for his stop.

Out here the wind blew hard. The bus stop was on the same side of the road as the shuttleport. There was nothing but a fence and then miles of flat ground and far off, the buildings. The very air thrummed with engine noise. I put my hands over my ears, but I could feel it in the back of my mouth, in my teeth, an unpleasant thing. A shuttle came in over us. It looked as if it was moving very slowly. I realized that it was not moving slow, it was just very big, as big as a building. The clansman beckoned us to follow him across the street.

This part of the town was very mean. The buildings were no more than two stories high, and wind rushed and rushed. I thought if I lived out here I'd go mad. The shops were small, and they had signs that showed joss sticks and bottles and candy. Nothing to really eat. Not good food.

The clansman put his head into the wind and walked down the dirty street, and we followed him.

Finally, the clansman went up to a little square building, and we climbed a staircase up the side of the building to a door. Inside the door I could still feel the rumble of the shuttles through my feet, but at least the wind was outside. The place was dark and stank like bad old meat.

I breathed out of my mouth, and as my eyes adjusted I could see that the room was shaped like a roof and that it was small. There was a stove, a chair, and a bed, and there was someone on the bed and that was where the stink was coming from.

At first I thought that the person had died, but the shaman bent over the bed and I could see the shine of someone's black eyes moving. It was an old woman. I could hear her breathing then, a sound more terrible than the wind outside. Her breathing was liquid, as if her lungs were a swamp.

I wanted to go back outside.

"Boy," the shaman said, so I carried his bag over. The woman had yellow skin, and the parts of her eyes that were normally white were yellow. But she watched me sharp.

It was the clansman's mother. She had been sick for two years, he said, but he had not been able to find anyone but women until now. Women have lots of medicine for illnesses but not for spirit things and he needed a spirit talker for that.

The shaman leaned over and spoke to her. "What is your name?"

She didn't answer. I was pretty sure that she understood. Her eyes understood everything. They looked at the shaman, at me, and at her son and then back at the shaman. The clansman told us her name was Katya.

"She needs her things," the shaman said.

The clansman blinked. "Can you make her better?"

The shaman shook his head. He leaned over the old woman. "It's all right now."

The clansman blinked again, blinked away tears.

The shaman got out his drum and sat on the floor next to the bed and tapped out a soft rhythm. He hummed through his nose. He motioned me to sit on the floor, and I sat down and hummed, too. The shaman rocked a little. I could see the woman's bright eyes looking at me. Her tiny body was under the blue blanket, but her bony yellow face was right there at eye level.

I closed my eyes and listened to the drum.

The shaman stopped humming and said, "Burn some calf's ear." Calf's ear was one of the plants that he burned. I got it out of the bag and put it into the fire-blackened pot. I lit it from the stove and set it on the bare floor in the middle of the room. The shaman motioned for me to bring it closer to the bed. Calf's ear smells bitter, but it was a cleaner smell than the stink of the dying woman. It burned out after a moment, but the bitterness lingered a bit.

I didn't know what calf's ear would do to help her dying. It didn't make trances.

The woman's breath bubbled and rumbled in her chest, and I tried not to listen. Her son went out. The wind rushed in the door and then was cut off. A shuttle passed overhead, and the walls and floor shook around us. A dish on the table rattled.

The way the drum worked was this. It played the same thing for a while, and then it did something a little different. Then it went back to what it had been doing. Then the different thing. You had to listen for the different thing. You had to follow the sound of the drum. But it was hard to concentrate on the sound of the drum when I could hear the woman's drowning breath.

The door opened after a while and two women came in. One of the women sat at the dying person's feet, so I knew that was the daughter, getting ready to go with the dying woman as far as she could.

I wished for something to drink. I didn't even smell death anymore, but I could still hear the dying woman's breathing.

"Get me some bellflower," the shaman said.

I found a little wood jar of bellflower. It was a medicine, really strong. For heart, the shaman had told me. It was an old medicine and since the shaman didn't have a garden, once it was gone, it was gone, unless he could find a place to plant his seeds.

His bellflower was a paste; he had already made medicine from it. The paste was blackened on top. "Scrape the top off, but don't get it on your fingers," he said. There was a piece of straw just for that. I scraped the hardened stuff off the top very carefully.

The shaman stopped playing the drum then. I didn't have a drum, so it was silent then in the room. The shaman smelled the paste and then, using the straw, put some on the woman's lips. Then he went back to playing the drum.

Her bright eyes watched him, but she didn't try to talk. She didn't even ask for water.

Her son came with another man and a woman. He got her things out of a drawer—a beaten metal bowl and spoon, a dress with blue and red embroidery, and a pair of beautiful red and black boots. He got her a necklace of yellow beads. Her daughter got her a pot to cook in and a blanket to be buried in. She had a needle and thread. They put the things on the bed, piling them against the wall to get ready to send her off with the things she needed. She looked at the people when they put something on the bed, and then she looked back at the shaman or at me. When she looked at me I closed my eyes and listened to the drum.

She had more things than my mother, who only had someone else's pants.

It was dark in the room. There was only one window, and I couldn't see it from where I was sitting on the floor.

It took hours while the shuttles rumbled overhead. Sometimes the other people hummed with us and sometimes they didn't. I knew I wasn't allowed to stop humming. After a while I realized that I was listening to the drum, not her breathing. Her breathing was more quiet and her eyes were half open now. She was dreaming from the bellflower, I thought. I hoped there was enough bellflower that she would dream all the way.

I don't know when she died, only that she was dead when the shaman stopped. The daughter wailed, sending her own spirit after her mother's, the way my mother wailed when my father died.

Someone brought us tea. My throat was so dry I couldn't even say thank you.

The room was full of people. A woman had a baby on her hip, and the little girl was fussy. The son and daughters asked everyone to go outside. Then the shaman and I burned more calf's ear while they dressed the old woman's wasted body in the embroidered dress and fine boots. They wrapped her in the blanket and laid all her things on the bed.

People came back inside. The shaman carried a third pot of calf's ear around the room, wafting the bitter smoke. We had never done that at the Mission. I didn't know if it was because people from the coast did things different or because JohnKisu just didn't do it.

The shaman said, "Bitter smoke."

The daughter was wailing. Some people took us outside and down the steps. The sky was pink where the sun had set, and it was already night on the other side of the horizon.

"Uncle," said a man, "you will come and eat with us."

We went to another place, as mean as the first one but a little larger and full of people. There were children in Taufzinner clothes, except the clothes were all either too big or too small. Everybody was dressed in refugee combinations of clansman clothes and Taufzinner clothes, and it made them all look kinless.

The shaman sat down and they talked about kin. They were all coastal people, of course, so I wasn't close kin to anyone. I didn't even know most of the clan names they were using. I sat quiet and ate soup that was too salty. The shaman wasn't talking to me anyway. He was still mad at me because I'd argued with him.

We had to stop talking every time a shuttle rumbled overhead. We all sat there, made mute and stupid by the noise.

I wondered if the doctor at the factory would have been able to help the old woman. Probably. If they could turn me into a man, surely they could have helped the old woman. I knew better than to say anything. The shaman would have just smacked me and these people couldn't have afforded to get a doctor who did offworld medicine. Clanspeople lived in Taufzin like poor relations.

This is how I would have ended up if I hadn't met Mika.

The shaman had appeared tireless while he was singing the old woman's spirit out and at dinner, but as soon as we got on the bus he started nodding. We were coming back out the next day to meet more people. I was angry. It was my weekend and Mika had kept me up all night Friday and now the shaman was going to work me Saturday and Sunday.

I thought about not going back. The shaman would be mad, but I had been surrounded by my own people the whole afternoon and I felt just as strange there as I did anywhere. They spoke my language, but they weren't my kin. And they lived like bafits in the corner of this city, feeding off scraps.

The night was clear and cold. The stars were far away. The air was so cold you could feel it inside your nose. At least once I got to Mika's I wouldn't have to go back outside to pee or worse, to get water. I missed the Mission but I didn't miss everything about it.

The shuttleport was not a place for a person.

It was good to be at our own bus stop, in front of the shop that cleaned people's clothes and down the street from Mika's apartment. I woke the shaman up and followed him off the bus.

There were people standing outside Mika's building, and there were two police cars and some police.

"Uncle," I said, "I think you should wait."

He frowned at me. "Wait for what?"

"There might be some trouble at Mika's."

I thought he was going to cuff me for a moment, but instead he sighed. "Go take care of it," he said.

I went up to the building, but when I tried to go in, one of the police stopped me.

"I live in here," I said.

"Where?" the police said.

I told them on the top floor.

He asked me something in Taufzin about Mika Tatason. He was nice enough but a little sharp.

"Ich spreche neine deutsch," I said, meaning I didn't speak Taufzin language.

They took the shaman and me and put us in one of their cars. I rode in a car for the second time in two days but this one smelled of sweat and coffee over the offworld odor of the material of the seats and floor.

"Where are we going?" the shaman asked.

"They are taking us to prison," I said. It was about the disks, I was certain.

"Because of Mika?" the shaman asked.

I nodded.

The shaman looked away and out the window.

"I'll tell them you had nothing to do with it," I said.

The shaman didn't answer.

The police station was large and cold. We parked in the back of the building, in a place where the cars were fenced in, and climbed steps up to an outside door. I didn't understand why there would be a door like that, but mostly I was worrying about the shaman. He was tired and his feet weren't steady.

We sat on a hard bench for a long time, until I finally took off my jacket and made a place for the shaman's head. He lay down on the bench with his legs folded, because there wasn't enough room. I sat on the floor.

I watched the clock. We waited for over two hours. It was almost three hours, each as slow as the long hour at work, before a policewoman stopped and said that we should come with her. I woke the shaman and helped him up, and we followed the policewoman to a room. There was a clanswoman in the room, a girl like Sissela, who was really more of the city than the clans.

The policewoman sat down and said something to the girl, and the girl asked us if we would like something to drink. She gave us sweet cold drinks. I opened the shaman's because he wasn't used to the containers. A policeman came in and sat down and said something to the girl and she said, "Do you know Mika Tatason?"

"I know Mika," I said. "I, um, I mean, we are staying at his apartment."

She asked us our names and the shaman told her he was JohnPekka of Nordstord clan. It was the first time I had ever heard his name.

The policeman said something to the girl, and she asked me how we had come to be staying with Mika. Did we know if Mika ever bought or sold drugs? When I said I didn't know, the policewoman said something and the girl said not to worry, we would not be in trouble if we told them about the drugs. So I said that he had. She asked if he had argued with anyone and I said no.

"Did anyone want to hurt him?" the policewoman asked through the girl.

I shook my head.

"Mika Tatason was shot in the head and killed in his apartment this evening," the policeman said through the girl.

I believed it the moment they told me. I wanted to tell them about Dolf, but I was afraid, so I said nothing, and after a while, they let us go outside.

We went back to the house of the dead woman. I wasn't sure I could find it, but I found the street because at the corner there was a little shop and it had a sign that glowed blue. The snow drifted in the streetlight and everything shivered in the sound of the shuttle. The shaman was stumbling on his feet.

I wouldn't have found the house if it hadn't been for kin visiting the family of the dead woman. They saw us and came to us.

"Uncle, you've come back," said a man.

"The man we were staying with," I said, "someone has killed him." Then I had to hide my face in the crook of my arm because tears choked me.

"Uncle," they said to the shaman, "are you all right?"

The shaman put his hand on top of my head. He had never been kind to me that way before.

They took us to the house of the dead woman. She was laid out on the bed, dressed in her things. We were given the son's room, where he and his wife usually slept. I lay down on the floor. Maybe he wasn't dead. Maybe he'd been shot and he needed a doctor. The floor vibrated like a drum under my head. I tried to tell myself that Mika might be all right. I tried to sleep. It was never really dark in the city. The artificial light rose up from the ground outside the window, and I buried my face in my arm and cried from tiredness.

People came to see the shaman the next day.

On Monday I went to work. The shuttleport was so far from my work that it took two hours and I had to change buses twice. I was an hour late for work and I got a warning from my supervisor. In the evening I took the disks out of my locker. At one of the places where I changed buses there was a restaurant, and behind the restaurant was a big trash container painted green. I threw the disks in the trash container. They had killed Mika, and if I kept them, they would kill other people.

I didn't get home until very late and then I overslept and missed the early bus. I was so tired, I didn't go to work. It had been so hard to always be on time and always do the right thing. I let the job go like water through my fingers. That day and the next, I assisted the shaman.

I wasn't very good at it. I was nervous all the time from the noise, the sound of the shuttles shaking all my bones. Everybody had to talk loud all the time. Mothers were always sharp with their children and everyone was on edge. It was no place for a human to be. Worse than the camp, I thought.

I kept thinking I saw my father or Teija, my little sister. Especially Teija. She was in the street, playing with the other children. She was dirty and running without a coat in the slush, laughing or crying—but it wasn't her. Or she was squatting in the gutter, using a twig to draw channels in the mud for the water to seep through, and she looked up at me and looked back down, utterly absorbed—but it wasn't her. Every time I mistook someone for her, the fear ran through my body like pain and I started inside myself. But worse than the fear was the realization that it wasn't her.

Clanspeople came from all over the city to see the shaman. They paid him. I was running out of money, but now the shaman took care of me. We moved into a place over a shop that sold whiskey and coffee. It was smaller than Mika's place had been, only a bedroom, a bathroom, and a big room with the stove and an old red couch. I slept on the floor of the big room at night, and during the day the shaman saw people there.

One day a man brought his son. The boy was about as tall as my shoulder, not yet grown but starting to get longer in the leg. He was healthy. "Maybe," the man said to the shaman, "he could give you another set of hands?"

I expected the shaman to say that he already had me, but he didn't. And after that, Sorj slept on the old red couch, except on weekends when he went home to his family. He spoke the language of the Taufzin people, and although he understood a lot of what we said, he didn't speak enough of our language for me to talk to him. Besides, he was a little boy—what was there for me to say to him?

Living over the whiskey store was hard because I had no money. I had nothing, in fact. The shaman never gave me anything except the money to go buy us food. One day the man who owned the whiskey store asked me if I would watch the store for him for an hour. I did, and when he came back he paid me, so I could buy some whiskey. After that he would ask me once or twice a week. But the shaman would take the money from me if he found out, so I always bought whiskey before I went back upstairs.

All through the gray spring I was afraid of catching a glimpse of my sister, or even once in a while, my father. I finally told the shaman. "Where is your mother?" he asked.

That night I had a nightmare. I was in the apartment, standing at the door. To leave our apartment, you went out the door and there was a long set of stairs on the outside of the house. They were wooden and they had old bits of paint still stuck in places. In my dream it was too dark to see to the bottom of the stairs, but I knew my mother was down there in the dark. In my dream, I was afraid to go down the steps. I knew it was my mother and

I knew that it was terrible, and I woke up and got my whiskey bottle from under the couch and drank some until I could go back to sleep.

The next night I dreamed I was dead. I was lying on the couch in my things and the shaman was spirit-talking for a woman. Sorj was holding the pot with the calf's ear leaves burning in it. Everything was rumbling with the constant sound of the shuttles going overhead. I woke up on the floor, and the shuttles were rumbling overhead. Sorj was asleep on the couch, curled with the covers half off him and the bones of his spine showing under his skin.

I couldn't tell any difference between being dead in my dream and alive when I was awake. I thought it was a true dream. I was afraid to go to the bottom of the stairs, but I couldn't stay here anymore.

The shaman would tell me that wasn't what the dreams meant, but I didn't care. I got my few clothes and the little bit of money I had, then I covered Sorj so he wouldn't be cold. And I went down the stairs and into the night.

My dream took me a long way away. It took me years away. I worked a few years as a security person on an ore train. It wasn't like Taufzin. They didn't much care who you were. After a while I stopped thinking that Dorf would be there one day, but everywhere I went I could see offworld things changing people. Offworld people didn't mean to, but everything they touched was changed and I didn't like it. After five years I quit the job on the train and started walking to a place where there would be no offworlders. It was a long walk.

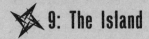 **9: The Island**

I WAS NEVER MEANT TO LIVE IN A PLACE SO hot as it was in the southern islands. The coolest place I could find was down on the docks, and since I had no work, I had a lot of time to sit there. I would sit in the sun and watch the boats with their saffron- and rose-colored sails and imagine that the breeze made me cooler. I hadn't had any work in days and hadn't had anything to eat for a while. I was sitting there, feeling hungry, and a woman stopped and tossed a copper coin at me.

"Are you blind?" she asked. "Do you tell fortunes?"

"Not blind," I said. "Blue eyes. I am a foreigner." I had learned how to say "foreigner" pretty quickly.

She squatted so her dress, which was about the same rose color as some of the sails, dragged in the dust. She stared into my eyes, frowning. "How can you see?"

"The same as you," I said.

Nobody had ever thought I had cataracts before. At least, if they had, they hadn't mentioned it. She had black eyes and yellow-gold skin. Like many of the people on the island, she looked as if she could have been kin to my old teachers, Wanji and Ayudesh. I felt she was a little put out that I could see.

"You're not an old man," she said, accusatory. "You're young."

Depended on what you thought of as young. "Do you want your coin?" I offered it back to her.

She hesitated only an instant and then shook her head. I already regretted offering it back, so I was relieved.

"So what is my fortune?" she asked.

It is hard to be mentally nimble when you haven't been eating well. I closed my eyes and tried to think of something valuable to say. "This thing that is troubling you," I finally said, "is at end soon, but for a great price. You think the price is more than you can pay, but in many tomorrows, it is a small price."

That seemed to satisfy her, or at least she seemed to think that she had gotten her money's worth. She straightened in a swirl of dyed cotton and the rattle of her many gold bracelets. I found it hard to use the language to talk about things that were going to happen, but I hoped that my mangling made it all sound more mystical.

After she had gone I sat there and thought about maybe trying to tell fortunes. It was either that or sell my rifle. I had bought the rifle four years ago in New Steubendorf because it reminded me of Aslak's rifle and because I had the money. It was hidden in some weeds behind a godown right now because I was broke and sleeping unclean.

The island of Hainandao was not the place I had thought it was going to be. There weren't many offworlders here, but there was no place for a blond clansman to get work, either.

It was easy to sit there and contemplate telling fortunes. I thought of mystical things to say. *You will be good to a person, and when you are in need that kindness will come back to you. You must be patient and not take the first thing offered.*

There was a ship with a great sail out in the water. The sail was a purple so deep that either it was new or the ship's owner was wealthy. I thought it might be a good-sized ship, but I didn't have much eye for that kind of thing. Island ships had eyes painted on the prows. The better to watch for shoals, I supposed.

Shipping was very controlled. Little fishermen could sail some, but they never went very far, and the bigger ships were all run by the navigation orders. Navigation orders were a kind of religion, I thought. But my command of the language was indifferent and it was hard to be sure.

The ship flashed suddenly with an unnatural light. I blinked and everything was as it was before. Great purple sail. Then the flash again.

The ship got closer, and I saw it was a huge three-masted thing. I couldn't make out people yet. It flashed again, light reflecting off metal so bright it made me think of offworlders. The islanders called the offworlders "the cousins" because they said that since we had come from their world so many years ago, even though we had lost touch, they had come back. I thought the islanders had a strange sense of kin.

I clasped my hands around my knees and watched the slow business of bringing the ship to dock. Whatever was making the flash was mounted on the mast. The ship was an island ship, made of wood like every other ship on the water here, but one of the people standing on the deck was in coveralls, which meant an offworlder woman. Her face, turned up, was as white as mine would have been if I hadn't spent so much time unclean, but her hair was darker, although not as dark as an islander's.

I watched her get off in a crowd of high members of some navigation order. They all had heads shaved almost bare except for a long tail of hair in the back. A lot of people had stopped to watch the procession down the wharf.

For no reason I can explain, as the offworlder passed, I said in English, "Good afternoon."

One of the order members swung around to kick me and I scuttled a bit away, but the woman held up her hand. "What did you say?" she asked.

"I say good afternoon," I said.

"Good afternoon," she said. "You speak English."

"A little," I said. It had been a long time since my English lessons in Taufzin.

"What's your name?" she asked.

"Jan," I said.

"Jan what?"

"Jan Hamra," I said. "What is your name?"

"Natalia Bodinskaya," she said. I knew that I would not be able to repeat it, much less remember it. "Where did you learn English?"

"Hamra Mission," I said. "And a—" I had to grope for the word "—a factory."

"What are you doing here?" she asked.

I was aware of what I looked like—after all, I'd just been mistaken for a beggar. What *was* I doing here? I gave her an old answer. "Putting off death." It struck me as funny, so I laughed.

One of the priests or whatever they were kicked out at me. "Show respect," he said in island speech.

"No," she said in island speech, motioning at him to stop. Then to me in English, "What was this place, Hamra Mission?"

"It was an appropriate technology mission."

"Wait," she said. "Hamra. Almost everyone was killed there. Years ago."

"Yes," I said.

"You speak English," she said. "You don't have to be like this."

I laughed again, but it sounded different even to my ears. Bitter. "Offworlder, I have worked in a factory. I have lived in a, what do you say, a slum? A slum. Here is good, thank you."

She reached in her pocket and tossed a coin at me, a silver bar. More money than I had seen in a long time. I let it lie in the dust. She was doing to me what offworlders did to all of us. It was offworlders who had created the Mission. Offworlders who made the guns available that killed us. It was offworlders who put us in refugee camps and fed us like pets. It was offworlders who kept clansmen in houses near the shuttleport where the sounds rattled the dishes on the tables. It was offworlders who made the market for ore so that Menno people worked in the mines and got metal poisoning from the quicksilver used to extract the metal. Here was an offworlder, faced with a problem, and all she could think to do was throw me a piece of silver.

But after they had walked on, I picked up the silver piece. I was not so proud.

The roads were full of midday traffic—people on foot, some with poles over their shoulders to carry buckets, donkeys in the road, the occasional bicycle.

In the market I headed for the food. There was a man
selling bright green wedges of pineapple on skewers. I'd
had them, dipped in saltwater to add an edge to the sweet-
ness, and the thought of them made my mouth water, but
I passed him up for chapati and dal.

I bought a bowl of spicy dal and vegetables and chapati
with green onions and ate it slowly. After I ate I went
down to the godowns and snuck around and checked my
rifle. My constant fear was that some children would find
it. It was wrapped with my last box of ammunition in
some offworld plastic, and the whole bundle was taped up
and buried in the ground right under a large black scrape
on the wall. Where I had buried it I had piled up trash.
The trash was undisturbed.

I walked away from the docks and into the stifling heat
of the town. The heat was hard to carry around, and it
made me tired. I found the bar where Ahi was. His bicycle
was tied up tight to a bicycle post. I would check with
Ahi because Ahi was a job finder. If he didn't have any
work for me I planned to buy a bottle.

Ahi was a pretty good-sized man. He wore a white
cotton shirt that was so thin I could see the color of his
skin through it. He looked up at me. He had a round face.
"Jan," he said. "Where have you been? I have a job if
you want one."

"A job?" I said.

"Yes, you unclean piece of trash," he said, "a job."

I didn't ask Ahi for work because he liked me.
"Doing what?"

"Guarding a boat."

"Okay," I said. The offworlder's silver was burning a
hole in my pocket, but Ahi wouldn't let me buy a drink
if he had a job for me. "Should I go get my rifle?"

"Get it," he said, and turned his back on me.

The rifle was probably the only reason that Ahi ever
offered to find me a job, and he found me damn few. Guns
were rare because offworld things had to be approved in
the islands. Islanders weren't supposed to have guns. I
could have one because I was a big-nosed, hairy blond
foreigner. The other people who Ahi found jobs for were
unclean people. They mostly lived at the west end of the

island. Unclean people were almost invisible to everyone else—unlike me; I was more like some exotic animal wandering around. Unclean people couldn't buy things at the market, no one would sell them anything. Unclean people didn't have guns because they didn't have money.

Ahi was a person in no-man's-land. He hired unclean people to do things no real person would do. Bad things. Against-the-rules things. But Ahi was a real person. Not much of a real person though, mostly people treated him with contempt. He, of course, treated us with contempt.

I went and got my rifle and the box of ammunition. When I got back, there were two unclean men sitting against the wall. The man who owned the bar wouldn't let them in. They glanced up at me and then went back to contemplating their feet or the dirt street.

Ahi said, "Come on."

We walked inland, away from the ocean: first Ahi, who didn't look behind him to see if we were following, then the unclean men, then me.

We tramped alongside a canal full of boats. Whole families lived on the boats. They were different from Ahi and the unclean men; they had strange eyes that folded and paler skins. I watched the children, mostly. The youngest ones had big hollow gourds tied around their waists, as floats, I guessed, in case they fell off. The older ones leaped from boat to boat, playing between them like we played between houses when I was growing up. The boats were small compared to the big purple- and rose-sailed ships in the harbor. The single masts were mostly bare, and the few sails that were tied around the rigging were faded so much that they were soft and rotten looking. The canal smelled of sewage, and sometimes, as we'd pass a boat, the brief sharp scent of a meal cooking, of meat and peanuts and onions and oil.

Oh, I was hungry again.

Ahi stopped for a moment and then climbed down into a boat. We followed. The boat rocked slightly. It appeared to be empty and we crossed it to another boat. A man and a woman were crouched at the prow of this boat and they watched us, flat-faced. The third boat was bigger than the first two, and we had to climb up to it.

This boat was of enough size that there was living space below. A big man came out, followed by a girl in a school uniform. The man looked over us and rubbed his hands together. "Good," he said. "Good."

"The foreigner has a rifle," Ahi said.

"Eh?" said the big man. "Let's see it."

I squatted and unwrapped the rifle.

He held out his hand, but I shook my head. "Careful," I said. It wasn't loaded, but islanders didn't know anything about rifles. I didn't let anyone touch it anyway.

The big man put his fists on his hips. His robe was open far enough to show a big belly and a smooth hairless chest with flabby breasts. "I am Kushio-shian," he said. "Shian" meant "sir."

The girl was watching. She looked old enough to have her menses. Her school uniform was the rose color of one of the navigation orders. It was high-waisted and too little-girlish for her, it strained across her chest. She was pretty in a sullen sort of way, standing there barefoot with one foot curled. I wondered what she was doing here.

He paid Ahi and told us we'd get five coppers cash for the night's work. He was going to be discussing a business deal and we were to guard the boat.

As far as I could tell there was nothing to guard on the boat. I didn't like this. I had assumed that we'd be guarding a cargo hold, like the work I did for the train, years ago. I thought about leaving.

Kushio-shian said to the girl, "Get them some dinner."

I was too easily swayed by my stomach to listen to my head. It's bad when your stomach thinks for you.

The girl brought us bowls of vegetables and grain with some chicken in it. The islanders have a vegetable called paprikeen that I really like. It's an onworld vegetable, not one that is poisonous but empty of nourishment, so you can eat it and eat it and still starve to death. It has a hot sweet taste better and hotter than any onion and more savory than a chili. I could smell it even before the girl gave me my bowl.

We squatted there to eat.

"Why don't you have a beard?" the girl asked. Islanders think that northerners are all hairy as termagents.

"Why don't you?" I asked.

"Because I'm a girl," she said. "Stupid." She watched me eat. I don't know if she expected me to eat differently than she did. Islanders eat with their fingers or with bread like chapati or naan. They only use their right hand, and they do it in a very special way which is kind of elegant once you get used to it.

"You need to wash," she said.

I nodded. I did.

"Where are you from?" she asked.

"A place very far north," I said, "where it snows all winter long. I come from a village called Hamra. It's gone now."

"What happened?" she said.

"There was a war. Everyone in the village died." The food was really good, much better than the dal I'd had in the market.

"Do you want some pineapple?" she asked.

"Yes, please," I said. She didn't offer any to the unclean men. They didn't seem to expect much. The pineapple was sweet.

"Ming Wei," Kushio-shian called. "What are you doing?"

"I'm here, uncle," she said. She didn't say "uncle" like she was being respectful but as if that was who Kushio-shian was.

He came out of the hold. "Did you get them something to eat?" he asked.

Her face was sullen again. She stood oddly flirtatiously, the heel of one foot against the instep of the other, her face turned away and her hair in her eyes. She was too old to go around with her hair down like a little girl. She leaned and spat over the side of the boat. I winced. They spat a lot here, and I hadn't gotten used to it.

"Come on," Kushio-shian said, "you don't need to be hanging around them." She followed him down into the hold. I didn't envy her, the hold was stuffy and the afternoon was clear.

One of the unclean persons was looking at my rifle. "Can I see it?" he asked.

"No," I said.

*   *   *

When it got dark the fat merchant came out and lit
lanterns—a momentary strong scent of the oil, and the
light flared and then dimmed a bit and shadows jiggered
on the deck. I loaded my rifle.

I was expecting the guests to come the way we did, so
when something thunked against the hull my first thought
was that some dimwit in a boat had run into it.

"Hallo," called a voice from the water.

"Get the rope ladder," Kushio-shian said to me.

The top part of the ladder was wood and it hooked over
the side of the boat. Below, in the water, was a single-
masted sailboat with its sail glowing golden in the light
of the lantern on the mast. A young man with a shaved
head was looking up at me. He wore a robe that left one
shoulder bare. It was the same color as the sail. He was
a member of one of the navigation orders. The one that
wore gold, obviously. I thought people like him were sort
of like shaman's boys but the way people talked about the
navigation orders, sometimes they sounded like worship
and sometimes they sounded like businesses.

I dropped the end of the ladder down to him. He held
a hand out to help another man and then knelt and put
the man's foot on the ladder. "Up with you," said the
young man in gold, and carefully guided the other man's
feet up the ladder. Kushio-shian was waiting at the top to
help the man.

The guest wasn't a member of an order, at least not as
far as I could tell. He was a little pale man wearing gray
and green who was one of the people who looked kin
to Wanji and Ayudesh. He didn't seem to be very good
in boats.

"What are you staring at?" he asked me.

"I am admiring your appearance, sir," I said and
bowed.

Kushio-shian snarled at me.

I had been polite. At least, I thought I had. Maybe I'd
been presumptuous. Maybe I was furniture and not supposed to talk. What the hell, I was foreign.

They had barely gotten into the hold when three more
men came across the boats and gangways.

Kushio-shian came halfway up and said, "You," pointing to me, "bring them down and don't talk to them."

"Yes, Kushio-shian," I said. I waited at the gangplank, trying to look as respectful as possible, and gestured for them to climb the steps down into the hold.

It was not a very big space, and out of the breeze it was close. Kushio-shian pointed to a spot beside the door, so I stood there. I envied the unclean men stuck on the deck. He sat behind a table that took up much of the space in the room. The man from the boat sat next to him. Ming Wei had changed out of the too-small school uniform, and now that she was dressed in dark red and indigo she seemed more grown-up. She glanced at me. I winked at her. She frowned and looked away.

The four businessmen sat down to eat in the stifling hold. Ming Wei poured wine for the men and put food on their plates. They talked about business and about buying and selling. I could understand a good bit of the language, but the talk was flowing too fast for me. I didn't even try. I just watched the one that had come up from the boat— the thin pale one in gray and green—and I noticed that he didn't drink very much.

Ming Wei drank some, more than was good for a girl. She needed someone to take her in hand. She was not being brought up properly at all.

I still didn't know what I was supposed to guard. The boat was bare of valuables and even though the boat itself was probably worth something, the little man in green and gray didn't seem likely to hoist it on his back and run off with it. Kushio-shian was vain. I supposed I was here as a sop to his vanity.

Five coppers wasn't bad, and with a meal thrown in, it was wonderful. I decided I would try a little harder to be properly respectful to Kushio-shian's guests. Maybe I could convince him that having a foreigner for a guard was exotic. I crossed my arms and shoved my fists under my biceps in a mildly laughable attempt to look like more muscle for the money. The rifle was better for that than any muscular show I was likely to make.

At five coppers a day I would be able to get off this

island in about four years. Kushio-shian would have to have a party every night. I wanted a drink.

The stuff they drank here was awful—clear and raw tasting like green whiskey. What I should do is save up enough money to build a little still. Then I could make money. I didn't know if I could even put a still together. Working with my mam and actually doing it myself were two different things. If the whiskey wasn't done right it could make you blind or kill you.

They were tossing off toasts to each other, calling "bottom of your cup" and drinking liquor down. At least Ming Wei wasn't doing that. There was a puddle of liquor at the gray and green man's feet, although I couldn't see how he was spilling it instead of drinking it. But Kushio-shian's was all going into that big belly.

Kushio-shian was quite drunk and red-faced and so was at least one of the other men.

Ming Wei stood up and cleared the table. She swayed a little on her feet, and the color was high in her face, too.

"So, Kushio-da," said the little man in gray and green, "you have something to show us?"

That seemed a little rude—besides the "Kushio-da," which meant "big Kushio"—there didn't seem to have been enough time for polite talk. Kushio-shian rumbled a bit in his chest. "I have," he said. "I have. A little something. Maybe not so little."

"You said you have charts," one of the other men said.

Charts? All shipping was controlled by the navigation orders, and charts were illegal. Having a chart could get you executed, if you were caught. Ming Wei brought back four long rolls of paper, and Kushio took one and unrolled it on the table, weighting the ends with a wine jug and glasses. I craned to see.

"What is this?" asked the little man in gray and green.

"Yueguang Straits," one of the other men said, reading the characters scrawled down the side. I couldn't read their language. Every word had a different symbol, and they all looked like bird tracks to me.

"How accurate is it?" asked the man in gray and green.

"It is accurate. It is yours," Kushio-shian said. "You,"

he nodded toward the man in gray and green, "you take it. Show it to your captains."

The little man hiked an eyebrow.

They pored over the four charts, asking questions about draft and depth. Kushio-shian couldn't answer them. "This is the best I can get, I am afraid," he said. "But you can use them, yes? And as I get more, if you find these valuable, you'll be interested."

"These are Hongde," gray and green said. Hongde was one of the navigation orders, the one that wore rose. "I recognize the style," the man said. "See the way the headland is marked for shoals? Hongde does it that way, with the lines that way. Qingde does it with lots of tiny little rocks."

Ming Wei was stealing them. She had to be. She wore a rose school uniform.

I was trying to think, furiously trying to. Maybe with these men I could get off the island. The little man in gray and green, he'd come on a navigation order ship— but anyone could hire one. I couldn't put it all together because I didn't understand enough about these people. I was such a foreigner.

The men gathered up their charts and went up on deck. Kushio-shian watched them off with satisfaction.

"I wish you hadn't given them away," Ming Wei said.

I did some ditch digging for Ahi. My back ached afterward. Days went past. I hid my rifle in a new place, still wrapped up in offworld plastic. I bought a bottle of the local whiskey and then another. I slept in a rented bed for a while, until my money was short and I decided to hoard the rest for food rather than shelter.

Then one morning Ahi told me that the fat merchant had asked for me. I refrained from remarking that Ahi was not so small himself. Just as no one is faster to note falsehood than a liar, few were more sensitive to observations about their size than Ahi.

Kushio-shian was awake and sitting on deck. He had hired a barber, who was working on him. His hair was wet and shining and smelled faintly of some oil. Kushio-shian didn't wear his hair in a braid; it wasn't long enough.

The barber was shaving the fine hairs from his high fore-head. The first thing Kushio-shian said to me was, "Where is your rifle?"

"I did not bring it, sir, but I can go and get it," I said.

"I am having guests tonight," he said. "For ten fen, you will guard."

I bowed and went to fetch my rifle.

"Here are two fen against your pay," he said. "Get yourself cleaned up."

In the market some yammerhead was giving a speech about the offworlders and how they were evil because they meant to defile the purity of the social order. He was right that they were evil, but he was wrong about how. If he saw me, his harangue would probably include the pernicious influence of foreigners, so I ducked between two tables selling cotton cloth. I found a seller of second-hand clothes and bought a black cotton jacket with a high collar to hide my lack of adam's apple. Since I had gotten the implant, back in Taufzin oh so many years ago, my arms and legs were thin but muscled and stringy and my face, when I had an opportunity to see my reflection, was harder and leaner, although some of that may just have been age. One nice thing was that I didn't bleed each month anymore.

It was easy to pass for a man, as long as I stayed clothed. I had been doing it so long that I didn't think of myself as a woman anymore. I didn't really think of my-self as a man, either. I was just me, whatever that was.

I took my second-hand clothes—besides the jacket I had found a narrow gray robe—and spent another two coins on a private bath. The bath house attendant braided my hair as if I were a gentleman. It wasn't really very long but long enough for a decent braid.

I went back to the boat, and not long after Ming Wei came down the road that ran alongside the canal. I watched her dawdling along the stone wall, stopping to spit into the water below. She trailed her finger along the wall. The breeze kicked up cat's paws on the open water on the other side of the boats. She was a pretty thing when she didn't know anyone was watching.

When she got to the place where she would come across, she stood for a moment, doing nothing, looking at nothing, a study. Her uncle called, "Ming Wei?" Her face clouded over and she got that sullen look that made her so odd.

She stood at the edge of the gangway, her bare toes curled in, and sulked.

"Ming Wei," he called again.

"What?" she said.

"Come down here."

It made me glad I wasn't a parent.

"What?" she asked.

Eventually she came back up and brought me a bowl of vegetables and grain and some flatbread to eat it with. She sat on the edge of the rail and watched me eat.

"You look different," she said.

"I'm older," I said.

She didn't quite know what to make of that, so she ignored it. "You look more like a regular person."

"Thank you."

"But you talk funny."

"Yes," I agreed. "I do. You have no manners."

That took her aback. She frowned at me. "I do, too," she said. "Better than a foreigner who doesn't know how to eat."

I laughed. "I can eat. You think I am hungry?"

"You show your teeth when you eat," she said.

"You tell other people they are wrong."

"But I am helping you. And you aren't a person, anyway."

"Ah. I am foreigner," I said.

"Right," she said.

I laughed at that, too.

She was discomforted, and she looked out across the water, but she didn't leave. "What is it like, where you're from?"

"It's cold," I said.

"I know. You told me before that it snows in the winter. I've never seen snow."

"It's pretty," I said, "but too cold. We have animals. Renndeer."

She didn't know what a renndeer was, and I lurched and stumbled through a bad explanation. I hadn't had a lot of reason to talk about toes and ear fringes and my vocabulary wasn't up to it.

"Why did you leave?" she asked.

"People come, soldiers, and kill everyone. My mother, my father, my little sister. Only I'm alive. I and my friend Aslak. So we leave."

"What happened to your friend?"

"He's dead," I said. "Everyone's dead. Except me. I am not good enough to die."

She laughed but I didn't, and that made her even more uncomfortable. So she stood up and went to the other side of the boat and eventually across the boats to the shore where another girl her age was waiting.

Had I ever been so young?

By dusk she was back and went below deck to change. Kushio-shian came up and lit the lanterns. I stood in the faint night breeze. It was the same as before. First the bump on the side of the boat, and I let the ladder down and helped the gentleman up. As far as I could tell, it was even the same young man in his golden robe in the boat below. Then the other guests—only two this time, the big man who had gotten drunk wasn't there—coming across the boats and gangplanks from the shore. I took them below and took my place by the door.

There were no unclean men to guard with me. They hadn't done anything but stand on deck anyway.

My jacket was too warm and my robe stuck to my back. I kept thinking I'd get used to the heat, but I didn't. Tonight the little sharp man who'd come on the boat was wearing white cotton, and he looked cooler than any of the rest of us. I had a headache. I had headaches a lot lately, from the heat, I was pretty sure. I watched the parade of dishes: vegetables in garam masala and milk, pancakes wrapped around onions stained purple red by spicy paprikeen, little pillows of dough stuffed with beans and dried fruit, garlic and more paprikeen.

I thought of snow. Of winter. Ming Wei poured wine and the dinner droned on. I thought about whiskey and about the pleasant dizzy feeling when I had drunk enough that I couldn't stay awake. I thought of sleep.

Finally, dinner was cleared away.

Kushio-shian had every appearance of being a man who could not hold his wine. Ming Wei was red-faced, too. The sharp-faced man sat with his feet in a puddle of strong liquor, his face still sober and wicked.

"How were the charts?" Kushio-shian asked.

The sharp-faced man shrugged. "They were vague."

"But better than nothing, eh?"

One of the other men said, "I already have charts of this place. Yours are no better."

"I knew they weren't so valuable," Kushio-shian said, "but I gave them to you so you could check them against what you knew. That way you could see that I was giving you good charts. You don't have charts of Aohong, do you?" Kushio-shian grinned, his eyes almost disappearing in his red face. "Eh? You don't, do you? Do you? Ming Wei! Get the charts!"

Ming Wei cleared the dinner bowls and dishes first, swaying a little, and then brought in more rolls of paper.

The sharp-faced man leaned back and crossed his arms, all his body expressing his disinterest, but Kushio-shian didn't notice. Kushio-shian spread one of the charts out, pinning the edges with wine jug and glasses. "Look, eh, look. Isn't that nice," he said. "Isn't that a fine job?"

One of the other men couldn't hide his curiosity. He leaned forward, frowning with concentration. "Aohong?" he said.

"Can you get Lingbian coast?" the sharp-featured man asked.

"Lingbian?" Kushio-shian said. "Not yet. Not yet."

"When can you get it?"

"It's hard to say," Kushio-shian said. "It's very hard to say. I can only get things as they become available."

"How are you getting these?"

"Ah," Kushio-shian said, "if I told you that, then you would know, wouldn't you?" He grinned again. "But I have Aohong. If you don't need it yourself, you can certainly sell it to someone who could use it, ey?"

"If you sell these things to just anyone, then anyone can copy them and have them, right?"

"Yes," Kushio-shian said, "but I do not sell them to anyone. Only to you."

Sharp-faced man sighed and thought about that for a while. "I don't need Aohong," he said.

"But—" Kushio-shian said.

The sharp-faced man stopped him with a hand. "I know, I know. You say I can sell copies. You say perhaps Lao Ma, here," he indicated one of the other men, "old horseface might use it."

Kushio-shian did not know how to answer this. He wanted desperately to argue, but he didn't have words to put to use.

"I have to think," the sharp-faced man said. "What else can you get me?"

"This is all I can get now," Kushio-shian said. "This is all that . . . I can get."

"How long until you can get something else?"

"Maybe a month, maybe a little more."

My heart sank. That meant a month before he would hire me again. A month of occasional ditch-digging jobs from Ahi. I would starve. I could sell my rifle, but once I did that there would be no reason to hire me at all. That would be just putting off the inevitable.

Raised voices. "It's worth more than that!" Kushio-shian said. "You can sell it for more than that!"

"Not without a buyer," the little sharp-faced man said.

"But you wanted me to sell only to you and your partners."

I straightened up. I'd been leaning.

"I don't need Aohong," the sharp-faced man said. "I don't want to spend four hundred cash silver for something I don't need. When you have something I need, then I'll buy it."

"I will sell this to someone else!" Kushio-shian said.

"I wouldn't recommend it." The sharp-faced man got up and walked past me.

The other two sat for a moment, caught unexpectedly, then they scraped back their stools and followed him up and out onto the deck. I watched Kushio-shian to see if he wanted me to go up after them to see they got off, but he just sat there. After a moment he started calling them sons of poxed dogs, yellow-light bastards, the product of incest—one vile term after another delivered in a monotone.

Ming Wei sat there, staring at the table. I did my best to be a piece of furniture, deaf as the door, staring into the center of the room at nothing at all.

I slept on the deck of Kushio-shian's boat. He told me I would have work the next day and told me to get up there and closed the door behind me. It was no worse than where I usually slept, which was in some weeds behind a godown where they stored cotton bales.

Ming Wei crept out of the hold early the next morning. The mist hung above the dull water. She rinsed out her mouth with tea, spitting over the side, then did her hair back in a long tail. I pretended to be asleep.

A girl called her from the shore and she crossed the boats, barefoot and sure. I sat up and watched them go, both so alike from behind with their dark hair and school uniforms that I didn't know which was Ming Wei.

I was awake and very hungry when Kushio-shian finally got up and came out on the deck to perform his morning ablutions. He glanced at me once but then ignored me. He was in a foul mood, but whether he was usually in a foul mood in the morning or if this was the result of the night before I wasn't sure.

He came back dressed in a loose wine-colored robe, looking, if anything, more dissolute than he had the night before. He handed me a note written in the impossible writing of the islanders. "Take this to Wang Jiu," he said, and gave me an address.

I didn't have the vaguest idea where the address was, but it didn't seem good to ask, so I took the note, bowed, and got off the boat as quickly as I could.

No one recognized Wang Jiu's address. I finally went and asked Ahi, my job broker, which turned out to be lucky because Ahi knew the address.

"What are you doing skulking around neighborhoods like this?" he asked.

"I am working for Kushio-shian," I said.

Ahi grunted and heaved himself off the bench. "Come," he said.

I trotted along after his bicycle. He was kind enough to ride pretty slowly and even stopped once when I grew so breathless from exercise and heat that I thought I would be sick. For Ahi this was thoughtful. "Where are we?" I gasped when he shifted as if to start the bicycle moving again.

"Down there," he pointed, "that is where the unclean men live."

Down there was a ravine with shacks climbing down the sides. From where we stood I could see where the creek at the bottom of the ravine emptied into a flat marshy-looking area and beyond that, ocean. No place to put a garden, no place to get good water except perhaps the creek, and hundreds of shacks upstream fouling the water before it got to the marsh. I could smell it from here.

He pointed down the narrow street that ran along the ravine. "I live down that way." On the edge of where the unclean people lived. Bicycle or no bicycle, if he lived here, Ahi was barely a person. We turned the other way, inland and uphill. Of course, uphill.

We followed alongside an old wall, and when we got to a break, Ahi said, "Someone in there will tell you where you are going."

I stood for a moment, watching him ride off. I was sick from the heat and sweating so much that it stung in my eyes. I thought unkind thoughts about fat men on bicycles.

There was a whole neighborhood beyond the wall. Faces with folded eyes everywhere. I went down a half dozen steps into a street so narrow that Ahi would have had trouble negotiating it on his bicycle. Laundry was strung across the street above my head and almost no sun got down here. People stared at me, but I told myself I was used to that. I asked a girl where Wang Jiu's address was, but either my accent was too much for her or my appearance was, and she just looked at me without answering.

The next person I asked pointed mutely, and after that I went from one person to another. "That way." "Turn there." I went deeper into the maze of shadowed little streets and found, at the center of it, a circle door and a sleeping servant and beyond, a courtyard surrounded by the balconies of a stone two-story house. A strange place to put a house this nice.

Wang Jiu, I was told, was taking his little sleep, what they called the nap people took in the afternoon. I said I had to deliver my message to his hand. The servant nodded, staring at the rifle I wore slung over my back, and left me sitting on the worn stone bench in the courtyard. In the center of the courtyard, where I would have expected a tree or a fountain, was a rock with more islander writing on it. It wasn't a very big rock, not even as high as my knee, and it looked very small sitting there.

Wang Jiu, when he came out from his nap, was no taller than my shoulder. He was old, with a wispy bit of white beard on his chin, and slumped shoulders and a concave chest. "What are you?" he asked me when he saw me. For a brief moment I thought he had seen me as a woman, but then I realized he was a bit startled by my foreignness.

"I am employed by Kushio-shian," I said. "I have a message." I held out the note.

"What does it say?" he asked.

"I don't know," I said. "I don't read your language."

He sighed and called for a servant. The one at the gate, a man even older than Wang Jiu, shuffled in. Wang Jiu told him to bring his spectacles.

The servant didn't move very fast, so I suspected that we would have a bit of a wait.

"Do you know what that is?" Wang Jiu asked. I was staring at the rock.

"No, sir," I said.

"It's old," he said. "It's very old. It's from offworld. From the world of the cousins."

I wondered why the offworlders had brought him a rock. I couldn't imagine an offworlder here, but stranger things had happened.

"It has been in my family since we came here from there," Wang Jiu said. "It was in my family back there, on the world where we come from. We used it to remember that we were people of the middle kingdom, far from home. Do you know the story of how this island was settled?"

I didn't even bother to shake my head.

"We were a mixture of people from my home, the yinduren who are darker than us and don't eat meat and keep their cows holy, and people from islands close to us. Men from my homeland would go out of their homes for years and years and when they had money, go back home. It was a tradition. First they crossed oceans, eventually they crossed the stars. But when we got here, it was too far to go back home. Still," he pointed to the rock with his chin, "we remember. Other people mixed themselves together. But some of us remember we are middle kingdom people and we eat with kuazi, not our fingers, and we remember our grandfathers."

I didn't understand why he was telling me this, unless it was to put me in my uncivilized place, but I bowed.

The servant came out with a pair of spectacles. Wang Jiu put them on and held the note out at arm's length to read it.

"Tell Kushio-shian I will eat with him tonight," Wang Jiu said.

I bowed again. It took me forever to find my way out of the neighborhood.

The whole feeling of this dinner was different. From the moment the old man came down the gangplank, Kushio-shian was solicitous, holding his elbow and apologizing for the discomfort. Wang Jiu was either frail or allowed himself to be helped. Maybe it was an island custom, I didn't know. There was wine at dinner, but Kushio-shian drank a lot less. Wang Jiu ate with two sticks that he held in one hand. Kushio-shian ate the same way, which surprised me, because at the other parties he had eaten like everyone else. Wang Jiu was very clever with the sticks. He held pieces of food in the air and examined them and complimented Kushio-shian on the dishes. Kushio-shian plucked the best bits off dishes and put them on Wang Jiu's plate.

Ming Wei drank no wine at all.

Finally, Kushio-shian sent Ming Wei in to get the charts. They spread them out on the table, and Wang Jiu bent over them, studying, stroking his beard.

"It is Aohong," Kushio-shian said.

"Ahhh," Wang Jiu said, although whether that meant he hadn't known that or what it meant I had no idea. Wang Jiu stroked his beard as if he were in a play. It was an artificial gesture. I had the idea that everything Wang Jiu did meant something. I wondered if it was wasted on this audience.

"Who else have you shown these to?" Wang Jiu asked.

"No one," Kushio-shian lied.

Ming Wei looked sharply at Wang Jiu and then at her uncle and then at the chart.

"This is not clear here," Wang Jiu murmured. "Is it a reef or does the shore come out . . . ?"

"It is the shore," Ming Wei said. "Here, see where it is connected? It is a spit."

Kushio-shian frowned. I was surprised that Ming Wei could read charts. Stealing them was one thing but reading another.

Wang Jiu did not appear to notice that Ming Wei knew quite a bit about the charts.

"I will have to discuss this with my brother," Wang Jiu said. "You know, he knows much more about this sort of thing than I do. I will let you know within two days, if that is all right?"

"Ahhh," Kushio-shian said. "Yes. How is your younger brother?"

Wang Jiu said, "We are both old men. He has trouble with his kidneys. Still, for old men, we are both doing well."

"That's good," Kushio-shian said. "You will give him my regards, I hope?"

Wang Jiu looked sideways at Kushio-shian. "Oh, yes," he said, smiling slyly. "Oh, yes, most certainly."

Wang Jiu tottered down the gangway and into the back of a pedicab. His driver stood up on the pedals and made a wide slow turn in the street. Wang Jiu sat back beneath the hood around the chair.

That night I woke when something clunked against the side of the boat. I was a little drunk. There was wine left over and I'd stolen some of it. I hadn't had money for a drink in so long and I was nervous, as if insects were running under my skin. I thought the wine would help me sleep, but instead it made my sleep light and troubled.

I was slow, though, and I sat for a moment, not sure if I had heard the clunk or dreamed it. Then they threw the hook for the ladder over the gunwale and I scrambled for my rifle, shouting to wake everyone up. I fired the rifle at the first shape to come over the gunwale and the sound echoed across the water. But my shot was high and wide.

I hit someone the next shot. I heard him grunt, and the sound was as loud in my soul as the hard crack over the water had been. I didn't move, didn't breathe. I didn't really know what was going on. They were silent—even the one I had shot—and it should have been clear that they were attacking us, but I really didn't know. The man I had shot came into the boat, and so did the man behind him, while I stood there with my rifle at my shoulder.

Kushio-shian came stumbling up out of the hold.

By that time they were too close to shoot, and I turned my rifle around and clubbed blindly with the stock. Something connected, and someone swiped at me. I felt a long stitch of pain, but the knife—it must have been a knife—got tangled in my jacket or more probably the bindings I used to hide my breasts, and I jumped out of the way.

The first one, the one that I'd shot, sagged against the rail and knocked the lantern over. The second one jumped away from me, pulling his knife from the fabric of my jacket, and stabbed Kushio-shian in his thick belly and yanked up, opening him like a rabbit.

Then I shot him.

The shot knocked him down, and he scrabbled around on the deck. Like my father in the snow, so long ago. Like the outrider. I walked up and shot him again. But he still scrabbled and moaned. I shot him a third time. He sighed, a wet, bubbling sound.

Kushio-shian was holding his open belly, trying to keep the edges together like a too small shirt. He sat down heavily. He was whimpering.

Ming Wei was standing there staring. I heard something moving on the gangplank, so I grabbed Ming Wei's arm and pulled her to the edge of the ship and looked over. A boy was standing in the boat, looking up at us. I could barely see his pale face. I jumped over the rail and landed on him, almost upsetting the boat. I thought I heard a bone crack. Maybe his arm—I didn't know. I pushed him over the side of the boat, water coming in as the side dipped, and he swam awkwardly, shouting for help.

"Ming Wei!" I called. "Climb down!"

She stood there.

"They're coming from shore!" I shouted.

She came over the side then, climbing down the ladder, and I pushed the boat away into the middle of the canal. There was a sail, but the wind was coming from the sea. I wanted to get out and away, so I unshipped the oars and started rowing. My side hurt and I could feel the blood tickling across my ribs. I pulled for my life.

The boat behind us started to burn. Maybe it was from the lantern knocked over, but I didn't think so.

I pulled and pulled. Ming Wei sat looking back, and the fire got bright enough I could see her face. The breeze pushed the smoke away from us, obscuring the canal behind the boat. I could only taste the faintest bit of it in the air. Finally she said, "Do you think my uncle got away?"

There was no way to say it nice. "Ming Wei, sweet, your uncle is dead."

She cried and I rowed. After she had cried a bit, she sat watching forward. Then she put down the sail for me and rowing got easier.

I woke up with the sun in my face. I'd only meant to sleep until dawn, but it was mid-morning. I hurt and I itched. I'd been dreaming of the Mission. I couldn't remember my dream, just that I had been getting married and I was wearing a Taufzinner wedding dress. This seemed to make sense, since I was older and knew about Taufzin. Sometimes the groom was Aslak and sometimes he was Mika.

We'd made the harbor and then put up the sail again—Ming Wei doing a much better job than I did. I'd learned quite a bit about sailing as we went down the coast—not the least of which was that you sailed faster if the wind was at an angle to you rather than directly behind you.

This defied all my expectations of sailing, since about all I knew was that the wind pushed the sails. It was a complicated business, and without Ming Wei I probably would have had to try to row.

We'd come down the dark coast, keeping the lighter beach on our left. Dogs barked at us in a chain, one starting and then the next, while the first gradually left off and then the next. I was afraid that someone would come after us, but we passed another boat with a lantern hung off its prow and Ming Wei explained that some people fished in the dark. We found a stream and came up it to hide for a while, and I'd decided to get a little rest, and now it was mid-morning.

I sat up and my side hurt. No sign of Ming Wei. I tried to explore my hurt with my fingers. As best I could tell it was little more than a broad scrape along the ribs, but the cloth of my bindings and my shirt and my jacket and one side of my pants were all stiff from bleeding and I felt sick.

"Ming Wei?" I called.

Her head popped up from inside the boat. We'd pulled the boat up on land when the tide must have been higher. Now there was a stretch of mud between the stream and the boat.

"What are you doing?"

She climbed out of the boat. "You were still sleeping and I didn't want to wake you up."

"You are a courteous girl," I said.

I expected to get a sneer out of her for that, but Ming Wei was very subdued this morning. Not so surprising. "Where are we going to go?" she asked.

"I thought we might hide where the unclean people live," I said.

"I'm not an unclean person," she said, surprised.

"And I'm a foreigner," I said, cranky. "Do you have a better idea?"

"We could go to my grandmama's. She lives across the channel, on Xin Haibeidao."

"Across the channel?" I said. I stood up, slowly, cracking and creaking and holding my ribs. We weren't far from the sea and standing up I could see the beach and the water stretching beyond, no sign of the land across the channel. "Child," I said, "I'm not a sailor." I could do what I was told, but I certainly wasn't a seaman.

"It's just there," she said, pointing.

"But I don't know how to get us there," I said, patiently.

"I can sail," she said. "And I drew the charts."

"Drawing them and having them now are two different things," I said.

"You don't understand," she said. "I can remember them. Well, I can remember the channel. The more complicated ones sort of leak out of my head after a couple of days, but the channel is the first one I learned and I can draw it. Here, I scratched it in the bottom of the boat." She grabbed my arm and pulled me over and showed me the lines she'd marked.

It was amazing. As full of detail as the ones that her uncle had been showing and far more than I could ever understand. She prattled on about currents and depths— not that we'd have to worry about depths, she said, since our little boat drew so little—and rocks and a point we could use to guide us to the river that would take us to her grandmother.

"How did you do this?" I asked.

"I can remember things," she said. "When I see them on paper. I can read a pamphlet and remember it, too. My uncle used to make me do it as a game. He'd take the pamphlet and say, 'third page, three paragraphs down, ninth word,' and I'd picture the page in my head and tell him the word. But after a couple of days, usually I can't remember it anymore."

I was struck dumb. "You cannot," I said.

"Yes, I can."

I didn't believe her. She was just a child, after all.

"Watch," she said, and crouched down on the dirty sand by the boat and using a twig started drawing again. It was like a trick. Like one of those little balls of colored paper they put in a cup in the market and when they poured hot water over them the paper opened up into an elaborate flower.

"We practice on charts at school, and then I come home

and draw them,'' she said. "Sometimes I can't draw them as well as I see them in my head, I'm not as good at copying—oh," she said.

"What?" I said.

She turned away from me, her eyes filling up with tears. I assumed she had just thought about last night and her uncle. I waited for her to get her composure.

Finally she gasped, "I won't be going back to school."

I let her cry on my shoulder for a while. When you're a strange foreign barbarian, you don't get much contact with other people, so even having someone cry on your shoulder is something.

We drank as much fresh water as we could. We didn't have anything to store it in, so it would be our last drink until we got somewhere. Ming Wei guessed it would take us about half a day to get across.

Then we pushed the little boat into the waves, and I rowed as hard as my aching side would let me to get beyond the breakers.

Ming Wei knew a lot more about sailing than I did, but that wasn't very much and what she did know was from the still canals and slow river of the city. The ocean was an entirely different thing. Pretty soon we determined that I was better with the tiller and she was better with the sail, partly because I was too stiff to clamber around much. She ducked under the boom and tightened and loosened things. Then she crouched in the prow.

The sun got awful pretty quickly. It was in front of us and the wind was almost behind us, coming just over my left shoulder. Then about midday it dropped and the sail emptied of wind and hung there.

"The current isn't very strong here," Ming Wei said. The lines she had scratched in the bottom of the boat were unreadable now that waves and spray had wet everything down, but she still pointed to it as if it were there. In her mind's eye it obviously was. "It's taking us this way," she said, gesturing off to my right, "and we want to go this way," toward my left, "watching for the point."

"The wind might come back up in the afternoon," I said.

"But we could be a long way that way," she said.

It didn't feel as if we were moving. The water seemed still all around us. I could see the shore behind us as a faint line but no sign of the island in front of us at all.

"Should I row?" I asked.

She cocked her head. "It wouldn't hurt," she said.

Actually it would and did, but I rowed for a while. My side bled, I could feel it. I was thirsty. At least I wasn't hungry.

I rowed and took a break, rowed and took a break. Ming Wei rowed a bit, too, but she nearly lost an oar and almost had to go in after it. I didn't mention that I couldn't swim. Aslak had been able to swim. He had learned fishing on the river. I thought about the summer camp with Toolie clan when the men would go fishing out on the water and we would sit on the shore and gossip. I thought about my daughter. When I wasn't rowing I sat with my blistered hands soaking in the water. It was silent except for the slap of the swell. The sea was deep, deep blue and looked colder than it felt.

The wind did pick up in the afternoon, filling the sail, but now it was coming in the direction we wanted to go and we had to tack against it. Sailing was contrary.

I had to pee, but there wasn't any place to do it. I was sure Ming Wei did, too, but I was equally sure she was too embarrassed.

"Turn your back," I said to her, "and don't look around." When I was done, I turned my back on her. "I'm not going to look," I said.

It was quiet for a while, then the boat tipped a bit. After a moment or two she said, "You can turn around."

She was sitting in the front of the boat as if she had never moved. The sea was unchanged.

By the time it got dark we had no idea where we were.

"I think we are too far down the channel," Ming Wei said. "We will have to sail more up that way."

"If we get swept too far we miss the island and we're out at sea, right?" I asked. It was bitterly cold as soon as the sun went down.

"Yes," Ming Wei said in a small voice.

"Maybe there will be some fishermen," I said. We had

passed fishermen last night. "Come sit against me and stay warm."

I couldn't see her face in the darkness, but she was very still. Probably not sure about sitting too close to a foreign barbarian who might ravish her. If I tried to ravish her, even if I could have ravished her, I would probably fall out of the boat and drown. Even if I had been able to ravish her I was thirsty and I'd spent all day in the sun and I felt too terrible to bother. "Don't worry," I said. "I won't do anything. I'm just cold and so are you. The tiller will be between us."

After a bit she clambered back and sat next to me. She sat there for a while and then she leaned up against me. She sat up and touched my face. "You're hot," she said.

"A little fever from the sun. Your face is sunburned." I didn't need light to tell me we were both burned. Ming Wei leaned back against me. Her teeth chattered. I tried to steer the little boat back in the right direction. Ming Wei fell asleep, and at one point I had to adjust the sail. I woke her up and she mumbled at me but didn't move. I didn't do a very good job with the sail. Ming Wei's knots looked simple, but I seemed to manage to get too much slack or not enough.

I was grateful for the dawn, and even more grateful for the long thin strip of land on the horizon. "Ming Wei, sweet," I said.

She sat up, rubbed her eyes with the heels of her hands, and stared at the land. "Where are we?" she asked.

"I don't know," I said. "But I think we should sail for land."

We covered a pretty good distance before mid-morning.

"I think that's waves breaking," Ming Wei said.

I nodded although I didn't really care. I was so tired and light-headed that all I wanted to do was rest. "We can come in there and then after we rest we can sail up the coast," I said.

"I don't think so," she said. "I don't think we can land there. I think we're still too far from the point."

"So we'll sail like we did the first night," I said.

"No," she said, "we can't get the boat up there. The

rocks will kill us. We need to get back out into the channel.''

Back out?

We sailed back away from the land and made our way up the coast. The wind was more favorable. Ming Wei's lips were cracked and the skin was peeling off her nose. We didn't talk.

I dozed and dreamed that I was home, at the Hamra Mission. It was after the outrunners had been there because everything was burned. Snow had collected on timbers and charred wood stuck up out of the white. I saw Aslak between two ruined houses and called him, but he didn't look around. I couldn't move very fast because my legs were so heavy in the snow. I stumbled after him. He was wearing his blue jacket with the gray fur on the shoulders. I couldn't catch up to him.

I was in the boat and Ming Wei was in the prow, watching ahead. "There's the point," she said, hoarse. It curved almost to us. "We have to get around."

I was so thirsty that my tongue was swollen in my mouth and I couldn't talk. I just nodded.

I fell into the dream whenever I closed my eyes except sometimes the Mission was in water instead of snow.

Aslak said, "I have to find Wanji."

"Wanji's dead," I said. "They're all dead."

"We have to get help from the offworlders," he said. Except he didn't look like Aslak, he looked like Mika.

"Offworlders ruin everything," I said. "Wanji apologized to me!" How did Mika know Wanji?

"Jan?" Ming Wei said. "Jan? Who are you talking to?" Ming Wei was crying.

"I'm just dreaming," I said with my thick tongue. "Where's the point?"

"We need to sail in," she said. There were waves and I kept seeing Aslak and sometimes Mika.

Ming Wei soaked the hem of her dress in the cold water and put it on my face and I blinked.

"Who are you talking to?" she asked.

"My friend," I said. "An old friend. He's dead."

"Are you going to die?" she asked.

"Death spits me out," I said.

The Mission was full of water and I was trying to sail the boat. The Mission was a river's mouth, and the sails emptied of wind. People were standing at the edge of the water, looking at us.

"I'm looking for Lili," Ming Wei said. "My grand-mama Lili."

People helped us out of the boat. I couldn't stand up and the world spun. Someone gave me water.

We had arrived.

I woke up naked except for an old shirt, not mine. It was soft from washing. I remembered being sick. I remembered people talking to me.

I remembered someone taking off my jacket and Ming Wei's voice saying, "He's hurt." I could remember the relief of having the bindings off and the cool air on my skin. Ming Wei saying, "What's wrong with his chest?" I could see her face when she said it.

A woman said, "It's a woman." And laughed.

I wanted to say, "Not really," and explain, but it was too difficult.

I could remember other things about Aslak and Mika and all mixed up. The world was made of hot metal and I flew and swooped around in it, trying to find a place where it was cool and I could be still. Fever dreams.

After a while an older woman looked in the door. "Ai-ya," she said, smiling, "you are awake." She brought me water to drink. "I'm Ming Wei's grandmama," she said. "Ming Wei says you brought her here."

"We came together," I said.

"Thank you for bringing her to me," Lili said and patted my hand.

I wondered if Ming Wei's uncle was her son, but I couldn't tell if there was much likeness or not. Island people tended to look too much alike to me.

I slept some more and then Ming Wei's grandmama brought me my clothes. They were clean. "Do you want something more suitable?" she asked.

I didn't understand her at first, but finally I realized she was asking me if I wanted to dress like a woman. "No,"

I said. "These are my clothes. For a long time. A dress would be uncomfortable."

She looked at me for a moment. "Where you come from, do women dress this way?" She was curious and direct. I didn't feel as if she meant it as a slight and I liked the way she talked to me.

"No," I said. "Women wear dresses. My husband is dead, my daughter is dead. There is a war. I want people to think I am a man. They don't hurt me if I am a man."

"You don't have to be afraid now," Lili said.

"It has been many, many years," I said. "Now, in my head, I am some part man, some part woman, I think." I couldn't explain the implant, I didn't have enough island speech to even begin to. I don't think Lili had a clue what I was trying to say, but she just shrugged and patted my hand again and left me so I could put on my clothes.

I didn't see Ming Wei until the next day. I was sitting breaking beans. Doing women's work in men's clothes. Not that I really minded, I'd done a lot of women's work in men's clothes. Ming Wei slid in the door and stopped there, looking at the beaten earth floor, one bare foot on top of the other. "Hello," she said.

"Hello, Ming Wei," I said. "How are you?"

"I'm fine," she said. She stood there for a moment. I didn't know what she wanted, so I broke beans until they were all done. Finally Ming Wei said, "Why didn't you tell me?"

It came to me then that she had been a little sweet on me, on this man, this strange foreigner, Jan. "Ming Wei, sweet," I said, "I am sorry. I tell no one. Never. I don't even think to tell a person."

"But you could tell me!" she flashed out angry. "I'm your friend. In the boat."

I shrugged. I had no answer for her. I could try to explain in my bad island, but she didn't understand. She didn't understand that when you are fighting for your life, the person you are with is like kin to you, but when the danger is gone, they go back to being a stranger. "I am sorry," I said.

She wanted to argue with me. She tried. She told me

that I wasn't fair and that I should have told her, but I just agreed and said I was sorry. It's hard to argue against someone who gives way.

"What are you going to do now?" she asked.

"I don't know," I said. I was just as trapped as I had been on Hainandao. More so. There weren't even navigation order ships leaving from here. Maybe I'd find a smuggler somewhere.

"Will you stay here?" Ming Wei asked plaintively.

I smiled at her. "I have no place to go."

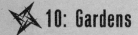 **10: Gardens**

MING WEI, GRANDMAMA LILI, AND I WERE
walking single file in the predawn gray. In the early morning it was easy to hear Grandmama Lili talk. Ming Wei's
grandmother dyed cotton kracken yellow and sold it at the
village of Shijing so it was worth it to go, even though it
meant getting up so early and walking on an empty
stomach.

Red foxbats were walking and chattering back and forth
in the early morning. Grandmama Lili stepped around a
puddle I wouldn't have seen.

Shijing was bigger than our village, but not very much
bigger. We passed raised garden plots. I looked carefully
at the gardens; I was learning to garden. In Hamra Mission
we'd grown whatever would grow that we could eat, but
here they changed the soil and then they grew a lot of
things like pineapple and tomatoes and green beans. In
Shijing some people even grew little fruit trees in tubs.

I was looking for a starter for my garden plot. I had
covered the soil in black offworld plastic and let it cook
in the sun for weeks, and now I would buy a good starter
that would make soil that would grow a lot of things.
Grandmama Lili was giving me the plot and money to
buy the starter. It was partly because she was too old to
garden and this way I would have to keep her in vegetables, and partly as thanks for bringing her Ming Wei. She
teased me, calling me *nushu,* "son-in-law," which always
made Ming Wei get that sullen look.

262

The path widened and became a muddy town with two-story houses sitting behind more garden plots. People had two-wheel carts with their goods covered in old plastic sheets. "Auntie Lili!" a woman called. "Who are these people?"

"This is my granddaughter," Grandmama Lili said. "This foreigner, she brought my granddaughter to me. She saved my granddaughter. And now she is like my own niece. She's making a garden to feed me in my old age."

The woman looked hard at me. "Ai-ya," she said, noncommittal.

"Have you eaten, yet?" I said politely.

The woman looked startled and then laughed.

"Why do you dress like a man?" another woman asked. She had the plastic on her cart pulled partway back to display pink meat and strips of pale fat.

"Bad fortune," I said. "A woman alone is weak. My family are all dead." I had given this explanation so many times. It always brought nods and murmurs.

"And this is your granddaughter."

"Tall. She is very tall."

"You have to get her married, soon."

Ming Wei looked at her bare, muddy feet.

"Let's get some noodles," I whispered. We had come with empty stomachs so we could get Shijing noodles. Ming Wei said they were wonderful.

"This way," she said.

The noodle woman didn't sell in the street but at her house. Her husband was making more noodles. He took the dough and swung it out away from him, stretching it between his two hands. It grew like a thick rope. Then he rolled it in flour and doubled it and stretched it again. Then he doubled it so there were four strands being stretched, then eight, then sixteen, and then a host of noodles. We watched him while we ate.

The noodles came in broth with a sheen of oil on top. The nut oil was infused with black mushrooms and chilies and things I didn't know and it was a wonderful dish.

We slurped and the woman stared at us. We were strangers. Her husband stared at us, too, while he was stretching noodles, but that was all right, we were staring at him.

"Do you know Cha-li?" the woman asked us.

It was a funny name, and Ming Wei giggled. "*Cha,* like green tea or black tea?" she asked. *Cha-li* meant "strong tea."

"It's some foreign name," the woman said. Ah, yes, since Cha-li was some foreigner and I was a foreigner and Ming Wei a stranger, we all must know each other.

"Is the person yellow-haired?" Ming Wei asked.

The woman shook her head, looking at my hair. "No, black hair."

"Where is the person from?" I asked.

"Somewhere else," the woman said. Then, perhaps realizing the inadequacy of this response, "Far away, though."

Not so far as me, I suspected.

It started to rain as we finished our noodles. It was a rainy time of year, but the rain was warm as milk. Ming Wei and I wandered back to the market. Grandmama Lili was squatting, still talking to the woman. She waved at us. "Go see Cha-li," she called. "He is a soil farmer. He has good soil starter. He's a foreigner." She pointed.

What did being a foreigner have to do with having good soil starter? I had found that being a foreigner meant that there were all sorts of things I supposedly was or wasn't, and a lot of them had nothing to do with me. I was supposedly good at soccer, for one thing, because sometimes a foreign team would come and play on the big island. They were foreign, they played soccer. I was foreign, therefore I played soccer, too. I didn't even know the rules.

From a distance—and not all that great a distance, we could see the entire market from end to end—Cha-li looked pretty much like everyone else, that is, small, dark, and wet. He was older than I was. He could have almost passed for an islander. Not the kind that Ming Wei and her grandmother were, not Han people, but the ones with big eyes, the yinduren. But he wasn't, somehow. Although I wasn't sure; I had been looking at Han and yinduren for so long that sometimes I saw foreign faces where there were none.

"Hello," Ming Wei said. She had been about to say "Hello, Cha-li," but couldn't bring herself to, and her tongue tripped itself, leaving her with her mouth open a little too long. She giggled and then she blushed.

"Hello, have you eaten yet?" Cha-li said mildly.

"We ate," I said politely.

"You're going to start a garden," he said. "Do you know how to garden?"

"A little," I said.

"She's already built her bed and covered her soil," Ming Wei said.

"Good," he said, "good. You've got plastic?"

I nodded. It struck me as strange that plastic had gotten out here where there were no offworlders yet. It was expensive, though. People used and reused it.

"So you know what you're doing?" he asked.

"A little," I said again. He was much better at the language than I was.

He had a face that was all eyes and nose. He was truly a big-nosed foreigner. He was almost ugly, but his eyes were lively and black. He showed us little green plants in pots. "This is what I use with my starter," he said. "Bean plants are good in starter soil because they give back. These are bush beans. They take more room than pole beans, but for new soil they are very, very good. And around them," he touched fronds, "these are flowers I call meilijin. I plant them at the edge of my garden because they help keep away pests. Everyone is always asking me about *dama*. I wouldn't plant *dama* for at least sixty to eighty days after I started my soil."

Dama was a plant that people grew to smoke. It made people quiet and a little silly. It was also good if you were sick to your stomach. "I don't want *dama*, not yet," I said. "I only want to plant vegetables. I am a student."

"You're smart," he said.

I shrugged. "Thank you," I said. I wanted to look for other people with soil starter. "We will think for a while, okay?"

"Okay," he said.

We wandered back down the street.

"It's smart not to act too interested," Ming Wei whispered to me.

"I'm not sure I am interested," I said.

She frowned at me. "Everyone says to go to Cha-li."

"I'll talk to other people."

A man with melons and a pregnant wife with a belly like a melon showed me his soil starter. "It's okay for a season, or in an established garden," he said. "But. for starting a bed, you want to talk to Cha-li."

So we ended back with Cha-li. "You are Auntie Lili's granddaughter," he said.

Ming Wei nodded.

"Do you miss school?" he asked.

"A little," she said. "I miss my friends."

"Ah, yes," he said. "It's lonely to move to a new place. But you have family here. You will make friends."

His ugly face didn't give away anything, but he didn't have kin here and I knew how lonely you could be without kin. I wondered if he was married.

He gave me careful instruction on how to make my soil. Soil had to be boiled a potful at a time to kill all the onworld spirits. "If you can't find anyone to ask at home, or if you aren't sure, come ask me," he said. "I live in Tailing."

I didn't know where Tailing was, but I thanked him as sincerely as I could.

The little pot of soil starter was very expensive. I was surprised. But the plants—the beans and the meilijin flowers—they were not so much. He sent me to other people's carts to buy other things. I bought a melon vine from the melon man with the pregnant wife. Ming Wei helped me fill a basket and then when Grandmama Lili was ready, Ming Wei balanced the basket on her head and we walked home.

I cooked soil from my garden beneath the overhang because of the warm rain. The mud stank and the smoke eddied back and filled the house.

"It stinks," Ming Wei said. "It's cooked enough."

"No," her grandmama said, "it needs to cook a long

time. Cook all the demons out. Demons don't mind a little heat; it takes a lot.''

It wasn't demons, it was amino acids. We needed the amino acids of Earth, and so did plants we could eat. This planet had different amino acids, and most of the stuff that grew we couldn't eat.

I told Ming Wei about my people. "There are three kinds of things: onworld, that will fill you up but not feed you or that will make you sick; in-between things like renndeer and potatoes, that we can eat but that can live on onworld things; and offworld things, like dogs and people.''

Ming Wei looked bored. "I'm going to talk to Mai-mi,'' she said. Mai-mi was newly married and talked about things Ming Wei was a lot more interested in than gardening.

My garden didn't look very big. It was only twice my height in one direction and three times my height in the other. I laid plastic in the bottom to cover the raw soil and then started pouring my cooked soil in. There wasn't enough cooked soil to fill a corner.

I stood there in the rain and looked at my tiny mound of cooked soil for a long time and thought about giving up.

Nothing to do but stir my soil food and cook more soil. Grandmama Lili cautioned me, "Don't expect much from a new garden,'' she said.

"Most of it died,'' I said to Cha-li. I had walked to Tailing to ask him for help, getting lost only twice. He was moving pots of dirt and plants out into the sun. Soil starter couldn't get rain in it or it would be contaminated by local organisms, so he gave it boiled water and moved it in his house when it rained.

"What's still alive?''

"Meilinjin flowers,'' I said.

"Meilijin,'' he corrected. He stood up and put a hand on his back. "The beans died?''

I nodded.

He thought. "It's hard to start a garden in rainy season,'' he said finally.

"I start over?'' I asked.

He shook his head. "Cover it in plastic and cook it for a while."

"The flowers? I cover the flowers?"

"I've got some pots. Pot your flowers and use boiled water." He went back into his house and brought out some old chipped pots. Inside his house looked like a man's. The bed was unmade and cooking things sat on a stool. A pair of wooden garden sandals caked with mud were lying in the middle of the floor, and there was dirt from where he had either been potting or making more seed dirt or something. He needed someone to come and make order for him.

"Would you like some hot water?" he asked and brought me a cup. We sat outside and drank hot water out of fairly clean cups. "You heard that in Lijing there are sick people?"

There were a couple of ways to say "sick." One was to say that people were "a little uncomfortable" and you said it when someone had a cold or something. He used the other one, the one that you said when someone was really ill. "I didn't know," I said.

"They got it when a cousin came from Shinjuang. Now a lot of people are sick and some have died."

I wanted to ask if it was a plague, but I didn't know the word for "plague." "You think people will get sick here?" I asked.

"What city did you live in?" he asked.

I told him a little about Taufzin and about the other cities I'd lived in.

"I've never been to those places," he said and scratched the dirt with his heel. "I come from Ahkmed."

I'd heard of it. I had stuck to the coast and it was inland, so I'd never been there. "How did you get here?" I asked.

"I ran away," he said, "the same as you."

"How do you know I ran away?" I asked. Something about his easy assumption irritated me. It was the same as everyone assuming that just because I was foreign I played soccer.

"If you've come this far, you had to be running from something. But I've discovered a secret," he said. He leaned forward and whispered, "No matter how far you go, you can't escape yourself." Then he grinned. It was the first time he'd smiled and it utterly changed his face.

It was months before my garden started to give vegetables. It didn't look anything to me like the vegetable gardens in Shijing. It was full of bare patches, and I remembered those gardens as full and green. But the potatoes were good and the melon grew. The onions were okay. We ate some green beans and dried some green beans, and I felt as if I had contributed a bit.

Ming Wei watched me weed. "Why don't you make friends with Cha-li?" she asked.

"Why should I?" I asked.

"Because you are both foreigners."

"He lives too far away."

"But you don't go to Shijing, not even when Grandmama and I go."

"It takes all day to go to Shijing," I said. "I have things to do."

She made a disgusted noise.

I straightened up. "Ming Wei, how many people are in this village?"

She stopped and thought. I could see her counting. After a moment she said, "A lot."

"How many of them would you be friends with?"

She flipped her hair back over her shoulder. "I have a lot of friends."

"Sixty?"

"No," she said and scowled.

"So if you were stuck in a city full of foreigners, with only one person from this village, does that mean that you would like that person? Especially if it were a man? Someone like Shiwa Zhuang, maybe?"

"Shiwa Zhuang? You mean Tsa-chi's husband? I don't even know him. I know who he is, but—"

"I don't know Cha-li."

"But you're a lot alike," she said.

"How are we alike?"

"You garden," she said.

"Lots of people garden."

"You're both . . . I don't know how to say it so you'll understand it. You don't know the word." She pulled a yellow and sickly weed out of the dirt. I thought if it was yellow and sickly then my soil must be all right, although it would get contaminated soon enough. "It is a word about your breath, you know, about inside of you. You both find strange things funny."

"What things?"

"Well, the way people eat. You have pretty good manners, but you eat like a foreign person, but sometimes you act like we are the funny ones."

I did think they were the funny ones, sometimes: The way people spit fish bones on the table, but if you sneezed or coughed at the table, even when you covered your mouth, they got green-faced and ill. Or the way you weren't supposed to eat all the noodles in your bowl if you were eating at someone else's table. Because, Ming Wei had explained to me, that was like saying that the food had been so inferior that you had to fill up on noodles.

"We both have big noses but that doesn't mean we look alike," I said.

"You do look alike," Ming Wei said, surprised.

"Ming Wei! I have yellow hair!"

"Yes," she said, "but you still look alike. I mean, you both have skin like yinduren and you have funny-shaped eyes, and you're alike in a lot of ways."

I snorted.

"It's true," she said.

"Did you know that Cha-li and I don't even speak the same language? I speak my own language, and English and some Taufzin. But he and I have to talk in your language."

This information didn't seem to appear germane to Ming Wei. "You are always cranky," she said, petulant.

I laughed.

"See what I mean? You find strange things funny."

I picked a flower and put it in her hair. It was vibrant orange against the smooth black. She was so young and so pretty.

"Your fingers are all dirty," she said.

"If I really were a man I'd marry you," I said.

"If you were my husband I would cry all the time," she said. But she didn't take the flower out of her hair. It was there, drooping slightly but still brilliant, while she made dinner. She chopped an onion from our garden and the smell of it rose up in Grandmama Lili's little house and filled me up. I didn't even know if I should bother to eat I was so full of the smell of that onion cooking in a little oil.

I ate a lot.

I thought about Cha-li, and then one day he was there, almost as if I had conjured him up.

He was shorter-legged than I had remembered, as short-legged as a lot of the islanders. Bowlegged, like my da. His face was nothing like my da's though. Something about Cha-li made me feel that he might be thinking things I wasn't smart enough to think.

"Hello," he said. "I came to see your garden."

"Did you eat yet?" I asked.

"Oh, yes," he said.

Ming Wei followed behind us, pretending a sudden interest in gardening.

One of my meilijin flowers had died and dried up, but it was still sitting in a chipped pot just outside the door. The rest I had planted. They were doing all right, although, looking, I could see that most of them didn't seem to be in flower right now and they all looked stalky.

I was embarrassed but he didn't seem to notice the pot and flower. I took him out to the back. "I am still learning," I said.

He nodded. "You put the garden the right way," he said, squinting into the sun. "It doesn't get shade, does it? That's good. For leafy things you can plant them under melons." He squatted and took a handful of my dirt and smelled it. Then he crumbled it in his hands.

"Would you like tea?" I finally asked.

"Hot water is fine," he said.

Grandmama Lili watched us. I couldn't tell, but I thought she was laughing a little. Or maybe she was angry.

Sometimes I didn't know how to behave. Ming Wei was trying not to smile.

"I thought you were going to Mai-mi's house, to help with the new baby," I said to Ming Wei.

"In a while," she said.

"Please have some tea," I said to Cha-li. Grandmama Lili always asked three times.

Cha-li looked up from the pot. "All right," he said.

Ming Wei giggled. I probably looked like the barbarian fool that I was. Ming Wei probably thought this was barbarian courting.

I brought him tea, and then we went to sit under the overhang, out of the sun and away from the heat of the fire. Inside, I could hear the rhythmic thunk of the grinder and smell the dust from the dye.

"So what did you do before you came here, since you obviously weren't a farmer," he said.

"I was a technician in a factory," I said, stung. "You were a farmer, I can see."

"No," he said, "I was," and he said a word I didn't know. "A person who writes down numbers, this many sold, that much bought."

"How did you become a farmer?"

He laughed, and again I noticed how his face changed. "Sheer stubbornness. I was a terrible farmer."

Grandmama Lili laughed, too, her voice coming from the darkness inside the house. "Oh, he got so thin. Like sticks. We all felt so sorry for him."

"Garden after garden died. No one would tell me things. Old farmers keep their tricks to themselves. But I watched you all," he said, gleeful.

"You were a wicked thief," Grandmama Lili agreed, her voice flowing bodiless in the heat. I was aware of the smell of my own sweat. Could Cha-li smell me? I smelled hot cloth and dust off of him, a dry pleasant smell. A road smell.

"I think I know what you need. You need si-chi," Cha-li said.

"What's that?" I asked.

"It is a plant that you can eat, but mostly it's good for the soil. It will really help."

Ming Wei made a face. "It's bitter."

"It's good in soup with melon," Grandmama Lili said.

Ming Wei shook her head. "Country food," she said.

"This is the country," I said.

"It's expensive, but you only need a little," Cha-li said. "It spreads. Most people don't like it because once you plant it, soon it will try to conquer your whole garden."

"Like mint," Grandmama Lili said. "But it would be good. I'd like you to do it." Which meant that she thought the money would be well spent.

"It will soften the soil," Cha-li said. "Then you can grow good garlic and carrots and root vegetables. And you can get worms. Then you can raise them and sell them. That's how I started."

"Okay," I said. "I'll try it. I'll go back with you and buy some."

"I don't have any," Cha-li said. "Not anymore. I don't do worms anymore; now I sell soil starter. You need to get it in Da-mou."

"Da-mou!" I said. Da-mou was a city. Not a very big city but the biggest city on the island. "I've never been to Da-mou."

"Then it's time," Grandmama Lili said.

"I'll go with you," Cha-li said.

"You have to stay and take care of your soil," I said.

"My soil will be all right for two days."

"I'll go, too," Ming Wei said, happy.

Da-mou meant "big mouth." The mouth was a harbor of bright blue water, not so big as the harbor of the big city where Ming Wei and her uncle had lived and more funnel shaped, with city all along it. It was all made of pale yellow stone and wood and it looked quite peaceful and pretty. We ate some fruit and frybread sitting on the hill beyond the city, looking at all the distance we would have to walk and admiring the way the jungle had been cleared for a long way around. Square ponds shined like metal in the sun. It was the middle of the day and people were probably taking their little sleep. There was almost no noise but the sound of dragonflies and daybats.

Around the village were rice paddies and as we walked,

Cha-li told Ming Wei and me about how the rice was grown in water and how rice had to be adapted from Earth to grow here because no one could have farmed it otherwise. Ming Wei was bored and even I thought Cha-li talked a lot, but I thought it was interesting. Some of the paddies had water in them. They shined silver like mirrors, with the green stalks of the rice sticking up out of them. Boiling enough water to fill all those rice paddies would have been impossible. Making the soil would have been impossible. We walked past rice paddies for a long time, coming to another village and then another, and then the villages crowded together more and more. As afternoon wore on people were out in the paddies, bent over, moving young rice plants from one place to another for no reason I could see.

Just outside the city we bought bowls of brown rice and fish and ate and ate. All the walking had made us hungry. In Da-mou they made their food so spicy that tears ran down our faces. It was good. We hadn't passed the city gates yet, but the city had long since sprawled over the walls. The people called this area Jongwen-juang. Cha-li bought us some strong white wine, and we found a man in the market outside the wall who would let us sleep under his cart. Cha-li sold him potatoes. Potatoes grown the normal way were reddish inside, but potatoes grown in boiled soil were creamy white. Most people grew potatoes around their gardens, not in them, because it was a waste of space for things that wouldn't grow outside. But some city people, it turned out, would pay a lot of money for white potatoes. The cartman smelled slightly sour, but not particularly distasteful, not like sweat.

"Some people don't like foreigners," he told us, "because of the sickness. You be careful with city people. You get a cloth, like this," he had one tied around his neck, "and you keep vinegar with you. When you see someone sick, you sprinkle vinegar on the cloth and put it over your nose and mouth."

We didn't know about the sickness, but he explained to us that in the part of the city upriver from the harbor, two men had died. They were from the big island, not from here. And the physician who had seen them said they had the plague. Then no one got sick for two weeks, and everybody thought maybe the plague wouldn't come. "But then the man who owned the house, he died. Then no one died for a while, except for normal things, until we found out that all up and down that street people had been dying of sickness and no one would say. Sixteen people died in one week, and their families buried them in the middle of the night, so no one would know. And now it's all over that part of town. Country people aren't sick, we're okay, but when you talk to city people, you need a vinegar rag."

He had a jar with vinegar in it and when people paid him, he made them drop the coins in the jar so he didn't have to touch them.

In my head I saw those coins drop, turning and gleaming, through the vinegar and hitting the bottom, tap, tap, tap. Even though I didn't see them, they were what scared me. More than the dried-up rag he had tied around his neck like a bandanna, like a bandit. The air around me smelled of vinegar. My eyes started to water.

Ming Wei looked scared.

I was thinking, maybe we should go back. Cha-li said it, "Maybe we should go home?"

As soon as he said it I felt all the tiredness in my legs from the long walk. To come so far and go back without anything!

"No, no," said the cartman. "If you are careful, you won't have a problem. I can get you all rags."

I wouldn't get sick. Or if I got sick, I wouldn't die. Death always spit me out. Besides, I had been immunized in the Mission. Probably I couldn't even get the sickness. But Ming Wei could. "Cha-li?" I asked. "Have you ever had offworlders give you something," I mimed pressing the dispenser against his arm. "Then you cannot get certain sickness?"

He looked blank for a moment, and then suddenly he nodded. He said something in his own language, and then pressed against my arm and made a hissing noise, like the dispenser.

"That's it," I said.

"You think we can't get sick?"

I shrugged. "I don't know. Ming Wei could, though."

"I have to stay here?" Ming Wei wailed.

A moment ago she had looked terrified. Sometimes I wished I were her mam and could just slap her. "We haven't even decided if we're going," I said.

"He says it will be okay with the cloth," Ming Wei said.

"Would you bring your daughter into the city?" Cha-li asked him.

The man looked at Ming Wei. "No," he said. "I don't bring my daughter or my sons."

"That's not fair!" Ming Wei said.

"We can't go back tonight," Cha-li said.

The cartman promised to bring us some rags in the morning, but he had to go to his family.

He had straw under his cart, and we put our blankets on that and sat there. Ming Wei asked us about what we meant by pressing each other's arms and I let Cha-li explain to her about immunizations because he spoke the language better than I did; and I was tired and my head was turning round the idea of sickness.

I drank a little wine, feeling it burn, and then passed it to Ming Wei, who drank too much.

"If you get the sickness," Cha-li said, "and you go home with it, then everyone in the village will die."

"But the cartman said if I'm careful I won't get it," Ming Wei said. "You're going to go."

I expected to hear Cha-li say that he wasn't, that we were going to go back home the next morning, but instead he said, "I am one person alone, and a foreigner."

"But you'll give it to everyone in Tailing," she said. "You'll get it and give it to me and I'll die and I won't even have gotten to go to Da-mou."

"That's stupid!" I said. "If you die, who cares if you ever got to see Da-mou!"

Ming Wei looked a little startled, but she knew Cha-li and I didn't really have good arguments. "You're going to go yourself," she said. "It's stupid for you to go. I'm not a child, anymore."

"Dogmeat," I said in my own language. Ming Wei laughed. She was so pretty and so young. She really didn't understand. "Look, I'm not going to die, but you could."

"Why couldn't you?"

"Because death doesn't want me."

Ming Wei laughed again and that made me really angry.

"My mother is dead, my father is dead, my sister is dead, and I saw them all die. My husband died, my baby daughter died. I watched my husband starve to death and then I waited in the snow to die, and when I woke up, it was spring. Winter had gone. My lover died in Taufzin. My whole village is dead, but I don't die, Ming Wei. I don't die. I should have died when my baby was born, but I didn't. Before that I walked out into the dark and I should have frozen to death. When they found my body there was no breath, and yet an hour later, I was breathing again. Death spits me out!"

There was a long silence. Then Ming Wei said in a hushed voice, "You had a husband and a baby?"

"You're not going into the city," I said.

"I'll go by myself after you and Cha-li go," she said. "Who can stop me?"

"You are as stupid as that fishhead uncle of yours," I said.

"Your mother," Ming Wei said.

I was up before dawn and so was Cha-li. I walked away from the cart, through the fog, and found a place to pee. I wandered part of the way back to the cart. I wanted to leave Ming Wei sleeping, but I wasn't surprised to see Cha-li standing there in the mist.

We squatted. Fog does funny things to sound. Sometimes things faraway sound close and sometimes things close sound as if they were under a blanket.

"What do we do?" I asked.

If you didn't look at Cha-li's eyes he was all nose and no face. It was a mobile face, when he wanted it to be, with a narrow chin and temples sunk deep. But his eyes were as pretty as a girl's, and when he smiled all I saw was black eyes and white teeth in a dark face and I forgot how ugly he was. He wasn't smiling. It was dark but I could tell that much.

"Do you want to go home?" he asked.

"Not really," I said, "do you?"

"No."

"Do you think vinegar will protect us?" I asked.

He shrugged. "The cart man said the plague was all up in that end of town," he said. "Maybe it won't be where we go."

We sat in silence and listened to the darkness.

"Do you really believe that," he said, "what you said about death spitting you out?"

I could tell he didn't understand it. He thought I was foolish. It made me sad and it made me feel farther away from everything than ever. "It's true," I said.

"Do you think you're ever going to die?" he asked.

"Yes. I hope so."

"You want to die?" he asked in the dark, and I wondered if it was the voice of someone who knew about that feeling.

I swallowed. Darkness is a place for truth telling, I think. "Sometimes. Doesn't everybody?"

"So that's what you were running from," he said. "Living?"

I had never thought of it that way, and it didn't seem exactly true, but then in another way maybe it was true. I laughed a little. "Maybe. You said, when you run away from yourself, you're still there."

He chuckled.

"So what were you running away from?" I asked.

"I stole money from my boss," he said.

"Why did you do that?" I asked.

"I don't know," he said. "Lots of reasons. I had a lot of problems and then I only had one great big problem. But it wasn't enough money."

I could see him smile.

"Is it ever enough money?" I asked.

He shook his head. "Only enough to get away."

We sat there awhile, and then we went back and sat on the straw while it got lighter. When it was light, Ming Wei was lying awkwardly asleep, vulnerable to the world, with her hair in tangles and her pulse beating in the skin of her throat. The words I had said before dawn were something I couldn't talk about anymore.

Ming Wei woke up long after dawn. Young people sleep

long. She untangled her hair, and we found some breakfast. The cart man came back and brought us cloths. We
bought vinegar in a jar, then we walked to the Jong gate.
The closer we got, the more afraid I became, until my
stomach was tight inside me, but when we walked through
the gate, everything was the same as it had been on the
other side. The streets were filled with people, and no one
looked sick. They stared at me, some of them, but people
always stared at me. The feeling stayed inside me, winding
tighter and tighter. I didn't see anyone else wearing their
cloths over their faces, but I kept wondering if we should
pull ours up over our noses.

Ming Wei walked close to me, sometimes bumping into
me because she was looking at the streets and the buildings. She was quiet except to whisper that it was smaller
than she expected. Cha-li pointed to a paper sign pasted
on a door with a word and a drawing of a circle with a
swirl. Underneath it was more writing, smaller. "Can you
read it?" he asked Ming Wei.

I expected her to sniff and say of course, but she just
went up closer and read. " 'Dr. Li, herbalist, from an
honorable line of physicians from all the way back to the
middle kingdom. Cure and preventative for sickness, made
with ancient techniques from offworld, remembered only
in this family. Consultations.' " I felt my heart lift a bit.
Usually, when reminded that these people remembered
where they came from while my people had utterly forgotten, I felt ashamed, but I was too relieved to care.

Cha-li shook his head and walked on.

"What?" I asked. "What?"

"It's just a way to rob poor, sick people of their
money."

"But it's from offworld," I said.

Cha-li stopped and pointed back at the house. "Look
at it. You've been in an offworld factory. Could someone
here make offworld things? Where are the machines?"

"In Hamra," I said, "we did things . . ." I wanted to
say that we used appropriate technology to create offworld
technologies, but I couldn't say that in anything but English. Not even my own language, much less in this language. "We did things offworld without offworld

machines," I said. But not medicine. Medicine always came from the city in beautiful foil packets, brought by shuttle to Ayudesh and Wanji. I didn't know what to think or what to say, and I was so frustrated that tears rose and I blinked them away. So I shut my mouth and kept walking.

It's hard to be scared for a long time. Eventually my stomach growled. The city went on and we stopped and got a bowl of spicy rice and mushrooms. Cha-li asked some people directions and they gave them, pointing. Ming Wei chattered about Mai-mi's new baby and how she wanted to get something from the city for Mai-mi.

"Do you think I'll make a good mother?" Ming Wei asked. "Mai-mi says I'm really good with the baby."

Personally, I thought she had been brought up head-strong and spoiled and a baby would be the first thing in her life ever to make real demands on her. But maybe that would be a good thing. "It's hard to tell what kind of mother you'll make until you become one." We turned a corner into another street.

"Give me the vinegar," Cha-li said.

The street around us was empty, and all the houses were shuttered tight. Paper signs were pasted on some of the doors with huge characters on them.

Ming Wei looked scared.

"What does it say?" I asked, although I already knew.

"It says 'sickness,' " she whispered.

"We should go another way," I said.

The street was a street of silence. Even the air was still and heavy. Bad air. We sprinkled our cloths with vinegar and pulled them up over our noses. The smell was so strong that tears ran from my eyes. We walked down the center of the street, as far from the shuttered houses on either side as we could get. My breathing was loud in my ears. I wiped my eyes with my arm, and the tears smeared the travel dust in streaks. Vinegar, I would never be able to use vinegar again, in fact it was hard to imagine that I had ever even thought of it as food.

I saw a window open on the second floor and I looked up and caught the eyes of a boy child, not much younger than Ming Wei, watching the street. Watching us. He was as silent as the street, as silent as death. All around him

was death. Even though his hair and eyes were black, he
looked as Aslak had looked all those years ago. Or maybe
as I had looked. It was like Hamra and the shuttle coming
and we were like the offworlders to him. He was on one
side and we were on the other, and death was between us
like a huge space we could not cross—like the glass in a
window in Taufzin.

I could see he was going to talk to me and I didn't
want to hear what he would say. I felt as if he were so
far away that I would barely be able to hear him, but of
course he wasn't far away at all.

"Help me," he said.

The shutters were made of bamboo, once painted white
but now mostly their natural red, with chunks missing
where pieces had fallen out. The boy had on something
without sleeves, like something somebody would sleep in,
and it was too big for him, so the neck hung down
exposing one dark nipple. His arms looked so thin.

We kept walking.

"They're all dead," he said. "Please?"

At least the offworlders had given us food and blankets.
We gave the boy nothing. We just walked.

I felt his eyes on my back, and I kept thinking he'd say
something more. My shoulders were drawn toward my
ears, but the silence stretched between us. I started to slow
down, not even yet thinking about going back, but here
was Ming Wei and I couldn't expose her to the sickness.

After a couple of blocks we passed some houses with
their shutters open. Then we crossed a big street, and on
the other side there were people walking and stores open.
Some people wore vinegar rags on their faces; and everyone avoided all the other people, each walking in his or
her own space. But the doors didn't have signs pasted on
them warning of sickness.

There were a lot of places that had signs posted telling
how you could buy cures and preventions. Each one made
me feel worse, because each one meant that Cha-li was
right, otherwise, none of us would be wearing vinegar-
soaked cloths. When there are a lot of cures for something,
you can be sure that doctors really don't know how to
cure it.

The place to buy si-chi was a huge garden in the middle of the city. It was laid out in regular squares of raised beds, some covered with green and some with new growth just peeking up and some just with dirt. Some were covered with domes of clear plastic. The dirt in some of them was beautiful, all dark and crumbly. Nothing like the hard bake that mine was.

I pulled my vinegar mask down and drank in the smell of dirt and plants. In the middle of the city it was a wonderful, reassuring smell and I felt a strong longing to be back in my own garden, working the soil, making it into this dark rich stuff that would grow anything.

Si-chi was a plant that didn't grow very tall, no taller than my finger, and it had tiny oval green leaves and little yellow weedlike flowers. Cha-li bought me two little containers of it to carry. He bought me worms and plastic to put over my worm bed so that the rain wouldn't contaminate the soil. Then he wandered for a long time, stopping to poke soil and sniff it and crumble it between his fingers.

Finally he bought little bags of soil from three different raised beds and some powder to grow mushrooms.

Then we walked back out of the city a different way and passed no more streets of silence.

Out in the villages the sickness was far away again. We walked well out from the city of Da-mou before we found ourselves a place to sleep in a farmer's shed. The sun had been up and the day had been clear. The shed smelled cleanly of hay and animal. We laid out our blankets, and Ming Wei talked about how she wished she had been able to buy something for Mai-mi. My shirt stank of vinegar and with it I imagined the spoiled-meat smell of sickness.

I was so tired all my muscles ached, but as soon as I relaxed I thought of the boy in the window and then of Aslak and Mika and the shaman and all the people I'd left behind in my life. I wanted to escape, I wanted to sleep, but all I could think were thoughts that twisted me around. I knew what I was. I was the kind of person who was dissatisfied with everything. I was the kind of person who ran away when it got hard.

I felt so bad for that boy. I didn't know which was worse: to die or to survive the plague and be alone. He was in the land of the dead, now, and when he came back nothing would ever be the same. I had brought Ming Wei out of the land of the dead, that was good. But nobody was going to bring that boy out of the land of the dead. No one had ever brought me out of the land of the dead. Here I was, neither woman nor man, foreigner with no home. Maybe that was what I was for, to be a guide out of the land of the dead. Crazy thoughts.

He was so clear in my head, that boy. I couldn't remember Aslak's face, not exactly. I couldn't remember Mika's face as clearly as I could the boy's.

I knew my thoughts were running like a bafit in a box, scrabble, scrabble, scrabble. Bafits must really be my spirit animal. I tried to think of the sweet smell of straw and feel the heaviness of fatigue in my chest and follow that down into sleep like wrapping myself in a blanket.

In the morning I was up before Cha-li and Ming Wei. Cha-li woke up, and we drank water from a clear pond where wind ran across it in ripples. The sky was brutally clear.

"You remember the street," I said, and paused. Cha-li nodded, knowing what street I meant. "Did you see the boy standing at the window, up above?"

He nodded again. "It was the only house with the shutters open."

"What do you think will happen to him?" I asked, knowing that Cha-li didn't know any better than I but wanting him to tell me something.

I thought he would shrug but he didn't. He was quiet for a bit. "What are you thinking?" he asked.

"I should go back," I said, which scared me. The words came out and I couldn't snatch them back. They were air, bad air, gone between my fingers.

"Don't be stupid," he said.

"Why did you ask, then?" I said.

"Because you were feeling responsible for something you can't be responsible for. I thought once you had to say something aloud, you would be sensible."

"You said that foreigners were all the same, that we

run away.'' I twisted a handful of grass between my fingers. ''So I decided you were right, and I'm not going to run away anymore.''

''It's not your city,'' he said. ''If you want to stop running away, go back to your home.''

''My home is gone,'' I said. ''My people, my people are all dead. All of them. There is nothing left.''

''There are lots of people left,'' he said.

''But not my people. The, the''—I didn't know the word in any language but English—''the *Mission* is gone. I tried to go to the *clans,* but I didn't belong. I have no place, so I make a place.''

''Make a place with Ming Wei's grandmother and don't be stupid.''

''What about the boy?''

''What if you get sick?'' he asked.

''I won't get sick,'' I said, although I was not as sure of that as I had been before. I was making things true with words, and I wasn't sure I wanted them to be true. I was going down a road of words and maybe it was the wrong road.

''What would you do there?'' he asked.

''I don't know,'' I said. ''Maybe I could help take care of people.''

''You are just trying to die,'' he said, and his face twisted with bitterness.

''I am not,'' I said, ''not anymore. I can help and then when the sickness is gone I can come home,'' I said.

''You will die,'' Cha-li said.

He was a good man, even if he had been a thief. ''Why did you steal money from your employer?'' I asked.

''That doesn't have anything to do with what we're talking about,'' he said.

''So tell me,'' I said.

''I stole money from my employer because he was, how can I tell you, a man who did business in bad things and who hurt people for business and when I found that out, I knew that I couldn't leave my job. I knew things that he didn't want people to know. I took money so I could leave forever.''

''That wasn't how you made it sound,'' I said. ''You

said instead of a lot of little problems you had one big problem." It occurred to me that if I went back to the city, maybe I was making a lot of little problems into one big problem, but I wanted to come back eventually.

"People who work for my employer, they have lots of problems," he said. "That's how my employer finds you."

I didn't know what that meant. "That's not an answer," I said.

"It makes as much sense as anything you've said," he said.

"Why are you so mad at me?" I asked.

"Because you're being stupid," he said. "You think you are smart. You think because you have lived in the city you're smarter than Ming Wei and her grandmother. I tell you there are many kinds of knowledge, and at heart you are still the foreigner who believes in spirits and that death would spit you out. You know a lot of little pieces of things, but you don't really know anything. You're a barbarian." Cha-li's cheeks were red from anger.

His words made me angry, too. "If you had to live the things I have lived, you'd be dead," I said.

"How do you know?" he shouted. "How do you know what I've lived?"

"Why are you shouting?" Ming Wei said, cross.

I was embarrassed, but Cha-li was too angry to care. "Because Janna has this stupid idea she's going back to the city."

"Why?" Ming Wei said.

"To help the boy we saw on the street where the plague was bad," he said, disgusted.

"What boy?" Ming Wei said. "What are you talking about?"

I walked back into the city, and I didn't know where to go or what to do. Now that I was looking for sickness I didn't see it anywhere. I had just a little money. I had given most of Grandmama Lili's money back to Cha-li along with the si-chi for him to plant in Grandmama Lili's garden. He was so angry I didn't know if he would or not.

Ming Wei just cried and wouldn't talk to me.

My mam used to tell me, when three people tell you you're drunk, lie down. So what was I doing in this city, looking for sickness? Part of it was my own words and my own pride, and part of it was the boy standing in the window, and part of it was something I didn't really know.

I tried to go the same way that Cha-li had taken us, but I lost track before long. I tried to guess, looking for the street. Twice I thought I'd found it, but I couldn't remember enough about the house to be sure, just that the shutters had once been white, and I didn't see the boy.

There were a lot of people leaving the city. They had carts and wagons piled with their goods. An old auntie or grandmama would be perched on top, wrapped in a blue quilted blanket, or maybe an old grandfather or uncle. The old people swayed with the motion of the cart, impassive. It was the best thing to do, I thought, but how many of these people already had the sickness and would take it with them to relatives in the country?

Along about afternoon I sat down by a pale stone wall because my feet hurt. I was dusty, and I was thinking maybe I should go back outside the wall to where the cart man was to see if he'd let me sleep under his cart again. It would take me hours to get back, so if I was going, I probably should start now.

So much dust had been kicked up by all the traffic that I was covered with it. I felt as if I looked like the refugee I had been years ago, when I came to Tonstad.

A wagon stopped in front of me, with two children sitting splay-legged on top of a bundle of blankets. They were craning to look backward. "Mama," the girl called. "Mama, a crazy man is coming this way. He doesn't have any clothes on!"

I got up to look. The woman grabbed the boy and then the girl off the pile of blankets and ran down a side street holding the girl in her arms. I could see a commotion and the flash of white. People were scattering. A man came running. He was naked. Not just nearly naked but completely naked. Some people, a woman and an older boy, were running after him, shouting for him to stop. He was looking back over his shoulder, so I stepped out and grabbed him.

He knocked me over, and when he hit the road I heard the air go out of him with a hard *uh!*

I sat on him, and he struggled against me, all wiry and strong. His cheeks had flushed spots as dark as wood, his skin was hot, and a rash ran down his chest.

"He is sick!" the woman said, sobbing with the effort of getting her breath. "Chang Li! You are sick! Be still!"

He struggled and grunted, and didn't appear to understand her at all.

"Chang Li!" she called. "Chang Li!"

"Baba!" the boy said. "Baba! Be still!"

We were gathering a crowd, but one that kept a respectful distance. The man was on his belly, so he couldn't do much but squirm and reach awkwardly back for me. "Hey," I said. "Hey, you are all right."

Suddenly the fight went out of him. He closed his eyes and sighed.

He was not so big a man, and his ribs stood out against his skin. His back was covered in the same fine rash, like pinpricks. Most frightening of all, his feet were black as if they were bruised. I had never seen anything like it.

"Chang Li?" the woman said.

I was afraid he was pretending and that if I got up he would leap off in wild flight again.

"Is he okay?" she asked me.

He had the plague, he was certainly not okay. And I imagined that if I was not immune, I would have it, too. "I think we need to get him home."

"I can carry him," the boy said. He was almost grown.

"No," I said. "You both shouldn't touch him. See if you can find someone with a cart."

"He got sick last night," the woman said. Then, looking at me, "What are you?"

"I'm a foreigner," I said, "but it's okay. I'll help you."

She didn't know what to do for a moment. She looked at the man on the ground. "I don't know anyone with a cart," she said.

I got out the last of my money. "Here's a bit of money," I said to the boy. "See if you can find someone." To the woman I said, "You go and get a blanket to cover him. I'll stay here with him."

"Get him out of the road," someone said.

"Get him out of the way."

"His name is Chang Li?" I asked the woman. She nodded. "Chang Li," I said, "I'm going to let you up but you mustn't run."

But there was nothing there but a dying man who had burned himself out. When I got up he didn't move. I pulled him to the side of the road, and the woman went off to get a blanket and the boy went to find a cart.

His lips were bluish and his eyes moved under his eyelids, but he didn't know we were there. When he breathed I could hear something in his chest like fluid. His saliva was pink with blood, and his breath stank like something foul.

"It's too late for him," a man remarked. "Once they start bleeding they always die."

"Was he going to the river?" another asked me.

"I don't know," I said.

"Probably," said the man who had said it was too late.

"Are you sound?"

I nodded.

"Why did you touch him?"

"I've had offworld medicine," I said. "I don't think I can catch the sickness. So I came to help."

A man spat, and his spit made a dark spot on the road. I wasn't the only one who checked to see if it looked bad.

"This disease comes from offworld."

"I heard that the offworlders want us all to die so they can have our world."

I didn't know if the man would live until the woman or the boy got back. He sounded as if he could never clear his throat. I rolled him over on his side. I didn't think it would help, but it was all I knew to do. I rapped him lightly between his shoulder blades, but it didn't seem to make any difference.

I couldn't tell how old he was. His front was dirty, his sex small and soft and dusty. He didn't have any hair on his chest. He seemed small to me. People seem smaller when they are not conscious. I think our selves, our spirits or our souls, make us bigger than we are. The dead almost always look reduced.

I started to sing through my nose because I didn't know what else to do, singing the man's spirit. It had been so long, so very long since I had sat with the shaman in Taufzin and sang to anyone. There was no spirit door here, and my hand drum was a long time gone. I didn't have anything to burn for him. But I could sing.

"What's he doing?" someone asked.

"I don't know."

"It's a kind of prayer," I said, and resumed.

"Is it a cure?"

I shook my head, humming. It was hard to do since it had been so long. It involves a kind of circular breathing and if you do it right you don't have to pause, but I kept having to take a breath.

"Are you a priest?"

I nodded.

The men and women talked around me while I watched the face of the dying man. Was this what I had come here to do? Sing to the dead? No one had sung to my dead. There were worse things to do.

The boy came back with a man with a two-wheeled cart. The boy didn't know where to look, with his father lying sick in the dust. The cart man came forward to help me lift him, but I shook my head. "You are sound, aren't you?" I asked. "After you take us back, wash your cart out with vinegar and water, and wash your hands." Ayudesh and Wanji used to tell us that when someone was sick we should wash our hands. "Do you have soap? Wash with soap if you can get it."

I remembered how red and chapped my hands would get in the winter from washing them when someone was sick. At least here it was always warm.

"I have a blanket," the woman said. It was an old indigo quilt. The people let her through, and I wrapped the blanket around the man. I was pretty strong, but not so strong that I could easily lift a man, but I was afraid to have anyone help me. I staggered and dumped him roughly in the back of the cart.

"I'm sorry," I said to Chang Li and to the woman and the boy. The boy started to weep.

I was shaking with fear. I wanted to walk away, to go

and hide somewhere to see if I was sick and if I was not to go back to Grandmama Lili's and plant the si-chi and start worms in the garden. The garden seemed suddenly clean.

I followed the cart to Chang Li's house. Chang Li lived in a little house in a maze of alleys. We turned off the main road into a warren barely wide enough for the cart to get through, and then we turned and turned deeper and deeper until the woman said, "Stop." They lived in two rooms, one in back of the other, in an airless alley so narrow the sun could only shine in when it was directly overhead. A little girl ran out of the neighbor's house calling, "Mama! Mama!" The girl broke off coughing and hid her face in her mother's shirt. She had the dark, brown-red flush on her cheeks.

The neighbor woman had a toddler on her hip. "What happened?"

"He ran until this one stopped him." She pointed at me.

I heaved Chang Li off the cart and carried him, staggering, into the back room. It was so dark I was afraid to move and run into something, so I lowered him to the floor as carefully as I could.

His breathing filled the room.

I heard the little girl cough again outside and I felt sick with dread.

"Do you have any soap?" I asked. "Any vinegar? Does the little girl have a fever? The neighbor and her family must wash their hands and wash anything the little girl has touched. You must wash everything."

"Are you a priest?" the boy asked me.

My eyes were adjusting to the darkness. There was nothing in this little room but bedding. "Yes," I said. I wasn't a priest, I wasn't even a shaman, but I didn't know how to explain it otherwise.

"Will you pray for my father?" he asked. He was standing in the doorway.

"I think your father will die," I said.

"Will you pray anyway? We don't have money. . . ."

"I'll pray," I said.

"Is my sister sick?"

"I don't know," I said, because I didn't want to say death words. "Does she have fever?"

He nodded. I could almost feel it rather than see it.

"Tell your mother to make her up a bed in here. You and your mother stay in that room."

"And the baby?"

"The baby in that room, too."

I made a bed from the blankets for Chang Li in one corner, and the mother put the little girl in the other corner. The little girl was afraid of me, afraid of my singing, and she whispered for her mama. Her mama sang to her from the other room, and she quieted, coughing fitfully sometimes in her sleep.

Chang Li died in the night without ever speaking to anyone or knowing where he was. I thought he was dead long before he really was, and I kept checking him and finding, to my surprise, that he was still faintly alive. His face was a strange color, paler than any human's could be, worse even than the dead. His eyes were drawn deep into his head and all the skin around them was black. He was already a skull. I couldn't even hear him breathe. But then suddenly he was cold.

I was wrapping him up in the blanket when the mother came in. "You should stay in the other room," I said.

"I already have the sickness," she said, and lit a little lamp. In the lamplight her face was all hollows, like an old woman's, and her cheeks had the mark of the fever. "Why are you here?"

"When my family died, no one helped me," I said.

"So you came to die with someone?"

No, I hadn't come to die. "Maybe I can keep someone alive," I said.

"Are you a physician?"

I shook my head.

"Are you sick?"

"Not yet," I said.

She shook her head. "Then you are crazy," she said and she bent over to rest her hand against her daughter's cheek.

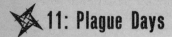 **11: Plague Days**

CHANG LI'S NEIGHBORHOOD WAS A WAR-
ren of long, dirty whitewashed walls and doorways. Each
doorway had a little green-tile door god over it, leering
down with bulbous eyes. The street was so narrow that if
I stood in the middle and stretched out my arms, I could
all but touch both sides. To cook, I sat in the doorway
and tended a charcoal fire in a grate.

The street wasn't empty. Everyone had cooking grates
outside, and lines were strung from roof to roof to hang
laundry. People stood in the alley to talk and watch me
cook. It smelled of charcoal smoke and people and
cooking.

I was making soup from onions and potatoes and rice
with a little pork fat. The woman two doors down had
given the pork fat to me, barely a spoonful but better than
nothing. I was trying to make something to give the little
girl who was coughing and whose fever was rising. Chang
Li's house was now the sick house, and the boy and the
baby were staying next door.

"*Daifu*," said the boy, who everyone called Young
Chang. He was squatting in the neighbor's doorway,
watching me.

"I'm not a doctor," I said.

"Yes," he said. "How is my mama?"

I shrugged. "How are you?"

"Not sick yet," he said.

The pork fat went in the pot first. "Don't come over

292

here," I said. "You'll get sick." The pork fat melted pale white to sizzling liquid in the bottom of the pot, the smell of it thick enough to coat my tongue, and then I put in the onions and let them cook a moment to release their flavor. I wished I had garlic or paprikeen, not so much for the sick people but for me. I was hungry and the soup didn't look like it would be very tasty. I poured water in and put the rice and potatoes in. Salt. I would very much have liked some salt.

"I don't think I'm sick yet," Young Chang said. "I can't tell if I'm sick or just scared. Maybe my throat hurts a little."

"If you get sick, you'll know," I said and smiled at him.

He smiled back at me. He was at the age where he was all elbows and ears, and he was probably even hungrier than I was. I suspected he had been hungry before.

"Will everyone die?" he asked.

"No," I said, not really knowing.

"*Daifu*," he asked—

"I'm not '*daifu*,' " I said.

"—why won't you get sick?"

"I don't know, maybe I will get sick. Maybe not. I worked for offworlders, they gave me medicine. I think it will help me."

"The offworlders are coming here," he said.

"Where did you hear that?" I asked.

"Bowlegged Yi told me."

"Maybe bowlegged Yi didn't know what he was talking about," I said.

"If the offworlders come, they can make us all so we don't get sick."

I shrugged. "Maybe."

Young Chang watched me.

I went in to check on his mother. There were no windows, and the room smelled of something black and rotten. It was so still and so hot inside that my clothing stuck to my skin. The smell of death coated me like perfume.

The sickness came on so quick; last night Young Chang's mother had been talking to me and now, this morning, she stared at nothing with vacant eyes. The little girl lay next to her. The little girl's face was blue-white, and when I pinched her arm the skin stayed wrinkled instead of smoothing out. I pulled the blanket off the little girl's feet, and they were bruised and black, fading to pale skin at her ankles and shins. I held her against my chest and tried to get her to take some water, but her mouth was slack, and anything I poured in just ran down her cheek. Her breath was foul.

I didn't know if I was doing it right. Maybe there was another way I could hold her that would help the water go down her throat. I tried tilting her head back, but I was afraid she would choke, and her breathing was so hard already. Her hot skin felt as if it would tear in my hands, as if it were paper.

I dipped the corner of the blanket in the water and washed her face. I gave her mother some water. The woman swallowed and murmured something.

It was so strange. I didn't know what the black feet meant. I was no healer, but with the shaman I had seen some sick people. I'd never seen anything like this.

I sat and sang to them, softly. It made me feel better, and maybe it did make a bridge to the spirit world. Maybe it made a bridge to my spirit world, though, not theirs. Maybe by singing I was sending them to the place of my people instead of their people.

In any event, they wouldn't go into death without their things. Not like my mam in borrowed pants and not like my daughter, with tight-clenched hands and nothing else, not even a blanket to warm her so that she had had to run to the strange world of machines to find her place.

"Daifu?"

In the doorway was a man I didn't know. He had a boy on his hip, maybe six or seven, with long limp legs hanging. The boy had his head resting against the man's shoulder and his eyes closed, and he had the mark of the disease on his face—the flush and the rash down his chest.

"Can you help my son?" the man asked.

"I can't help anyone," I said. "I can only look after him."

"I've brought rice," the man said, "not much, only a few caddies. It's all I have."

The boy's feet weren't black. Did that mean that he might survive or only that he wasn't as sick as the others?

"When did the fever start?" I asked.

"Yesterday, I think," the man said, laying the boy down on the dirt floor. He didn't even have a blanket.

"I have no medicine," I said. "I don't have anything to help him."

"You have your spells," he said.

I shook my head. "No, the songs I know aren't healing songs."

"There's nobody else," the man said.

I'm nobody else, I thought. The man's want was little fishhooks in my skin. Save my child. Save my child. If I could save a child, I would have saved my own. Or maybe I wouldn't—I don't know. Maybe I never wanted my daughter in the world. Crazy thoughts.

"I have to move the body out of here," I said.

The man looked at Chang Li's body, and I could see he was afraid.

"It's wrapped," I said. If he had carried his sick son, then he could carry the body. "I'll take the head, you take the feet."

"Where should we take it?" he asked.

"Where do you take bodies when people die?"

"We get a cart and take them to *fenshilu*." Fire something. I didn't know the word.

"Well," I said, "we can take him outside. You don't want your sick child lying with the dead." I went and took the head. Grudgingly, the man picked up the feet. Chang Li's body was heavy but stiff, which made it easier to lift. We took it outside by the door. The man dropped the feet and stepped back, wiping his hands on his breeches as if there was something greasy on them.

"You must help me," I said. "Find someone who can take the body."

The man shook his head. "His family must take care of him."

"His family is sick," I said. "Soon they might be dead."

"I am not his family," the man said.

"I am not your son's family," I said.

"You are *daifu*," the man said.

"There is no one else."

"I woke up this morning," the man said, tears in his eyes. "My son is sick. I didn't know what to do, so I brought him to you because they said you were a *daifu*." He started backing up. "I am afraid for my other children. I didn't know what to do! Why do you help Chang Li's family but not me?"

"I'll watch your son," I said. "I will take care of him. But I'm a foreigner and I don't know how to take care of the body—"

But he was backing up, not listening to me, tears of fear running down his face, twisting his mouth.

"It is all right," I said, talking like he was a spooked renndeer. "It's all right. . . ."

But he turned and ran, bare feet leaving no marks in the street.

I didn't know what to do. The neighbor woman came out in the street. I felt foolish, so I went back into the sick house. The mother was trying to sit up. I remembered how Chang Li had run down the street. "It's all right," I said.

"I have to," she panted, "I have to . . ."

Then I smelled shit. Thin watery stuff soaked the blanket. She leaned her head against my arm and made dry little sobs either for air or from shame, I couldn't tell which. The only other blanket I had was my own.

"*Daifu,*" Young Chang was silhouetted in the daylight of the door so that I couldn't see his face. "*Daifu?*"

"Don't come in here!" I snapped.

"The body of my father—" His voice cracked and he swallowed. "The body of my father is lying in the street. What should I do?"

The little girl died in the afternoon, but the little boy woke up enough to take some soup. The woman drank some soup and vomited it back up. Her feet weren't black, but I thought she would die anyway. But she took some more soup and then some water and they stayed down. Her skin wasn't papery yet like the little girl's had been.

The next day, the neighbor's father was sick. He was

an old man with the wispy beginnings of a beard. They brought him over to the sick house and lay him down just inside. I used his blanket to pull him out of the doorway and over by the wall away from Young Chang's mother. Young Chang's mother had fouled my blanket, but I had boiled hers in a pot of water. It was still stained but it didn't stink. I had wrapped her in hers and boiled mine and now it hung drying.

"*Daifu?*" said Young Chang's mother.

"Do you need to pee?" I asked.

"No," she said. "Will I die?"

"I don't know," I said. I sat down and held her hand. Her lips were chapped and cracked, but she was talking. I thought that was a good sign. She seemed a little better. "You should drink some water."

"It will make me sick," she said.

"You should try," I said.

"In a moment. But talk to me first."

"I don't speak your language so well," I said.

"It is better than being alone," she said.

We are all alone, I thought, but I didn't say it. Anyway, I knew what she felt and I couldn't have said no.

"Will you take care of Young Chang for me?" she asked.

I opened my mouth and closed it, not knowing what to say.

"I shouldn't call him Young Chang anymore," she said. "He is Chang Jiang. His father is dead so he isn't little anymore."

"Chang's mother," I said, "I have no home."

"We will all be dead, so you can live here," she said. "You are good. A doctor can make money. He can be your assistant."

"I am not a doctor," I said.

"You talk foolish," she said. "Look at you. You are taking care of sick people."

"I am foreign," I pointed out.

"Not in your heart," she said. "It doesn't matter. You think about it."

"I am a woman, not a man," I said, knowing that would change everything.

She looked at me and frowned. "I can never tell with foreigners, I can't tell one of you from the other. But you don't have a beard." She sighed, not very interested in whether I was a man or a woman.

At least I wouldn't have to worry about peeing in front of her anymore.

"Now I can die," she said.

"Your sickness makes you sad," I said. "You might surprise yourself and live." I kept my voice light, as if we were joking about something inconsequential. I soaked a shirt and used it to wipe her face.

"That feels nice," she said. "You have a woman's touch."

"Do you have any brothers or sisters?" I asked, thinking about where Young Chang might go.

"Ai-ya," she said, "my brother. He is worthless. He smokes *dama* all the time with his wife, and she has babies no one looks after. My niece—only as tall as my daughter, so little—she is running in the street all day with no one watching, and she runs in front of a cart and it breaks her bones, both legs. My sister-in-law, she cries and wails and lets the child lie there until I tell Chang Li that we have to take her home. I take care of her like my own and she lives, although her legs are bent. Then my sister-in-law, she says that I am whispering poison against her in her own daughter's ear and takes her back. I say, you have to take care of her, she is not strong, but does that one listen? No, she sits in her blue smoke all day. So the little one, the little thing, she is left lying and of course she gets sores on her backside and legs and she gets sick and dies. Murdered by her own mother, I say." Young Chang's mother starts to cry and turns her face from me. "I am sorry," she said. "Everything makes me cry. I am usually not like this."

I stroked her forehead. "It's okay. Sickness makes you weak. You save your strength to be well."

The room stank, and I was so hot I could barely breathe. The old man's breathing was like the sound of someone drowning. I turned him on his side and thin bloody liquid drained out of his mouth on his blanket. I tried to clean his face but he kept drooling. The shirt was soaked and it was all over my hands. I went back out front and saw Young Chang. "Get me a pot of water," I said and stood back away from the pot.

I waited in the doorway because I couldn't go back inside. I wondered why I was staying. I didn't have to. I could just leave anytime. I could walk out of the city and then wait—how long? Ten days? Twenty days? One hundred days? How long until I could go back to Ming Wei and her grandmother, to Cha-li and the garden.

I had been stupid.

I picked up my pack, everything except my blanket. The air felt so cool and smelled so good. Young Chang would be back before too long. He could nurse his mother and the old man and the boy. I didn't know what I was doing and I couldn't keep them alive any better than he could. I could get out now and then figure out what to do.

I stood in the door, wanting to go and knowing that if I did, Young Chang would surely get sick, and watched him come back from the well with the pot of water. I would boil the shirt clean. I would wait to see how his mother did. Then I would go.

"*Daifu!*" Young Chang called. "*Daifu*, the offworlders are here! They are coming to houses and counting sick people!"

The old man died in the afternoon. I boiled the shirt and we waited for the offworlders.

Chang Li's body was smelling. The old man's body and the girl's body, both wrapped next to him, would soon smell, too.

The neighbor came out of her house. She was a stocky woman. "How is Young Chang's mother?" she asked.

"The same," I said. We talked over a distance, from one door to the other. "I don't know what to do about that," I said, nodding at the bodies.

"Those people," she pointed to a house. "They have run away to the countryside, to his mother's house, to escape the sickness. You could put the bodies in there for now."

There was no one to help me, since I wouldn't allow anyone who wasn't sick to come near. Young Chang and the neighbor woman watched as I grabbed the blanket-wrapped feet of Young Chang's father and dragged him toward the door. The body wasn't stiff anymore. The blanket unwrapped and the swollen arm fell out and open. The smell made me gag.

I stopped and tried to wrap it up again, but I didn't have anything to secure the blanket.

"Young Chang," said the neighbor woman, "go check my baby."

I was grateful when Young Chang went inside.

She came over and grabbed the head.

"No, don't!" I said.

"I am already sick," she said. "I just don't want to say it to myself. We'll get this done."

The house was empty of everything except the bed that was too big to move. We put the body in the corner of the back room and then came out and got the old man. Young Chang was watching from the door with the toddler on his hip. The neighbor woman coughed hard for a moment while we were carrying the old man, so we stopped and I waited until she caught her breath. "Young Chang," she called, "you get my blanket and put it by the door."

We put the old man next to Young Chang's father.

"I will take care of the girl," I said. "You go and lie down."

"She was a sweet girl," the neighbor said.

All children are sweet after they die, but even if it's not true that doesn't make death any easier. I picked up the blanket. I heard her say, "Young Chang's mother! I had no one to talk to so I came here!"

Three more sick people came from the neighborhood, so I had six to take care of. The little boy cried until I held him against me and fed him spoonfuls of weak soup. He laid his red face against my shoulder, shining with fever and swollen with crying, and fell asleep. I held him until my legs were numb.

I thought he was doing better. He wasn't as pale as the others had been and he was fractious.

Young Chang's mother was worse.

Young Chang came and told me that the offworlders

were still going from house to house, but that they had a long way before they got here. No one came that day.

At night was the worst.

I didn't have a light, so I sat in the dark and listened to the body sounds of the sick. In silence you can hear the bellows of the lungs and the roiling belly. Their breaths rose up around me, and I breathed them in and breathed them out. Their air was part of me.

Chang Li's house had an indigo cloth hanging in the doorway, but even if there had been a door I wouldn't have closed it. It was too hot and there was nothing to steal. The doorway was a faint opening, barely lighter than the darkness of the room. I slept on the hard-packed floor of the front room. Above me, the wet shirts and blankets I had washed hung in the room, still in the stagnant air.

I was tired but I kept listening, wondering who had fouled their blanket—not that I could clean them up in the dark. Wondering who I should give water to. Wondering who had died in the blackness. My throat ached and I felt feverish. I didn't know if I had it or not. I didn't think so, I didn't think I was sick enough.

I got up and sat in the doorway.

"*Daifu?*" someone whispered in the dark.

"Go to sleep, Young Chang," I said gently.

"I have the fever," he said, a voice out of nothing. He coughed.

"Oh, Young Chang," I said. He came in the darkness and sat next to me, and his skin felt hot.

"It's all right," he whispered. "I was lying there and I was thinking, soon everyone will have it and everyone will die, and what—what if I am one of the last ones? What if I am last and I am all alone?"

"Those are the kind of thoughts you have when you are sick," I said, and put my arm around him. "Remember, the offworlders are coming."

"You don't like the offworlders," he said.

I sighed. "They will help sick people."

"Everyone says that the offworlders won't help people, because you're an offworlder and you can't help everyone."

"An offworlder?" I laughed in the dark. "Who says that?"

"Everyone," he said.

"Everyone?"

"Well, not everyone."

"Bowlegged Yi," I said.

Young Chang didn't answer, which I took as a yes.

"No, I'm not an offworlder. I'm just a foreigner. I'm not even a *daifu*."

"You take care of sick people," he pointed out.

I didn't have an answer for that.

I didn't want to take him inside because I didn't want to go inside, so we sat. He leaned against me, and eventually I dozed and he fell asleep. He was a good boy. We sat until my shoulder ached from holding still, and then I finally woke him up and took him in with me.

In the morning his mother was dead, and he sobbed and rocked back and forth. I reached out to hold him, but he shrugged me off, angry, so I left him be.

I wrapped his mother in the blanket and pulled her body into the dead house and when I came back, Young Chang had put his blanket in his mother's place and lay with his face to the wall.

He lay that way all afternoon, until the offworlders came.

And finally, they were here. Two of them, a man and a woman, in shirts the same color blue that had been at the refugee camp all those years ago.

The man moved through Chang Li's house as if it were his own. "How many sick?" he asked. His language was much worse than mine.

"Six," I said in English. "Four die, six sick here."

"I don't understand," he said. "How many sick?"

"I speak English," I said.

He shook his head.

"He's speaking English," the woman said. "He said six are sick and four have died. How do you speak English?"

"I am tech in Taufzin," I said. "My name is Jan."

She said something I didn't understand at all. It had been a long time since I used English.

"I don't understand," I said. "I forget . . ."

She crouched down next to me. "You come with me, with us." She pointed to the man and herself.

"Why?" I asked.

"You translate," she said.

I shook my head. "My English is bad."

She laughed and said something I didn't understand.

"I . . ." I wanted to say I was taking care of these people, but I didn't know how. I pointed to the people in the hut. "Not good," I said. "I am here for them."

"We'll give them medicine," she said. "They'll get well."

I could understand a lot of what she said, a lot more than I could speak.

"Please," she said. "You can help."

I pointed to Young Chang. "He come," I said.

They talked quietly, just a moment or two. I didn't even try to understand.

"Yes," the woman said. "He comes." She knelt over him and tapped some things into her pad, then she put a dermal patch on his arm. She and the man did the same for everyone.

"Young Chang," I said, "Young Chang. Your mother told me to take care of you. Come with me. We will go with the offworlders."

"I am sick," he whispered.

"It'll be all right," I said. "I'll help you."

We walked out of Chang Li's house into the air. I lifted my face to the sun and breathed deep. My chest was tight, as if I had not taken a deep breath in days.

They would have done anything I asked—they would have taken everyone at Chang Li's, but I didn't know that. They took Young Chang and me back with them, poor Young Chang stumbling with fever. The offworlders were living in a big gray stone house with a courtyard. I looked to see if in the center of the courtyard there was a stone from Earth, the way there had been in the house of old Wang Jiu, back when I delivered the message for Ming Wei's uncle, but here there was only a pond filled with lazy fish.

But everything was strange, neither island nor offworld

but some awkward mixture of both. The courtyard was full of offworld things. Jackets were draped over the old softstone balustrade, and there were metal chairs everywhere and papers and drinking cups and a music player. Two offworld men were sitting slumped in chairs like big children, their legs long and bare and hairy, looking at tablets and tapping things out. Under their feet, the courtyard stones were uneven, but the offworld men were like all offworld things—smooth, maintained, almost unused.

The music was loud and it sounded as if the musicians were right there. It also sounded as if it were raining.

"What's this?" one said, and the woman answered, but I didn't catch it. She shrugged off her jacket.

"Hello," I said.

"This is Jan," the woman said, "and this is Chang Jang." She said Young Chang's name so badly that I'm not sure he would have recognized it.

One of the men jumped up. He was tall, so tall, much taller than me, and he was wearing bright yellow short pants and sandals of almost the same color. "I'm Paul," he said and held out his hand. I knew to shake it. His big hand was soft, like someone's who has never done work.

"Hello, Paul," I said. "I have forget my English."

He said something with "okay" in it and then said, "This is Henri."

Henri was almost as big as Paul, but dark, even darker than Ayudesh or Wanji. "You are from India?" I asked.

Henri looked surprised. "No," he said, "I'm from—" But I couldn't get the name of where he was from.

The rooms were cool and bright, and they made a place for Young Chang to lie down. They were sorry they did not have one of the clever little pallets they used, but I didn't care. They gave us both water.

"You are fine," I told Young Chang, smiling at him. "You will get better now."

"I'm tired," he murmured.

I made him drink some water.

Paul wanted to examine me. "I am a doctor," he said, "umm, *daifu*."

"Yes, doctor," I said. Now that Young Chang was taken care of my own tiredness fell on me like a pleasant weight. Doctor Paul examined me. "I am woman," I said, trying to be helpful.

He nodded and said something, but I wasn't trying to follow him. He was so big and so young. He was like a renndeer calf or a dog, all friendly and wanting to be liked.

"Jan," he was saying, "do you understand?"

"Yes?" I said.

"Food? You want to eat?"

"Yes," I nodded emphatically. "Eat, yes, Doctor Paul."

He took me through the courtyard to the kitchen in the back. I smelled rice and pork. There was a nice garden. He sat me down and served me, big pieces of pork, very spiced, and rice and lots of leaf vegetables. There was so much food and so many pots and pans. Food was everywhere, some of it offworld and some of it familiar. He sat and watched me eat.

I remembered how to hold a fork and a knife and a spoon, but I was not so good with them. He just grinned and watched.

"You are a doctor?" he asked.

I shook my head.

"Lisa called you *daifu*."

"No," I said, my mouth full of rice. "Young Chang call me *daifu*. I, um, I says, I mean I say, 'No, I am not *daifu* . . .'" My English ran out.

He nodded anyway. After I ate he brought me sweets, in foil. "Cookie," I said, and covered my mouth in surprise. I had not had a cookie since I left Taufzin.

"Yeah." He grinned and nodded as if I were his student. "Where did you learn English?"

"Hamra Mission and Taufzin," I said.

"Hamra Mission?" he said.

"Appropriate technology mission," I explained. "Um. One, economic development should be gradual. Two, that analyzing economic growth by the, um, production of goods rather than the needs and—um, and um—of people leads to . . . um, I forget much." Actually I was pleased that I remembered as much as I did. The familiar words came up from the dark of my memory. Sometimes, trying to sleep at night, I had said them like a prayer.

"That's great," Paul said. "Lisa!" he shouted.

After a moment she came.

"Say it again," he said, "Appropriate technology . . ."

I stumbled through it again.

She seemed surprised.

He asked her something. "Hamra Mission" was in it.

She shook her head. "Where is Hamra Mission?" she asked.

"North," I said. "Very north. Very, very north. But people are dead. No Mission there now." I wished I remembered my English better. I felt like a child.

Lisa gave me a shirt and pants. "For a woman," she said. "Is that okay?"

I smiled. "Okay."

Behind the kitchen was a place they had made to shower, a little tent, just big enough to stand under the water in private. I stripped and washed in warm water, and washed my clothes as well. The soap. I had forgotten how wonderful offworld soap could be. It was like the soap in the factory in Taufzin, all slippery in my hands like a fish. I turned the water off and dried and dressed in clean clothes.

I felt like new.

English came back to me, not as well as I had spoken it in Taufzin. We went out in the morning, Lisa and Sasha—the one who had been with her who hadn't been able to understand my English—and me, and we walked through the city and counted the sick and the dead. Sasha had a tester that told him if people had already had the cure. He would put their finger in it, Lisa would mark down the numbers that came up, and I would ask, "How many have died? How many are sick? How many have left?"

Lisa would tap in the numbers. We would distribute medicine. Sometimes we were too late. Sometimes people were so sick that the medicine would not save them.

Sasha had trouble with my English; he couldn't understand it. His English was not so good either, but most of the time I could understand him. So I talked to Lisa.

"On Earth," I said, "people all speak English?"

"No," Sasha said. "Most people do not. In my family, I am the only one."

"So," I said, "these people," I gestured around us, at the city, "they are from Earth. They remember. Why no one speak their language?"

Lisa said, "They don't speak a language spoken on Earth. Their language is very difficult. It's a, well, it's a tonal language that's a mixture of Southern Chinese and Indonesian with a huge vocabulary of words borrowed from Hindu and Malayam and other Indian languages. It's a new language, just here."

I was silent, trying to figure out all of what she said. I got the idea, though.

"Besides," she said, "China and India sent more settlers to space than any other places. They didn't send as many here as they did the other three settled worlds, so people who speak the languages this language comes from go other places."

People asked me questions; I asked Lisa as best I could.

"The disease come of where?" I asked her.

"Earth," she said. "People from Earth came here—and they didn't know it, but they were sick. For us, it's like a cold. But for you, it's very bad."

"Why did you bring it?" the man asked. He was squatting outside the door to his house. His son and two daughters were dead. There was only him and his wife left.

"We didn't bring it on purpose," Lisa said. "If you went to visit someone in a village, and you didn't know you had it, they would get sick because of you."

"You have this thing," he waved at Sasha's tester, "you can tell you have it, so why did you bring it?"

"Everyone has a lot of diseases in them," Lisa said. "But most of them don't make us sick. We are strong and our bodies keep them from making us sick. It's hard to tell what will make someone else sick. Sometimes something that won't hurt me will hurt someone else, and I don't know until they're sick."

The man spat at Lisa's feet and looked away.

"Are you sick?" I asked the man.

He shrugged, he didn't care.

Sasha crouched to test him, but the man wouldn't let Sasha take his finger.

"Leave me be!"

"We need to see if you are sick," I said.

"What difference does it make?" he asked. "My son is dead. There's no one after me."

"Because if you are sick, you can make someone else's son sick," I said.

"What do I care about someone else's son?"

It was like something from a story, but it was real. The man was there in front of me. He needed to shave and he smelled of sweat. His feet were broad and the skin around his heels was cracked. He wasn't a story at all.

"He says no," I said.

"We have to," Lisa said. "We have to treat a lot of people."

I reached down and took the man's arm. He was a little startled, so he stood up when I pulled him up. Then I twisted his arm behind him. I had worked security on an ore train and they had taught us how to do this.

"Let him go!" Lisa said.

"Treat him," I said.

The man arched to get the pressure off his shoulder, standing on tiptoe. There wasn't much he could do that wouldn't hurt. Lisa didn't move, but Sasha did. He put a patch on the man's arm and then took it off.

I released the man. "I am sorry," I said, "but if you are not given medicine, maybe you make other people sick." I rubbed his arm.

He didn't say anything, just stared at the dust.

Inside his house, his wife was sitting where she could see us. I took a patch from Sasha and walked inside.

"I am sorry, *taitai*," I said.

She held out her arm. "He is just crazy with sadness," she said.

I put the patch on. "I know," I said.

"It's cold," she said.

I took it off. "That's all," I said.

"What does it do?"

"It sends spirits into your blood to fight the disease," I said. I didn't know the word for antibodies. There probably wasn't one—and I had only a dim notion of what antibodies were. "Spirits" was the best I could do.

"Why did you do that!" Lisa said to me, angry and quiet.

"You said we had to treat him," I said.

"He's right," Sasha said.

"*She*," Lisa corrected.

Sasha grinned at me.

Lisa said some things I didn't understand. Sasha put his hands up. "No," he said. "You must do things sometimes. You don't like them, you do them. It saves lives."

"People must have a say in their treatment," she said.

"Not always," Sasha said.

We were collecting a crowd. People watched us talk in English.

The next house we entered was full of the dead.

Lisa and Sasha backed out, and I held my breath and counted seven dead, three of them children, and then went back out gagging. I told Lisa and she put it on her tablet.

"At least there aren't flies," she said.

I bent over and put my hands on my knees. "I don't understand," I said, catching my breath.

"Flies," she said. "Little, um, *insects,* um, animals, in the air." She showed me the difference between thumb and forefinger to show me how very little. I tried to think of what she meant, but nothing came to mind. We didn't have bats that small that flew, at least none that I'd seen.

"On Earth," she said, "bodies have *insects,* little animals only not animals."

I looked at her, not comprehending.

She shrugged. "It doesn't matter."

I straightened up and then I realized what she meant. When something onworld died, it was covered with bugs, eating it. On Earth bugs ate people, too. I could picture it in my mind.

I leaned over and threw up.

"Are you okay?" Lisa asked.

"I am sorry," I said. I held the idea away from me. "I understand now, about the, what did you call them? On the dead?"

Sasha laughed and then covered his mouth. "Sorry, Jan," he said.

Lisa was embarrassed. She kept asking me if I was all right. As always, people were watching us.

"The offworlder is sick," a man said.

"No," I said. "It is the smell, the dead."

The people of the neighborhood looked at me with flat eyes. If an offworlder could get sick, then what good was the medicine?"

"I'm not an offworlder," I said. "I'm a foreigner."

"What is it?" Lisa asked.

"They think I have disease," I said. "They think I am offworlder."

Sasha said, "Walk slowly."

We went to the next house. It was empty, no bodies, no living. Fled to the countryside, I thought.

A rock hit Lisa in the shoulder and she grabbed the hurt place.

I turned. "Stop it!" I said. I wished I had my rifle. "Go," I said to Lisa and Sasha. "Go."

They backed away.

"If I am sick," I said, "I touch you and maybe you die. You have stones, but I can touch you before I die."

They were poor people in dirty clothes. Mostly young men with narrow faces and bad teeth and hard hands. A dog pack, bored and scared.

"I go now," I said. I looked at a couple of them in the face, made them look at me. They did not drop their eyes. That scared me a lot, but I tried to keep it from my face. I took a step back and then another.

They stood there, watching me. Someone threw a rock. I ran.

Luckily, they did not follow.

I ran up the steps to the room I shared with Young Chang. Young Chang was lying on his blankets with one arm across his eyes.

I sat down on my blankets. "Terrible day," I said.

"Umm," Young Chang said, not moving his arm.

He had been getting better and yesterday had seemed perfectly well. "Are you sick?" I asked.

"I'm fine," he said.

"What's wrong?" I asked.

"I hate it here!" he said and sat up. He'd been crying. "I hate the offworlders!"

I didn't know what to say.

"No one talks to me and I can't understand what they're saying and their food makes me sick!"

"Their food?" I asked, a little stupidly.

"It smells bad! The white food, that they put on meat!"

"Cheese?" I asked.

"It smells bad! And they don't cut their meat up and they don't use chopsticks! And you are always gone with them! My mama said you were supposed to take care of me and you don't!" His face was red with emotion.

I didn't know what to do. "I have to go," I said. "This is their place."

"I don't want to stay here!"

"Where would we live, what would we eat?"

"You could be a doctor," he said. "I would help. I could learn."

I shook my head. "I'm not a doctor."

"Stop saying that!"

"It's true."

"You take care of sick people."

"I was a farmer."

Young Chang shrugged and looked away. "Can we leave?"

"Today was very bad. People—" I didn't know how to say that they threw stones. "People . . ." My head ached and I was tired and I couldn't think of the words. "You think no one understands you," I said. "No one understands me. I talk to you in your language, I talk to offworlders in *English*, no one talks in my language."

"Nobody made you come here!"

"You were sick, they make you well!"

"I wish I were dead!" Young Chang shouted.

"Death is easy," I said.

It didn't make sense in Young Chang's language. It stopped him a moment though. Then he fell back on his blankets. "You don't understand," he said.

Of course I did. I tried to think of how to tell him that

my whole clan was dead, my mother and father and sister and aunties and cousins and husband and daughter. It was too hard. I got up and went back downstairs, but Lisa and Paul and Henri and another doctor, Sara, were all talking and drinking tea and listening to music. There were so many offworlders here, I could not keep them straight. I went through to the back even though I knew someone was always in the kitchen.

The only one there was Sasha, but I didn't want to see him at all.

"Jan!" he said, "Hey. I want to talk to you!"

"Yes, Sasha?"

"I am making a cup of tea. Do you want a cup of tea?"

"No, thank you," I said.

"It is not tea, you know. Tea is from Earth and this, it does not taste like tea, but it's better than nothing."

I didn't really care, but I nodded. "You want to talk?"

"You don't like me," he said and grinned a dog's grin. "No, it is okay. But we are more alike than you think." He sat down on the bench beside the long table. "They, most of them, are all together. They speak English, they think English. Even Henri, his English is good. It is a little piece of their home—all this English. You and I, we are the outsiders. We have no one to talk to. So we should be friends." He frowned at the expression on my face. "Okay, not friends. I am trying to think of how to say it. We are like soldiers, together. We are on the same side, yes?"

I shrugged.

"Come up to my room. I have something for you, I think you will like it."

Sasha was not a handsome man, but he was not a big puppy like Paul and Henri and so many of the offworlders. He had a face that looked already too old. The skin always looked dark and bruised under his eyes and his jaw was always blue with hair. I still thought there was something in him that was a little mean. But I didn't want to be rude.

Up we went to his room. It was like Young Chang's and mine, except that he had things in it. He had a folding bed in a metal frame. The blankets were all tossed on it and the mattress showed. He had a table and a mirror and a couple of boxes of clothes. Mostly he had papers everywhere and all his work things.

I looked at myself in his mirror. It had been a long time since I had seen my reflection in anything larger than a brass mirror you could hold in your hand. I was surprised.

If you had asked me I would have said I did not really think of myself as a man or a woman. When I told Young Chang's mother I was a woman, it was because that was an easy way to tell her that I wasn't what she thought. But my face was hard, like a man's. There were lines around my mouth. I was not so old, not any older than Sasha, but I looked older.

I touched my face.

"What?" Sasha said.

I pointed. "The mirror. I not see me for a long time." I had to smile. "Not so pretty, ai?"

He grinned. "Not so pretty. But smart. Today when they were about to stone us, you were smart."

" 'Stone us'? It is what you say?"

He nodded.

"They were stoning us."

"Yes. Your English is not so bad. You need to work on verb tenses." He shrugged. "Me, too." He dug in a box and pulled out a bottle of clear liquid. "This is like whiskey. It is from my home. It is called vodka."

He took the cap off and took a drink and passed it to me. I smelled it. It smelled sharp, like whiskey, and had another smell, like something spicy. I took a sip.

"It is a kind of vodka called pepper vodka. Do you like it?"

I wasn't sure.

"Take another drink. I have been saving it, but it is not so good to drink alone."

It was good. Two kinds of fire. "It would be good in the snow," I said.

"It is good in winter," he said.

"Where you come from, there is snow?"

"Snow?" He laughed. "You have never seen so much snow. You have never been so cold."

"At my home, very cold," I said.

Sasha had to tell me about snow. He told me how cold

it had been where he lived, using numbers. "Sometimes, where I am from, there is no day."

I nodded. "The sun, it—" I made a gesture of a circle, to show the sun circling below the horizon, but he didn't know what I meant. "At my home, the same," I said.

He squinted at me. His face was flushed. I suspected mine was, too.

"You see," he said. "We are more alike than you know."

I took a drink of pepper vodka. I liked it. He was trying very hard to be friendly. I knew that. And he was right about one thing: we were both alike in that we were foreigners here. We were children in their eyes and they were children in ours. Our lack of language made us appear simple to each other when we weren't. I saw them as big and soft and awkward and they saw me . . . how did they see me? I wasn't sure, but I was certain it was not the way I saw myself.

How did Sasha see himself? I saw him as a man with a mean streak, a bit sentimental now that he was drunk, but just as likely to get mad and start swinging his fists. He was bigger than me—they were all bigger than me. Maybe that was true, but it wasn't all. My troubles with language, it made me make everyone smaller than they really were.

"Why you come here?" I asked Sasha.

He was talking about cold and snow, but he stopped, "Here?" he asked. "To cure plague."

I shook my head. "This, so far of your home," I said.

His lips moved as he parsed my sentence silently. "Ah, you mean why did I leave Russia to come to this planet?" He laughed. "You should wonder. This planet . . . you know there are only four colonized planets? And this one is good one. Most like Earth. Amino acids are all right-handed, so unless animal is genetically engineered you can't eat it—" I understood enough to know he meant renndeer and sheep and oxen; at the mission we had studied about the change in renndeer "—and people can live. Like paradise, eh?"

He rattled on some more, but I was trying to remember what "paradise" was. I thought it was something that made you sick, but I wasn't sure. I was drunk on pepper vodka and he was talking too much.

It didn't really matter what he said anyway. Men like to talk about themselves—anyone does. He probably thought I was a smart person, too.

He leaned forward. "You do not know. Russia, my home, it was a strong place. Do you understand?"

I shook my head.

"Many guns, guns with bullets this big." He showed a foolish distance between his hands, a bullet as long as the length of my arm from wrist to elbow. "No," he insisted, "it is true. Some of these guns, they are on wheels, you know? Trucks pull them."

These people could make the shuttles that landed in the shuttleport. Why couldn't they make giant guns?

"But sometimes this place is powerful, then time passes and they are not so powerful and that one is more powerful—do you know?"

I thought about it. Sometimes one clan was powerful, then another. Did that mean that someday maybe we would be as powerful as the offworlders?

I doubted it.

"Now my home is not strong, it is weak. I wanted to be rich. I wanted to be strong. I thought I wanted to escape, I thought I did not like my home. But now, I am homesick," he said. "I want to speak Russian with someone who will understand. I want a Russian wife, a home, all those things. I want to see the moon. I miss the moon."

We had two moons, although they were sometimes hard to tell from stars. Ayudesh had fussed about moons, too. I didn't want to hear about homesickness. I took a pull on the vodka.

"I can teach you a Russian song," he said. "We sing together."

"No," I said, "not sing."

"The song, it is easy," he promised.

I shook my head. "No, Sasha, not sing. I am too sad."

"The song is good. Sometimes, it is good to feel sad," he said. "This is big sadness, sadness of whole people."

"No, Sasha," I said.

"I sing for you," he said.

He had a surprising voice. The music was nothing like the music they played in the courtyard. It was human music, it let you in—not like the wall the other music made, where you could listen and admire but not ever imagine being able to make it yourself. Sasha could sing. He sat down next to me where I was leaning up against the wall and put his arm around my shoulders and sang a soft song like a love song or a lullaby. He closed his eyes and sang to himself as much as to me, and the weight of his arm was a great comfort.

When he had done he let his chin sink to his chest and sat that way for a moment, his eyes closed, while the feeling from the song was all around us. Then he opened his eyes and said to me, "You sing."

I sang a song we used to sing while we were fishing, one that I had sung that summer before the war, after the baby had died but while Aslak was my husband. It made me think of kin and summer and it made me cry.

"There, there," Sasha said. "See, it is good to cry sometimes. You need to feel or you die inside, eh? You do not cry like a woman, though."

"I am not a woman, not long, long time," I said.

"What are you, man?" Sasha asked.

"No," I said. "I am Jan. Just Jan."

"Just one," he said, holding up a single, careful drunken finger.

I nodded. "Just one."

He kissed me, a drunken bleary kiss, and I let him. I kissed him back.

"You kiss like a woman," he said.

"How man kiss?" I asked.

"The same," he said, and we laughed.

We kissed some more. His cheeks were scratchy with stubble and his lips were soft and very red, like a girl's. I was thinking he would want to fuck and I was not sure if I wanted to or not. I didn't want to say no after kissing him—it would be like saying yes and then saying no. And I liked kissing him. It would be nice to have sex and sleep here and then I wouldn't have to argue with Young Chang, especially since I was drunk. All the while I was feeling his soft lips and his scratchy beard and smelling the faintly sweaty smell of him.

"Come here," he said, and tugged me over to the bed.

"It is too small," I said. I pulled the blanket on the floor.

"Not floor," he said.

I didn't care because I knew he would give in. It was the little man thinking and the little man only had one thought.

We lay down on the blanket, Sasha on top of me, and kissed some more. "You are so hard," he said and touched my flat chest. I didn't want to think about how I looked.

A baby. But I didn't think I could get pregnant. I hadn't gotten pregnant after Rahel and now I was as much man as woman, even like this, with Sasha. "You are so hard," he said. There was no place in me for a baby.

"Take off your shirt," he said.

I took off mine and he took off his. He found my scar from the night Ming Wei and I had fled her uncle's burning ship and traced his finger across my ribs. Offworlders had such nice hands. His hands were small for a man and very, very clean. They were soft, almost as soft as his lips, and I closed my eyes. It was as if he were kissing me with his fingers.

I felt the little man hard against me.

Sasha made me lift my hips so he could slide my pants off.

He wore pants and offworld underpants, smooth white tight things as soft as baby's skin. They were as warm as his skin, and when he pulled them off I could smell the musky smell of him. He had tightly curled black hair that went down the insides of his thighs. His chest was covered in stiff curls, too. He was the hairiest man I had ever seen.

I wrapped my legs around him, but I was dry and it hurt, so he put his fingers in his mouth and rubbed inside me until he could go in.

We fucked each other, smelling of sweat and vodka and sex, first for his pleasure and then for mine, and he was very good and very thoughtful. I was satisfied and then all soft inside and sweaty behind my knees and tired in that way, easy. Then I fell into drunken sleep on the floor, waking up once in the dark, not knowing where I was and finding the gray square of the window in the greater darkness of the room and seeing outside that there were stars, very far away.

In the morning I picked up my clothes. My room was across the courtyard, so I went down the steps and back out past the kitchen to pee. No one was up. Back up the stone steps. They were cold. The door to my room was open.

Young Chang was gone.

The blankets were tousled, but he'd been lying in them the afternoon when he had been so angry with me. I leaned against the door frame and rubbed my head. I shouldn't have left him, of course. His few things were gone.

I could only think of one place he might have gone and that was home, although I didn't know very much about him, really, and he might have known a number of places to go.

I washed my face and rinsed out my mouth. I was afraid to drink anything because after all the vodka the night before, if I drank anything now I might be drunk again.

It was late enough for people to be up and making breakfast when I got to Young Chang's neighborhood. People turned their heads to watch me walk down the alley, but no one said anything. At least that made me think that Young Chang was there.

Young Chang's father's house was empty and the door was like a missing tooth, but next door the neighbor's house was full of life and Young Chang was there. The neighbor nodded at me and said, "Hello, *daifu*," but Young Chang, who was holding the baby, would not meet my eyes.

The neighbor, cheerful and round-faced, beckoned me outside. She looked recovered from her sickness, although her wrists were thin when she gestured. "Ai-ya." She sighed. "He is a good boy, you know that."

I nodded. "I'm sorry. His mother told me to watch him."

"Yes, yes, yes," she said. "And you have been very

good to him. Oh, it is hot already, isn't it? I feel like steamed rice." She smiled and I smiled.

"I have not been good to him," I said.

"No," she said. "No, you do not understand, he has always been spoiled. You know what that is? He was her favorite. But I think, it is best if he stays here, with us."

"I said I would take care of him," I said.

"Yes, yes, yes," she said, and patted my arm. "You are good. But you know, a young boy, he needs to be with us. You're a foreigner. . . ." These people's word for foreigner was "outside-of-the-center person." They called themselves "center-kingdom people."

"It's best," I said, nodding. My head ached from vodka. "It is best."

She patted my arm again.

"Maybe I'll come back, see him again," I said.

"Yes," she said, "that'd be very good."

"Can I tell him that?"

She hesitated. "Maybe, *daifu,* you should come back some time."

I didn't argue. I just went away.

I was late to go out with Lisa and Sasha. Lisa was beside herself, but Sasha, hungover, sat slouched in one of the folding chairs in the courtyard. He raised his face, swollen and dark. "You are okay?" he said.

"Young Chang ran away," I said.

"He was not your family, you know," Sasha said.

"I feel too sick today," I said to Lisa. "I am sorry."

"Christ!" Lisa said.

I went upstairs and lay on my blankets and thought about what I was doing. I thought about going back north, to my own people. I thought about Ming Wei and Grandmama Lili. I was thinking when Sasha knocked on the frame of my door and looked in.

"You are okay?" he asked.

"Okay," I said. I thought about how unexpected it was for a man to come to see how I was and I smiled at him. Sasha was unexpected.

"You know," he said, awkward, "last night . . ."

I shrugged. "It is nice. We are drunk. Now," I shrugged again. "It doesn't matter."

He squeezed his nose. "Yes," he said. "Me, too. Very good. Um, I am thinking, about, um, contraception. You know this word?"

I shook my head.

"You, I mean, I did not think last night, about, you know, a baby. About if you might have baby? Do you have implant to make no baby?"

"I have implant make me like man," I said.

"But nothing to stop a baby?" he said. "Come, I will check you out. I am doctor, you know."

That made me laugh. Sasha was not like a doctor at all. He was rough and he didn't know people. But offworlders had odd ways. I knew that they thought of him as a doctor, even if he wasn't a *daifu* in my eyes.

"What is funny?" he asked.

"I can't," I said. "No words."

We went down to the room where they did their science. It was a beautiful gray stone room, with high windows and shutters and a long table made of bluewood, but they'd filled it with offworld machines that made the old room seem raw and unfinished. "Sit up here," Sasha said.

I sat up on a metal table covered in paper, and Sasha got his instruments and laid them out. In my experience, the doctors at the factory in Taufzin had treated people the same way they taught me to repair their machines, which explained why someone like Sasha could be a doctor. The table was cold and felt good. Sasha's hands shook a little from the night's vodka.

"You have many implants," he said, frowning.

I shook my head. "One."

"No," he said, "you have surveyor's kit."

I didn't know what he said, much less what it meant.

"In your head, you have communications unit to call, in emergency, don't you? And stasis unit? And a slowtime? But the slowtime," he peered at his instrument, "it did not implant right, it does not work."

I didn't know what he was talking about at all, and then I realized. They were from Wanji. I hadn't thought much about them in years. "Very, very old," I said. "Very old."

"The stasis unit is old? Jan, you should not have it more than a year, you understand? It's bad."

"Bad?" I said. "Why?"

"Many things can go wrong." He looked at an indicator. "You are not pregnant," he said. "It can cause cancer," he said. "In your blood, in your brain. You'll be very sick and die."

"Okay," I said. "But no baby, right?"

"If you have stasis unit and you get pregnant, the baby would not be right, maybe born dead, maybe not right."

I nodded, although what he said was hard for me to understand.

"I take it out," he said.

"Okay," I said.

"I take it all out, all implants," he said.

"Not the one that makes me like a man."

"No?" he said.

I thought about it a moment. "Maybe take it out," I said. I didn't really care about any of the implants anymore. Even the one that made me like a man. I didn't care what people thought I was. Grandmama Lili knew what I was, so did Ming Wei and Cha-li.

"It make changes," he said, "in your body. Your arms not be so strong, but you be more woman, okay?"

"Not as strong?" I shook my head. "Okay, not the one that makes me like a man."

"How about only the metabolic stasis? You still have communications. In emergency, you can send signal."

"You can take that out," I said. "I don't care."

"No," he said. "It is not bad. It is okay to keep."

I shrugged. I didn't care.

He started making up a solution. "You want to be a man, all the way?" he asked. "We can do that."

"No," I said. "I am not a man."

"Then I can take it out."

"No," I said. "No." I didn't want to be a man all the way. But I wanted to be strong and I wanted to be able to do lots of things. I knew women could be strong, like my mam, but I didn't want to be just a strong woman.

Why were there only two choices, man and woman? "I am not man or woman," I said, "just Jan."

"Okay, just Jan," he said, loading an injector.

"It hurts?" I asked.

He shook his head. "You will feel sick, a little. You lie down, okay?"

"Okay." I held out my arm and he pressed the injector against my skin. I felt the cold for a moment. I looked at my arm. There was a red square.

"Done," he said. "Go lie down."

I went back and lay on my blanket and after a while I felt sick, the way he said, sick to my stomach, and my head still aching from the vodka. I let my mind wander, but it kept returning to the here and now. I wanted to go home. I didn't want to be among strangers anymore. Funny how even when the world is all strangers there is still home in my head, a place/no place. If I tried to think about it much, there was nothing there, like fog.

Once when I was with Toolie clan and I was sick, I heard the sound of my mother moving about and that was home. I heard her pouring water and the sound of the spoon in the pot, stirring slow-cooking beans. I could almost remember her smell—I remembered smelling it, like the scent of sleep in a bed. I couldn't remember Aslak's scent but I could my daughter's, the milky baby scent. If I had gotten pregnant from Sasha I would have to make a life for me and a child. Would that make me home?

I thought about life with a daughter and then life with a sickly daughter—Sasha said the implant would have hurt or killed the baby—and I realized that it already had. I had gotten pregnant with my daughter after Wanji gave me the implants.

I felt sick.

I turned on the blankets and cried for my baby who never should have been born.

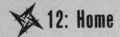 **12: Home**

WALKING TO GRANDMAMA LILI'S VILLAGE
I had a feeling it was gone. I thought it was a premonition.
It wasn't a dream or a vision, I didn't know what would
have happened, it was a feeling of disaster, and I watched
for signs that the spirits were telling me something. The
signs I knew were all from the north—one winterbaby was
sorrow, two were joy, three meant a girl, and four meant
a boy—but here I only saw whistling flocks of foxbats,
their wingclaws hooked on branches, and I smelled the
sharp-green smell of the forest. The path meandered, and
I bent and stooped beneath prickly vines and crossed
streams that soaked through my boots. It wasn't raining
so much as the clouds had touched the earth and everything was wet. I was enclosed, and the sounds came oddly,
things sometimes closer than they really were and sometimes muffled. The humidity made me gasp and in my
heavy boots it was all like a dream, one where I
couldn't run.

Then the village was there. Smoke curled up from the
houses, and the gardens were green and square. My garden
outside Grandmama Lili's was green, too, and the plants
were bigger. The si-chi that I'd bought with Cha-li and
Ming Wei was planted in the new soil and it had taken
hold.

"Son-in-law," Grandmama Lili said from the darkness
inside the house. "You've come back."

"Is everything okay?" I asked.

"My back hurts and Ming Wei is useless and that Cha-li keeps coming here. You left the garden for an old woman to take care of."

"It looks better than when I took care of it," I said.

"Sit down. Sit down," she said. "Have you eaten yet?"

"Are you angry at me?" I asked.

"Of course," she said, snappish. "But when has an old woman's anger ever stopped someone from doing something?"

"I am sorry, Grandmama," I said.

"Ming Wei is with Ta Fen."

"Ta Fen? Why?" I said. Ta Fen was Widow Hehua's son. I knew who he was, but he had never come around before.

"Why does any young woman keep company with a young man?" Grandmother Lili said.

"Ta Fen?" I said. "He—he is boring."

"Not to Ming Wei," Grandmama Lili said tersely.

I thought it prudent to change the subject. "Grandmother Lili," I said, "in the city, offworlders stopped the plague. I worked for them, giving medicine. They paid me." I poured cash into her lap—coins with holes in the middle and silver bars, a handful. "I brought it home."

It was a frightening thing to say. What if this wasn't my home? What if she gave it back?

"I'll use it for some of Ming Wei's dowry," she said. "Did you eat yet? Now you eat." She gave me a bowl of spicy soup. "You are like my husband, always going somewhere. He was never satisfied. That is why I had so few children, only five. Only two grew up and now they are all dead and Ming Wei will be married."

"To Ta Fen?" I asked. I hadn't been gone that long.

"Maybe to Ta Fen, maybe to another. She is as wild as her mother. She was not raised right and now she has no modesty."

"What happened to her mother?"

"Ai-ya," Grandmama Lili said. "You have a cup of tea."

She boiled water and I thought she wasn't going to tell me. I climbed up into the loft and checked on my rifle. It was still there, wrapped in plastic. I unwrapped it and checked it—keeping it in plastic worried me because water condensed inside at this time of year. It wasn't rusting, but tonight I would clean it. The loft was smaller than I remembered and smelled of wet straw gone green. I came back down to get my tea.

Grandmama Lili sat down on her heels and sipped her tea. She was all sinew and loose skin about her neck, but she was still strong. "Ming Wei's mother was pretty. Maybe not so pretty as Ming Wei, maybe a little more. It is memory and that makes it difficult. Her name was Yuyu and she was perhaps a little spoiled. She was my youngest and so many had died. And her father was gone a lot when she was young, so maybe I talked too much to her. Then when her father drowned, I talked to her as if she was older than she really was. You should not do this with children. They need to be children, not adults. They can have many friends and you can have many friends, but they only have one mama."

"Were you pretty?" I asked.

She laughed. "A little bit. My husband built me this house to get me to marry him, so he must have thought so."

Grandmama Lili's house was old, and the batberry wood that framed her door was almost black with age and smoke. Pretty wife and a pretty daughter with a waterfall of black hair. Not like my mam, who didn't spoil anyone. A whole different life, just the two of them, talking to each other in this neat house with the square garden outside.

"Yuyu, I don't know that you would have liked her. She was like a daybat, always here and there and chattering, not quiet like you. I was a talker then, too."

That made me smile because it was what I had known. It made it feel as if what was in my head was real.

"We'd have to eat a week on a caddy of rice. But she was easy to feed, and she wasn't fussy, not about that. We were here when they told me that my husband had drowned and that they had pulled his body up, caught in the net. They fish at night, with a lantern and a net, and he had fallen overboard. Maybe he was sick or maybe he was drunk, I don't know. Her brother didn't say anything, he was almost as tall as I am and his father was never pleased with him. You know how it is with some fathers and sons, when he would go out and hoe out the weeds his father would always say 'you're cutting too deep, you should use the hoe like a knife and cut them off' or 'you're cutting the stalks,' and take it from him and do it himself. I used to try to turn his look from the boy. It was better when he was fishing because then the house was not tight like a drum, where every step booms loud in everyone's ears.

"YuYu and her brother fought all the time. Yuyu carried a little pointed stick. He was bigger than she was. She was this pretty little thing that would sing and talk nice while he was too big too young and full of temper, but she was nasty, nasty-nasty," Lili said. "She put a hole in the palm of his hand. I saw it. He cupped his hand and it was full of blood, like water. I screamed at her, but she never turned a hair. She never felt any pain where he was concerned. Her elder brother. Yes. And since her father was dead, the head of the household."

The tea tasted of flowers, fragrant and bitter.

"In the evening, she would take the bucket and go out on the porch to empty it," Grandmama Lili pointed. "I would watch her. It would be late and her hair would be down, you see. Not decent. I could tell, if she stood there a moment. She wouldn't look at the trees, but I could tell. Maybe by the way she swung her hair or maybe by the way her body would be listening even though she didn't want to show it and my eyes couldn't see it. I would know that some boy was out there, in the trees, hoping to see her with her hair down. You think I was just a mother who saw boys everywhere. But it isn't so. If you had seen her standing there, barefoot, and the way she would bend to pour the bucket out and her hair would swing down and the air would smell of rain. Everything would be so quiet. We had a dog and it wouldn't bark, because it knew all the boys—but I would tell it to go, very soft, and it would trot out there with its tail held up and I knew the dog was going to see who was out there. I would tell her to shut the door. She always did. She didn't sneak out at night, but I knew some poor boy was lying in the dark, eating his own heart to ease his hunger for her.

"After she was married, I would think about that.

"She married a boatman. I didn't want her to, not after my husband that drowned. I wanted her to have a big family and grow old. I don't know if he is still alive or not." She frowned, thinking. "No reason why not. I found him in the city. I took her with me when I sold dyestuff. Once in a while I used to go to the city and sell there. There was so much dyestuff for sale that it had to be something unusual. In those days I grew my own plants to make some of my dye and if I saved the madder flowers and hung them up where you sleep and let them dry and if they didn't mildew, once I got enough of them I could make a rose dye. It wasn't very common and I could sell it in the city, so I would take Yuyu with me and we would go. Remember, I was a widow, and there was no one to do anything for me and I needed money for a dowry. I used to call that dye dowry rose. Only to myself, no one else—it's not right to talk that way to your daughter. Yuyu didn't talk to me when she got older. Some daughters, they turn away, do you know? Sometimes two women under one roof is too much.

"I wasn't looking for a husband in the city. I had a cousin there—we would stay with my cousin while we were there—and my cousin introduced me to him. My cousin was go-between. He helped my son get to the big city, across the water, to work for a man in a godown and learn about those things, because he knew that I didn't want her to marry a man who lived on the water. She wanted to live in the city, so she ran away to him. He was a man, grown, and she ran away to him. What could I do? She couldn't marry anyone else then, that's why she did it. Then she died after Ming Wei was born. They told me she was weak after the baby and a doctor gave her tonics, with a needle, you know how that is done? They took her across the water to the big city and lived there for a while. The boatman, I think he really loved her. Then she got a fever and she was in a coma for a while, and they say that when she woke, her mind was like a child and her back was curved, like this," Grandmother Lili hunched her back so her chin touched her chest. "Eventually she died. Ming Wei fought with her step-mother and my son took her. And you brought her home, but she'll leave again. It's the way with children. With all people. You don't really have them, you know.''

I knew. I sipped the tea tasting of bitter flowers.

"With this,'' she jingled the silver in her lap, "I can pick a better husband for Ming Wei. You have to help me bury it.''

We went out to the garden, and Gandmother Lili picked a corner where the flowers were full. She held them back and I dug a hole next to the wood of the edge of the raised bed. Not very deep, just down to the layer of plastic underneath.

"So she won't marry Ta Fen?'' I asked.

"I don't know,'' Grandmother Lili said. "But I would like her to marry someone with a little land and maybe a business. Someone like a carpenter.''

She wrapped the money in cloth and I shoveled dirt back over the bundle and patted it down.

"Ming Wei will be angry,'' I said.

Grandmother Lili nodded. "She is headstrong. She needs someone to decide some things for her.''

"Jan!'' someone shouted. I looked up. Ming Wei came running down the street, skipping through the puddles and splashing, her bare brown legs flashing. "Jan! Jan! You came home!''

In an afternoon, when the heat made the hair on my head too hot, I went looking for Ming Wei because her grandmother wanted her help. It was early. Ming Wei had said she was going to help the neighbor with the baby, but the neighbor hadn't seen her. I'd checked Ta Fen's mother. The widow had been surprised to see me. No, she had said, Ta Fen and Ming Wei weren't here—they were helping Lili.

"I missed them,'' I said. "I will go back.'

I went back down the street for a ways and then cut between Ciu Fei Han's house and the boathouse. Out among the trees I followed a narrow sandy path, pale gold, down to the glimmer of fresh water, and with the water I walked down to the sea. Even I knew where young people went around here when they wanted to be alone. The path went crooked. Then on the other side of the dune I heard them, so close to me I could have taken four steps and touched them. I crept to where I was looking at the back of their heads.

"No," Ming Wei said. "I'd know."

I had not meant to overhear.

"You did for your uncle," Ta Fen said.

I should have kept walking over the dune and made some noise so they would look up, but the wind was whipping Ming Wei's hair into her face and mouth and any sound my feet made wasn't heard over the waves.

"My uncle was, he was, was a *pig,*" Ming Wei said and her voice was sharp with anger.

I didn't know if that anger was because of the charts or something else and I felt myself on the edge of something too much to hear. I thought the boy would lean forward and kiss her. Instead he said, "My cousin would sell them. I wouldn't even tell him where I got them."

"Stop it or I'll go back."

Ta Fen did lean forward, but it was just to argue. He had a small face with a mouth full of teeth too big for it, but he was not so bad looking as that would sound. "Listen," he said, "with the money I would have enough to make us a house on our own."

Ming Wei shrugged. "We can live with my grandmother. We don't need a house." She didn't know about the dowry money or that her grandmother was looking for a husband for her.

"I don't want to live with your grandmother," Ta Fen said. "There are too many people in that house. I want things for you. A red wedding dress. A tree, a fruit tree, with flowers."

"I don't need a fruit tree," Ming Wei said. "I just need you. When I want flowers I can get them from the batberry."

"You can't eat a batberry," Ta Fen said. "And you can't wear it on your wedding day. We could grow oranges. It would just be once, to get us a start. My cousin would take care of it."

"No," Ming Wei said. "I won't."

"We should try," Ta Fen said.

"I'm going back," Ming Wei said. When I saw her start to get up I stepped back on the path, back out of sight, and started walking as if I was just coming up. "Ming Wei?"

Her face was open and innocent. "Ai, Jan!" she said.

"Your grandmother wants you," I said. "I asked your mother," I said to Ta Fen, "but she thought you were at Grandmother Lili's."

"What did you say?" he asked.

"I said thank you," I said, "and came to look for you here."

He grinned at me, nervous and complicit. Ta Fen had a way of smiling at me that I didn't trust, although mostly I liked him well enough. But he wanted me to like him too much. I followed them back to Grandmother Lili's.

To tell or not?

I worked in the garden, cooking some more soil and turning it into my soil bin. I straightened up and saw Cha-Li coming through the village. The road dipped a bit in the center of the village and he picked his way around where the water stood. I waved but he didn't.

"Did you eat yet?" I asked.

"You're back," he said.

"I am," I said. I pulled the pot off the fire to let the dirt cool. It smelled. I didn't know why boiling the mud made it stink so much, but it did.

"Did you cook it long enough?" he asked.

"Longer than I needed to," I said. "Are you angry?"

"No," he said. "Did you find what you were looking for?"

"Yes," I said. "When I came back it was right here."

He smiled and the smile transformed his ugly face as it always did and I saw what wonderful eyes he had.

"Tell me what you did," he said.

"I found some sick people and stayed with them and took care of them until the offworlders came. Then when the offworlders came I worked as a translator for them."

"You were a translator?" he said.

"I speak English," I said, irritated. "Do you?"

"No," he said, his eyes laughing at me. "But I speak this country's language."

"I'm learning," I said.

"So you are," he said, noncommittal. "I thought you didn't like offworlders."

"I like them. It is just that, when they go somewhere, they make things go wrong."

"For example?"

"Walk with me," I said.

We walked away from the house and from Ming Wei and Ta Fen. I was not going to make the mistake of being overheard. "When I worked for the offworlders, they paid me. I brought the money home and gave it to Grandmother Lili, and she decided maybe she would use it for a dowry for Ming Wei."

Cha-li nodded. "This doesn't sound bad."

"Ming Wei has a boyfriend. Ta Fen—do you know him? The Widow Hehua's son?"

"The one with melon-seed teeth?" I didn't know what he meant. "You don't know that saying? Melon-seed teeth? He has big teeth in front? Good for picking out seeds?"

"That doesn't make any sense," I said.

"It's something people say, so if you're a translator, you should learn it. Is that the boy you mean?" Cha-li shrugged. "She'd be better off with someone else. He's young, he doesn't have anything."

"Ming Wei is strong-minded, and he's, he wants her to do something with him. Something black market. To get money for them to marry."

"What kind of thing?" Cha-li said, serious and curious. Why do we always want to know the details of a bad thing? How did he die? What did she do? Who was the father?

"Smuggling," I said. "With his cousin. It makes no difference what it is, it's wrong."

"Did you tell her grandmother?"

"Ming Wei won't do it. I feel bad. I'm not a person who tells."

Cha-li shook his head. "You should tell the grandmother. Did Ming Wei tell you this?"

I shook my head. "No, no, no. I overheard them. They don't know. Ming Wei won't do it."

"Tell Lili," he said.

I shook my head.

He argued with me. My people, mostly we picked our own husbands and I had some sympathy for Ming Wei, even if I wasn't sure about Ta Fen, but Cha-li thought that Ming Wei was too silly to decide whom to marry. We walked around and around the village, talking, and the talk slipped from Ming Wei to my own choice of husband, to Aslak.

"You were too young," Cha-li said.

"I was not. You weren't there."

"I didn't say it was your fault," Cha-li said.

"Listen," I said, "you say that if Lili marries Ming Wei to someone she doesn't like, they will come to know and love each other. So if I choose someone I like, then we grow up together, and we love each other, and we become used to each other and maybe our love grows."

He held his hand up. "That is not love, you know, two young people. That's young bodies. Animals. Love is being with each other for a long time. Better to marry someone who has something and grow to love him than marry a boy and have nothing. Then love has a hard time. The ground is too bitter, too poison, with wanting and being hungry and babies with nothing in their bellies. You can love someone with something as easy as you love a poor man."

He is lonely, I thought. It is longing. He wishes someone would pick him for a husband. Maybe because he's so ugly he can't get a wife. But he wasn't that ugly and when you were talking to him, you forgot because he had such beautiful eyes. "Why don't you marry Ming Wei," I said, feeling wicked. "You have a good business."

He stepped back from me. "Don't be stupid."

"Why not?" I said. "You two could grow love like you grow your garden."

"I'm a foreigner," he said. "No one would let a girl marry me."

I had hurt him in some deep way I didn't mean to. When you are a foreigner, you're lonely all the time and I thought I had touched that loneliness. "I'm sorry," I said. "I was teasing."

We walked back to Grandmother Lili's and drank some tea, and he laughed and was easy, but we didn't talk about personal things anymore that day.

That night I was lying in the loft. I had thrown out all the mildewed straw and now there wasn't anything up there but my blankets and the hard wooden floor. The rain was beating on the roof. It was close and hot and damp, and my shirt stuck to my skin. I lay on my back with my arms underneath my head and thought about nothing as much as I could or I'd never go to sleep.

"Jan?" Ming Wei called.

I crawled to the edge of the loft and looked down at her. I couldn't even make her out in the dark. "What?" I asked.

"Can I come up?"

"Okay," I said.

I heard her on the ladder and I scooted back to give her room.

"It's hot," she whispered, and her voice was close to me.

"It is," I said. I wondered why she'd come up. She slept down below. I thought of Ta Fen and the dowry money.

We lay in the darkness for a while, and I could hear her shift. It was so humid that the night felt heavy. It was still, not even the sound of the sinkers singing in the green by the water. "Jan," she said. "Are you going to marry Cha-li?"

"No!" I said.

"Why not?" she said. "Aren't you lonely?"

At the moment I wasn't lonely at all. I didn't talk to people much, and today I had talked a long time to Cha-li. Now I was talking to Ming Wei, and I didn't want to talk to anyone at all. All this talk was more than I could stand. "I'm old, I dress like a man, and I like things the way they are," I said.

"But I'll be getting married and then things will change," she said.

I tried not to think of the dowry money buried under the flowers. "So you'll move down the street and have babies and I'll come and hold them and pretend that I like them."

She laughed a little. "But what if I move away? Would you still live here?"

"Someone has to take care of your grandmother," I said, trying to be light. "But you're not going to go far."

"What's it like to be married?" she asked.

I sighed. "I don't know, sweet one. It was a long time ago. Sometimes it makes you angry; sometimes it's wonderful."

"Did you love your husband?"

"I did," I said. "I still miss him sometimes."

"How did you know you truly loved him?" Her voice was breathless.

"I don't know," I said. "It was a long time ago. Sometimes I don't think I did. Sometimes I hated him. We were young, I was younger than you. It was too young, I think." Not that I would ever admit it to Cha-li. Not that I could ever tell my mam that she was right. My poor mam.

She sighed in the dark, a soft tired sound.

"I'll go back down," she said after a while.

I listened to the creak as the ladder took her weight and she swung down. I was awake for a long time, thinking about ghosts.

Grandmama Lili had tended my worms, and they had started to multiply. I covered the dirt with leftovers from the garden—carrot tops and onion skins—but was careful not to let it get too hot, and my worms multiplied.

I put some soil and some worms in pots and sold them at market. I didn't sell much and I didn't make much, but I bought some garlic bulbs to plant. One day a man appeared at my garden saying he wanted some si-chi and that Cha-li had sent him to me. I sold him some cuttings. The si-chi was doing well, spreading a little. I spread plastic over another place to start another garden plot. I wasn't sure what I would do with it, but I could either grow si-chi in it or plant more vegetables. When I got some more money I planned to buy another sheet of plastic so I could make another worm bin and keep the rain from them.

Ming Wei seemed to be seeing less of Ta Fen. I hoped

they were growing apart. She was cranky in the mornings, though, and she spent a lot more time with Mai-mi. I came upon her twice and thought she'd been crying. It made me angry at Ta Fen. He certainly wasn't worth heartbreak.

Grandmama Lili was thinking about raising ducks. She ticked off the reasons on her fingers: eggs, meat, and feathers. "Son-in-law," she said, "you should go to the market in Tailing and get me ducks. You can see your friend Cha-li." Grandmama Lili had kept ducks for years but had stopped a few years ago.

"You said they were too expensive. You have to buy feed," Ming Wei pointed out.

"We can feed them some grain and some greens and some of Janjan's worms. They aren't so expensive to keep." Grandmama Lili had started calling me Janjan because she said that Jan was too short a name, that it didn't sound like a real person's name. I said that she could call me Janna, but she didn't like that either.

I woke up before dawn to go to the market. Ming Wei wasn't in her blankets. I slid down the ladder and looked out and saw her by the trees, bent over crying. I walked out to her through the wet, and as I got closer I realized that she wasn't crying. She was sick to her stomach. I pulled her hair back out of the way and held her elbow while she retched.

"You're sick," I said.

"I'm okay," she said. She wiped her mouth. "I'll be all right in a little bit."

I took her back and sat her under the awning and brought her some water. "Rinse out your mouth," I said.

She spat the water out and leaned against the red bamboo that held the awning up. I rubbed her back and worried, thinking about plague.

"It'll go away," she said.

"I think you're sick." She was sweaty, which was good since it meant that any fever she might have was breaking. "Your grandmama can make you some tea."

"Don't tell Grandmama!" she said.

And then I knew. I didn't know how, maybe it was a dozen different things. The way she suddenly hated the smell of garlic. The way I had noticed before that her face seemed to have the suggestion of a mask, darker around her eyes and on her chin and light around the edges of her face. "You're going to have a baby," I said.

She looked wild. "Don't tell Grandmama," she whispered.

"Who is it?" I said, quiet. "Is it Ta Fen?"

She nodded.

"Does he know?"

She nodded again. "We're going to get a little money, then Grandmama won't mind."

"How are you going to get money?"

"Oh, ah, he's going to work for his cousin for a while," she said airily. "His cousin can make a lot of money."

"His cousin the smuggler?" I asked.

"No," she said, too fast. "His cousin is a trader."

"No," I said. "No cousin. I'm going to tell your grandmama."

"No," she hissed. "No, don't."

"If you get involved with something illegal, the same thing could happen to you that happened to your uncle," I said. "I won't have it."

She looked over her shoulder. "Grandmama is getting up. Don't say anything! Let me talk to you first. I promise, no cousin."

"What is all this?" Grandmama Lili asked. "Secrets, secrets?"

"Jan says she won't marry Cha-li," Ming Wei said.

"You are too nosy," Grandmama Lili said. "Your nose is in everyone's business."

"You just want Jan to stay and take care of you." Ming Wei acted easy and happy. I couldn't bear to watch.

"I've got to check the garden," I said.

I walked out to the meilijin flowers spilling over the edge of the raised garden and pushed them back as if I was checking for weeds. I glanced over my shoulder to see if anyone was watching, but Ming Wei had gone inside and it was too dim to see. Still, I thought Grandmama Lili would be wanting some tea and Ming Wei would fix it for her. I dug under the flowers through the loose dirt until I touched the bundle of coin and reassured myself it was still there. I did this almost every day. Then I packed worms and si-chi to take to Cha-li. He had offered to sell them for me when he was selling soil starter from his cart.

I didn't know why I still wanted the bundle to be there, since it didn't look as if Ming Wei would need it for a dowry, but I did. I would talk to Ming Wei. I would explain to her that since there was a baby coming, her grandmama would have to help them anyway, so there was no reason for risking smuggling. Maybe I would hint a little that Grandmama Lili could help better than Ming Wei thought. Then we could tell Grandmama Lili together and once the shouting was over, everything would be all right again. Ming Wei could go to her husband's house or Ta Fen could come live here. Either way, Ming Wei would be close and that would be good for Grandmama Lili. And good for me, too.

I came back in and said, "After the market, Ming Wei will help me with the ducks."

"She can go with you," Grandmama Lili said.

"No," I said, "she says her stomach is a little uncomfortable. She can help Mai-mi with the baby."

Ming Wei smiled up at me as if nothing was wrong.

I came back that evening, driving a pair of ducks and carrying a basket of eight ducklings. Packed inside with the ducklings was a couple of pots of soil starter that I was going to sell for Cha-li.

I'd never driven ducks before. I expected to be home in late afternoon, but the ducks didn't make very good time, and the man who sold them to me said that if I hurried them too much they'd start dropping weight. By the time I got them home I was ready to eat them for dinner.

Grandmama Lili came to the door. "Where's Ming Wei?"

"I thought she was over at Mai-mi's," I said. I set the basket down and the ducklings peeped. "These are misbegotten creatures. She stayed home, remember?"

"No," Grandmama Lili said, "she left at mid-morning to find you. Did she miss you?"

"She couldn't have missed me," I said. "She must have changed her mind and gone to Mai-mi."

"She was bringing you something you forgot," Grand-mama Lili said.

"She's run away," I whispered. Then I ran to Mai-mi's. Mai-mi was sewing a shirt while her husband, just in, was eating noodles. She looked up, not at all surprised to see me, then her eyes slipped away and down toward the floor. "No," she said. "Ming Wei hasn't been here." From there I ran to the widow's. Ta Fen was gone. I ran back to Mai-mi's.

"Where did she go?" I said.

"I don't know," Mai-mi said. "Isn't she home?"

"I know about the baby coming," I said. "Where is she?"

Mai-mi looked frightened. "I—I don't know," she stuttered.

"Did she go to Ta Fen's cousin?"

"I—I don't know!"

Mai-mi's husband said, "Ming Wei is going to have a baby?" He turned on his wife. "You knew?"

Mai-mi shrank back. "No," she whispered.

"What's the cousin's name?" I asked.

"I—I don't know. I didn't know she'd run away!"

I was so angry I raised my hand as if to backslap, and she lifted her arm to protect her face. Her husband grabbed her arm and pulled her up. The shirt and needle and thread fell to the floor. "Silly girl!" he shouted. "Tell the truth!"

"I don't know!" She sobbed.

The baby started to cry.

"Do you know what they are doing?" I said. "Do you know?"

"No," she said. "The baby is crying!"

"They're smuggling charts! Do you know what the nav-igation orders will do if they catch them? They'll kill them!"

"That's where they got the money?" Mai-mi said. "Ming Wei said it was her grandmother's—"

Money? How had she found the money buried in the garden? Ming Wei didn't garden.

"Where did she go?" I asked.

"Neigang," Mai-mi said, "a village called Neigang."

"Where is it?"

"I don't know," she said. "I don't—truly, I don't."

I ran again, back to Grandmama Lili's to the garden. There was a hole under the meilijin flowers and the money was gone.

"Where is she?" Grandmama Lili asked.

"She's run away with Ta Fen," I said. Maybe, if they'd taken the money they weren't going to try to sell charts to Ta Fen's cousin.

"Did you tell her about the money?" Grandmama Lili asked.

"No," I said.

"Why did you tell her about the money!"

"I didn't!" I said.

"How did she find out about it?"

"I don't know!" I said.

"You are lying! I trusted you," Grandmama Lili wailed. "I trusted you! I treated you like my own!"

"I didn't tell her!" I said. "Where is Neigang?"

"I don't know," Grandmama Lili said.

I wanted to shout at her, shake her, demand that she tell me where it was. People were being so stupid. I made myself take slow breaths. "I will find her," I promised Grandmama Lili. "I'll bring her back."

Mai-mi and her husband were watching us from under the awning of their house. One of the ducks was in my worm bin. Liu Liming and his wife were standing in their garden watching us. Liu Liming was a fisherman, and he went up and down the coast. He'd know where Neigang was.

I stalked over and grabbed the white drake and threw him out of my worm bin. In the dusk he was an offended explosion of wings so white they almost seemed to glow. "DOGMEAT!" I screamed after him in my own language. He and his mate fled across the yard to hide in the bush beyond my garden plot.

It made me feel a little better.

Neigang was a village on the edge of a stretch of beach that curved slightly inward. I wouldn't have called it a harbor. I didn't smell smoke. Dogs barked at me, but nobody shushed them. I started down the slope, and the village and sea were hidden by the trees.

It was too quiet. I didn't hear anything except the dogs. I kept waiting for someone to halloo or something, but there was only the empty sounds of forest and waves—sounds that wouldn't have seemed empty if the village wasn't somewhere ahead of me. There should have been the smell of kitchen smoke.

I stood long moments in the falling twilight, long enough that the sinkers started talking to each other and the dragonflies got fearless enough to buzz around me. I had walked all day and it would get dark if I waited much longer. I started on down to the village, past neat gardens, squared off, lettuces under tall bean plants and rings of flowers and tomatoes and melons. Old gardens, long worked, where the soil had been worked and boiled and worked and boiled and built up and built up until it was black. But nobody was getting onions for dinner.

It started to mist. I hadn't been dry since morning, but the rain on my face felt like fog and it was like breathing in a cloud. I wanted to bat it away and get a breath of air.

A man was standing by one of the houses and he startled me. He was dressed to garden, pants to his knees and a shirt, but he had a cloth tied over the bottom part of his face. "Don't come here," he called. "We have plague. Everyone is sick, except the dead."

"I'm looking for two people who came to visit a cousin," I called. The space between us was awkward, too far too talk but too close to shout. "Ta Fen and Ming Wei. Did they come here?"

"Two young people? They came last night, but they can't leave now; they'll take the sickness with them."

"Are they sick?" I asked and fear bit my heart.

"Not yet," he said.

I rubbed my face, trying to think. "Can I talk to them?"

"No. You have to go."

"I'll stay here with them."

He squinted at me. "You're a foreigner?"

"Yes. I can't get the plague."

"If you stay here you'll get it," he said.

"All right."

The man shook his head and coughed.

"I can help," I said.

A lot of the houses were dark already. More than half-way through the village I finally smelled a cookfire and saw a place with a lamp lit. It was a big house, at least by village standards, and it had been turned into a kind of hospital. Even from outside I smelled sickness and bodies left lying in their own foulness. I felt the breath lock within me and the muscles of my hands and across the back of my shoulders drew tight like a bow. Someone was moaning "ah . . . ah . . . ah . . ." very softly, probably without even knowing it, but mostly there was quiet and sometimes a cough.

"Are you giving them water?" I asked.

The man shrugged. "We try. Not enough hands, too much work."

I couldn't count the people in the lamplight. Shadows came in from the walls and covered some of them, but the rest lay on mats or blankets. The shadows made a sharp hip visible or the curve and hollow of a collarbone like a spoon. The air inside was close, and the dampness felt thick and cloying.

"In the back," the man said.

There was another room off to each side and a door in the back. In the back it was dark, but I whispered, "Ming Wei?"

From the darkness she said, "Jan?"

"Ming Wei," I whispered, "how are you?"

"Have you come to take me home?" she asked.

"No, sweet," I said. "But I'll stay here with you."

At dawn I was making soup. I found a big pot used for rendering fat, built a fire, and put in water and salt. Then I went through the gardens and picked anything I could find that was ripe. I found tomatoes and cucumbers, orange cantaloupe, bitter melon, beans and onions and garlic. I carried them back in armfuls and cut them into the pot. I didn't know how it would taste, but if I didn't use the vegetables, they'd rot. I smelled faintly of vinegar but the salt wind off the ocean was clean on my face.

Two men from the village walked down the beach and then cut up toward a ridge. They carried shovels for graves. Five people had died during the night. A young girl and boy were playing at the edge of the water. The girl knelt, digging in the sand, while the boy squatted, watching her. They were normal in the silence.

I unbraided my hair to let it free so the air would blow through it and felt for a moment the luxury of letting it loose. In a while it would feel in the way and it would be good to bind it back up; but for right now it was a little like having kept still too long and finally being able to stretch.

Ming Wei and Ta Fen were still asleep. Ta Fen was on his back, and Ming Wei was curled up with her back against him. The back room was full of people sleeping, and it was hard to step over them. Ta Fen started and pushed away from me when I woke him up, but Ming Wei just sat up and said crankily, "You look fierce."

"You two go find bowls," I said.

"Find bowls? Where?" Ming Wei asked.

"In the houses," I said, irritated.

"We can't go in people's houses and take things," Ta Fen said.

"If we don't, more people will die," I said. "Get going."

"I feel sick," Ming Wei said.

"Go outside, then."

"I don't have to take orders from a woman," Ta Fen said.

"I'm not a woman," I said.

"What are you then?" Ta Fen said.

"I'm what you see, and I've got too much to do to argue with you." I grabbed his arm and hauled him to his feet and twisted his arm behind him.

"Ai-yah," he said. "That hurts!"

"Jan! Leave him alone!" Ming Wei said.

"Be quiet," a woman said. "There are sick people here!"

I was embarrassed but I was furious with the two of them. "Bowls," I said and went outside to see if my water was anywhere near boiling. It takes a lot of time to get a big pot boiling.

Ming Wei and Ta Fen went from house to house and came back with bowls.

"I am sorry," Ta Fen said. "I should not have been so disrespectful."

"Don't be polite," I said. "I should not have been so bad tempered."

He was a nice enough kid, I thought. Just not good enough for Ming Wei. We filled bowls with broth and took them to people who were well enough to try to eat on their own. Then I had them fill more bowls, and we started trying to get some liquid into the people who were too sick to feed themselves. Some people would sip from a spoon if you held them up sitting, and some people you had to trickle the broth into their mouths. Some people were too sick and wouldn't open their mouths, and four people were so gone that when we put soup in their mouths it just ran out and down their chins. Two more couldn't be roused at all, and both of them had black and bruised-looking feet. Their faces were paler than mine, clay white, and their eyes were so sunk in their heads they looked like skulls.

"They will die," I told Ta Fen. "Don't try to feed them."

"Jan?" Ming Wei whispered, "when are the offworlders going to come?"

"What? The offworlders? They're not coming, are they?" I had been awake thinking about the offworlders until late, trying to decide if I should go to Da-mou to find them or if it would take too long. If they were even still in Da-mou. But when Ming Wei said it I felt fear.

"They're not? But people are sick and they came to Da-mou. . . ."

"Da-mou is a city. By the time they could find out the sickness would have passed here."

Ming Wei grabbed my arm. "You've got to tell them! Jan, you've got to tell them!" Her voice rose to a shriek. "You've got to, or we'll die, we'll all die!"

"I can't tell them," I said. "I'd have to go to Da-mou—that would be a couple of days."

Ming Wei folded down and grabbed her knees. "My baby," she keened, "my baby."

I thought about going to Da-mou. It would take me a day and a half, at least. And then to come back. Ming Wei's hair was up, but some of it had fallen loose around her face.

"I'm sick," she said, her eyes closed. "Oh, help me, I'm sick. I'm sick."

I knelt down and felt her forehead. "You're not sick," I said. "You're just upset."

She put her head on her knees and cried, a high sound like a tired child. Ta Fen looked at me, aghast. People were watching us from pallets, some with interest, some blankly.

Then I remembered the implant from Wanji, the one that called the skimmer. Did it only call Tonstad? I couldn't even remember if Sasha had taken it out. He'd asked me, and I couldn't remember if I'd said yes or not. I hadn't ever thought I'd need it.

If the offworlders came here, what would happen? In my experience, nothing good. I didn't want them to come here. I couldn't even explain why, it wasn't as if Ming Wei would leave me, the way Young Chang had. But every time I was around offworlders, bad things had happened.

I stroked her hair. "Sweet," I said, "you'll be all right. I'll take care of you. I will."

She reached out, her face red and wet. "I want to go home," she said. "Jan, I don't want to die here. I want to go home." I hugged her and stroked her hair and shushed her, but nothing could console her. I thought of my baby, all those years ago, crying and crying as if something inside was broken. Rahel would be almost as old as Ming Wei. I hadn't kept track of the years, but I thought she'd be a bit younger. Maybe not.

Ta Fen stood there in that helpless way some men did, hands hanging as if broken at his sides.

I stood up and walked back out to the pot of soup, trying to think past the fear inside me. My hair whipped into my face and in my mouth and I tied it back.

Whistling was bad luck, but I remembered the song. I

didn't whistle very well, so it took a couple of tries to get sound, but when I whistled the song and everything got dark and my head felt hot and then I could see again, I knew it had worked. I didn't know what it would do, if anything.

I went back inside. Ming Wei had gone into the back room and was sitting against the wall with her knees drawn up. I crouched in front of her. "Sweet," I said, "I've just sent a message to the offworlders. I don't know if they'll get it." I brushed her hair back behind her ear and out of her face. "I will try again in a while."

"I don't want to die," Ming Wei whispered.

"You're my sweet," I said. "I'll take care of you."

They came, three of them, Lisa, Henri, and Sasha, in a loud and noisy boat that sailed off the water and up across the beach in a swirl of air and wet sand before settling with a bump.

"Jan!" Sasha said. "You are in trouble?"

I walked across the beach to them. "Here is plague," I said. "I call you. My family, one is sick."

Lisa climbed out, looking around. "You live here?"

"No," I said. "A day, that way."

Lisa looked confused.

A handful of villagers came out to stare at the offworlders and the boat. Lisa had her notebook to mark down numbers, and Henri carried the tester. Sasha, it turned out, had come to see me. "I know it is you. Who else can it be? I think of you and I wonder how you're doing," Sasha said. "I think you are the perfect friend, you know? Both a man and a woman, everything somebody needs at once." He grinned.

I took them to Ming Wei. Her fever had come up and she wasn't doing so well, but she was still aware. To Lisa I said, "My family. She has baby." I touched her stomach. "No problem?"

"No problem," Lisa said. She smiled at Ming Wei and said hello.

I stroked Ming Wei's hot forehead. "They will cure you," I said.

I had forgotten how tall Henri was. "Is there a lot of

plague out here in the countryside?'' he asked. Henri was
gentle as a girl, maybe because he was so tall.

''I think,'' I said.

''We should start going village to village,'' Henri said
to Lisa.

''Can we do that?'' she asked.

''Can we not?'' he asked. To me he said, ''Jan? Would
you help us? Would you translate?''

I didn't want to help them, I wanted to go home. ''I
have business,'' I said. ''I think a moment?''

''Okay,'' he said. I took them from person to person,
explaining what they would do, explaining that it would
stop the sickness. They stayed to help me feed people and
to clean pallets and sick people. Even Sasha was good to
the sick. I had not known that he was so gentle.

We sat by the fire in the evening and ate offworld food
from packets.

I thought about what they had asked me, about translat-
ing for them. I thought about plague. I was so tired of
sickness, but I couldn't think of anyone else who could
do what they needed. I spoke English, because I had
grown up in a mission and because I had lived in a city.
I could talk to the people of the villages because now I
lived here. It was a long way to come.

It was a good technology. Even in the mission we had
used offworld medicine. Maybe it would cause problems.
Probably it would cause problems, but I couldn't let people
die. So if there were more problems later from all this
offworld technology, well, then I would take those problems as they came.

I realized my shoulders ached, as if I had been carrying
something for a long time. I thought about going home,
to Grandmama Lili. To my garden.

''When do you go home?'' I asked.

They were all quiet. Finally Lisa said, ''Not for a
long time.''

Henri said, ''Maybe never.''

''Why?'' I asked, surprised.

''It costs a lot to come here,'' Lisa said. ''We have
come here to work for many years, and then they will
give us a lot of money, enough to pay to get home, but

then when we get there we won't have anything, or we can stay here and be rich."

I didn't know what to say. I didn't know if I had the words in any language—not my own, not English, or the language of these people or even my bit of Taufzinner. "You . . . you choose to come? To be foreign?"

Henri said, "This will be home for my children. They'll have more than I do."

"We aren't any different than whoever came here and started your clan," Lisa said.

It was true; someone had to come from Earth to live here, to start the clans.

Sasha said, "This is the best colony world. Almost like Earth. Not like Kobayashi."

"What is Ko-Kobo—"

"Kobayashi," Henri said. "It is another world. But it isn't like Earth and it isn't like this. Most places, people cannot live. Too hot, too little water, too cold at night. They are trying to make it more like Earth, but it will take hundreds of years."

"Some ways," Lisa said, "this is better than Earth."

"No," I said. Look at them, with all their technology, all their strength. They could do anything they wanted.

"Earth has problems. Too many people," Henri said, "too many things—chemicals in the soil, in the air. Do you understand?"

"Pollution," I said. I knew about pollution. We had to worry about it all the time at the factory. It had been in my English lessons. I had thought of it as one more example of the way offworlders liked everything clean and new.

My head was full of these things.

"There isn't any place like this anymore," Lisa said. "If this were Earth, there would be a hundred people here. There would be buildings. It would be like the city."

Sasha said, "Koziko is the best colony world. The others, very much more hard."

"What is Koziko?" I asked.

Lisa and Henri and Sasha looked surprised. Lisa said, "Your planet. That's its name. What do you call it?"

Name a world? What a foolish thing. It was the world. I looked out at the water and shrugged. "Home," I said.

We hope you've enjoyed this Avon Eos book. As part of our mission to give readers the best science fiction and fantasy being written today, the following pages contain a glimpse into the fascinating worlds of a select group of Avon Eos authors.

In the following pages experience the latest in cutting-edge sf from Eric S. Nylund, Maureen F. McHugh, and Susan R. Matthews, and experience the wondrous fantasy realms of Martha Wells, Andre Norton, Dave Duncan, and Raymond E. Feist.

SIGNAL TO NOISE

Eric S. Nylund

JACK WATCHED HIS OFFICE WALLS SPUTTER malfunctioning mathematical symbols and release a flock of passenger pigeons; his nose was tickled with the odor of eucalyptus. Inside, the air rippled with synthetic pleasure and the taste of vanilla.

"I need to get in there," he told the government agent who blocked the doorway.

"No admittance," the agent said, "until we've completed our investigation on the break-in."

Puzzles, illegalities, and dilemmas stuck to Jack—from which he then, usually, extracted himself. That gave him the dual reputation of a troubleshooter and a troublemaker. But the only thing he was dead sure about today was the "troublemaking and sticking" part of that assessment.

The agent stepped in front of Jack, obscuring what the others were doing in there. National Security Office agents: goons with big guns bulging under their bulletproof suits. And no arguing with them.

Today's trouble was the stuff you saw coming, but couldn't do a thing about. Like standing in front of a tidal wave.

Jack hoped his office *had* been broken into, that this wasn't an NSO fishing trip. There were secrets in the bubble circuitry of his office that had to stay hidden. Things that could make his troubles multiply.

"I'll wait until you're done then."

The agent glanced at his notepad and a face materialized: Jack's with his sandy hair pulled into a ponytail and his hazel eyes bloodshot. "You have an immediate inter-

view with Mr. DeMitri. Bell Communications Center, sublevel three.''

Jack's stomach curdled. ''Interview'' was a polite word
that meant they'd use invasive probes and mnemonic shadows to pry open his mind. Jack had worked with DeMitri
and the NSO before. He knew all their nasty tricks.

''Thanks,'' Jack lied, turned from the illusions in his
office, and walked down the hallway.

From the fourth floor of the mathematics building, he
took the arched bridge path that linked to the island's outer
seawall. Not the most direct route, but he needed time to
figure a way out of this jam.

Cold night air and salt spray whipped around him. Elec-
tromagnetic pollution filtered through the hardware in his
skull: a hundred conversations on the cell networks, and
a patchwork of thermal images from the West-AgCo satel-
lite overhead.

Past the surf and across the San Joaquin Sea, the horizon
glowed with fluorescent light. Jack regretted that he'd
stepped on other people to get where he was. Maybe that's
why trouble always came looking for him. Because he had
it coming. Or because he was soft enough to let little
things get to him. Like guilt.

Not that there was any other way to escape the main-
land. Everyone there competed for lousy jobs and stabbed
each other in the back, sometimes literally, to get ahead.
He had clawed his way out with an education—then
cheated his way into Santa Sierra's Académe of Pure and
Applied Sciences.

But it wasn't perfect here, either. There were cutthroat
maneuvers for grants, and Jack had bent the law working
both for corporations *and* the government. All of which
had helped his financial position, but hadn't improved
his conscience.

He had to get tenure so he could relax and pursue his
own projects. There had to be more to life than chasing
money and grabbing power.

Now those dreams were on hold.

His office had been ransacked, and the NSO had got
too curious, too fast, for his liking. Had they been keeping
an eye on him all along?

He took the stairs off the seawall and descended into a red-tiled courtyard.

In the center of the square stood Coit Tower. The structure was sixty meters of fluted concrete that had been hoisted off the ocean floor. It had survived the San Francisco quake in the early twenty-first century, then lay underwater for fifty years—yet was still in one piece.

Jack hoped he was as tough.

The whitewashed turret was lit from beneath with halogen light, harsh and brilliant against the night sky. Undeniably real.

Jack preferred the illusions of his office; sometimes reality was too much for him to stomach.

No way out of this interview sprang to mind, and he had stalled as long as he could. The crystal-and-steel geodesic dome of the Bell Communications Center was across the courtyard. Jack marched into the building, took the elevator to sublevel three, and entered the concert amphitheater.

On the stage between gathered velvet curtains, the NSO had set up their bubble.

Normal bubbles simulated reality. Inside, a web of inductive signals and asynchronous quantum imagers tapped the operator's neuralware. It allowed access to a world of data, it teased hunches from your subconscious, and solidified your guesses into theories. They made you think faster. Maybe think better.

But this wasn't a normal bubble. And it was never meant to help Jack think. It was designed for tricks.

THE DEATH OF THE NECROMANCER

Martha Wells

SHE WAS IN THE OLD WING OF THE HOUSE now. The long hall became a bridge over cold silent rooms thirty feet down and the heavy stone walls were covered by tapestry or thin veneers of exotic wood instead of lathe and plaster. There were banners and weapons from long-ago wars, still stained with rust and blood, and ancient family portraits dark with the accumulation of years of smoke and dust. Other halls branched off, some leading to even older sections of the house, others to odd little cul-de-sacs lit by windows with an unexpected view of the street or the surrounding buildings. Music and voices from the ballroom grew further and further away, as if she was at the bottom of a great cavern, hearing echoes from the living surface.

She chose the third staircase she passed, knowing the servants would still be busy toward the front of the house. She caught up her skirts—black gauze with dull gold striped over black satin and ideal for melding into shadows—and quietly ascended. She gained the third floor without trouble but going up to the fourth passed a footman on his way down. He stepped to the wall to let her have the railing, his head bowed in respect and an effort not to see who she was, ghosting about Mondollot House and obviously on her way to an indiscreet meeting. He would remember her later, but there was no help for it.

The hall at the landing was high and narrower than the others, barely ten feet across. There were more twists and turns to find her way through, stairways that only went up half a floor, and dead ends, but she had committed a map of the house to memory in preparation for this and so far it seemed accurate.

Madeline found the door she wanted and carefully tested the handle. It was unlocked. She frowned. One of Nicholas Valiarde's rules was that if one was handed good fortune one should first stop to ask the price, because there usually was a price. She eased the door open, saw the room beyond lit only by reflected moonlight from undraped windows. With a cautious glance up and down the corridor, she pushed it open enough to see the whole room. Book-filled cases, chimney piece of carved marble with a caryatid-supported mantle, tapestry-back chairs, pier glasses, and old sideboard heavy with family plate. A deal table supporting a metal strongbox. *Now we'll see,* she thought. She took a candle from the holder on the nearest table, lit it from the gas sconce in the hall, then slipped inside and closed the door behind her.

The undraped windows worried her. This side of the house faced Ducal Court Street and anyone below could see the room was occupied. Madeline hoped none of the Duchess's more alert servants stepped outside for a pipe or a breath of air and happened to look up. She went to the table and upended her reticule next to the solid square shape of the strongbox. Selecting the items she needed out of the litter of scent vials, jewelry she had decided not to wear, and a faded string of Aderassi luck-beads, she set aside snippers of chicory and thistle, a toadstone, and a paper screw containing salt.

Their sorcerer-advisor had said that the ward that protected Mondollot House from intrusion was an old and powerful one. Destroying it would take much effort and be a waste of a good spell. Circumventing it temporarily would be easier and far less likely to attract notice, since wards were invisible to anyone except a sorcerer using gascoign powder in his eyes or the new Aether-Glasses invented by the Parscian wizard Negretti. The toadstone itself held the necessary spell, dormant and harmless, and in its current state invisible to the familiar who guarded the main doors. The salt sprinkled on it would act as a catalyst and the special properties of the herbs would fuel

it. Once all were placed in the influence of the ward's key
object, the ward would withdraw to the very top of the
house. When the potency of the salt wore off, it would
simply slip back into place, probably before their night's
work had been discovered. Madeline took her lock picks
out of their silken case and turned to the strongbox.

There was no lock. She felt the scratches on the hasp
and knew there had been a lock here recently, a heavy
one, but it was nowhere to be seen. *Damn. I have a not-
so-good feeling about this.* She lifted the flat metal lid.

Inside should be the object that tied the incorporeal
ward to the corporeal bulk of Mondollot House. Careful
spying and a few bribes had led them to expect not a
stone as was more common, but a ceramic object, perhaps
a ball, of great delicacy and age.

On a velvet cushion in the bottom of the strongbox
were the crushed remnants of something once delicate and
beautiful as well as powerful, nothing left now but fine
white powder and fragments of cerulean blue. Madeline
gave vent to an unladylike curse and slammed the lid
down. *Some bastard's been here before us.*

SCENT OF MAGIC

Andre Norton

THAT SCENT WHICH MADE WILLADENE'S flesh prickle was strong. But for a moment she had to blink to adjust her sight to the very dim light within the shop. The lamp which always burned all night at the other end of the room was the only glimmer here now, except for the sliver of daylight stretching out from the half-open door.

Willadene's sandaled foot nearly nudged a huddled shape on the floor—Halwice? Her hands flew to her lips, but she did not utter that scream which filled her throat. Why, she could not tell, but that it was necessary to be quiet now was like an order laid upon her.

Her eyes were drawn beyond that huddled body to a chair which did not belong in the shop at all but had been pulled from the inner room. In that sat the Herbmistress, unmoving and silent. Dead—?

Willadene's hands were shaking, but somehow she pulled herself around that other body on the floor toward where one of the strong lamps, used when one was mixing powders, sat. Luckily the strike light was also there, and after two attempts she managed to set spark to the wick.

With the lamp still in hands which quivered, the girl swung around to face that silent presence in the chair. Eyes stared back at her, demanding eyes. No, Halwice lived but something held her in thrall and helpless. There were herbs which could do that in forbidden mixture, but Halwice never dealt with such.

Those eyes— Willadene somehow found a voice which was only a whisper.

"What—?" she began.

357

The eyes were urgent as if sight could write a message on the very air between them. They moved—from the girl to the half-open door and then back with an urgency Willadene knew she must answer. But how— Did Halwice want her to summon help?

"Can you"—she was reaching now for the only solution she could think of—"answer? Close your eyes once—"

Instantly the lids dropped and then rose again. Willadene drew a deep breath, almost of relief. By so much, then, she knew they could still communicate.

"Do I go for Doctor Raymonda?" He was the nearest of the medical practitioners who depended upon Halwice for their drugs.

The eyelids snapped down, arose, and fell again.

"No?" Willadene tried to hold the lamps steady. She had near forgotten the body on the floor.

She stared so intensely as if she could force the answer she needed out of the Herbmistress. Now she noted that the other's gaze had swept beyond her and was on the floor. Once more the silent woman blinked twice with almost the authority of an order. Willadene made a guess.

"Close the door?" That quick, single affirmative blink was her answer. She carefully edged about the body to do just that. Halwice did not want help from outside—but what evil had happened here? And was the silent form on the floor responsible for the Herbmistress's present plight?

With the door shut some instinct made the girl also, one-handedly as she held the lamp high, slide the bolt bar across it, turning again to find Halwice's gaze fierce and intent on her. The Herbmistress blinked. Yes, she had been right—Halwice wanted no one else here.

Then that gaze turned floorward, as far as nature would let the eyes move, to fasten on the body. Willadene carefully set the lamp down beside the inert stranger and then knelt.

It was a man lying facedown. His clothing was traveler's leather and wool as if he were just in from some traders' caravan. Halwice dealt often with traders, spices, and strange roots; even crushed clays of one sort or another arrived regularly here. But what had happened—?

Willadene's years of shifting iron pots and pans and dealing with Jacoba's oversize aids to cooking had made her stronger than her small, thin body looked. She was able to roll the stranger over.

Under her hand his flesh was cool, and she could see no wound or hurt. It was as if he had been struck down instantly by one of those weird powers which were a part of stories told to children.

THE GILDED CHAIN
A Tale of the King's Blades

Dave Duncan

DURENDAL CLOSED THE HEAVY DOOR SI-
lently and went to stand beside Prime, carefully not looking at the other chair.

"You sent for us, Grand Master?" Harvest's voice war-
bled slightly, although he was rigid as a pike, staring
straight at the bookshelves.

"I did, Prime. His Majesty has need of a Blade. Are
you ready to serve?"

Harvest spoke at last, almost inaudibly. "I am ready,
Grand Master."

Soon Durendal would be saying those words. And who
would be sitting in the second chair?

Who was there now? He had not looked. The edge of
his eye hinted it was seeing a youngish man, too young
to be the King himself.

"My lord," Grand Master said, "I have the honor to
present Prime Candidate Harvest, who will serve you as
your Blade."

As the two young men turned to him, the anonymous
noble drawled, "The other one looks much more impres-
sive. Do I have a choice?"

"You do not!" barked Grand Master, color pouring into
his craggy face. "The King himself takes whoever is
Prime."

"Oh, so sorry! Didn't mean to twist your dewlaps,
Grand Master." He smiled vacuously. He was a weedy,
soft-faced man in his early twenties, a courtier to the core,
resplendent in crimson and vermilion silks trimmed with

fur and gold chain. If the white cloak was truly ermine, it must be worth a fortune. His fairish beard came to a needle point and his mustache was a work of art. A fop. Who?

"Prime, this is the Marquis of Nutting, your future ward."

"Ward?" The Marquis sniggered. "You make me sound like a debutante, Grand Master. *Ward* indeed!"

Harvest bowed, his face ashen as he contemplated a lifetime guarding . . . whom? Not the King himself, not his heir, not a prince of the blood, not an ambassador traveling in exotic lands, not an important landowner out on the marches, not a senior minister, nor even—at worst—the head of one of the great conjuring orders. Here was no ward worth dying for, just a court dandy, a parasite. Trash.

Seniors spent more time studying politics than anything else except fencing. Wasn't the Marquis of Nutting the brother of the Countess Mornicade, the King's latest mistress? If so, then six months ago he had been the Honorable Tab Nillway, a younger son of a penniless baronet, and his only claim to importance was that he had been expelled from the same womb as one of the greatest beauties of the age. No report reaching Ironhall had ever hinted that he might have talent or ability.

"I am deeply honored to be assigned to your lordship," Harvest said hoarsely, but the spirits did not strike him dead for perjury.

Grand Master's displeasure was now explained. One of his precious charges was being thrown away to no purpose. Nutting was not important enough to have enemies, even at court. No man of honor would lower his standards enough to call out an upstart pimp—certainly not one who had a Blade prepared to die for him. But Grand Master had no choice. The King's will was paramount.

"We shall hold the binding tomorrow midnight, Prime," the old man snapped. "Make the arrangements, Second."

"Yes, Grand Master."

"Tomorrow?" protested the Marquis querulously.

"There's a ball at court tomorrow. Can't we just run through the rigmarole quickly now and be done with it?"

Grand Master's face was already dangerously inflamed, and that remark made the veins swell even more. "Not unless you wish to kill a man, my lord. You have to learn your part in the ritual. Both you and Prime must be purified by ritual and fasting."

Nutting curled his lip. "Fasting? How barbaric!"

"Binding is a major conjuration. You will be in some danger yourself."

If the plan was to frighten the court parasite into withdrawing, it failed miserably. He merely muttered, "Oh, I'm sure you exaggerate."

Grand Master gave the two candidates a curt nod of dismissal. They bowed in unison and left.

KRONDOR
The Betrayal

Raymond E. Feist

THE FIRE CRACKLED.

Owyn Belefote sat alone in the night before the flames, wallowing in his personal misery. The youngest son of the Baron of Timons, he was a long way from home and wishing he was even farther away. His youthful features were set in a portrait of dejection.

The night was cold and the food scant, especially after having just left the abundance of his aunt's home in Yabon City. He had been hosted by relatives ignorant of his falling-out with his father, people who had reacquainted him over a week's visit with what he had forgotten about his home life: the companionship of brothers and sisters, the warmth of a night spent before the fire, conversation with his mother, and even the arguments with his father.

"Father," Owyn muttered. It had been less than two years since the young man had defied his father and made his way to Stardock, the island of magicians located in the southern reaches of the Kingdom. His father had forbidden him his choice, to study magic, demanding Owyn should at least become a cleric of one of the more socially acceptable orders of priests. After all, they did magic as well, his father had insisted.

Owyn sighed and gathered his cloak around him. He had been so certain he would someday return home to visit his family, revealing himself as a great magician, perhaps a confidant of the legendary Pug, who had created the Academy at Stardock. Instead he found himself ill suited for the study required. He also had no love for the burgeoning politics of the place, with factions of students rallying around this teacher or that, attempting to turn the study of magic into another religion. He now knew he was, at best, a mediocre magician and would never amount to more, and no matter how much he wished to study magic, he lacked sufficient talent.

After slightly more than one year of study, Owyn had left Stardock, conceding to himself that he had made a mistake. Admitting such to his father would prove a far more daunting task—which was why he had decided to visit family in the distant province of Yabon before mustering the courage to return to the East and confront his sire.

A rustle in the bushes caused Owyn to clutch a heavy wooden staff and jump to his feet. He had little skill with weapons, having neglected that portion of his education as a child, but had developed enough skill with his quarter-staff to defend himself.

"Who's there?" he demanded.

From out of the gloom came a voice, saying, "Hello, the camp. We're coming in."

Owyn relaxed slightly, as bandits would be unlikely to warn him they were coming. Also, he was obviously not worth attacking, as he looked little more than a ragged beggar these days. Still, it never hurt to be wary.

Two figures appeared out of the gloom, one roughly Owyn's height, the other a head taller. Both were covered in heavy cloaks, the smaller of the two limping obviously.

The limping man looked over his shoulder, as if being followed, then asked, "Who are you?"

Owyn said, "Me? Who are you?"

The smaller man pulled back his hood, and said, "Locklear, I'm a squire to Prince Arutha."

Owyn nodded, "Sir, I'm Owyn, son of Baron Belefote."

"From Timons, yes, I know who your father is," said Locklear, squatting before the fire, opening his hands to warm them. He glanced up at Owyn. "You're a long way from home, aren't you?"

"I was visiting my aunt in Yabon," said the blond youth. "I'm now on my way home."

"Long journey," said the muffled figure.

"I'll work my way down to Krondor, then see if I can travel with a caravan or someone else to Salador. From there I'll catch a boat to Timons."

"Well, we could do worse than stick together until we reach LaMut," said Locklear, sitting down heavily on the ground. His cloak fell open, and Owyn saw blood on the young man's clothing.

"You're hurt," he said.

"Just a bit," admitted Locklear.

"What happened?"

"We were jumped a few miles north of here," said Locklear.

Owyn started rummaging through his travel bag. "I have something in here for wounds," he said. "Strip off your tunic."

Locklear removed his cloak and tunic, while Owyn took bandages and powder from his bag. "My aunt insisted I take this just in case. I thought it an old lady's foolishness, but apparently it wasn't."

Locklear endured the boy's ministrations as he washed the wound, obviously a sword cut to the ribs, and winced when the powder was sprinkled upon it. Then as he bandaged the squire's ribs, Owyn said, "Your friend doesn't talk much, does he?"

"I am not his friend," answered Gorath. He held out his manacles for inspection. "I am his prisoner."

MISSION CHILD

Maureen F. McHugh

"LISTEN," ASLAK SAID, TOUCHING MY arm.

I didn't hear it at first, then I did. It was a skimmer.

It was far away. Skimmers didn't land at night. They didn't even come at night. It had come to my message, I guessed.

Aslak got up and we ran out to the edge of the field behind the schoolhouse. Dogs started barking.

Finally we saw lights from the skimmer, strange green and red stars. They moved against the sky as if they had been shaken loose.

The lights came toward us for a long time. They got bigger and brighter, more than any star. It seemed as if they stopped, but the lights kept getting brighter. I finally decided that they were coming straight toward us.

Then we could see the skimmer in its own lights.

I shouted, and Aslak shouted, too, but the skimmer didn't seem to hear us. But then it turned and slowly curved around, the sound of it going farther away and then just hanging in the air. It got to where it had been before and came back. This time it came even lower and it dropped red lights. One. Two. Three.

Then a third time it came around and I wondered what it would do now. But this time it landed, the sound of it so loud that I could feel as well as hear it. It was a different skimmer than the one we always saw. It was bigger, with a belly like it was pregnant. It was white and red. It settled easily on the snow. Its engines, pointed down, melted snow underneath them.

And then it sat. Lights blinked. The red lights on the ground flickered. The dogs barked.

The door opened and a man called out to watch something but I didn't understand. My English is pretty good, one of the best in school, but I couldn't understand him.

Finally a man jumped down, and then two more men and two women.

I couldn't understand what anyone was saying in English. They asked me questions, but I just kept shaking my head. I was tired and now, finally, I wanted to cry.

"You called us. Did you call us?" one man said over and over until I understood.

I nodded.

"How?"

"Wanji give me . . . in my head . . ." I had no idea how to explain. I pointed to my ear. "Ayudesh is, is bad."

"Ask if he will die," Aslak said.

"Um, the teacher," I said, "um, it is bad?"

The woman nodded. She said something, but I didn't understand. "Smoke," she said. "Do you understand? Smoke?"

"Smoke," I said. "Yes." To Aslak I said, "He had a lot of smoke in him."

Aslak shook his head.

The men went to the skimmer and came back with a litter. They put it next to Ayudesh and lifted him on, but then they stood up and nearly fell, trying to carry him. They tried to walk, but I couldn't stand watching, so I took the handles from the man by Ayudesh's feet, and Aslak, nodding, took the ones at the head. We carried Ayudesh to the skimmer.

We walked right up to the door of the skimmer, and I could look in. It was big inside. Hollow. It was dark in the back. I had thought it would be all lights inside and I was disappointed. There were things hanging on the walls, but mostly it was empty. One of the offworld men jumped up into the skimmer, and then he was not clumsy at all. He pulled the teacher and the litter into the back of the skimmer.

One of the men brought us something hot and bitter and sweet to drink. The drink was in blue plastic cups, the same color as the jackets that they all wore except for one man whose jacket was red with blue writing. Pretty things. I made myself drink mine. Anything this black and bitter must have been medicine. Aslak just held his.

"Where is everyone else?" the red-jacket man asked slowly.

"Dead," I said.

"Everyone?" he said.

"Yes," I said.

AVALANCHE SOLDIER

Susan R. Matthews

IT LACKED SEVERAL MINUTES YET BEFORE actual sunbreak, early as the sun rose in the summer. Salli eased her shoulder into a braced position against the papery bark of the highpalm tree that sheltered her and tapped the focus on the field glasses that she wore, frowning down in concentration at the small Wayfarer's camp below. They would have to come out of the dormitory to reach the wash-house, and they'd have to do it soon. Morning prayers was one of the things that heterodox and orthodox—Wayfarer and Pilgrims—had in common, and no faithful child of Revelation would think of opening his mouth to praise the Awakening with the taint of sleep still upon him.

The door to the long low sleeping house swung open. Salli tensed. *Come on, Meeka,* she whispered to herself, her breath so still it didn't so much as stir the layered mat of fallen palm fronds on which she lay. *I know you're in there. Come out. I have things I want to say to you.*

The camp below was an artifact from olden days, two hundred years old by the thatching of the steeply sloped roofs with their overhanging eaves. Not a Pilgrim camp by any means. No, this was a Shadene camp built by the interlopers that had occupied the holy land in the years after the Pilgrims had fled—centuries ago. A leftover, an anachronism, part of the heritage of Shadene and its long history of welcoming Pilgrims from all over the world to the Revelation Mountains, where the Awakening had begun. Where heterodoxy flourished, and had stolen Meeka away from her. And before the Awakened One she had a thing or two to tell him about that—just as soon as she could find him by himself, and get him away from these people . . .

Older people first. Three men and two women, heading off in different directions. The men's wash house was little more than an open shed, though there wasn't anything for her to see from her vantage point halfway up the slope to the hillcrest. The women's wash house was more fully enclosed. That was where the hotsprings would be, then.

Where was Meeka?

The sun would clear the east ridge within moments, and yet no man of Meeka's size or shape had left the sleeping house. In fact the younger people were hurrying out to wash, now, and there were no adults whatever between old folks and the young, so what was going on here?

Then even as Salli realized that she knew the answer, she heard the little friction of fabric moving against fabric behind her. Felt rather than heard the footfall in the heavy mat of fallen palm fronds that cushioned her prone body like a feather-bed. Well, of course there weren't any of the camp's men there below. They were out here already, on the hillside.

Looking for her.

"Good morning Pilgrim, and it's a beautiful morning. Even if it is only a Dream."

She heard the voice behind her: careful and wary. But a little amused. Yes, they had her, no question about it. She could have kicked the cushioning greenfall into a flurry in frustration. But she was at the disadvantage; she had to be circumspect.

"How much more beautiful the Day we Wake." And what did she have to worry about, really? Nothing. These were Wayfarers, true, or if they weren't she was very much mistaken. But there were rules of civility. She had meant to get Meeka by himself, without betraying her presence; but she had every right to come here on the errand that had brought her. "Say, I imagine you're wondering what this is all about."

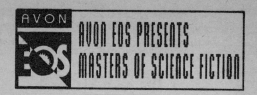